S0-BCO-163

Light in Shadow

Also by Jayne Ann Krentz

Summer in Eclipse Bay
Smoke in Mirrors
Dawn in Eclipse Bay
Lost & Found
Eclipse Bay
Soft Focus
Eye of the Beholder
Flash
Sharp Edges
Deep Waters
Absolutely, Positively
Trust Me
Grand Passion
Hidden Talents
Wildest Hearts
Family Man
Perfect Partners
Sweet Fortune
Silver Linings
The Golden Chance

By Jayne Ann Krentz writing as Jayne Castle

Harmony
After Dark
Amaryllis
Zinnia
Orchid

Light

A WHISPERING SPRINGS NOVE

DOUBLEDAY LARGE PRINT HOME LIBRARY EDITION

G. P. Putnam's Sons New York

in Shadow

JAYNE ANN KRENTZ

This Large Print Edition, prepared especially for Doubleday Large Print Home Library, contains the complete, unabridged text of the original Publisher's Edition.

This book is a work of fiction. Names, characters, places, and incidents either are the product of the author's imagination or are used fictitously, and any resemblance to actual persons, living or dead, business establishments, events, or locales is entirely coincidental.

G. P. Putnam's Sons
Publishers Since 1838
a member of
Penguin Putnam Inc.
375 Hudson Street
New York, NY 10014

Published simultaneously in Canada

ISBN 0-7394-3149-8

Printed in the United States of America

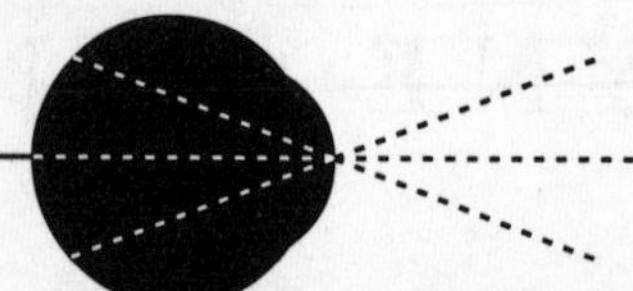

This Large Print Book carries the Seal of Approval of N.A.V.H.

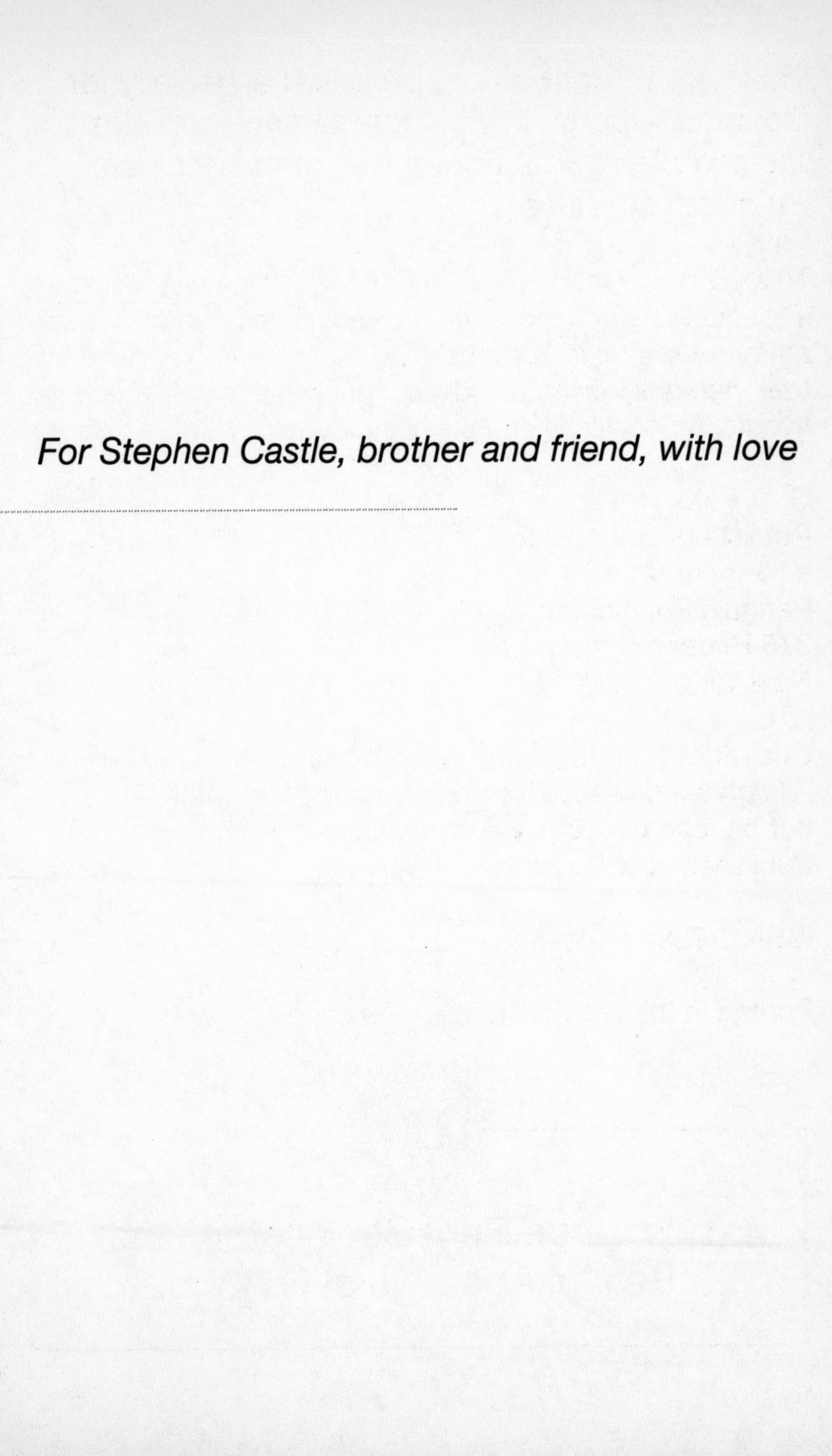

For Stephen Castle, brother and friend, with love

Light in Shadow

Chapter One

The walls screamed at her.

"Oh, damn," Zoe Luce whispered. She halted in the doorway of the empty bedroom and stared at the white walls. *Not now. Not today. Not this time. I really need this job.*

The walls sobbed. Terror pulsed through layers of Sheetrock and the fresh coat of stark white paint that covered it. The silent shrieks ricocheted off the floor and ceiling.

She put her fingers to her temples in a purely instinctive, utterly useless gesture. She squeezed her eyes shut, bracing herself against the ragged bolts of icy lightning that were shooting through her and pooling into a glacial pond somewhere in the vicinity of her stomach.

Davis Mason had followed her so closely down the hall that he was only a pace behind her when she came to a sudden stop. He bumped awkwardly against her.

"Oops, sorry." He caught his balance. "I wasn't paying attention."

"My fault." With what she hoped was an unobtrusive movement, she eased out of the doorway back into the hall. Things were much better out here. She could cope. She gave Davis what she hoped was a bright, assured smile. It wasn't easy, what with the muffled cries still leaking out of the bedroom.

She wanted out of this house. Fast. Whatever had happened in the bedroom had been bad.

"Hey." Davis touched her shoulder lightly. "Are you all right, Zoe?"

She gave him another shaky smile. It was relatively easy to smile at Davis. He had elegant lines and cleaning styling with just the right touch of roguish flair. If he'd been a car, he would have been a sleek, European roadster. Judging by the spacious home, the hand-tailored shirt and trousers, and the onyx and diamond ring he wore, he was also wealthy. In short, she thought sadly, until that moment, she had considered him the ideal client.

Everything had changed now, of course.

"Yes, I'm fine." She did a little on-the-spot deep breathing, using the techniques she had learned in her self-defense class. Summoning up her teacher's instructions, she sought the calm, stable center that was supposed to be somewhere deep inside her. Unfortunately, she had not yet mastered that part of the program. All she could feel was a bad case of the jitters coming on.

"What's wrong?" Davis was looking seriously concerned now.

"Just the start of a headache," Zoe said. "I often get one when I forget to eat breakfast."

The lies came so easily these days. But, then, she'd had a lot of practice. Too bad she wasn't yet clever enough to convince herself, she thought. A little self-delusion would be very welcome right now.

Davis watched her intently for a few seconds, and then he relaxed. "Missed your morning shot of caffeine?"

"And food. It's a blood sugar thing. I should know better." Feeling an urgent need to change the topic of conversation, she looked back into the bedroom and blurted out the first thing that came into her mind. "What happened to the bed?"

"The bed?"

They both looked at the large, empty stretch of uncovered hardwood flooring between two massive, mission-style bedside tables.

Zoe swallowed uneasily. "The rest of the residence is fully furnished," she said. "I couldn't help but notice that there's no bed in here."

"She took it," Davis said grimly.

"Your ex-wife?"

He sighed. "She loved that damned bed. Spent months shopping for it. I swear, it meant more to her than I did. When she left, it was about the only thing she insisted on taking with her in addition to her personal stuff."

"I see."

"You know how it is in a divorce. Sometimes the biggest fights are over the smallest, dumbest things."

Whatever else it had been, Zoe thought, the missing bed had not been small.

"I understand."

Davis searched her face. "Headache getting worse?"

"It'll be all right once I've had lunch and a cup of coffee," she assured him.

"Tell you what. You've seen the rest of the house. I'm sure you've got the general picture. Why don't we take a break and get something to eat at the club? It will give us a chance to talk over your initial impressions."

The thought of eating made her stomach churn. She knew from experience that she would not be able to keep any food down until the chills stopped. That could take a while. This had been a really bad experience, and it had caught her totally off guard.

It was her own fault. She knew better than to enter a room so recklessly. But she had been caught up in her plans for the interiors, completely focused, and the rest of the spacious residence had seemed so new, so *clean.* She simply had not been expecting trouble, and, as often happened, she had paid the price.

"I'd love to join you for lunch, but I'm afraid I'll have to take a raincheck." She made a show of glancing at her watch. "I've got another appointment this afternoon, and I need to prepare for it."

Davis looked hesitant. "If you're sure—"

"I'm afraid so." She tried to inject a note of apology into her tone. "I really do have to run and you're right, I've seen all I need to see for now." *And sensed far more than I ever wanted to know, thank you very much.* "I've got the floor plan you gave me earlier.

I'll make some copies and do some sketches that will you give you an idea of what I have in mind."

"I'd appreciate the drawings." Davis glanced into the bedroom and shook his head somewhat ruefully. "I'll admit I'm not what you'd call a visual person. It's easier for me to grasp the concept when I can see a picture."

"It's always easier when you can look at a drawing. Hang on while I check my calendar."

She reached into her voluminous tote, one of six similar bags in different colors that she owned. Each functioned as a combination briefcase and purse. She had chosen the chartreuse green one today because she liked the way it contrasted with her deep violet pantsuit.

Groping in the vast depths, she pushed aside the small camera, a sketchbook, measuring tape, a clear plastic box containing an array of colored pens and felt markers, a folder of fabric samples and the large, antique brass doorknob attached to the ring that held the keys to her apartment.

The appointment calendar was at the

bottom. She hauled it up to the surface and flipped it open.

"I'll get some ideas down on paper," she said briskly, "and I'll try to have some preliminary layouts ready for you by the end of the week. What do you say we meet in my office Friday afternoon?"

"Friday?" Davis was clearly disappointed. "That's a week off. Do we have to wait that long? I'd like to get started as soon as possible. The truth is this house has been damn depressing since my wife walked out."

Yeah, I'll bet it has, she thought.

"I understand," she said aloud, trying to sound sympathetic. It wasn't easy, given the fact that the fine hairs on the nape of her neck were still tingling and there were goose bumps on her arms beneath the sleeves of her lightweight jacket.

"I'm trying hard not to be bitter," Davis said. "But the divorce is costing me a bundle. Got a feeling I'll be getting bills from the lawyers for a long time."

All the available evidence indicated that Davis Mason had come out of the divorce in excellent shape, financially. From what she could see, he possessed a very expensive residence, the interiors of which he was prepared to pay her handsomely to have redesigned, and a membership in a pricey country club. But she did not raise those points aloud.

She was rapidly learning to be diplomatic with the newly divorced, having discovered that they constituted a hot market niche for interior designers such as herself. People emerging from shattered marriages frequently yearned to redo their living spaces as a form of therapy to help them get past the negative emotional fallout caused by the breakup.

She flipped through the pages of her calendar, pretending to study her schedule. Abruptly she snapped the leather-bound volume closed with a decisive air. "I'm afraid I'm booked solid. Friday is the only day I can give you the time this project deserves. Will two o'clock work for you?"

"Looks like I don't have much choice." Davis was not pleased. He was used to getting what he wanted. "Friday it is. Didn't mean to sound so impatient. It's just that I'm very anxious to get moving on the project."

"Of course. Once you've made the decision to redesign a personal living space, there's a natural urge to rush into the job." She spoke quickly, trying to inject a professional, businesslike quality into her voice. "But redoing an entire residence is a major undertaking and mistakes at this stage can be extremely costly."

"Yeah, I found that out the hard way." He took one more look at the bedroom. "I got as far as repainting this room and realized I needed expert help. I didn't think I could go wrong just putting a coat of white paint on the walls, but as soon as I finished I realized it didn't look right. I wanted to make it seem light and airy in here and instead—" He shrugged and let the sentence trail off with a *who knew* expression.

And instead the bedroom had all the cozy ambience of an autopsy room or an embalming chamber, Zoe concluded silently. No amount of the bright Arizona sunlight dancing on the surface of the sapphire pool outside could counteract that effect. Some of the unpleasant sensation was attributable to the stark white paint, but she knew that the real problem had been created by whatever it was that had happened in this bedroom. Some things could not be covered with a coat of paint.

She also knew that Mr. Ideal Client was not consciously aware of the emotions trapped in the walls. To her everlasting regret, she had never encountered anyone else who picked up on that kind of stuff the way she did—as pure, raw energy. But she had seen enough instances of others reacting in subtle, unconscious ways to the atmosphere of a particular room to be convinced that a lot of people responded to a space on some deep, psychic level.

She had also learned the hard way to keep her inner knowledge to herself.

"You chose a stark bright white." She took another step back, putting more distance between herself and the bedroom doorway. "I know it seems like pure white should be simple and straightforward, but it is actually very difficult to work with because it reflects so much glare, especially here in the desert. It also tends to create very cold shadows when you add furnishings. Ultimately that makes for a lack of harmony and tranquility. You were right to stop painting after you finished this room."

"Knew it wasn't the right direction." Davis made a casual gesture that invited her to go ahead of him down the hall. "I have to tell you, Zoe, when I decided I needed a professional designer, I didn't really put much stock in this feng shui thing that you do."

"A lot of people have doubts about it until they experience the result."

"I knew it was trendy and all. The women at the country club are really into it. When Helen Weymouth gave me your name, she went on and on about how you had completely transformed her home after she got her divorce. She'd been on the brink of putting it up for sale because of all the bad memories, she said. She credits you with changing the whole atmosphere of the place."

"The Weymouth project was an interesting one." Not much farther to the front door. A couple more minutes, and she would be out of here. "Mrs. Weymouth gave me a free hand."

"She advised me to do the same thing. A few months ago, after Jennifer left, I would have said that all this business of arranging the furniture to regulate the flow of negative and positive energy was way too far out for me. But the longer I live here alone with everything just the way it was when she was here, the more I'm convinced that there may be something to your design theories."

"I don't practice one particular school of feng shui." To her horror she realized she was talking much too fast. *Act normal. You know how to do this.* "I use elements of several different approaches combined with organizational principles from other classic design traditions such as Vastu."

"What's that?"

"An ancient Hindu science that sets out principles for architecture and design. I also incorporate what I consider the most useful elements from contemporary theories of harmony and proportion. My style is really quite eclectic."

Actually, I pretty much make it up as I go along, she added silently. But clients did not like to hear that.

She walked swiftly toward the front of the house, desperate to escape into the fresh air. Now that she had been sensitized by the experience in the bedroom, she was picking up wispy tendrils of dark, unwholesome emotions from other walls in the residence. She had to get out of this place fast.

She reached the terra-cotta foyer at last. Davis was right behind her. He opened the front door, and she escaped into the reassuring warmth of the early October day.

"Are you sure you're feeling well enough to drive back to your office?" Davis asked.

Act normal.

"I've got an energy bar in the car." Another lie. Was she getting good at this or what?

"All right. Well, take care. And I'll see you on Friday."

"Right. Friday."

She gave him what she hoped was a bright, professional-looking smile, tightened her grip on the chartreuse tote, and went briskly toward her car. She tried not to appear as if she was rushing away from the screaming house.

She breathed a sigh of relief when she reached the vehicle. Yanking open the door, she tossed the tote onto the passenger seat, slid behind the wheel, put her dark glasses on, and fired up the engine, all in what felt like a single motion.

Her hands were still trembling. Aftershocks from the surge of adrenaline, she surmised. This wasn't the first time. She could handle it.

But she had to grip the wheel very tightly

in order to steer her way out of the exclusive community. To her left was the long stretch of impossibly green fairway that served as the approach to the sixteenth hole of the Desert View Country Club. Elegant homes similar to the Mason residence were scattered artfully around the golf course.

Beyond the vivid green links stretched the rugged expanse of the Sonoran Desert and low, rolling mountain foothills. The golf club community and the adjoining town of Whispering Springs were a little more than an hour's drive from Phoenix, close enough to catch some of the spillover from the tourist trade but far enough out to avoid the traffic and congestion of the city.

The harsh, dry landscape had seemed a strange and alien place to her when she had moved here a year ago, but somewhere along the line her new environment had begun to feel familiar, even comfortable. She had discovered an unexpected beauty in the desert, with its spectacular sunrises and sunsets and the astounding depths of light and shadow. She had always been drawn to contrasts, and there was nothing subtle about this place.

The decision to move to Whispering

Springs had been a good one, she mused, but maybe she should reconsider the career move she had made at the same time. Interior design had seemed like a natural, logical way to go. After all, she had a background in the fine arts and a good, trained eye, and she certainly knew how to get the feel of a living space. Best of all, she hadn't needed any additional degrees or qualifications in order to set herself up in business legally. But today's encounter was enough to give her some second thoughts.

A uniformed guard came out of a small building located at the gated entrance. The emblem on his snappy khaki jacket declared him to be an employee of Radnor Security Systems. He greeted her politely, wished her a good day, and went back inside his air-conditioned sanctuary to make a note on his log.

Security was tight here in this carefully planned enclave of wealth and status, but someone in the Mason residence had not benefited from it.

She waited until she was clear of the gates and on her way back toward the downtown section of Whispering Springs before she picked up her phone. She punched in the only number that she had coded into her speed dial.

Arcadia Ames answered on the third ring, giving the name of her gift shop in her low, throaty voice. "Gallery Euphoria."

Arcadia sold unique, expensive gifts to an upscale clientele, but Zoe was pretty sure her friend could have sold sand here in the desert with that voice.

Arcadia was her best friend, make that her only friend. She had once had other friends, Zoe thought. But that was a long time ago, back when she had had a real life and had not been living in the shadows.

"It's me," Zoe said.

"What's wrong? Something happen with Mr. Ideal Client?"

"You could say that."

"He decided not to hire you after all? That idiot. But don't worry, there will be other good clients like him. The divorce rate doesn't seem to be going down very much."

"Unfortunately, Mason didn't change his mind," Zoe said evenly. "I wish he had."

"Did the creep make a pass at you?"

"He was a perfect gentleman."

"He must be rich because everybody who lives in Desert View is, by definition, a high roller," Arcadia said patiently. "So what went wrong?"

"I think Mr. Ideal Client may have murdered his wife."

Chapter Two

Twenty minutes later, Zoe left her car in one of the landscaped parking lots that served the shops and businesses of Whispering Springs. She walked down the sidewalk and turned into the palm-shaded entrance of Fountain Square, an upscale outdoor shopping mall. Arcadia waited for her at a small table set out on the shaded patio adjoining one of the numerous cafés.

Arcadia was, as usual, a study in ice and silver hues. Her very short, gamin-cut hair was tinted platinum and matched her long acrylic nails. Her eyes were an unusual shade of silvery blue. She was tall and slender and as languidly graceful as a haute couture model. She wore a pale glacier blue silk shirt and flowing white silk trousers. Silver and turquoise gleamed at her throat and ears.

Zoe was not precisely sure how old Arcadia was. Her friend had never volunteered the information, and there was something about her that made you think twice before you intruded on her very private space. Zoe assumed that she was in her mid-forties but she would not have put money on it.

In another time and place, Zoe thought, Arcadia could have been an expatriate living in Paris, drinking absinthe and recording her observations on soon-to-be famous people in a journal. There was about her an air of sophisticated ennui that implied too much knowledge of the world. In reality, she had once been an extremely successful financial trader.

There was a small cup of espresso in front of Arcadia. A glass of iced tea waited for Zoe. The neighboring tables were unoccupied.

Zoe dropped her tote onto a vacant chair and sat down, aware, as always, of the sharp contrast between herself and her friend. On the surface they looked like they had nothing in common. Her own hair was a dark shade of auburn brown. Her eyes were that vague, hard-to-describe mix of green and gold that ended up going down as hazel on a driver's license. And, unlike Arcadia, she loved bright, vivid colors.

Opposites they may have been, Zoe mused, but the bond between them was as strong as any that could have existed between sisters.

She glanced briefly at her fingertips. They were no longer trembling. She took that as a good sign.

Arcadia's platinum brows drew together in a delicate frown. "Are you okay?"

"Sure. The worst is over. I got caught by surprise, that's all. I should know better than to just blunder merrily into an unknown room like that."

Zoe picked up the pleasantly cold, damp glass in front of her and took a long swallow of the iced tea. The adrenaline that always accompanied an episode was wearing off, but it would take a while to wash out of her system. The aftermath inevitably left her restless and oddly hungry.

"I ordered a couple of Caesar salads," Arcadia said.

"Oh, good. Thanks."

A waiter appeared bearing bread and rosemary-scented olive oil. He arranged the items on the table and departed.

Zoe tore off a large chunk of bread and plunged it into the olive oil. She paused just long enough to sprinkle a little salt on the oil-saturated bread, and then she took a very large bite.

"Are you sure you're all right?" Arcadia remained unconvinced. "No offense, but you look somewhat the worse for wear."

"I'm fine," Zoe said around the mouthful of dense, chewy bread. "The problem is: what do I do now?"

Arcadia leaned forward and lowered her voice even though no one else was seated nearby. "You're absolutely sure this guy, Mason, killed his wife?"

"No, of course, I'm not sure." Zoe swallowed. "I have no way of knowing exactly what happened in that room. I only pick up on the emotions of the events, not the events themselves. But I'll tell you this much, whatever it was, it was bad." She shuddered. "And fairly recent."

"You could tell that much from those weird sensations you get?"

"Yes." She thought about her impressions. "Furthermore, I've got some evidence to back up my conclusions. At least, I think I do."

Arcadia pounced on that. "What kind of evidence?"

"Well, nothing that would stand up in court. But the bed was gone."

"The bed?"

"He claimed that his ex took it with her."

"Maybe she did. A missing bed isn't going to get anyone's attention."

"I know, but the bed wasn't the only thing that was gone. I could see some fading in the finish on the wooden floor, but there was a rectangular area near where the bed had stood that was not faded."

"A rug?"

"Uh-huh." Zoe ate more bread. "But it's gone, too. Mason didn't say anything about the ex taking it. Also, the walls in that room have been recently repainted with a coat of white paint that is all wrong for that space. Mason told me that he did it himself, and it looks like it. Lousy job. A wealthy man like that living in a high-end neighborhood, you'd think he would have hired a painter if he didn't know what he was doing around a bucket of paint."

"Hmm." Arcadia tapped a platinum nail lightly against the small espresso cup. "I admit this is not sounding good."

"As far as I'm concerned it was his choice of stark white that bothered me the most. It had a certain symbolism to it. Almost as if he was trying to cover up something very dark."

"I see what you mean."

The waiter reappeared with the salads. Zoe picked up a fork and went to work.

"Unfortunately, he really wants to hire me," she said between bites. "Apparently Helen Weymouth gave me a glowing reference. I've got another appointment with him on Friday."

"You could cancel it. Tell him that you can't take on the job of redoing his residence because there's been a huge glitch on one of your other projects that won't leave you any time for him."

Zoe was briefly amused. "Not a bad excuse. You're good, you know that?"

"Well?"

"The thing is, I got the distinct impression that Mason isn't going to like it if I back out of this. He's very anxious to get his house redone. Maybe on some unconscious level, he's picking up a few of the bad vibes in that bedroom. Or maybe he's living with a guilty conscience and thinks a change of environment will make him feel better. Either way, I've got a feeling he'll make an unpleasant scene."

"What's he going to do? Report you to the Better Business Bureau?"

"You're right. There isn't much he can do, is there? If he is guilty of something really awful, he certainly won't want to draw a lot of attention to himself by creating a scene in the office of a respectable local business person."

"So why aren't you rushing to back out of that Friday appointment?"

"You know why." Zoe ate the last anchovy, sat back and met Arcadia's eyes. "What if he really did murder his wife?"

"All you know right now is that something nasty occurred in that bedroom."

"Yes."

Arcadia studied her for a long moment and then sighed softly with an air of surrendering to the inevitable. "And you, being you, can't let it go."

"It's sort of a hard thing to block out of my mind," Zoe said apologetically.

"Okay, okay, I understand." Arcadia took a dainty bite of salad. "We've got to think this through before we make any decisions."

"Well, one thing is for sure, I can't do the logical thing and go to the cops."

"No," Arcadia said immediately. "That's not an option. They'd laugh in your face if you told them you thought you'd picked up some bad energy vibes from a client's bedroom."

"Maybe I could phone in an anonymous tip? Pretend I saw something suspicious happening at that house and ask them to inquire into the current whereabouts of Mrs. Jennifer Mason?"

"If no one has filed a missing person report, I doubt you'd get their attention," Arcadia replied. "You're not a member of the family. You never even met the woman."

"True. And even if I somehow managed to convince them to search Mason's residence, they wouldn't find much in the way of evidence. I ought to know. I went through every room myself, this morning, including the linen closet."

"It's possible that whatever took place in that bedroom had nothing to do with the Masons. Maybe it occurred before they bought the house."

"Maybe. But Mason told me that he and his wife moved in shortly after they were married. I got the impression that was about a year and a half ago. I think that what I felt in that bedroom occurred more recently."

"But you can't be sure, right?"

"No," Zoe admitted. "When the emotions are very powerful, they can linger for a long time."

"Then it is possible that the events in the bedroom could predate the arrival of the Masons."

"Well, yes. It's possible." *But not likely,* Zoe added silently. There was a faded quality to the old stuff that she had learned to detect, even if she could not describe the difference. What she had felt this afternoon was fresh. "Look, it shouldn't be too hard to find out if Mrs. Mason is still alive and well. If she's happily sunbathing topless in the South of France, I can relax and assume that her husband did not murder her."

"Right." Arcadia looked somewhat relieved.

"What I need," Zoe said, "is a private investigator. I'll bet an expert could go online and get me the answers I need in half an hour."

She jumped to her feet. "Back in a second."

"Where are you going?"

"Inside to find a phone book."

She hurried into the interior of the small eatery and spotted a worn set of yellow pages on the desk behind the front counter. She asked if she could borrow it. The clerk shrugged and handed it to her.

She carried the phone book back outside, sat down at the table, and opened it. There were two listings under *Investigators.*

The first was for Radnor Security Systems. It featured a full-page display ad that offered employee background and due diligence checks, corporate security seminars, security guards for businesses, and the latest in online investigative technology.

The second company was named Truax Investigations. The tiny ad occupied a small space approximately two inches long and one inch high on the page. It claimed that the firm had been in continuous operation in Whispering Springs for more than forty years. It also guaranteed privacy and confidentiality to all clients. There was a phone number and an address on Cobalt Street.

"Looks like I've got a choice between a large company with a corporate emphasis or a small firm that has been in business here in town for quite a while." Zoe studied the Truax Investigations ad. "Probably a one-man operation."

"Go with the big company," Arcadia advised. "More resources and more guarantee of getting someone who knows how to do the online stuff. But it will probably be pricier."

"How expensive can a simple search like this be?" Zoe dug her phone out of the tote. "All I want to know is whether or not Mrs. Jennifer Mason has used her charge cards or accessed her bank account recently. Piece of cake for an investigator, I'm sure."

She entered the number for Radnor Security Systems and was promptly greeted by a professional-sounding receptionist. She made a quick inquiry regarding fees and hung up fast when she got the answer.

"Well?" Arcadia asked.

"In hindsight, it appears that my observation of a moment ago was somewhat naïve. It turns out that, contrary to what I assumed, this sort of search can be very expensive. Not only was the hourly rate very high, but in addition, there is a nonrefundable minimum fee which is equivalent to three hours of investigative time."

Arcadia raised one shoulder in a small, resigned shrug. "Obviously they don't want to encourage small accounts. Try the little agency. Might be hungrier." She paused. "Also might be less chance of complications."

Zoe looked at her. There was no need to go into the fine nuances of just what the term *complications* meant. They both knew how carefully this matter would have to be handled if they were to avoid attracting unwanted attention to themselves.

"Okay, I'll call Truax." Zoe picked up the phone again, trying to stay positive. "It's probably the best way to go, anyway. After all, if he's been in business for more than forty years, he must be getting on. A real old-fashioned kind of investigator. I'll bet he has a ton of contacts in the community and with the police. If Jennifer Mason is, indeed, missing, he might even be able to convince the cops to look into the situation without explaining why."

"Just make sure he keeps your name out of it."

Zoe glanced at the ad for Truax Investigations again while she listened to the ringing on the other end of the line. "It says right here that he's really big on privacy for his clients. I'll bet he's built his reputation on his ability to maintain confidentiality."

"What reputation?" Arcadia asked. "Neither of us had ever heard of him until you opened that phone book."

"Just goes to show how good he is at keeping a low profile." She frowned when she realized that no one was rushing to pick up the phone at Truax Investigations. She waited through a few more rings and then gave up.

"Out to lunch?" Arcadia asked dryly.

"Looks like it. The address is on Cobalt Street. That's just a few blocks from here. I'll walk over and talk to the person in charge as soon as we finish."

"You're sure you want to do this?"

"Yes." She closed the phone book and picked up her unfinished tea. A sense of satisfaction flowed through her, lifting her spirits. Or maybe that was the food and caffeine taking effect, she thought. "You know, I've got a good feeling about this. Hiring Truax is the right way to go. I know it."

"Think so?"

"Yes."

Arcadia shook her head once, her silver-glossed mouth curved slightly in a rare, wry smile. "The thing that never ceases to amaze me about you, Zoe, is your seemingly bottomless well of optimism. If I didn't know you better, I'd swear you took drugs to maintain such an irrational view of the universe."

"So I'm a glass-half-full kind of person."

"And I'm a worst-case-scenario type. Do you sometimes wonder why we get along so well?"

"The way I see it, we sort of balance each other, and we did both graduate from the same alma mater."

"To good old Xanadu." Arcadia raised her espresso cup and clinked it lightly against Zoe's tea glass. A fleeting rage glittered briefly in her eyes. "May it sink into an undersea volcano and disappear forever."

Zoe stopped smiling. "I'll drink to that."

Chapter Three

Zoe's bright bubble of optimism threatened to burst when she turned the corner into Cobalt Street. It was amazing how fast the character of a town could change within a few blocks. The fashionable shops and the modern business district were only a short distance away, but they might as well have been in a different dimension. Here on Cobalt Street there was a dated, slightly seedy air.

The buildings were mostly two-story structures done in the classic Southwestern version of the Spanish Colonial style. The stucco exteriors had rounded edges, arched doorways, and deep-set windows. The roofs were red tile. The old trees, no doubt planted many years ago before the city council had begun to fret about water conservation, created a shady canopy.

In the middle of the block, Zoe paused to check the address she had written down. There was no mistake. She was standing in front of 49 Cobalt Street.

She crossed a small patio and studied the grimy-windowed directory. Truax Investigations was on the upper floor. Most of the other offices appeared to be empty except for one on the ground floor labeled SINGLE-MINDED BOOKS.

She opened the front door and hesitated a fraction of a second on the threshold. She had already learned one lesson today, she reminded herself. And older buildings were often the worst.

Nothing terrible happened. No fierce or violent emotions emanated from the walls. The hallway in front of her was sunk deep in gloom, but she didn't think anyone had killed anybody here. At least not lately.

She went toward the staircase. When she passed Single-Minded Books, she noticed that the door was closed. The proprietor was evidently not keen on encouraging walk-in business.

She climbed the squeaky, badly lit stairs to the second floor and went warily down a dingy hall. There were two closed, unmarked doors. The third one had a small sign tacked to it. TRUAX INVESTIGATIONS. It stood partway open, revealing a dim interior.

She hesitated, wondering if she was about to make a serious mistake. Maybe it would be better to go with the larger, corporate security agency on the other side of town. So what if its services cost three or four times as much? You got what you paid for in this world.

On the other hand, she was here and time was of the essence. And money, unfortunately, was a factor, especially now that it looked like Mr. Ideal Client might not be quite so ideal.

She pushed open the door and stepped cautiously inside. But once over the threshold, she relaxed. There was nothing alarming in these walls.

She took stock of the surroundings. You could tell a lot about a business and its owner by the manner in which the office was maintained, she reminded herself.

If that dictum was true, it looked like Truax Investigations was in bad shape financially. Either that, or the proprietor had not seen fit to invest any of the profits back into the reception area.

There was an old-fashioned vintage look to the heavy wooden secretarial desk and the large overstuffed leather chairs, but they were not the kind of period pieces that would interest an antiques dealer. People didn't collect furniture like this, but it was sturdy and built to last. The desk and the chairs were used and worn, but they would never break down or wear out. If you ever decided to get rid of them, you'd have to haul them off to a landfill.

She was half tempted to take out her camera. The place would have made a great black-and-white shot. She could see the picture in her head, brooding and moody and atmospheric with the hazy afternoon light slanting through the blinds.

There was a phone on the desk, but she saw no evidence of a computer. That did not bode well. She had been counting on an investigator who was conversant in technology to get her the answers she wanted in a hurry. The lack of a secretary or receptionist was not encouraging, either.

What really worried her, though, was the stack of cardboard packing boxes that occupied a third of the small space. Many of them were sealed. A few stood open. She crossed to the nearest one, glanced inside, and saw a gooseneck lamp and several shrink-wrapped packages of new, unused notepads in various sizes. Half were the small three-by-five type that fit into a man's shirt pocket. The rest were large, eight-and-a-half-by-eleven legal rule tablets. There were also several old, well-thumbed books.

Someone was packing up the office. Her heart sank. Truax Investigations was in the process of closing its doors.

For some reason, she was unable to resist the compulsion of curiosity. Reaching into the box, she plucked out one of the heavy volumes and glanced at the title on the spine. *A History of Murder in Late 19th Century San Francisco.*

She put it back into the box and took out another. *Investigating Violence and Murder in Colonial America.*

"Cheerful bedtime reading," she muttered.

"Jeff? Theo? About time you two got back."

Zoe started and dropped the book back into the box. The voice came from the inner office. A man's voice—not loud but dark and resonant with a natural air of authority.

Voices like that made her wary.

"I hope one of you remembered my cof-

fee. We've still got a lot of work ahead of us this afternoon."

Zoe cleared her throat. "This isn't Jeff. Or Theo, either, for that matter."

There was a short silence from the inner room. The door squeaked on its hinges as whoever was on the other side pulled it wide.

A man came to stand in the opening, one powerful-looking hand gripping the edge of the door. He looked out from the shadows, contemplating her with an enigmatic expression that was probably meant to pass for polite inquiry. He didn't have the kind of eyes that could do polite inquiry well, she thought. They were an interesting shade of amber brown. She had seen similar eyes on the Nature Channel and in wildlife shots in *National Geographic.* They usually went with the creatures that possessed the sharpest teeth.

He was dressed in a pair of close-fitting khaki trousers, which rode low on his hips, and a crisply pressed white shirt. The collar of the shirt was open and the sleeves were rolled up on his forearms, revealing dark hair in both places. The spiral wire binding of a three-by-five notepad stuck out of the chest pocket.

His stance in the doorway implied supple muscles and an innate confidence. Her self-defense instructor would no doubt describe him as *centered.* He was not exceptionally tall, only about medium height, but there was a sleek, compact power in his shoulders. He gave the unmistakable impression that he was in complete command of himself. Maybe to a fault, she thought.

His hair had no doubt once been so dark as to be mistaken for black in the shadows. But there were shards of silver at the temples and elsewhere now. They harmonized well with the crinkles of experience at the corners of his eyes and the brackets that framed his mouth.

The face fit that quiet, authoritative voice—not handsome but strong and compelling. Both belonged to the sort of man others would automatically look to in a crisis but who could be extremely irritating the rest of the time because he would always be in charge and would not hesitate to let you know it.

He had a lot in common with his furniture: well used and worn around the edges, but he would probably never break down or wear out. Like the desk and chairs, you'd have to haul him off to the landfill if you wanted to get rid of him, and that would be no easy task.

If this was the Mr. Truax of Truax Investigations, the ad in the phone book was guilty of severe misrepresentation. This man had some interesting mileage on him, but he certainly wasn't heading into his dotage.

"Sorry. I was on the stepladder. Didn't see you come in. What can I do for you?" he asked.

The dark voice brought her back to her senses. She realized that she had been holding her breath, as if this moment and this man were very important in some way she did not yet fully comprehend.

Let's try to stay focused here, she thought. *Breathe. So you haven't had much of a social life lately, that's no excuse to stare at strange men.*

"I came to see Mr. Truax," she said with what she thought was commendable aplomb under the circumstances.

"That'd be me."

She cleared her throat. "You are *the* Truax of Truax Investigations?"

"As of three days ago according to the date on my business license. The name is Ethan Truax, by the way."

"I don't understand. The phone book ad stated that you've been serving the community for more than forty years."

"My uncle put that ad in the book. He retired last month. I'm taking over the business."

"I see." She waved a hand to indicate the packing boxes. "You're moving in, not out?"

"That's the plan."

"Do you mind if I ask how long you've lived here in Whispering Springs?"

He gave that some thought. "A little more than a month."

So much for dealing with an investigator who had extensive contacts in the community and with local law enforcement, she thought. There was still time to call Radnor Security Systems. Of course there was the not-so-little issue of price, but maybe she could negotiate an extended payment schedule with the larger firm.

She took a step back toward the door. "You're new to this profession, then?"

"No. I owned and operated an agency in Los Angeles for several years."

That should have been reassuring news. Why wasn't she feeling reassured?

"This probably isn't a good time for you," she said quickly. "I'm sure you're very busy getting unpacked and organized."

"Not too busy to take on a client. Why don't you come into my office and tell me why you need an investigator?"

It was not exactly a request, she noticed. Not quite a command, either. More of a glittering lure designed to draw her into striking distance.

She had to make a decision. The bottom line here was time and money. She did not have a lot of either.

She tightened her grip on the handle of the chartreuse tote and tried to look like a woman who hired seedy private investigators on a frequent basis.

"How much do you charge for your services, Mr. Truax?"

"Come in and sit down." He moved deeper into his office, beckoning her closer with the subtle invitation. "We can discuss the financial aspects of the arrangement."

She could not come up with a good reason not to at least get a cost estimate.

"All right." She looked briefly at her

watch. "But I don't have a lot of time. If we can't agree on your fees, I will have to call someone else."

"The only other agency in town is Radnor."

"I'm aware of that," she said coolly. This was business. She did not want him to think that she had not done her research as a consumer. "They appear to be very cutting-edge. I was told that they use the latest high-tech methods."

"They've got computers, if that's what you mean, but I've got one, too."

"Really?" She looked around very pointedly. "Where?"

"In here. I'm still working on getting it set up."

"Oh."

"I can guarantee you that I'm less expensive than Radnor."

"Well—"

"And there's another aspect you may want to take into consideration." His mouth curved faintly at the corners. "Being new in town, I'm also a hell of a lot hungrier."

She almost bolted for the door. "Yes, well—"

"And more flexible."

She braced herself and walked toward the inner office. It was like walking through Door Number Three on a television game show, she thought, the door that concealed the mystery prize. You might get an all-expense-paid trip to Paris, or you might lose everything you had managed to win up to that point.

She paused briefly at the threshold, waiting to see what would greet her. But there was nothing terrible in the room, just the faint traces of sensation that she had learned to expect in old buildings. She picked up a few whispers of sadness, some anxiety, and a little residual anger—all of it from long ago and very low-level. Nothing she could not block easily.

"Something wrong?" Ethan asked.

With a start, she realized he was watching her very intently. Most people never seemed to notice her slight hesitation upon entering a room. The fact that Ethan Truax had observed that tiny pause worried her for some reason. She reminded herself that he was a private investigator and people in that line were supposed to notice things.

"No, of course not," she replied.

She went quickly to the huge, overstuffed, oversized armchair that sat in front of the desk. It almost swallowed her whole when she sat down in it.

Ethan went behind his desk, a massive, scarred hunk of oak that was even larger and sturdier than the one in the other room, and sat down. The chair gave a squeak of protest.

She examined the room with what she told herself was professional interest but which she suspected was actually deep personal curiosity. Everything connected to Ethan Truax fascinated her for some strange reason, and you could tell so much about a person by the space he or she inhabited.

The inner office was furnished with the same kind of window treatment and the same type of substantial, old-fashioned, masculine pieces she had seen in the other room. She had to admit that they invoked a certain period atmosphere and made a statement that suited the fictional image of the private investigation business.

But in her opinion, the client chair in which she sat was far too large and too overwhelming to make a visitor feel comfortable. Furthermore, Truax's massive desk was not in the right place in the room to create the best energy flow. In addition there was a mirror hanging on the wall that was both badly proportioned and badly positioned.

Several heavy metal filing cabinets were lined up side by side against the rear wall. They were ancient and not particularly attractive, but she supposed an investigator needed a place for files.

New bookshelves had been recently installed on either side of the door. Unfortunately, Truax had chosen to go with inexpensive metal shelving that did nothing to add to the ambience of the room. Half of the shelves were already loaded with volumes. She could see more of the same sort of impressive, academic-looking tomes she had seen in the packing box outside.

Who would have expected a private investigator to possess a serious book collection? Maybe her concept of the profession, formed as it had been by mystery novels, television, and old films, was not entirely accurate.

Ethan's surroundings did not answer her silent questions; instead they raised new ones and made her all the more curious about him.

One thing was clear, he commanded his space; it did not command him.

Ethan opened a desk drawer, took out a yellow notepad, and put it on the desk in front of him. "Why don't we start with your name?"

"Zoe Luce. I own a design firm here in town. Enhanced Interiors."

"You're a decorator," he said flatly.

"Interior designer."

"Whatever."

"Do you have some sort of underlying hostility toward people in my profession?"

"I had a bad experience with a decorator once."

"Well, for the record," Zoe said, "I think that I'm having a really bad experience with a private investigator. This could color my attitude toward folks in your field for years to come."

He tapped the pen on the notepad and contemplated her in silence for a while.

"Sorry," he said eventually. "Let's try this again. What do you want me to do for you, Zoe Luce?"

"I thought we were going to talk about money first."

"Oh, yeah. I almost forgot." He put down

the pen, rested his arms on the desk, and linked his fingers. "Like I said, if you're shopping by price, you're stuck with me. My hourly rates are considerably less than those charged over at Radnor, and I have only a two-hour minimum."

That news had an elevating effect on her mood. "What about expenses? Mileage and meals, that kind of thing?"

"You aren't responsible for mileage or meals within the city limits. You will be billed for miscellaneous expenses and for any costs incurred if I have to travel outside Whispering Springs. Don't worry, you'll get receipts."

He thinks I'm an idiot. Annoyed, she crossed her legs very deliberately. She sat back into the depths of the voluminous chair, trusting to fate that she would not get eaten alive by the monster, and smiled coolly.

"In that case, I would like to purchase the minimum two hours," she said. "I'm sure the job won't take even that much time."

"Background check on a new male acquaintance?" he asked with no inflection.

"Good heavens, no, nothing like that."

She frowned. “Do you get a lot of requests like that?”

He shrugged. “Not yet. You’re my first client here in Whispering Springs. But it was a fairly common request in L.A.”

“I guess that isn’t so surprising.” She considered the subject for a few seconds. “I mean, it makes a lot of sense to check out a potential date if you think things might get serious.”

“Especially in L.A.,” he agreed dryly.

“All I want you to do is locate someone.”

“Who do you want me to find, Miss Luce?” He paused with an air of grave politeness. “It is, Miss, isn’t it? Or should I call you Ms. or Mrs.?”

“I’m not married,” she said very precisely. She did not want him calling her Miss or Ms. Luce. It sounded ridiculously formal. She also did not want him inquiring into her past marital status. “Make it Zoe.”

“Fine. Who do you want me to find, Zoe?”

She breathed deeply and prepared to pick her way through the minefield. She needed to give him enough information to do his job but not enough to make him conclude that she was loony-tunes. And she definitely did not want to give him the kind of details that would arouse any curiosity about her personally.

"I would like you to find a woman named Mrs. Jennifer Mason. I can give you her last address here in town. I believe she lived there until a few months ago."

He unlinked his fingers, picked up the pen again, and began making more notes on the yellow pad.

"Friend of yours?" he asked without looking up. "Relative?"

"Neither. She's the wife of a man named Davis Mason. He lives in Desert View."

Ethan did glance up at that. "The fancy gated golf-course community just outside of town?"

"Yes. Mr. Mason recently hired me to redesign the interiors of his residence."

"Residence," Ethan repeated neutrally. "Would that be what you interior decorators like to call a house?"

Ethan Truax was becoming more irritating by the minute.

"In the field of interior *design,*" she said, emphasizing the last word, "the word *residence* is generally felt to be a more gracious term for a client's living space. The term conveys a sense of permanence and elegance. It implies a cultivated lifestyle. People like to associate those qualities with their homes."

"A lifestyle thing, huh?" He looked amused.

"Of course, if you have trouble with the longer word," she added sweetly, "please feel free to use the shorter one."

"Thanks, I'll do that. Any idea where Mrs. Jennifer Mason may have gone?"

"No. Davis, her husband, told me that she walked out on him a couple months ago and that they are in the process of getting a divorce. I just want to confirm that fact."

Ethan raised his brows. "Are you sure this isn't a background check on a potential date?"

"Davis Mason is a client," she said coldly.

"If that's the case, why are you so concerned with the whereabouts of his not-quite-ex-wife?"

The question worried her. "Do you need to know my reasons before you agree to take the job?"

"No. Not at this point, at any rate."

"Your ad in the phone book stresses your concern for privacy and confidentiality."

"That was my uncle's ad, not mine."

A whisper of uncertainty tingled through

her. She rested her hands on the overstuffed arms of the big chair, preparing to push herself up out of its cushioned jaws.

"If you intend to alter what I took to be the long-standing business practices of this agency," she said, "I'd like to know about it before this conversation goes any further. As you pointed out, I do have another option."

He put down the pen and leaned back in the chair. "There will be no change in this firm's concern for client confidentiality."

"Good." She relaxed a little.

"But I like to know as much as possible about what I'm getting into before I start an investigation."

It was her turn to raise her brows. "I'm here because I was under the impression that one consults a private investigator when one does not wish to explain all the reasons why one needs that particular type of professional assistance."

His hard mouth quirked a little. "Is that right?"

She was simmering now, but she felt trapped by financial considerations and the tight time frame. She needed answers and she needed them before Friday. "Do you want this job or not, Mr. Truax?"

"I want it. Sorry, if the questions bother you, but I'm just gathering information. It's what I do, Zoe."

"All I want is for you to locate Mrs. Jennifer Mason. How hard can that be for a professional investigator? Surely it's just a matter of checking to see if she's using her credit cards or checkbook, right? Any high school kid could probably do it."

"Yeah. Lately I've started to worry a lot about the competition from high school kids."

Now she knew for certain that he was mocking her. She shoved herself halfway up out of the chair. It wasn't easy disengaging herself from the mouth of the beast.

"If you feel that the job is beyond your abilities," she said grimly, "or that you can't do it without additional information, just say so and I'll go find myself a bright high school kid."

"Sit down." He paused. "Please."

It was not an order, not exactly. How could it be? It wasn't as though he could force her to sit back down in the big chair. The problem was that she had been bluffing, and he had guessed as much.

She sat. "Do you or do you not intend to investigate?"

"I'll find Mrs. Jennifer Mason for you. But I'd better make one thing clear. I'm not going to give you any contact information unless and until I'm sure she wants you to know where she is. Understood?"

That caught her off guard. "Wait a second. Do you think I want to know her current address so that I can do something to her?"

"It happens."

She shuddered. "Yes, I suppose it does. Well, rest assured, I don't care where she lives. I have no intention of contacting her."

"You just want to know that she's out of Davis Mason's life, is that it?"

He wasn't going to let it go until she came up with a convincing reason for wanting to check on the whereabouts of Jennifer Mason. Maybe the easiest way to handle this was to take the first excuse he had offered.

"All right," she said, trying to sound resigned. "As you suggested, this is a personal matter for me. Davis is a client but he is also a successful, intelligent, attractive man, and he seems interested in me, if you know what I mean."

"Uh-huh. I know what you mean."

She glared, suspicious of his tone, but he just sat there, waiting. She recognized the tactic. Dr. McAlistair, her therapist at Xanadu had employed it. The interrogation technique was based on the fact that most people were uncomfortable with silence, got nervous, and tended to start talking to fill the vacuum.

The realization that Truax was attempting to use the same approach as McAlistair pissed her off. She reminded herself that it was nothing personal in Truax's case. He just wanted answers.

"As I told you, Davis led me to believe that he's getting divorced. I'd like to be sure that he's genuinely free, or about to become free, to engage in another, uh, serious, committed relationship."

Ethan did not move, but his eyes never left her face. "Okay."

She was not sure how to take that. "Okay? You mean you'll get busy and investigate now?"

"No."

"That does it, I've had enough." She did get out of the chair this time. All the way out. "I've asked you to do a simple search and I've given you my reason, even though it was extremely personal and I resent the probe into my private life. What more can you possibly want?"

"An advance for two hours' worth of my time. Credit card, check, or money order will be fine."

"Does this mean you're taking the job?"

"Yes, ma'am. Like you, I'm not in a position to be real choosy at the moment. I'm trying to get a business up and running here."

She yanked open the tote and pulled out her wallet, removed a credit card, and tossed it onto the desk. "Here. Get busy."

He picked up the card, got to his feet, and went to a small side table where a credit card machine sat.

She watched him punch in some numbers and swipe her card. "You know, I can't help but notice that even though you haven't had time to set up your computer, you've managed to get your credit card authorization machine connected."

"First things first."

"I can certainly see how you rank your priorities, Mr. Truax. Always get paid in advance, is that it?"

"I'm not running a charitable foundation."

"Don't worry, I'd never in a million years make the mistake of thinking that you might be the benevolent type." She gave the office another critical glance while she waited for the machine to spit out the credit card slip. If she had any sense, she would keep her mouth shut, she thought. But she could not resist the urge to give him some free advice. "You know, if I were you, I'd get a smaller client chair. This one is too large. It's not inviting."

"Maybe you're just too small for the chair." He sounded supremely disinterested. His attention was fixed on the slip of paper coming out of the machine.

That's it, she thought. *Not another word, so help me.* If the man was too stubborn to take some good advice, that was his problem. But the desk worried her even more than the chair. And then there was the poorly positioned mirror.

She cleared her throat.

"It would also be a good idea to move that desk over there near the window, and I'd suggest that you take down the mirror or at least shift it to the other wall," she said in a little rush. "It would create a more calming energy flow."

He gave her a sidelong look. "Energy flow?"

She had been right. This was a complete waste of time. "Forget it. You're probably not familiar with design theories such as feng shui that are used to organize a harmonious environment."

"I've heard of them." He ripped the paper out of the machine and handed it to her. "But I'm not into decorating trends."

"Why am I not surprised?" She snatched the credit card slip from him, glanced at the total amount, and winced. Less than Radnor but certainly not exactly a bargain, she thought.

As if he knew what was going through her mind, Ethan's mouth curved humorlessly. "I'm cheap, but I'm not free."

She sighed, picked up a pen, and scrawled her name.

He took the signed slip from her and examined it with an expression of keen satisfaction. "You know, this is a special moment for me."

"In what way?"

"This represents my first professional business transaction here in Whispering Springs. I should probably frame this. Just think, your name could hang on my wall for years."

"Along with my credit card number. No thanks. If I were you, I wouldn't get too excited about this, Mr. Truax. I have no intention of becoming a repeat client."

"You never know. If this Mason guy doesn't work out as a suitable candidate for, what was it you called it? Oh, yeah, a *serious, committed relationship.* If he doesn't make the grade due to failure to obtain a divorce, you may want me to run a background check on some other man for you."

For some idiotic reason, she suddenly wondered if Ethan Truax was into serious, committed relationships. She glanced at his hand and noticed that he was not wearing a wedding ring. What would she discover if she had someone run a background check on him? A lot of ex-girlfriends, no doubt, maybe an ex-wife.

Damn. Now she was speculating on his marital status. This was not good.

She dropped the pen she had used to sign the credit card slip into her tote and gave him a very bright smile. "Don't hold your breath."

She hoisted the tote over one shoulder,

swung around, and went toward the door. At least she would have the last word, she thought.

"Just a minute," Ethan said.

She glanced back over her shoulder. "Now what?"

"That's my pen you're walking off with in your bag. Mind giving it back? I'm trying to keep a lid on overhead and office expenses."

Chapter Four

Leon Grady's heartburn always flared up in the hushed atmosphere and plush surroundings of his employer's office suite. He had grown up in a working-class neighborhood where, if you were lucky, walls got painted, not paneled, and the furniture was trimmed in plastic made to look like wood, not veneered with exotic species of actual trees.

Dr. Ian Harper had once told him that his office had been designed to calm patients and reassure their families. But all the fancy carpeting and the expensive pictures on the walls had the opposite effect on Leon. He really hated this room. Talk about stress triggers. Hell, he'd been standing here, waiting for Harper to get off the phone for only a few minutes and already he could feel the fire starting in his chest.

Maybe it was one of those weird psychological hang-ups, he thought, the kind of crazy shit the folks who worked here at Candle Lake Manor were always going on about. A phobia or something. Maybe he didn't like being in this office because he associated it with his worsening stomach problems. In his position as head of security for the Manor, he'd endured several extremely unpleasant conversations in this office over the course of the past year.

Things had been going halfway decently until the two female patients had disappeared. The job here at the Manor had been the best one he'd ever had. Bonuses, even. For the first time in his life he'd seen some good money coming in. And going out just as fast. Not his fault; he had expenses. The payments on the Porsche and the fancy sound system were steep.

He'd never been much good with money, mostly because he'd never had enough of it. Cash went through his fingers like water, but here at the Manor that had been okay because there was always another paycheck next month.

But then the two patients had skipped, and his cozy setup had gone sour. His stomach had followed.

The time right after the escape had been especially bad. Harper had ranted and raved and blamed the lousy security. Leon had feared for his job. It wouldn't be easy turning up another one, and he sure as hell wouldn't find anything else with the kind of perks he got here at the Manor. He had some problems with references.

He'd felt cornered and panicky when Harper demanded that the two patients be found and returned to the Manor. He'd had no idea how to conduct a serious investigation. The Bitch Goddess, Fenella, who served as Harper's administrative assistant, had acidly suggested that he hire a real investigator, one of those modern, high-tech types who used a computer.

To his private astonishment, he'd gotten lucky. A few weeks after the patients had disappeared, word had come back of a small story in a Mexican newspaper detailing the deaths of two women who had perished in a hotel fire. No identification had been found at the scene, and the authorities had been unable to locate any next of kin. The only clue to the women's identities were a ballpoint pen and some slippers. All three items had been monogrammed with the words Candle Lake Manor.

Leon had been relieved just to have an answer. Sure, it meant a loss of income for

Harper, but the guy was a businessman. Harper had to understand that sometimes you took a financial hit, but that life went on and you brought in new sources of revenue.

Actually in this case, Harper was still mining the old sources. Leon was impressed. The doc had balls. Shrewd operator that he was, Harper continued to bill the Cleland woman's relatives and the other woman's trust fund for the very expensive fees charged here at the Manor.

It was conceivable that Harper's clients might remain in blissful ignorance for a very long time. The Manor was a very private, very exclusive, very expensive psychiatric hospital situated on the shores of a remote lake in the mountains of Northern California. The sleepy little town of Candle Lake was nearby, but other than a scattering of summer boaters and campers, and some hunters in the fall, the place was all but forgotten on the maps.

Leon knew that the hard-to-reach location was one of the things that made the Manor attractive to Harper's clients. The hospital raked in big bucks from folks who wanted their crazy family members warehoused out of sight and out of mind. Like so many other patients whose relatives had paid dearly to have a relative committed indefinitely, the two women had not had any visitors.

But Harper could run his scam on the clients who were paying the fees for the two women only for a limited time, Leon thought. Sooner or later someone connected to one or both of the missing patients would have a reason to come to Candle Lake. When that day came, Harper would be in a bind because he would not be able to produce them.

After learning that the two patients had apparently died in Mexico, Leon had begun to hope his problems might be over. Then, last week, he'd been contacted online by the creep who called himself, simply, GopherBoy.

". . . understand you are looking for a missing patient. I can help. My fees are as follows and are nonnegotiable . . ."

That was when Leon's heartburn had kicked in again, big time. It was getting worse by the hour.

Harper put down the phone, slowly removed his glasses, and looked at Leon.

"I'm very busy today, Grady. I have two

intakes to deal with this afternoon. I trust this is important?"

Even Harper's voice affected his heartburn, Leon thought. It was classy sounding, a rich man's voice. It reminded him of all of the differences between them. Harper was a hustler, but unlike himself, the doc had gotten all the breaks.

Harper was good-looking, with a lot of thick, silver-gray hair and a trim, tennis player's build. Somewhere along the line, he'd gotten a good education. He also had the kind of charm that he needed to snow his wealthy clients.

"The hacker came through," Leon said. "It cost us, but it looks like we may have some hard information on the Cleland woman."

"Not the other one?"

"No."

Harper frowned, but he did not look severely disappointed, just mildly regretful. It was as if Leon had told him that one of the stocks in his portfolio had tanked but that another had turned in a higher-than-expected earnings report.

"Well, she wasn't nearly as lucrative as the Cleland woman," Harper said. "What have you got?"

"According to GopherBoy, she's alive and well and living under another name. He says some online ID broker set up a program to feed false and misleading information about her to anyone who goes looking. That was why that investigator we hired back at the beginning didn't turn up any real leads."

"Where is she?" Harper asked sharply. "I want her picked up immediately."

The fire in Leon's chest flared higher. He needed some of the tablets he kept in his pocket, but he didn't think it would look good to chew them in front of his boss. He wanted to look like he was calm and in control here.

"Not gonna be that easy, sir," he said. "She's being real careful. All GopherBoy could tell me is that she's somewhere in L.A. He did not have an exact location."

"Somewhere in L.A.?" Harper's well-manicured hand clenched around a gold pen. "What good does that do us? L.A. covers a lot of territory."

"Yeah, but now that I've got a name and some details about her new ID, it won't take me long to track her down. With your permission, sir, I'll leave this afternoon."

"Don't try to bring her in on your own.

When you've located her, stay out of sight and keep her under surveillance. Call me immediately. I'll send Ron and Ernie to assist you. They can handle the medications that will be needed."

"Yes, sir." Leon cleared his throat and tried to keep his tone respectful. "But I'd like to point out that once I've found the patient, we're gonna need to think about how we want to bring her in."

"The meds will make her easy to handle."

For all his fancy degrees, Leon thought, sometimes Harper could be as dumb as a brick.

"The thing is, sir, the Cleland woman has been living under another name for a year. She probably has a job by now. That means there will be co-workers. Friends. Neighbors. Folks who will notice if we just grab her off the street."

"Yes, of course." Harper tossed the gold pen aside and got to his feet. He went to the window. "I see what you mean. We'll have to do this discreetly."

"Right. So what I'm thinking is, I go to L.A., find the woman, and watch her for a while. Get a feel for her daily routine. When we nail that down, we can figure out the best way to pick her up without causing a fuss."

Harper gazed fixedly out at the lake while he considered Leon's logic.

Leon's chest burned.

"All right," Harper said eventually. "That makes sense. The last thing we want to do is to draw attention to this situation. The retrieval must be handled as quietly as possible."

Leon allowed himself a small sigh of relief and took a step back toward the door. "I've already made my plane reservations. All I need to do is go home and throw some things in a suitcase. It's a long drive to the airport, so I'd better get moving."

"Keep me informed."

"Yes, sir."

"I don't like this," Harper muttered. "But I suppose we can only be grateful that this GopherBoy person contacted us instead of Forrest Cleland."

Leon shrugged. He knew there was no mystery about why the hacker had approached someone at Candle Lake Manor first. GopherBoy was clever enough to figure out how the place worked. He obviously understood that the management here had solid financial reasons for wanting to get the Cleland woman back without raising a fuss and that privacy and a real low profile were crucial to Harper's profitable operation.

Leon cleared his throat. "Going to Cleland would have been a whole lot riskier. Cleland is a wealthy, powerful man, and he has no particular reason to keep things quiet. Hell, he might have called in the cops, which would have screwed GopherBoy's plan royally."

Harper frowned. "How did GopherBoy reach the conclusion that I would be willing to pay for this information?"

"Who knows? Probably something in that ID broker's files he hacked into that mentioned just how much money Cleland is paying to keep his relative under wraps here at Candle Lake. GopherBoy's gotta know what that income means to this place. Maybe more important is that he's figured out that the big thing you're selling here is a guarantee of silence. This place can't afford any bad press."

Harper clenched and unclenched the fingers of one hand.

Satisfied that he had made his point,

Leon turned and walked swiftly across the thick beige carpet to the door.

In the outer office, Fenella Leeds looked up from a file she had open on her desk. She was a centerfold dream, blonde, blue-eyed, and gorgeous. She was probably the most beautiful woman he had ever seen in real life, but he treated her pretty much the way he would have treated a cobra that happened to be coiled on the chair behind the desk.

He was fairly certain she had screwed Harper for a while, but there was now some gossip going around that she was getting it on with the guy in accounting. He did not envy either man. If you slept with snakes, you tended to get bitten.

"You're going to L.A. to find the Cleland woman?" Fenella queried.

It did not surprise him that she had somehow listened in to the conversation he'd just had with Harper. He wouldn't put it past her to have a tape recorder under her desk. He had a hunch she kept real good tabs on everything that went on around Manor. It was one of the reasons why he had to be very, very careful until he was clear of the place.

"Yeah." He glanced at his watch and kept moving. "Gotta get going or I won't make my flight."

Fenella did not wish him a safe trip. She went back to work on the file.

By the time he reached the relative safety of the hall, the burning in his chest was the worst it had ever been, almost unbearable. He took the bottle out of his pocket, unscrewed the lid and poured several tablets into the palm of his hand. He shoved them into his mouth and chewed frantically.

He knew why the heartburn was so bad today. It was because he had made his decision and that had involved lying outright to Dr. Ian Harper. It was a scary thing to do because it meant that he was burning all of his bridges.

He had told Harper that GopherBoy had given him only the Cleland woman's new name and the fact that she was somewhere in L.A. But that was pure crap. GopherBoy was a hell of a lot better than Leon had led Harper or Fenella to believe.

According to the information the hacker had provided, the Cleland woman was not in L.A. She was in a place called Whispering Springs, Arizona. GopherBoy had come up with an address and phone numbers, office and home. Everything, in short, that Leon needed to find her.

If the information had come through a year ago, right after the women had escaped, Leon knew that he would have gone straight to Harper with the data. But at some point, probably the day he noticed that he was popping the antacid tablets every couple of hours, he'd arrived at a blinding realization. He no longer wanted to work for Dr. Ian Harper, regardless of how much the bastard paid.

The problem was that, due to his expensive lifestyle and his lifelong inability to hang on to a dollar, he lacked the kind of nest egg he required for a comfortable retirement. When the hacker had turned up the location of the Cleland woman, however, Leon had been struck with a rare burst of creativity.

Chapter Five

"Jeff and Theo told me that you got your first client today," Bonnie said from the other end of the table.

"Sure did." Ethan forked up a bite of grilled halibut and looked at his nephews, sitting on either side of the dinner table. "I wouldn't say she was overly impressed by my professional style, though. She was in such a big hurry to leave that she nearly ran you guys down on the stairs on her way out."

"But you got her to pay you in advance," Jeff said around a mouthful of mashed potatoes.

"I may not have graduated first in my class from charm school," Ethan said, "but I do know something about running a business. The first rule is always get the advance before the client leaves the office."

Jeff grinned. He was eight, two years older than his brother. He still had all the awkwardness of boyhood, but when he smiled like that, Ethan thought, the kid looked exactly like his father.

Ethan glanced down the table and caught the wistful expression that came and went in Bonnie's eyes. It had been almost three years since Drew's death, and he was pretty sure that his sister-in-law had come to terms with the loss, but he knew that she would never be able to look at her sons without thinking of her husband. She had loved Drew deeply.

She was not the only one who thought about Drew Truax whenever Jeff or Theo smiled their father's smile, laughed their father's laugh, or exhibited his keen intelligence and outgoing nature. Ethan thought about his brother in those moments, too.

Drew had been four years younger. They had been close, but no one who knew them well was quite sure why because, when it came to personality and temperament, they had been polar opposites. Drew had been the enthusiastic, optimistic visionary. Whip-smart and endowed with gifts for management and finance, he had been a natural for the corporate world. He had risen far and fast.

Drew had disappeared seven months after the board of directors of Trace & Stone Industries had voted him into the CEO's chair. A big chunk of the company's financial assets vanished at the same time.

The police arrived at the logical conclusion that Drew had taken the funds, blown off his family, friends, and the life he had known in L.A., and was probably living under another name somewhere in the Caribbean. It happened, the cops said.

Ethan and Bonnie had known better. But while Ethan had sensed deep in his gut that his brother was dead, Bonnie had held fast to hope. The situation had become a thousand times worse after the con artist claiming to be a psychic had fueled Bonnie's belief that Drew would be found alive.

Ethan had dealt with his grief the only way he knew. He had gone after the truth with a vengeance and a fury that stunned even those who knew him well, including his wife.

Shortly after he started asking questions, a walking skeleton of a man with basset hound eyes had paid him a visit in his office at Truax Security. He had worn a cheap brown suit distinguished only by its incredibly poor tailoring.

"I represent some people," the man had said in a voice that had been damaged somewhere along the way.

"Sort of figured that out for myself." Ethan had leaned back in his silver-gray leather desk chair. "Can I assume these people are concerned about my ongoing investigation?"

"Yeah. The general opinion seems to be that your brother is not dead, but if it turns out that he is, these people want you to know that they are sorry for your loss."

"Compassionate."

"Very. But they also want you to understand that they had nothing to do with it."

"Swell. Then they have nothing to worry about, do they?"

"Thing is," the man had said, "they got a lot of money invested in a certain company, and they would prefer that you did not meddle in this situation at this time. This is a delicate stage, financially speaking."

"What do they suggest I do?"

"Leave the investigation to the cops."

"Who are getting nowhere fast."

"My employers urge you to be a good citizen and rely on the duly authorized forces of law enforcement to handle this case."

"Tell me, if you were sitting where I'm sitting would you rely on the duly authorized forces of law enforcement to deal with this?"

The man had not responded to that. "My employers also want you to know that if you stop asking questions, they will see to it that a large amount of money will be placed in your company's bank account."

Ethan had thought about that.

"Who are your employers?" he had asked.

"I am not authorized to provide you with that information."

Ethan had sat forward. "In that case, you can give them a message from me. Tell them I said to go fuck themselves."

"This is not a good idea, Mr. Truax. Trust me."

"Get out of here," Ethan had said softly.

The man had studied him for a long time. "You're not gonna change your mind, are you?"

"No."

"I can see that."

Then he went to the door without further comment and walked out.

Ethan's investigation into Drew's death produced far-reaching consequences that ultimately destroyed a Trace & Stone competitor and the powerful man who had been attempting to manipulate it from behind the scenes. The fallout from the scandal also sent shock waves through a shadowy consortium of power brokers, politicians, and businesspeople, many of whom had invested heavily in the rival firm on the basis of insider knowledge.

Ethan eventually found Drew's body in a shallow grave in the desert. The contract shooter and the man who had hired him, Simon Wendover, a majority shareholder in the competing firm, were both arrested. The shooter got killed before he could testify against his employer, and Wendover walked out of the court room a free man.

Wendover died a month later in a boating accident.

Karma was a funny thing.

Trace & Stone's rival was forced into bankruptcy. It was not the only firm that went down in flames as a result of the investigation. Truax Security, the company Ethan had built from the ground up, foundered the following year.

His third marriage disintegrated at about the same time. Everyone else in the family blamed the collapse on the stress of the investigation and the tumble into bankruptcy. Ethan didn't correct the impression, but privately he came to the conclusion that he wasn't any good at marriage.

The small mention of the demise of Truax Security in the business section of the L.A. papers attributed the financial failure to poor management.

But Ethan knew what had really happened. So many abrupt decisions made by so many Southern California firms to shift their business to other corporate security companies at precisely the same time had not been an unhappy coincidence. The mass exodus of clients was engineered by his visitor's angry employers in retaliation for obliging them to weather some annoying losses.

The man had paid Ethan another visit. The occasion was the public auction of the last remaining assets of Truax Security.

He had approached Ethan, who was leaning against his former office desk, arms folded, watching the progress of the sale. The desk was an impressive piece of furniture composed of polished steel and a massive slab of curved glass. The decorator who had done the interiors of Truax Security had assured Ethan that it made a *statement.*

For a while the man had not spoken. He

had seemed fascinated by the patter of the auctioneer, who was trying to work up some enthusiasm in the crowd.

"You ever wonder how they learn to talk like that?" he had asked eventually.

Ethan had said nothing.

The man had released a world-weary sigh. "You shoulda stopped when you had the chance. You woulda come out of this okay, you know? You woulda been sitting in a very nice place right now if you hadn't meddled. Maybe still be behind that desk."

Ethan had looked at him. "You never got around to telling me your name the last time you came to see me."

"Name's Stagg. Harry Stagg."

"How does it feel, Harry Stagg, to sell your soul for a bunch of bastards who probably can't even remember your last name and who could not care less if you have a heart attack or crash your car tomorrow because they know that you can be replaced in five minutes?"

"It's a living."

Ethan had gone back to watching the auctioneer.

Stagg had stirred a little. "You asked me a question that time I talked to you in your office. You wanted to know who I was working for. I didn't answer."

Ethan had said nothing.

"They're all members of a fancy private club," Stagg had said. "Got everything in that club, you know? Two big swimming pools and saunas and steam rooms and handball courts. There's this big golf course and a bar and everyone who works there, male and female, looks like a fashion model. They say that if you're a member of that club, you can get just about anything you want."

Ethan had listened to the auctioneer labor heroically to elicit bids for a pair of leather and steel chairs that had once graced the reception lobby of Truax Security. The chairs had come from Italy, and they had cost a bundle. He had objected strongly to the purchase, but the frustrated decorator had waged a passionate campaign on the grounds that first impressions on potential clients were crucially important. The chairs, according to the decorator, were an *investment.*

The chairs had finally sold for a tiny fraction of their original cost. Some investment,

Ethan had thought. *As God is my witness, I will never trust another decorator.*

"What's the name of this private club?" he had asked, not really expecting an answer.

"Won't do you any good. You can't touch those guys. No one can. They're always real careful to keep their hands clean."

"You going to give me the name?"

"They call the club The Retreat," Stagg had said. "The man who told me to talk to you back at the beginning of this thing? His name is Dorney. He was the president when the situation involving your brother first went down."

Ethan had recognized the name. You could conjure with it in Southern California.

"If it means anything," Stagg had said, "the club's board of directors fired Dorney and elected themselves a new president a few months ago. Presidents only get to hold the job as long as things are going the way the club members want them to go. Mistakes are expensive."

"Sounds like The Retreat runs pretty much like any other business enterprise."

"Yeah." Stagg had turned to leave. He had paused. "By the way, I quit working for them right after I heard you were having financial problems."

"What are you doing now?" Ethan had asked.

"I'm a security consultant."

"Any money in it?"

"It's a living. Even got my own business card." Stagg had pulled out a small leather case, removed a cream-colored card, and handed it to Ethan. "Let me know if you need any consulting."

He had walked away through the crowd and disappeared.

Ethan had stayed at the auction until the bitter end. His personal desk had gone for a lousy one hundred seventy-five bucks. Some statement. On the other hand, maybe it had said it all.

Bonnie glanced at Ethan while she passed the potatoes to Jeff. "What kind of job does your new client want you to do?"

Ethan pulled his mind back to the present and reached for another dinner roll. "Routine background check on a guy she's thinking of getting involved with. Take about ten minutes."

"Did you do it already?"

"Not yet." He buttered the roll. "Ran into

some glitches when I tried to set up the office computer this afternoon."

"Uncle Ethan is going to have to update his apps," Jeff said. "They're not compatible with the operating system on the new computer."

"I've got my laptop back at the house," Ethan said. "I'll run the check on it when I go home tonight. My client will have her answers in the morning."

Bonnie frowned. "Speaking of that pink monstrosity you now call home, did you give any more thought to my idea of putting it on the market?"

"Who'd buy it?" Ethan took a bite of the roll. "The only reason I got it so cheap from Uncle Victor is because he couldn't sell it before he moved to Hawaii. At one time or another, he had it listed with every broker in Whispering Springs."

"I think Nightwinds is cool," Theo announced. "And it has a pool."

"And a real theater with a big-screen TV," Jeff added. "And a popcorn machine."

"The TV and popcorn machine were Uncle Victor's only serious upgrades, outside of some work on the wiring," Ethan said. "At least he had his priorities straight."

"I wish we lived there instead of here," Jeff said. "That way we could watch TV on a giant screen *every* night."

"Yeah, this house is really, really boring," Theo said.

"The only problem with Nightwinds," Jeff said with a grimace, "is that it's pink."

"That's because the wife of the original owner liked pink," Ethan explained. "A lot."

"Uncle Victor told me that it's haunted by her ghost," Theo said. "Mrs. Legg or something."

"Foote," Ethan said. "Her name was Camelia Foote. She was an aspiring actress."

"What's *aspiring* mean?" Theo asked.

Ethan exchanged a look with Bonnie. "It means she never became famous."

"Oh." Theo digested that and evidently did not consider it important. "Well, anyhow, what happened was, she died and old Mr. Foote went crazy. He lived all alone in that house for the rest of his life and never changed a thing."

"Unfortunately, none of the later owners changed very much either," Bonnie said dryly. "You'd think that somewhere along the line someone would at least have had it painted."

"It stood empty most of the time until Uncle Victor picked it up for a song ten years ago after Aunt Betty died," Ethan said. "He couldn't afford to have the place remodeled either."

"You'll notice that your great-uncle did not choose to retire in Nightwinds," Bonnie pointed out. "He headed straight for Hawaii the day after he sold his business to you."

"He told me he was tired of the desert." Ethan helped himself to more potatoes. "Said he wanted an ocean and a beach."

"He told *me* that he wanted to look at girls in bikinis, all day," Jeff announced.

"Yeah," Theo added. "He said there's even beaches where some of the ladies don't wear any swimsuits at all."

"No kidding?" Ethan paused, a forkful of potatoes halfway to his mouth. "I've got Uncle Victor's address in Maui. Maybe I'll pay him a visit next time I get a few free days. Take a tour of the beaches, or something."

Jeff chortled so hard that he nearly fell out of his chair.

Theo kicked the bottom rungs of his chair.

"You really like to watch bare naked ladies, Uncle Ethan?"

"Well," Ethan said. "Given a choice between working and watching naked ladies on the beach, I've gotta say that—"

"I think," Bonnie interrupted firmly, "that you've all said enough on the subject of naked ladies." She looked at Ethan. "Getting back to Nightwinds, Jeff said something about your new client being an interior designer?"

"Decorator. What's that got to do with Nightwinds?"

Bonnie ignored that. "It occurs to me that after you handle her case, you could hire her to help you do something with that pink elephant."

"Residence," Ethan corrected.

"I beg your pardon?"

"I have it on good authority that you're supposed to call a house a residence. Classier sounding word. But, trust me, there's not a chance in—"

He realized that Theo and Jeff were watching him with thinly veiled anticipation. Catching him in the act of using a forbidden word was one of their favorite spectator sports.

"I will definitely not be hiring Ms. Luce to remodel the place," Ethan finished smoothly.

Disappointed, Jeff and Theo went back to their food.

"Why not?" Bonnie asked.

"Two reasons." Ethan finished the last of the potatoes. "First, I can't afford to hire a decorator at this point even if I were inclined to redo the place. Second, I doubt that Zoe Luce would make it past the front door of Nightwinds without fainting."

Jeff stopped in mid-chew, eyes bright with curiosity. "Why would she faint, Uncle Ethan?"

"You think maybe she'd be scared of the ghost?" Theo asked.

"I doubt that Zoe Luce would be scared off by a ghost," Ethan said. "But I'm sure that her delicate designer sensibilities would be severely traumatized by the sight of the inside of my new residence. Let's face it, Nightwinds isn't going to win any house-of-the-year awards."

"That's putting it mildly," Bonnie murmured. "Talk about Hollywood tacky."

"You think Ms. Luce would be so stunned

she'd just fall down right there in the front hall?" Jeff asked.

"Wouldn't surprise me," Ethan said.

"Maybe she'd start to twitch or something," Theo suggested.

"Yeah, like this." Jeff jerked his left arm wildly.

"Or like this." Theo wobbled his head from side to side.

Both boys began to cackle gleefully. Their spasmodic movements got more creative.

Ethan watched both performances with open admiration. "Not bad. Yep, I'll bet she'd collapse and start to twitch just like that."

At the other end of the table Bonnie gave a long-suffering sigh. "Why does dinner always end like this when you eat with us, Ethan?"

"What can I say? It's a gift."

He drove back to Nightwinds an hour later. When he got out of the car, he stood in the drive for a moment and surveyed his new *residence,* wondering for some inexplicable reason what Zoe Luce would think of it. Okay, so the place did look like a Hollywood fantasy version of a Spanish Colonial mansion. And it was definitely pink, not the faded, sunwashed pink of old adobe—more like bubblegum pink. So what? It had character. Or something. And it was spacious. Plenty of room for his books and personal stuff.

Best of all, it was fully furnished, which was a very good thing because the combined financial disasters of his business and his last divorce had left him with very little in the way of furniture.

The hell with Zoe Luce's opinion. Why should he care what she thought of Nightwinds?

He summoned up his impressions of her that afternoon. Sleek red-brown hair in a stylish-looking knot, vivid, compelling face, and smoky, mysterious eyes that probably held some interesting secrets. And a very strange taste in clothes. If he recalled his kindergarten painting lessons properly, that shade of acid green wasn't supposed to go with that purple color. There were rules about these things. At least there had been back in kindergarten.

Something told him that Zoe had probably never stuck to coloring between the lines. But, then, neither had he.

He knew that he should definitely not be thinking about her in such personal terms. She was a client, and long ago he had learned the hard way not to date clients. Besides, she would probably clash against the pink interiors of Nightwinds.

He climbed the steps, crossed the front entry with its pastel pink stone pillars, and let himself into the flamingo pink hallway.

In fairness, the interior of the house was not one hundred percent pink. There was a lot of gilt work and some white wooden molding. The giant leaves of the huge, deep pink orchids woven into the carpeting were green.

Switching on lights as he went, he made his way through the sprawling house to one of the rooms overlooking the gardens and the shallow canyon beyond.

He wove a path through the boxes of books that he had not yet had time to unpack and sat down at the grand gilt-and-pink desk near the window. Switching on the laptop, he opened a drawer to retrieve the notes he had made when he had interviewed Zoe Luce that afternoon.

He started with the usual online information resources. If all went well, it would take him about ten minutes to locate Mrs. Jennifer Mason, just as he'd told Bonnie. Easy money and Lord knew he needed it.

All did not go well.

There was no indication that Jennifer Mason had used her credit cards or written any checks in the past few months. Intrigued, he went deeper.

He found no evidence that Jennifer Mason was involved in the process of obtaining a divorce from Davis Mason. There was no sign that she had hired any of the local moving companies to assist in relocating to another town or city.

Forty-five minutes later he sat back, stretched his legs out under the desk, shoved his hands into his pockets, and contemplated the glowing screen.

Jennifer Mason had disappeared. He had a hunch Zoe Luce had already guessed as much before she hired him to find the woman.

Chapter Six

Zoe picked up the desk phone on the first ring.

"Enhanced Interiors."

"You lied to me," Ethan said on the other end.

He made the accusation in a stunningly casual tone, as if he was accustomed to having people lie to him. Maybe that was true, given his line of work, Zoe thought.

She went very still in her chair, staring unseeingly at the three framed black-and-white photographs that hung on the opposite wall.

She had taken three photos of the fanciful old house steeped in the shadows of the desert twilight. Later, she had tried to choose the most evocative shot but each had caught some elusive element, and she had been unable to select just one. She had wound up framing all three.

A client had noticed the photos hanging on the wall a few days later and had informed her that the house was known locally as Nightwinds.

"Are you there?" Ethan asked.

Don't panic yet, she thought. *Maybe it's not as bad as it sounds.*

"Yes, of course," she said tonelessly.

How much had he learned about her in the process of searching for Jennifer Mason? Had he somehow stumbled onto the truth? Had he found a chink in the firewall that had been erected between her past and her present? And what about Arcadia? Oh, Lord, what if she had blown her friend's cover as well as her own? She had been an idiot to hire a private investigator.

Get a grip, she told herself. *Breathe. Think.*

The new identities that she and Arcadia had purchased had been first class. Arcadia had insisted on paying the huge amount of cash required to get the very best quality. Ethan Truax could not have dug deep enough to uncover the truth, she assured herself, not in such a short period of time.

Besides, he'd had no reason to go looking into her past. She had paid him to search for Jennifer Mason. Why would he waste time probing into his client's background, instead?

"I don't know what you're talking about," she said, trying to keep her voice cool and even. "Did you locate Jennifer Mason?"

"No," Ethan said.

She clutched the phone more tightly to her ear. "You couldn't find her?"

"No," Ethan said again. "What's more, I don't think you expected me to find her. And that's what makes this all so damn interesting, you see."

"I don't understand."

"We need to talk," Ethan said. He ended the call abruptly.

Anger shafted through her. "Damn it, don't you dare hang up on me, Truax."

The door of her office opened without warning, jolting her. She swung around in her office chair.

Ethan walked into the room looking as if he had just come from a construction site. He wore a pair of grungy paint-stained jeans, a denim shirt, scuffed work boots, and a peaked cap emblazoned with the logo of a local tavern, Hell's Belles. She recognized the name of the establishment. It was a sleazy dive that catered to guys who drove trucks and motorcycles. She had never been attracted to the kind of male who frequented such places.

So why was she experiencing these little hot and cold chills of awareness at the sight of Ethan? She had clearly gone a little too long without a date.

Ethan slid his phone into the pocket of his shirt. "I happened to be in the neighborhood. Thought I'd drop by."

She put down her own phone with great care and tried to compose herself. At least this time she had the advantage of being the one on the business side of a desk.

"Is the dramatic entrance one of the tricks of the trade, Mr. Truax?"

"Like I said, we need to have a conversation and we need to have it right now." He started toward one of the two client chairs positioned across from her desk. Then he noticed the three black-and-white shots of Nightwinds and stopped. "Who took those?"

"I did."

"Huh."

"Forget the pictures, Mr. Truax." She sat forward, impatient and anxious, and folded her hands on the desk. “Sit down and tell me exactly what is going on.”

He took one last look at the three photos and then obligingly settled into a chair. She immediately regretted asking him to take a seat. The expensive upholstery on her client chairs had never been intended to withstand dirty work clothes.

Ethan appeared oblivious to any impact he might be making on her precious chair. Lounging back against the honey-colored leather, he extended his legs and crossed his booted feet at the ankles. He removed a small notepad from the pocket of his shirt and flipped it open.

“I found no evidence to indicate the Mrs. Jennifer Mason is celebrating her newly acquired status as a soon-to-be divorced woman.” He studied his notes. “She has not used any credit cards recently. She has not used an ATM machine to remove any cash from the couple’s joint checking account nor has she written any checks on that account.” He looked up. “The account is still open, by the way. Davis Mason has not bothered to close it.”

“What does that mean?”

“Wild guess? He’s not particularly worried

that his soon-to-be-ex will clean out the account."

"Oh." This was going to be as bad as she had feared.

"Jennifer Mason appears to have had no close friends here in town. I'm still checking that angle, but it's not looking good. She was not a longtime resident of Whispering Springs and apparently the only socializing she did after her marriage was when she helped Mason entertain business clients. That was not a frequent occurrence."

"Relatives?" Zoe inquired.

"Just a couple of distant cousins and an elderly aunt who live in Indiana. I called them this morning. None of them have heard from her recently nor is anyone concerned. They all said that they hadn't seen Jennifer since she was a child and had lost contact years ago. Not what you'd call a close family."

"In other words, no one is going to rush to file a missing persons report."

"Unlikely," Ethan said. "There is one more thing. I checked the legal angle. There is no divorce in progress."

This was definitely the worst-case scenario, she thought. Jennifer Mason fit the classic profile of an abused wife who enjoyed no close contact with family or friends. What was she going to do now?

She picked up a pen to give herself something to do, clutching it so tightly that her knuckles whitened. "Thank you for looking into the matter for me, Mr. Truax. Do I owe you anything more than the minimum I paid you yesterday?"

"Oh, yeah. A lot more."

She frowned. "How much?"

"Let's start with some answers. What do you think happened to Jennifer Mason?"

She said nothing.

"Did you know her before she disappeared?"

"No. Never met her."

"You think Mason murdered his wife, don't you?"

She hesitated and then nodded, saying nothing.

"That's a fairly serious conclusion," Ethan said dryly. "Mind if I ask what it was that made you jump to it?"

"Just a bad feeling I got when I went out to view his residence yesterday."

"A bad feeling," he repeated neutrally.

"Call it intuition."

"Okay, I've got some respect for intuition. Been known to use it myself. Anything else?"

Act normal. Think normal.

"The bed in the master bedroom is gone," she said evenly. "It and a small area rug are the only furnishings that are missing. There's a fresh coat of paint on the walls of that room."

His brows rose. "And that was enough to make you think Jennifer Mason had met with foul play?"

She decided to try a more assertive approach. "Mr. Truax, I am a professional interior designer. I get the strong impression that you don't think much of my career choice, but I assure you that designers are, by training and inclination, observant. Something is wrong at the Mason residence. I'm sure of it."

"Okay, take it easy. You sure Mason didn't sell the bed?"

"Davis told me that his wife had taken it because it was important to her. It was a very large, very expensive bed, he said. But—"

"Yeah?"

"But I saw two full sets of three-hundred-

and-twenty-thread-count Italian sheets in the linen closet. The sheets and pillowcases were still in the original packaging."

"So what?"

She tapped the tip of the pen on the desk top. "Do you have any idea what two full sets of king-sized sheets of that quality cost? If Jennifer Mason took the bed, I'm sure she would have taken the sheets that she bought to go on it."

Ethan meditated on that for a few seconds. Then he nodded. "You've got a point. Did Mason indicate that his wife put the bed into storage?"

"No."

"Did he say how she arranged to pick up the bed?"

"No." The steady litany of questions was getting on her nerves. "You're the private detective here, not me."

"Oh, yeah, that's right. I keep forgetting." He took a pen out of his pocket and wrote something down in the notebook. "Was there anything else that made you suspicious when you went through Mason's house yesterday?"

Aside from the screaming walls? She

wondered silently. *Gosh, no, that was enough for some obscure reason.*

"There was one other strange thing," she offered slowly.

"What?"

"The shower curtains."

"What about them?"

"The master bath has a large, glass-walled shower and separate tub arrangement but the other two bedrooms were obviously designed as guest rooms. They each have adjoining baths with standard combination shower-tubs with curtain enclosures But the shower curtains in both of the guest baths are gone."

He gave her a politely blank look. "Explain."

"Both rooms were fully outfitted with soap, towels and amenities. The shower curtains should have been there, too. But they were gone." She shrugged. "I just found that a little odd, that's all."

He looked at her for a long time.

"You do realize," he said eventually, "that we haven't got enough yet to take to the cops?"

"Of course I do. That's why I hired you to look into it."

"Correction, you came to me because Radnor was a lot more expensive, but we'll let that pass for now." He closed the notepad and dropped it into his shirt pocket. "We've got other things to do."

"Such as?"

"I want to get a look inside the Mason house. I beg your pardon, the Mason *residence.*"

She stared at him, intrigued in spite of her misgivings. "You're going to break in?"

"Hell, no. Private investigators only get to do stuff like that on television. You think I want to risk my license?"

"No, I suppose not."

His reaction to her question was entirely logical, but for some reason she felt a flicker of disappointment. Maybe she had allowed her fantasies about private investigators to run amuck.

"It probably wouldn't be possible for you to sneak in, anyway," she said coolly. "Desert View is a very secure, gated community. I doubt if you would have been able to get past the guards."

Ethan said nothing, just sat there doing enigmatic. For some reason, she was suddenly uneasy.

She wondered if she'd offended him or, worse yet, made him feel awkward or embarrassed. Truax Investigations was a one-person agency, she reminded herself. He did not have the resources of a large security firm such as Radnor. She could not expect miracles. And you got what you paid for, she reminded herself for the ninth or tenth time.

She cleared her throat. "I assume you've used up the two-hour minimum advance I gave you."

"You assume right," he assured her a little too easily. "Blew right through it last night."

"I was afraid of that." She drew herself up and fixed him with what she hoped was a steely glare. "How much more is this investigation going to cost me?"

"Can't say for sure, yet. Could be another day or two before I figure out what's going on here."

"Another *day* or *two*?" She was appalled. "I can't afford to pay you for that much time. Not at your rates."

"Relax. I think we can work something out. After all, I'm trying to get my business up and running here in Whispering Springs and you're my first client. I want to make a good impression. Got to think of future referrals."

"What terms are you offering?" she asked warily.

"My sister-in-law came up with an idea. I didn't pay any attention at the time, but last night when I realized this case was going to take longer than expected, it occurred to me that her plan had some possibilities."

"Describe these possibilities."

"I need a little interior decorating work," he said.

That made her pause. "I rather like the look of your office. It has a certain shabby charm."

"Shabby charm?"

"If you just replaced that oversized client chair and moved your desk into a better position and got rid of that mirror, I think you'll find that the energy flow works very well."

"The energy flow works fine the way it is. The oversized chair is useful because it makes clients aware that they aren't the ones in control in that room. Makes 'em want to turn all their problems over to me. And if the desk interrupts the energy flow that's okay, too. I like it right where it is.

Ditto with the mirror. It's not my office that needs redecorating."

"What, then?"

"My new house." He smiled. "I mean, my new residence."

"Your *residence*?" She flattened her hands on the desk and shot to her feet. "Are you serious? You expect me to redesign your entire living space in exchange for a little more detective work?"

"Sounded fair to me."

"Well, it certainly doesn't sound that way to me. It sounds like you're trying to—" she broke off abruptly, aware that the phrase, *screw me* did not seem appropriate.

Ethan watched her, politely expectant. Something in his expression told her he knew exactly what she had been about to say. She felt the heat rise in her cheeks.

She straightened her shoulders and folded her arms. "It sounds as if you intend for me to get the raw end of this deal. My fees for redesigning an entire residence are quite high, Mr. Truax. There is no way that I would spend that much on your detecting services."

"Okay, like I told you, I'm flexible. How about one room?"

She hesitated and then shrugged. “Okay, one room.”

“Deal. But I get to pick the room.”

“Fine. Deal. Now tell me: how you plan to get into the Mason residence?”

“That’s the easy part,” Ethan replied. “You’re going to get me inside.”

“How?”

“You can start by calling me Bob.”

An hour later Ethan stood in the center of the master bedroom of the Mason house and tried to ignore the little tingle of adrenaline that was humming through him. He understood the source of the sensation. If he and Zoe were right about Jennifer Mason’s fate, they were standing in the same room as a killer.

At least he was standing in the same room with Mason, he thought. Zoe, on the other hand, still had both feet out in the hall. She hovered in the bedroom doorway, arms crossed tightly beneath her breasts. Until now she had been doing a very good job of acting but he had noticed a new level of tension in her when they had reached this bedroom.

Davis Mason watched him from a short distance away. Zoe had reported that he'd sounded somewhat surprised when she'd phoned to say that she wanted to bring a contractor to his house. But he had not had a problem with the suggestion. In fact, he had offered to leave his office early to meet them.

"What do you think about my lighting ideas for this space, Bob?" Zoe asked from the door.

"No problem," Ethan said easily. "Plenty of room in here to drop the ceiling and put in recessed lighting. You want me to work up a detailed estimate?"

"Not at this stage," she said. "I just wanted your opinion on whether or not you thought the concept was feasible."

"Hell, yeah, it'll work. The lighting won't be a problem. Picture on the ceiling sounds weird, though."

Davis looked at Zoe. "You're going to paint a picture on my ceiling?"

"It's an option that interests me. There are some excellent mural artists here in town who could do something very special in this space. An evening sky scene, perhaps."

Davis nodded thoughtfully. "I like the

idea. Never would have thought of it myself."

"Gonna be expensive," Ethan warned him. "The recessed lighting she wants to illuminate the ceiling doesn't come cheap, and Lord only knows what the artist will charge."

Zoe fixed him with a steely look. "The cost is not your problem, *Bob.*"

"She's right," Davis said. "Price is no object for me. My wife and I recently parted ways. I want a whole new look for this bedroom."

"Oh, man," Ethan whistled softly. "Been there, done that a few times myself. I know all about the bedroom thing."

He caught Zoe's startled reaction to that comment, but he ignored it. He was more interested in Davis's frown.

"The bedroom thing?" Davis stood unmoving. "I don't understand."

Ethan shook his head. "This is the voice of experience talking. I've had three wives walk out on me and file for divorce. Just no pleasing some women, I guess."

"No," Davis said evenly. "Women can be difficult." He did not look in Zoe's direction.

"Difficult and damned expensive," Ethan

said. "Especially when it comes to beds. Beds cost a lot of money, you know."

"What does this have to do with beds?" Davis asked.

Ethan shrugged. "The first thing you do, after you finish paying off your ex and the lawyers, is you start dating again, right? Hell, maybe you don't even wait until the paperwork is finished. Maybe you need some understanding companionship right away, know what I mean?"

"No, Bob," Zoe said coldly from the hall. "I, for one, don't know what you mean."

"No offense, Ms. Luce," he said, making a show of exaggerated patience, "but these are facts of life for a guy in this situation. Like I was saying, you want to start dating again so you bring a new lady friend home. You turn on the music, have a couple of drinks, and you tell her your sad story." He winked at Davis. "Am I right?"

"I don't know yet," Davis said. "I haven't resumed my social life."

"Yeah, well, take it from me, this is how it works. Anyhow, things are going fine out in the front room, so you suggest that the two of you adjourn to the bedroom. She's okay with that. So far, so good. The two of you walk down the hall, enter the bedroom, and wham, no warning at all, the lady takes one look at the bed and stops cold."

Davis and Zoe were both watching him as if he had turned them to stone.

"Why does she stop?" Davis sounded baffled.

"Because of the damned bed, of course," Ethan said. "She gets this weird expression on her face and she looks right at you and she asks you if that's the bed where you and your ex-wife slept. Talk about a loaded question."

"Loaded is right," Davis grimaced. "I think I'm beginning to get the picture here."

"Women don't like to sleep or do anything else in the same bed you used with the ex, you see?" Ethan said. "Some kind of female thing, I guess."

He glanced at Zoe. She looked pained, but she kept silent.

Davis, on the other hand, was at ease again, relaxed and smiling. He gave Ethan a knowing, man-to-man look. "I must admit, I hadn't thought about that angle. Now that you've pointed it out, I can see where an old bed could be a bit awkward. However, that is one problem I'm happy to say that I don't have."

"Yeah." Ethan surveyed the large empty space in the center of the room. "I can see that. The bed's gone."

"My ex took it with her when she left."

"Just backed up a truck and hauled it off, huh? Talk about insensitive."

"Along with the rest of her personal possessions. To be honest, I helped her pack."

"Yeah, I've done that a few times, too," Ethan admitted. "I know where you're coming from. Well, as far as the bed goes, count yourself lucky. It'll cost you to replace it, but in the long run, it will be worth it. Trust me."

"I'll take your word for it, Bob," Davis murmured. "As you said, yours is the voice of experience. Three divorces?"

"My lawyer sends me cards on my birthday and most major holidays."

"Sounds like he should send flowers," Zoe said tightly. She took a decisive step back, moving away from the bedroom door. "I think we've seen enough, Bob. We'd better be on our way. If you will work up a rough idea on where you think the fixtures and electrical outlets could be located, I'll include the information in my presentation to Davis on Friday."

"Sure." Ethan paused in front of Davis and stuck out his hand. "Nice to meet you, Mason. Good luck with the remodel. You can't go wrong with Ms. Luce, here. She really knows her stuff."

Davis shook hands briefly, but his eyes were on Zoe. "I'm looking forward to working with her."

"Me, too," Ethan said. "It's always interesting, know what I mean?"

Zoe did not respond. She turned on her heel and disappeared down the hall.

She was certainly in a big hurry to leave the bedroom, Ethan thought. He wondered about that as he followed her outside to her car. He was aware that she had been tense when he had explained his plans for getting inside Mason's home, but she had cooperated willingly. Her nerves had seemed steady enough throughout the tour of the house. But all that had changed when they'd reached the master bedroom.

He got into the passenger seat and closed the door. Zoe slipped behind the wheel, fastened her seatbelt, started the engine, and drove away very quickly.

He put on his dark glasses and studied her taut profile. Her delicate jaw was tight. She had a death grip on the wheel. She drove with the focused concentration of a professional race car driver closing in on the checkered flag.

"Are you okay?" he asked when she slowed to approach the guardhouse.

"Of course, I'm okay."

"You did fine back there at Mason's place," he offered. "If I didn't know you were a decorator, I'd have said you'd had some experience in my line."

Her knuckles whitened. "What's that supposed to mean?"

"Just that you did the undercover thing with flair."

"Flair."

"Yeah. Flair. At least until we got to the bedroom. You started to get a little shaky at that point."

"Maybe it was because you and Davis got into that ridiculous conversation about changing beds when you changed wives."

"Wasn't ridiculous. It's a fact. Like I told Mason, I've run into the problem a few times."

"You really have been through three divorces? I thought maybe you'd made up that story to get him to talk about the missing bed."

"It was the truth."

"Good grief." She sounded dazed. "Children?"

"No." Okay, so she obviously did not think that he was Mr. Perfect. He already knew that. Why the hell did he care about her opinion on the subject? "What about you? I take it you're not married?"

"No."

"Divorced?"

"No." She braked for the guardhouse. "I was with someone for a long time. It didn't work out."

He could have heard the slamming of that door from a mile away, he thought. Whatever it was that had happened in that relationship, it had left scars.

Slammed doors always piqued his curiosity. He wondered what would happen if he probed a little deeper.

At that moment, the guard emerged from the security station. Zoe lowered her window and murmured something brisk and polite. The guard nodded and wished her a good day.

Zoe put her foot down on the throttle and sent the vehicle hurtling through the gates and out onto the main road. She was obviously keen to get away from Desert View.

"Well?" she said. "Did you pick up any useful clues back there?"

"Maybe."

She shot him an irritated look. "That's the best you can do? Maybe?"

"For the moment." He glanced back over his shoulder. The security guard was making an entry in a log. Methodical type. Radnor Security Systems was big on procedures. It was probably the secret of their success.

"What do we do now?" Zoe asked.

He turned his attention back to the road. "Now I find the missing bed."

"Why on earth do you want to waste time tracking down the bed?"

"Something tells me that when I find it, I'll find out what happened to Jennifer Mason."

Chapter Seven

The following afternoon, Zoe stood alone in the front hall of the Taylor residence and savored the gracious warmth that flowed through the space.

After a year in her new profession, she had discovered that this was her favorite moment in the design process. Every detail from window treatments to carpets was in place. The furniture had been delivered and positioned. The craft and construction people were gone at last. Her creation was complete, but the owners had not yet moved into their new home.

She had the place to herself. It was the only chance she would ever have to walk through the spaces alone and critique her own work. It was her one opportunity to decide whether or not she had achieved her design goals.

This large residence had been one of her first big projects, and it had been a challenge. She had worked on it for months. After giving her a detailed list of their requirements, the Taylors had announced that they were leaving everything in her hands and had taken off on a world cruise.

"My husband and I went through one complete interior design experience together early on in our marriage," Mary Taylor had explained with a shudder. "We almost got divorced because of the stress. We do many things well as a couple, but interior design is not one of them. This time around, we want a turnkey operation. When we get back, I want to walk back into a complete, finished home."

The Taylors were due to return next month. Zoe thought they would be pleased. They were in their sixties, successful, high-energy, gregarious people with an active lifestyle. She had set out to create a serene background against which their vivacious natures would shine.

The residence was brand-new with well-proportioned lines, high ceilings, and sweeping vistas. She had worked closely with the architect because she had wanted to be certain that her designs enhanced his well-executed spaces. Granted, she had been new at the job, but her instincts and her degree in fine arts had both told her that harmony was best achieved when the architectural and interior elements worked together.

She slipped the heavy crimson tote off her shoulder, put it down on the tile of the front hall, and walked into the spacious great room. The small, intimate seating groups that she had used to bring a comfortable sense of scale to the vast interior worked well. She imagined the room filled with a hundred guests. The energy and noise of a lot of people gathered in one space could be difficult to orchestrate, but she was confident that this room could handle the job.

She continued her walk-through, making tiny adjustments here and there. A sense of calm and tranquility enveloped her. It occurred to her that she had come here today not just because it was a good opportunity to take one last look at her work, but because she had been badly in need of the serenity she had designed into this residence.

The second visit to the master bedroom in Davis Mason's house had left her more disturbed than ever. The screaming in the walls had not dimmed. The invisible pain was at such an intense level that she could not understand why others failed to notice it.

Davis had appeared oblivious, just as he had the last time. But there had been a few seconds there when she had wondered if Ethan had unconsciously picked up some trace of what she felt emanating from the terrible room. It had to do with the way he had moved in that space, she decided. It was as if he'd become more alert or something. He hadn't walked or strolled through the room; he had prowled.

Then she had realized that it wasn't a subliminal awareness of the energy in the walls that was affecting him. What she had seen in Ethan was the anticipation of the hunter on the trail.

She came to a halt in the center of the gleaming copper-and-granite kitchen and thought about that. A tiny chill flickered through her. Ethan Truax could be dangerous under certain circumstances.

That realization would not have bothered her quite so much were it not for the extremely unsettling knowledge that she was attracted to him. She had finally faced that fact today. She did not understand the little tingles of excitement she experienced in his presence, but there was no point denying them.

The really weird part was that she had not given any man so much as a second glance for two years, and now, here she was, fantasizing about a low-rent private investigator who had admitted to three marriages and as many divorces.

Ethan Truax was very definitely not her type. Preston, with his love of art and history and his gentle ways, had been her type. Whatever it was she was feeling for Truax, it probably only involved a lot of hormones that had been dormant for a long time.

She left the kitchen with its large adjoining pantry and walked past the handsome, polished steel door of the new walk-in, climate-controlled wine-cellar. In addition to their extensive entertaining needs, the Taylors collected rare and exotic vintages. The cellar was empty and unlocked at the moment because the valuable collection of wines had not yet been moved. Edward Taylor had made it clear that he wished to supervise that delicate process personally when he returned from the cruise.

She continued along the spacious central

hall, admiring the artful patterns worked into the floor tiles. When she reached the fully equipped exercise and sauna room, she paused to check that all of the high-tech machines were properly positioned.

She was on her way to the guest wing when she heard the faint whisper of sound from the back of the house.

She froze; her palms felt as though she had just plunged her hands into ice water.

It had been only a tiny, hushed creak that could easily be written off as a figment of her imagination. It was just the sort of thin little noise that you could expect to hear in a large empty space where small sounds tended to echo. But it seemed to her that the flow of air down the hall had altered a little. One of the French doors that separated the kitchen area from the pool terrace had just been opened.

She was no longer alone in the big house.

"Hurry up, okay, man?" The storage locker attendant worked the code to open the door on the second floor of lockers. He glanced nervously over his shoulder. "Someone might come along, y'know? If the boss finds out I let you in, he'll fire my ass."

"This will only take a couple of minutes." Ethan shoved a few crisp bills into the man's hand. "Go back to your desk. I'll give you the rest on my way out."

"Just make it fast, okay."

"Sure."

The attendant pocketed the money and hastened off toward the stairwell.

Ethan went down the long hall of locked doors until he came to number 203. According to the attendant, this was the one that had been rented to a man matching Davis Mason's description. Mason had used another name and paid in cash, but the attendant had remembered the bed. *A really big one. Said his wife had left him and he didn't want it. He gave me twenty bucks to help him unload it and get it into the locker.*

Ethan opened the small box of tools he had brought along and selected the pick he thought would do the job.

He got the standard issue padlock open in less than fifteen seconds and rolled the garage door–style closure up into the ceiling.

He saw the headboard first. It was propped in the shadows against the left wall, a massive, ornate chunk of furniture.

The cold glow of the fluorescent fixture in the hall did little to illuminate the interior, but he could see the ends of the supersized box spring and mattress.

The mattress was wrapped in several yards of opaque plastic.

He took out the small flashlight he had brought, switched it on, and played the beam around the room. In addition to the bed, there were a number of packing cartons stacked inside the locker.

He took a knife out of the tool kit and slit open the nearest carton. He was not surprised to find a tangled heap of feminine clothing inside.

A good start, he thought. His new client might even be impressed. But it would be nice to have a little more to take to the cops.

He found what he needed when he went to work cutting away the layers of plastic that shrouded the mattress.

The massive bed was badly stained with a liquid that had dried to an unmistakable shade of brown.

Blood.

Panic hit hard and fast. Had the bastards from Xanadu managed to track her down? Or had she had the extremely bad luck to time her lonely walk-through on the same afternoon that a burglar had decided to enter the vacant residence? She had deactivated the sophisticated alarm system when she had entered a few minutes ago, making it all too easy for him.

Whatever the answer, she was trapped. Her tote, with the phone inside, was a million miles away in the front hall. Even if she had it in her hand, she could not risk using it because the intruder would hear every word she said in the echoing silence of the empty house.

The phone was not the only thing that was a long way away. Her car keys were also in the tote.

The only advantage she possessed was an intimate knowledge of the interior spaces of the large residence.

Pulse thudding heavily, she slipped out of her sandals and began to work her way back along the guest wing hallway toward the kitchen.

"I'm going to have to punish you, Zoe." Davis Mason spoke from somewhere in the great room area. "Just as I did Jennifer. You're like her in some ways. I couldn't trust her, either. I didn't want to hurt her, but she forced me to punish her frequently. And then she started talking about getting a divorce. Well, I couldn't allow her to do that, could I? I had to kill her, you see."

She almost stopped breathing. Davis Mason. Not someone from Xanadu or a passing burglar. Talk about your good news, bad news days.

"You're probably wondering how I figured it out." Davis sounded as though he was addressing the weekly meeting of his business club. "I'm not stupid, you know. That first day when you came to look at my house, I realized that you must have seen something in the bedroom. Until that moment, everything had been fine. But then you suddenly tensed up. I could tell that you were nervous. You couldn't wait to get away. And you asked about the bed."

She could hear his footsteps on the tiles of the grand central hall. He was not making any effort to conceal himself. He sounded so arrogant, so confident that she knew he must have a gun.

"I followed you back to your office," Davis said. "I saw you meet your friend at that café. I thought maybe I'd been wrong about you. Maybe it was all okay, after all. But just as I was about to drive away, you got up from the table and walked several blocks to the office of that private investigator on Cobalt Street."

Her bare feet made no sound on the cool tile. She took another step toward her goal.

"I told myself that you might have some personal reason for meeting with a PI. A reason that had nothing to do with me. After all, if you suspected I'd killed Jennifer, you'd have gone straight to the police, right? But then you called me yesterday morning and asked to bring a contractor to the house. After telling me that you didn't have any time for me until Friday. I knew then that you were lying, just like Jennifer used to do."

He was getting closer.

"When that damned contractor started talking about beds, I knew that he was probably that PI from Cobalt Street and that you must have asked him to find Jennifer. I knew then that the reason you didn't go to the cops was because you had no proof."

She took another step.

"You know what, Zoe? Your investigator never will find any proof. I put that bed into storage. Got any idea how many hundreds, maybe thousands of rental storage locker companies there are in this state?" Davis chuckled. "Neither do I. Talk about a needle in a haystack. Even if it occurs to Truax to check out the storage locker angle, he wouldn't know where to start."

Her hand brushed against a cool, steel surface.

"I'm afraid you're going to be the victim of a burglar you surprised when you walked into this house alone today, Zoe. You know, it's really too bad things had to end this way. I could have used some good feng shui."

Ethan stood in Zoe's office and listened to the ringing of her cell phone. Eventually he fell into voice mail.

"This is Zoe Luce. Please leave a message."

"This is Truax. Call me as soon as you get

this message." He rattled off the number and dropped the phone into his jacket pocket.

The edgy tension vibrated through him like electricity through a wire. Everything felt wrong.

He looked at Zoe's calendar again, but nothing had materialized in the space reserved for that afternoon since he had last checked it a few seconds ago.

Where the hell was she? He hated it when clients disappeared like this. It always meant trouble.

He flipped through her telephone card file, found Mason's office number, and dialed it. A woman with a pleasant voice answered.

"Mason Investments."

"Davis Mason, please."

"I'm afraid Mr. Mason is out of the office this afternoon. May I take a message?"

"No, I'll be in touch."

He checked the speed-dial function on the phone and found only one number had been entered. There wasn't even a name, just the letter A.

He called it.

"Gallery Euphoria," a woman said in a voice that belonged to a nightclub singer.

"I'm looking for Zoe."

"Who is this?"

"Ethan Truax. I'm working for her. It's important that I locate her immediately. Any idea where she is?"

"Truax Investigations?"

"Yes."

"I'm a close friend of Zoe's. Is something wrong?"

"She's not here. Her calendar is blank for the afternoon."

"Is this about Davis Mason?"

"Yes," he said trying to hang on to his patience, "Just tell me where you think she might be right now."

"I saw her at lunch. She told me that she was going to do a final walk-through at the home of a client today."

"Give me a name."

"The Taylors. There should be a number and an address in Zoe's files. What's this all about? Did you turn up something important, Mr. Truax?"

"The bed."

....

Zoe's car was parked in the drive. There was no indication that Mason or anyone else was in the vicinity.

Ethan told himself that was a good sign, but his gut wasn't buying it.

He removed his pistol from the center console and got out of the car. There was no need to worry about alarming the neighbors. The lots were large in this neighborhood. The nearest house was almost a quarter mile away.

He went to the front door. The knob turned easily in his hand.

He let himself into an elegant front hall. The first thing he noticed was a red tote. The second thing was a slight draft. There was another door or a window open in the house.

"Zoe?"

There was no response.

There was an intercom panel on the wall. At the top was a button labeled SEND ALL. He pressed it.

"Zoe, this is Truax. Talk to me."

The words echoed through every room in the house.

"Ethan, get out," Zoe shouted through the intercom. She had also hit SEND ALL. Her warning blared from every speaker in the place. "Mason's here. He's got a gun."

"Big deal. I've got one, too. Are you okay?"

"Yes, I'm inside the wine cellar." She sounded breathless, but coherent. "The door is locked. He can't get to me. A few seconds ago he was in the kitchen, but I don't know where he is now. For God's sake, get out of here. Call the cops."

He did not respond. He was out of his shoes, moving silently down a long, airy central hall with arched openings. He could see the living room and kitchen area.

Footsteps erupted suddenly from the vicinity of the kitchen. Mason burst into view, fleeing toward French doors that opened onto a walled patio and pool.

"Stop. It's over, Mason."

Mason spun around, gun coming up.

Ethan dove behind the nearest solid object, an ornate wooden chest.

Mason fired wildly.

A glass case containing a collection of antique silver and turquoise jewelry exploded nearby. A cold rain of shards fell around Ethan.

"You can't touch me," Mason shouted. "You'll never prove anything. You hear me? You'll never prove it."

The gun roared again. Shots thudded into the heavy chest.

The guy had gone over the deep edge, Ethan thought.

He made his way to the far end of his wooden barricade, leaned around the corner and squeezed off a single shot.

Mason yelped, jerked, flailed wildly, and then crashed headlong onto the tile floor. He dropped the gun to clutch his right leg.

Ethan counted to five before getting to his feet. Pieces of glass fell from his shirt and hair and skittered on the tile.

"Ethan, wait." Zoe was flying toward him down the hall, sandals in her hand. "There's glass everywhere and you're already bleeding."

He did not take his eyes off Mason. "You shouldn't have come out here alone today."

She ignored that and slid her feet into her sandals.

"Hang on," she said with startling gentleness. "I'll get a rug to cover the glass."

She was talking to him as if she thought

he was in shock, he realized. Maybe she didn't know he was just furious.

"Get Mason's gun first," he said.

"Right." She scooped up the weapon and brought it back to him. Then she seized a long carpet runner and tossed it down across the worst of the glass.

When she straightened, he got a good look at her face. She appeared too pale, but she was obviously in control.

She gave him a quick, frowning survey, and then she untied the little red and orange silk scarf she wore at her throat and handed it to him. "That cut doesn't look too bad, but it's getting messy."

He felt something warm and wet and realized that a trickle of blood was running down his jaw. Absently he dabbed at it with the silk scarf as he crossed the living room to where Mason lay, moaning.

Zoe followed.

Mason clenched his thigh with both hands, gritting his teeth. A pool of blood had formed on the tiles.

"You can't prove anything." Mason looked up, his face twisted with pain and rage. "You can't prove a damned thing."

"Don't bet on it." Ethan brushed a couple of slivers of glass off his shirt, reached into his pocket, and took out his phone. "I found the bed."

Chapter Eight

"Okay," Zoe said, "How did you find that bed?"

Ethan took a swallow of the champagne Arcadia had insisted on ordering for the table and put down the glass. Champagne was not his beverage of choice, but Zoe seemed to like it and he was trying to go along with the client. He consoled himself with the thought that he could always pour himself a stiff shot of whiskey later when he got back to Nightwinds.

It was late, and the trendy little Fountain Square restaurant was starting to empty out. A few couples lingered, and there was one large group on the far side of the room. He recognized a familiar face and figured it for a business dinner.

It had been Zoe's idea that they go out to eat after the long session with the police. They were both exhausted, and she said she was concerned about their stress levels. They needed to unwind.

"Dinner is on me," she said. "It's the least I can do after what happened today."

The offer had sounded too good to be true, and, as was often the case with such offers, it proved to be exactly that. Zoe invited Arcadia Ames to join them. The result was that instead of an intimate dinner for two during which he could have told her in great detail why she'd had no business taking off alone that afternoon, he was stuck with this not-so-cozy threesome.

He was acutely aware that he had no real grounds for complaint. If it had not been for Arcadia, he might still be looking for Zoe.

Every time he thought about Zoe locking herself inside the high-tech, steel-doored wine cellar to escape a crazy wife killer, he felt the inchoate anger and got the freezing sensation in his gut all over again. It had been so damned close.

So here the three of them sat, squeezed into a snug corner booth, sipping champagne. Maybe it was better this way, he thought. His relationship with Zoe was supposed to be all business, and the truth was he probably would have tried something really stupid if he'd found himself alone with her tonight.

The problem was that even though he was well and truly pissed, he also wanted very badly to take her to bed. The resulting tension had made him a little surly, and it was hard work trying to conceal his bad temper.

"The bed," he said, focusing on the neutral topic. "Right. In the end that proved to be Mason's biggest problem. It was easy enough to wrap his dead wife in the shower curtains and bury her in the back garden. But he couldn't quite see digging a hole big enough to bury a king-sized box spring and mattress."

"That might have gotten the attention of some of his neighbors," Zoe said dryly.

"But he couldn't just haul them off to a landfill, either. People prowl through landfills looking for things to salvage and the bed was in pretty good shape."

"Except for the stains, of course." Arcadia turned her champagne flute slowly between her fingertips. "He knew that if the blood-soaked mattress ever turned up it could be used as evidence of foul play."

Ethan nodded. On the surface he could not see what Zoe and Arcadia had in common, but the emotional tie that bound them together was unmistakable and it worried him.

He wondered if the connection between the two women was sexual. His instincts told him that it was not, but he did not trust his gut reaction when it came to that kind of thing. Women were a mystery. His instincts might be in denial tonight because all he could think about was having hot, sweaty sex with Zoe.

Get your mind out of the gutter, Truax. You're supposed to be a professional.

Zoe smiled at him. She looked better than she had a few hours ago when she had emerged from the wine cellar, but there was an unnatural brightness in her eyes. He knew what was causing it. She was feeling the aftereffects of the adrenaline, just as he was.

"Davis was sure that you would never be able to find the bed," she said. "He claimed that even if you guessed that it was in storage somewhere, there was no way you could find the right rental facility. He said there were hundreds, maybe thousands of them in the state."

"Probably are." Ethan removed the lid of the clay warmer in the center of the table and removed another plump corn tortilla. He dipped it into one of the three salsas that the waiter had brought to the table. They'd finished the salads, but the main courses had not arrived yet and he was ravenous.

"So?" Zoe prompted.

"The thing is, I didn't need to search every storage locker facility in the state." He took a bite of the tortilla. "I only had to check out the ones that could be reached within about a thirty-minute drive from Desert View. I also assumed that in order to remain as anonymous as possible, Mason would have gone with a large operation that had lots of lockers, not a small outfit where someone was more likely to remember him. That cut the number of possibilities down to a manageable number. I got on the phone and started calling."

"Wait a second." Zoe held up a hand. "How did you know that the storage facility had to be located within a thirty-minute driving radius of Desert View?"

"I got the pickup and drop-off times of the rented truck that Mason used. I knew almost exactly when he left Desert View with the bed. It wasn't hard to calculate how far he could have gone, allowing for the time to unload the bed at the locker facility."

He paused to take another bite of the salsa-laced tortilla and noticed that the business dinner on the other side of the room was breaking up. At the head of the table, the big, sandy-haired man in the expensive linen blend jacket picked up the tab for the other five people with an easy flourish.

It was nice to have a large budget for entertaining clients, Ethan thought. He turned his attention back to his own client and her companion.

Zoe gave him an admiring look. "I'm impressed. You make it sound so simple and logical. The mind of a detective is an amazing thing."

"Thanks," Ethan said. "I've always wanted to be loved for my mind."

Damn. That was not quite what he had wanted to say, he thought. Maybe he had better lay off the champagne. It did not seem to be mixing well with the aftermath of the adrenaline cocktail that still flowed through his system.

Arcadia looked faintly amused, but she did not say anything. If Zoe found the crack about being loved for his brain inappropriate, she gave no indication.

"I'm still a little confused though," she said, serious again. "How did you figure out which truck rental company Mason used and how did you find out precisely when he left Desert View?"

Ethan started to answer, but he broke off when the big man in the stylish jacket suddenly loomed over the table.

"Truax." Nelson Radnor gave him an easy grin. "Good to see you. I hear you closed a big one today. Congratulations."

"Word travels fast," Ethan said.

"I've got my sources." Nelson examined the bandage that covered a portion of Ethan's jaw and raised his brows. "Looks like you got knocked around a little."

"Just some flying glass." Ethan glanced across the table. "Zoe Luce, Arcadia Ames. This is Nelson Radnor."

Zoe made the connection immediately. "Radnor Security Systems?"

Nelson gave her an approving smile. "Right. A pleasure. I understand there was a woman at the scene this afternoon when Truax took Mason down. Can I assume it was one of you two lovely ladies?"

"I'd appreciate it if you wouldn't make any assumptions," Ethan said evenly. "My client would like to keep a low profile in this matter."

"No problem." Nelson switched his attention to Arcadia. "Truax is a lucky man to be enjoying such charming companionship tonight. Got a hunch he's having a lot more fun than I did."

The best that could be said for Arcadia's smile, Ethan thought, was that it was polite. There certainly wasn't much warmth in it. Not that Radnor seemed to notice.

Ethan angled his head toward the small group of people making their way toward the front door. "Client dinner?"

"Yeah. Routine." Nelson cast a quick, satisfied glance at the departing members of his dinner party. "The manager and some of his people from Las Estrellas."

"The new resort outside of town?" Zoe asked.

Nelson nodded. "Looks like Radnor will be handling security for them."

"Congratulations," Ethan said. "Nice contract."

"Thanks. You know, I may give you a call one of these days, Truax. We're running at full steam over at Radnor. Might be able to throw a little of the small stuff your way. You interested in some subcontracting work?"

"Depends," Ethan said carefully.

"I'll be in touch." Nelson appeared to realize that he had overstayed his welcome. He nodded at Zoe and Arcadia, his gaze lingering an extra second or so on Arcadia, and then he moved back a pace. "I'll let you folks get on with your dinner. See you around, Truax."

He walked off toward the door of the restaurant.

"I call him my competition," Ethan said. "But the truth is, we're not even playing in the same league."

"Maybe not." Zoe sounded amused. "But if I had to guess, I'd say he's jealous."

"Of the fact that I get to have dinner with you two instead of those folks from Las Estrellas?" Ethan nodded. "As well he should be."

Zoe shook her head. "He's not jealous because you're eating dinner with us. It's because of what you did today."

"She's right," Arcadia said with quiet certainty. "Radnor might be the big-time operator here in town when it comes to the security business, but his position as the CEO of a large corporation means he'll probably never have an opportunity to play the heroic private investigator who comes to the rescue in the nick of time the way you did today."

Zoe chuckled. "Probably not much opportunity for swashbuckling when you're in the business of doing routine employee background checks and supplying guards for places like Desert View and Las Estrellas."

"Got news for you," Ethan said. "My swash nearly buckled permanently today when I realized you were in that house alone with Mason. Talk about stressing out on the job. Thank God you had the presence of mind to get into that fancy cooler."

"It's not a cooler. It's a state-of-the-art wine cellar complete with its own refrigeration and humidity control systems." She spoke very evenly. "The room was designed to be physically secure because the Taylors collect extremely valuable old vintages."

"And another thing," he continued, getting into it now. "You should have stayed inside that state-of-the-art cooler until the coast was clear."

She said nothing.

Arcadia stiffened. "I hadn't," she said slowly, "thought about the size of the wine cellar." She broke off and gave Zoe a sharp, searching look. "Are you sure you're okay?"

"Yes," Zoe said firmly. "It was just a room, Arcadia. I can only thank heaven it was available when I needed it."

Arcadia's mouth tightened. "Have some more champagne."

She did not wait for a response. Hauling the bottle out of the ice bucket, she refilled Zoe's glass.

Ethan watched the two women in silence. *I'm definitely missing something here.* It wouldn't be the first time, of course, but he had a feeling this was something important, something he needed to know.

Zoe looked at Ethan. "I believe you were about to tell us how you came to learn so many of the details about the timing of Mason's movements the day he rented the truck."

"Yes." Arcadia watched him with a speculative expression. "Finish your story. How did you come by all those facts and figures?"

"Radnor's a cheap employer," Ethan said.

"He charges the Desert View Community Association a lot of money to supply security guards, but he doesn't pay his men very well."

Zoe's eyes widened. "You bribed one of the Desert View guards to let you look at the gate logs?"

"Yeah."

"The straightforward approach. I like that," Arcadia stated.

"So elegantly simple. Why didn't I think of that?" Zoe marveled.

"Probably because you are not a trained detective," Ethan said.

"That must be it," she agreed. "How much does it cost to bribe a Radnor security guard?"

"You'll find out when you get my bill. That bribe, as well as the one I used to get the attendant at the storage facility to look the other way while I opened Mason's locker, will be listed under miscellaneous expenses."

Outside the restaurant, the desert night felt good but it did nothing to dispel Zoe's strange mood. She wondered if she had drunk too much champagne. Arcadia had refilled her glass several times. She knew why her friend was deliberately trying to get her a little drunk. Arcadia was worried about the time in the wine cellar. *A small room with a locked door.*

As Arcadia suspected, the experience had brought back a lot of unpleasant memories that tonight might well trigger a few bad dreams about her time in Xanadu. But it was not as if there had been a lot of options this afternoon. The wine cellar had kept her safe until Ethan had arrived. That was the important thing.

Too bad there had been no Ethan Truax to come to the rescue at Xanadu. She and Arcadia had been forced to find their own way out of that nightmare.

She watched Ethan from the corner of her eye as he walked beside her toward the car. His hair gleamed darkly in the light of the street lamps. His face was in shadow. He moved through the night with an easy confidence, relaxed but aware of his surroundings. She had the feeling that the trick was a habit that came naturally to him.

The three of them got into Ethan's SUV. Arcadia gave directions to her condo. When they arrived, Zoe and Ethan walked her to her door.

She paused in the white carpeted hall to look searchingly at Zoe one last time.

"Are you sure you'll be okay alone tonight?" she asked. "You're welcome to stay here. You know that."

"Thanks, I'll be okay." That was a lie. It was going to be a bad night. But there was nothing anyone could do about the nightmares. She had to deal with them on her own. "Don't worry about me. If I can't get to sleep, I'll spend the time thinking up ways to explain to the Taylors why their antique Spanish chest has bullet holes in it."

"All right. I'll see you tomorrow." Arcadia looked at Ethan. "You probably need rest, too."

"Probably," he said, not sounding overly concerned.

Arcadia closed the door. Zoe heard her slide the heavy bolt into place. It was followed by the muffled clink of a chain.

Ethan glanced back at the door as he and Zoe turned to go down the stairs. "Sounds like your friend takes security seriously."

"We both do. A woman can't be too careful."

"Yeah, you did sort of prove that today, didn't you?"

The too-neutral, give-nothing-away tone was back in his voice, she noticed. He was in an edgy, unpredictable mood, just as she was, but she did not have a clue to what he was thinking. She reminded herself that he had been through a very traumatic experience that afternoon.

Outside on the street, they got back into his vehicle. The interior seemed a good deal smaller and the atmosphere far more intimate than it had a few minutes ago when there had been three of them.

She was very conscious of Ethan sitting so close. He was not one of those beefy men like Nelson Radnor who looked as if he'd played football in college and who always seemed to crowd a woman. Nevertheless, Ethan somehow managed to take up more than his share of the available space. His nearness did things to her nerve endings, unfamiliar things, things she could not remember experiencing before around a man, not even in her other life.

She wondered if she was suffering some form of delayed shock.

He drove the short distance to the two-story building that housed her apartment and parked in the lot.

Without a word, he got out of the car and opened the door on the passenger side. She knew what he was probably thinking. Ace detective that he was, he could not help but notice that the Casa de Oro Apartments did not exactly live up to its grand-sounding name. But while the place was no house of gold and although it was considerably more down-market than Arcadia's luxury condo, it was everything it had claimed to be in the newspaper ad she had answered: clean, quiet, and, most important of all, *affordable.*

Clutching her tote, she extricated herself from the close confines of the interior and walked with him to the green wrought-iron gate.

It was late, she realized, reaching into her tote for the heavy key ring, almost midnight. It was strange to think that, after all she and Ethan had been through together today, she hardly knew him. Yet here he was, taking her home. She wondered what he would say if she informed him that he was the first man to get this close to her front door since she had moved to Whispering Springs.

Then again maybe he would not be interested in that small factoid. Probably just hand her his itemized bill and ask her when it would be convenient for her to take a look at the room he wanted her to design.

"Here, I'll do that for you." Ethan took the key chain from her hand and muttered something beneath his breath when he felt the heft of it. Holding it up to the light, he examined the large metal ball attached to the ring. "Why don't you just get yourself a nice rock if you want to add a little extra weight to your purse?"

"It's an antique doorknob. I found it in an old residence I redid a few months ago. I took it to a local craftsman who works in metal and had him attach the key ring to it."

"I can see that it's a big old doorknob." He twisted the key in the gate lock. "What I don't understand is why you're using it for a key ring. Some kind of design statement?"

She gave him a cool smile. "It's big enough that I can find it easily in my tote."

"Uh-huh." He did not look impressed with her explanation. "You sure as hell don't want to drop it accidentally on your big toe. You'll limp for a week."

"I'm careful." She slipped quickly through

the gate and led the way along the walk to the door that opened onto the small lobby. He followed, carrying the brass doorknob in his hand.

"It's the long, silver key," she said.

He opened the door and stood aside. She moved into the lobby and stopped, locked up with indecision. Should she say good night here or allow him to see her to the door of her apartment? Did one offer a cup of coffee to a man who had arguably saved one's life?

Another chill of awareness went through her at the thought of taking him upstairs to her apartment. This was a no-brainer. Clearly the smart thing to do was to bid him good night here in the lobby. So why was she dithering?

Ethan studied her with an assessing expression. "You sure you're okay? You don't look good."

"Thanks. You really know how to flatter the client, don't you?"

"Think of it as a professional observation."

"I'm still feeling a little jumpy, that's all. I told Arcadia that I'm exhausted, and that's true as far as it goes. But I'm all revved up inside. I feel like I'll never sleep again."

"You overdosed on adrenaline today," he said. "We both did. Too much of that stuff does a real number on your nervous system. Takes a while to get past the jag."

"I know," she said automatically, not stopping to think.

"Been through it before, huh?"

That had been dumb, she thought. It occurred to her that, between the events of the day and the champagne, her defenses were dangerously low. She had better get upstairs to her apartment before she said anything else equally stupid.

"I've heard about the syndrome," she said smoothly. "Sounds like you've experienced it personally."

"Once or twice. Goes with the job, occasionally." He looked at the stairwell. "I'm betting you're upstairs."

"Yes." This was the moment when she should thank him once again for coming to her rescue and say good night. But the words seemed to have gotten stuck in her throat.

He gave her another critical survey and then grasped her elbow in a firm grip. "I'd better see you to your door. I don't think you should be wandering around loose in your present condition."

"I'm all right, really." She clung to her tote as if it were a flotation device and she was about to jump into some very deep water. "You're the one who got the worst of it today."

But she did not resist when he steered her up the staircase. She could feel the power in the hand wrapped around her arm. If he were to tighten his grip fractionally, she knew she would be unable to escape. But she also sensed the control that seemed to be so much a part of him. The combination of strength and self-discipline was disconcertingly sensual.

Maybe it was just this strange mood she was in tonight. She reminded herself for what was probably the two-hundredth time that he was not her type.

At the landing Ethan paused to study the doors that lined the hall. "Which one?"

"The corner apartment."

He walked her to the door, selected the correct key from the heavy ring, and let her inside her snug little home.

She moved quickly into the miniature

foyer, turned on the overhead light, and looked at him. "Have I thanked you for what you did today?"

He propped one shoulder against the door frame and folded his arms. "You've mentioned it a couple of times. If you do it again, I'll probably start back in on my lecture about how you shouldn't have gone out alone to the Taylor place this afternoon."

She shuddered. "I'd just as soon not hear that particular speech again. But I do want you to know I'm very grateful for what you did today."

His mouth curved faintly. "I guess this is the point where I get to say, *all part of the job, ma'am. You'll get my bill in the morning.*"

For some reason she found that incredibly funny. She smiled. The smile turned into a giggle. And then she realized she could not stop.

Something was wrong. She *never* giggled, at least not in this unnatural, high-pitched way.

I'm losing it.

Horrified, she dropped the tote on the floor and slapped her palm over her mouth.

Intensely aware of Ethan watching her, she took a deep breath. Then she took another.

Mercifully the runaway laughter subsided. Cautiously she took her hand away from her mouth. She could feel herself turning red with embarrassment.

"Sorry," she mumbled.

"Me, too," he said. "That wasn't my best line."

"Maybe the champagne was not such a good idea tonight," she said.

"I'm sure it seemed like it at the time."

"Yes, it did."

"Mind if I ask you a personal question?"

"I don't know." Something in his expression made her cautious. "What's the question?"

"You and Arcadia. Are you two, uh, a couple?"

It took her at least two beats to process that query. Then she managed to grasp his meaning.

"No," she said. "We're friends. Very close friends. But we're not lovers. I'm not gay and Arcadia is, well, I'm not sure what she is, to be perfectly honest. Arcadia is Arcadia. We've never discussed her sexual orientation."

"That was the way I had it figured, but I just wanted to be sure."

She could not seem to look away from him. Time was slowing down and turning viscous. She felt like a butterfly trying to move through thick honey.

"Why?" she whispered.

Ethan straightened very deliberately, unfolded his arms, and took one step forward into the hall.

"Because I didn't want to make a complete fool out of myself when I kissed you," he said.

Time stopped altogether. This was one of those deer-in-the-headlights moments, she thought. She groped for something intelligent to say, tried to come up with a smart, sophisticated way to break through the heavy spell that held her in thrall. But her brain refused to engage.

All of the restless, chaotic energy that had been ebbing and flowing through her for the past few hours surged abruptly to high tide. Every nerve in her body was shimmering with a tension that was not unlike what she had experienced when she had heard the gunshots outside the wine cellar.

The memory of that moment of horrified dread jolted her out of the silence.

"I was terrified that he'd shot you," she whispered.

Ethan put his hands on her shoulders. He flexed his fingers, tightening his grip experimentally, as if waiting to see if she would try to run. He drew her slowly toward him.

"All the more reason why you shouldn't have gone out there alone today," he said.

He really *was* angry, she thought. Or maybe not.

It was impossible to be certain of anything except the heat in his eyes. It was so intense it could have thawed an iceberg. It was certainly doing a terrific job of melting something deep inside her, something that had been frozen for a long time.

She raised her fingers to the small bandage at the edge of his jaw. He had gone home to shower and change after the session with the police. Evidently he had taken the time to shave, too.

It was incredibly exhilarating to touch him like this.

"Are you really mad at me?" she asked, intrigued.

"I'm not sure," he muttered. "Maybe I'm

just pissed off at myself for letting the situation get out of control. I should never have allowed you to get into that mess."

"It wasn't your fault."

"Yeah, it was my fault." He pulled her hard against him and put his mouth very close to hers. "And this is going to be my fault, too. No one to blame here but myself. I really hate when that happens."

His mouth closed over hers, fierce and demanding. Her response was immediate and electric. Excitement crashed through her. She was literally shaking with it.

With a tiny, muffled moan, she wrapped her arms around his neck and clung to him. Sensation poured through her, leaving her dazzled and breathless. She had known desire in the past but never like this. She could feel herself growing damp, and he was *just kissing her.*

She was aware that what was left of the rational part of her mind was trying to get a message through, but she ignored the warning. She knew that she had drifted into some uncharted danger zone, but she no longer cared.

She and Ethan had survived a brush with death at the hands of a cold-blooded killer.

As far as she was concerned, the events of the day had created a bond that would exist between them for the rest of their lives even if they never saw each other again. Then again, maybe that was how you rationalized a one-night encounter, she thought.

Works for me.

She was vaguely aware of Ethan closing the door with one hand while he pinned her to him with the other. She was too busy kissing his throat, his ear, his mouth—too busy rejoicing in the elemental thrill of being crushed into his unyielding body.

It seemed to her that, in spite of his shower and fresh clothes, the aura of the day's violence still clung to him. She wanted to free him from it and replace it with the same euphoria that was coursing through her.

Ethan reluctantly pulled his mouth away from hers. He was breathing heavily. He shoved his fingers through her hair and clamped her head very gently between his palms.

"This is probably not a good idea," he said thickly.

"Probably not."

"But I can't seem to think of a better one."

"Neither can I."

The urgency welling up from some deep place spilled through her, leaving showers of sparks in its wake. She could feel the same electricity crackling through Ethan. It was a wonder they didn't short out the apartment's wiring, she thought.

He lifted her into his arms, angled her out of the hallway and carried her into the close shadows of the small front room. There he settled her down onto the nearest piece of furniture, a dainty, elegantly curved little sofa. For a moment, she feared the graceful little piece would crumple beneath their combined weight.

The sofa shuddered, but it stayed upright. It was not large enough to hold the two of them, however. When he came down on top of her, Ethan rolled with her in his arms onto the carpet.

He did not seem to notice the sudden change in elevation.

She could hardly catch her breath, but breathing was the last thing on her mind now. She clawed at the buttons of his shirt. The knowledge that he was as caught up in this moment as she was acted like a potent aphrodisiac.

She was aware of him fumbling with her blouse. He got it off and it disappeared. Cool air flowed over her hot skin. Her bra vanished. His palm rasped lightly over her nipple. She shivered and dug her nails into his back.

He put a hand under the lower edge of her skirt and slid one warm palm up the inside of her bare leg until he touched her already dampened panties. He pressed his hand against her briefly. When she arched in response, he whispered in her ear—raw, earthy, incredibly sexy things. No man had ever talked like that to her. She was shocked.

"Yes," she said. "Oh, yes, please."

He tugged her panties off and pushed her skirt upward until it bunched at her thighs.

"Tell me if I'm going too fast here," he said into her mouth. "I feel like I'm in free fall."

"You are not going too fast."

She curved one leg around his thigh and felt the heat of him through his trousers. When she moved her foot along his calf, he sucked in his breath and groaned.

Buttons popped, flew, and skittered

across the little coffee table. She had done some damage to the shirt, she thought, but at least she had got it undone. That was the really important thing right now.

She flattened her hand on his bare chest and felt the smooth glide of muscle beneath skin.

Oh, yes, getting his shirt off had certainly been the right thing to do.

She went to work on his belt buckle.

"Hang on," he said against her throat.

"I'm trying to."

He started to smile and then he gave a husky groan and put a hand down between their bodies. He covered her fumbling fingers.

"I'll get it," he said.

He wrenched himself away from her again and got to his feet. She watched him strip off his low-cut boots, trousers, briefs, and shirt. The curtains were closed on the windows overlooking the swimming pool and garden, but enough light seeped through to reveal the contours of his hard body. He looked larger than life here in the confines of her small living room.

She looked at his heavy arousal and caught her breath. A *lot* larger than life.

A moment later he came back down on top of her. Excitement flared. She turned her head and bit him lightly on the arm. *Bit him.* She never did things like that in bed. He laughed softly in the shadows.

His hand tightened around the curve of her hip. She felt his mouth on her breasts, her belly and lower. When he found the hidden, exquisitely sensitive little button, she nearly screamed.

She had not expected this. It was too much for her overwrought senses, especially given the fact that it had been so long since she had shared any kind of sexual intimacy. She sank her fingers into his hair. Her entire lower body was clenched as tight as a fist.

"Ethan." Her fingers tightened fiercely in his hair.

He moved up to cover her, sinking into her. *Larger than life.*

The too-tight feeling was right at the knife edge that separated pleasure and pain. She could not stand it, she thought. She could not take this.

Without warning her climax rocked through her. This was not the sweet, pleasurable release she remembered from the past. This was a powerful, sweeping cascade of sensation that stole her breath. She could not even cry out with the astonishment and wonder of it all.

The furious release rode her, wringing her out and throwing her to the winds.

Ethan retreated an inch or two and then plunged back into her. She felt every muscle in his back go taut just before his own climax slammed through him.

At the last possible instant, he covered her mouth with his own. She swallowed most of his hoarse, triumphant shout of satisfaction.

A long time later, Ethan managed to rouse himself from the seductive lethargy that had stolen over him in the aftermath of passion. He glanced at his watch. It was after one in the morning. Beside him Zoe was wedged into the angle of his body, spoon fashion. He could feel the soft, silken skin of her sweetly rounded rear tucked warmly against his thighs.

He could not recall the last time sex had been this good. True, it had been quite a while since the last time, and he was old enough to know that bouts of abstinence, spiked with adrenaline overload, tended to make the heart grow fonder. Still, it had been pretty damn memorable. At least it had been memorable for him.

He thought about how good it had felt to be inside her, how she had wrapped herself around him and shivered in his arms. His satiated body began to stir.

She opened smoky eyes and looked up at him.

"You're leaving," she said calmly.

It was a casual, straightforward observation, not a question or a plea or even a protest. It shook him more than he would have believed. He tried to read her expression in the shadows and realized that she *expected* him to go, maybe even *wanted* him to leave.

He sure as hell did not consider himself to be the romantic or sentimental type, but it bothered him that she had no problem with the concept of showing him the door. Hadn't what had just happened between them meant anything to her? Maybe he was the only one here who was not accustomed to sex that good.

"Depends," he said. He decided to force

the issue out into the open. Better to know the truth than to leave wondering what it was he had done to screw up. Because he had a feeling that as soon as he walked out the door he would be trying to think of a way to get back inside. "Do you want me to go?"

For an instant he was certain that she was about to say yes, and he went a little cold inside. But she hesitated. In the shadows, her expression was very serious, as if she was attempting to make a profound decision, one that scared her.

"No," she said on a soft sigh. "I don't want you to go."

"Good." His insides reheated. "I don't want to leave yet, either. But I would like to request a move into the bedroom." He sat up cautiously. "I'm assuming that your bed is at least somewhat larger than that itty-bitty sofa over there."

She blinked a couple of times. He got the impression that she was already having second thoughts about inviting him to stay. His stomach tightened.

Then she smiled. "I think my bed is big enough for both of us."

Chapter Nine

. . . The white-jacketed orderly seized her arm and pulled her around the corner into the long hallway. Fear crested within her. She hated this passage more than any other place in the hospital. Desperately, she dug in her heels and tried to struggle free.

The attendant shook her angrily. "Get with the program, bitch. You've got an appointment with Dr. McAlistair this afternoon. I don't have time for this crap."

His name was Ron but she had privately given him and the rest of the orderlies the generic label of *Hulk.* She hated them all, but she hated Ron and Ernie the most. The pair always pretended to treat the patients with concern on the rare occasions when there were family members or visitors present but when they were alone with a *resident*—the director's diplomatic term for an inmate—they were rough, rude, and occasionally cruel.

She had managed to fake swallowing

her morning meds as usual, but she suspected that McAlistair had ordered something new to be slipped into her hot cereal. There was something wrong with her again. Her head was spinning and her balance was off.

Another one of McAlistair's little experiments, no doubt.

Ron was in a hurry today. He jerked her swiftly along the hall. She saw the red metal emergency fire extinguisher box on the wall and knew that the entrance of the screaming room loomed ahead on the right.

Sometimes the door was closed, and that was better because then the screams were muffled. But today the door stood open. Dread seized her. Some of the sobs trapped in the wall were fresh. Something bad had happened in that room again last night.

Ron hauled her past the entrance to the terrible little chamber. She braced herself but nothing could soften the blow. The white walls of the room shrieked silently, just as they always did. Pain, rage, and fear mingled together, assaulting her senses. Lately she had begun to wonder if some of the meds McAlistair was using on her were making her more sensitive.

She did not want to look through the doorway, but she could not bring herself to look away. There was no one inside the room. It looked quite normal with its white cabinets, blood pressure gauge, sink, small desk, and chair.

The examination table stood in the center, a fresh sheet of pristine white sanitary paper pulled neatly down the padded top. The cold metal stirrups were extended.

It was a common, ordinary medical examination room in every way except for the fact that the walls screamed . . .

He came awake instantly when he felt Zoe's body stiffen. He had fallen asleep with her nestled against him. He had one hand resting comfortably on her bare thigh when he first became aware of the tension that had invaded her sleep. Her skin went cool beneath his palm. Tiny goose bumps roughened her flesh.

"No." Her arm jerked but she did not awaken. *"No."*

She started to writhe as if in torment or terror.

"Zoe." He jackknifed upright and hauled her up into his arms. "Zoe, take it easy, honey. You're dreaming."

She shuddered, and then her eyes snapped open. She stared at him with a shocked, dazed expression. He could see that she was still trapped in the nightmare. She did not recognize him.

"Zoe, pay attention." He did not speak gently this time. He made the words a command, and he delivered it the way he would have in any other type of emergency, coldly, firmly, demanding a response. "Wake up. Now."

She shivered again, and then she seemed to come back to herself. He wondered where she had been.

Her muscles loosened and went limp. She gave her head a little shake.

"Sorry," she mumbled. "I get bad dreams sometimes. Didn't mean to scare you."

"Don't worry about it. Are you okay?"

"Yes, thanks."

But she was not okay, he thought. The nightmare had taken a toll.

"Come on." He rolled to the edge of the bed, got to his feet, and found his trousers.

"Let's go into the kitchen. I'll fix you some warm milk."

"Please, don't worry about it. I can cope with the dream."

"You'll cope better after you've had some warm milk." He reached down and pried her out of the rumpled bedding.

When she was on her feet, he took the dark blue satin robe down from the brass hook on the wall and draped it around her shoulders.

At that point she evidently decided to concede the field to him. Without another word of protest, she tied the sash of the robe and allowed herself to be steered to the kitchen.

He sat her down on one of the tall chairs at the high, round table near the window and went to work in the miniature kitchen. He found a half-full quart of nonfat in the refrigerator and a small sauce pan in a cupboard. He could feel her eyes on him, pensive and uneasy, but she did not speak.

When the milk was ready, he set a mug full of it in front of her and sat down in the one other chair. He folded his elbows on the table.

"Drink," he ordered.

"It was very kind of you to do this, but I really don't like warm milk."

"Drink," he said again. "It may not do anything for you, but it will make me feel better."

"Okay, okay." She raised the mug with both hands and took a tentative taste. She swallowed and made a face. "You're inclined to be rather dictatorial, but I suppose you already know that."

"Others have mentioned the trait on occasion over the years, but I feel that I have been sadly misunderstood."

She nodded. "Of course."

She drank some more of the milk.

"Want to tell me about the dream?" he asked after a while.

"No," she said quickly. "I'd rather not talk about it. Makes it too real, if you know what I mean."

"Suit yourself."

"Did I, uh, say anything?" she asked cautiously.

"While you were caught up in the nightmare?" He shook his head, wondering why that possibility concerned her. "Not much. Just the word *no* a couple of times."

She looked relieved. "That's all?"

"Yeah. Why?"

"I just wondered. It's a little embarrassing, to tell you the truth."

"Do you remember saying something in the dream?"

"Not really." She looked down at the milk. "It was one of those bad dreams in which you find yourself running away from some unseen threat. A common, garden-variety nightmare."

She was lying, he thought. It made him curious, but he let it go. This was not the time to push her.

"Given the events of the day, it's not surprising that your dream would follow that script," he said.

"I guess not."

He watched the remnants of her tension dissipate as she drank the milk.

After a while, he rinsed out the empty mug and led her back to the bedroom.

They got into bed, and he cradled her close. She relaxed against him.

He had just decided that she was safely asleep when she spoke.

"Thanks for the milk," she mumbled.

"Any time."

Chapter Ten

The door of Ian Harper's office opened. Venetia McAlistair, clutching a set of files, walked into the room. Her round face was crimped in disapproval.

With her halo of gray curls, her little glasses, and her frumpy suits, Venetia made Ian think of his grandmother. There had always been cookies in the oven and a heavy leather belt hanging close at hand in Granny's house. Granny had not hesitated to use the heavy leather strap on her *little man* if he failed to follow all of the rules. *Can't have you turning out like your father, now can we?*

"I brought my notes regarding Sara Cleland," Venetia said. "But I can't understand why you want to go over them, and I'm rather busy this afternoon."

"Please sit down," Ian said. "I have some news."

He had not been looking forward to this conversation. He did not like Venetia, but there was no getting around the fact that she knew more about the Cleland woman than anyone else at the Manor. Furthermore, she had a strong personal interest in seeing Sara Cleland returned to the hospital.

"What news?" Venetia demanded.

"Leon Grady found the Cleland woman."

"I don't understand." Venetia sat down hard in one of the two chairs on the other side of the desk. The jacket of her skirted suit bunched up around her thick waist. She held the files she had brought with her in both hands on her lap. "You told me that she and the other patient who escaped that night died in a hotel fire somewhere in Mexico."

"Apparently they faked their deaths or at least the Cleland woman faked hers."

"I see." Venetia removed her glasses and absently polished the lenses with the hem of her white blouse. "This is really quite astonishing. I had no idea."

"Several days ago, Grady was contacted online by someone calling himself GopherBoy. This individual claimed to have hacked into the files of someone who sells false identities over the net. He managed to steal some of the files before that person realized there was an intruder."

"Incredible. I've heard of such things, of course, but I never—"

"The hacker claimed that he had information regarding our patient and that he would give it to us for a price," Ian said, impatient with the interruption.

"I see." Venetia positioned her glasses back on her nose. "What did you do?"

"I authorized payment of a large sum of money to him. Grady handled the transaction. He told me that in exchange for the money, he had been given a name, some personal data, and the information that the Cleland woman was in L.A. We both agreed that he should try to find the woman and verify her identity before we arranged to have her picked up and returned to us."

"Of course. It certainly wouldn't do to snatch the wrong person off the street, would it? There are laws against that sort of thing."

Ian gritted his teeth. Once in a while he got the uneasy feeling that Venetia McAlistair did not have a great deal of professional respect for him.

"Grady left for Los Angeles a few days ago," he said. "And then he disappeared."

"Disappeared?"

"He has evidently betrayed this institution and my confidence. I do not know for certain what he plans to do with the information he has regarding the Cleland woman, but I think we can be sure that he does not intend to see her safely returned to the Manor."

"But where is he?"

"Fortunately, Ms. Leeds became suspicious of his behavior almost immediately and took action. She instructed Al Drummer in accounting to keep tabs on Grady by tracking his charge card expenses. Grady did indeed use his Candle Lake Manor card to get to L.A. There he rented a car and that is when he vanished."

Venetia looked baffled. "Where did he go?"

"Ms. Leeds believes that he has gone to wherever the Cleland woman really is, of course. She is currently trying to come up with that information."

"But what on earth does Grady intend to do?"

"I'm not sure, but I suspect he has figured

out a way to make a profit on the information he got from the hacker. Some form of blackmail, I imagine."

Outrage glittered in Venetia's birdlike eyes. "I must tell you, Dr. Harper, that I have long had serious doubts about Leon Grady's professional attitude and dedication. I've never been convinced that he put the best interests of this hospital or the patients first."

No shit, Ian thought. But he managed to maintain his carefully honed facade of the dedicated professional. "Unfortunately, your impression was correct. Hindsight is always twenty-twenty, is it not?"

"She has gone without her therapy and medication for an entire year. There is no telling how much ground has been lost."

"I agree. The situation is quite critical."

Venetia sat up very straight, gripping her files. "We must bring her back at once. For her own sake."

You mean because you've got plans for her, Ian thought. But he did not say that out loud. Whatever McAlistair wanted to do with the Cleland woman once she had been retrieved did not interest him. His only goal was to get his extremely profitable patient back.

The door opened again. Fenella Leeds entered.

"I've got an address for the Cleland woman," she said coldly. "Found it in some email correspondence that Grady conducted with that hacker. Grady deleted the email, but I was able to recover it. He was always very sloppy about records of all kinds."

Fenella's beautiful face was as composed and impassive as ever. Ian still could not believe that he had had her in his bed for a while. At the start of their brief affair, he had considered himself a very lucky man. By the time she had lost interest in him and ended the relationship, he was profoundly relieved.

Fenella was the only woman he had ever met besides his grandmother who had the power to terrify him.

"Where is Sara?" Venetia demanded.

Fenella glanced at her notes. "A town called Whispering Springs. It's in Arizona. She's living under the name Zoe Luce."

"What about Grady?" Ian asked. "Did you find him?"

"No. Evidently he's smart enough not to charge his lodging and meals to his corporate credit card. He probably realizes that we could track him that way."

"Well, he's the least of our problems," Ian said. "We'll deal with him later. The chief priority is to get Sara back. I'll send two of the orderlies who know her and who have been trained to handle difficult patients. Get Drummer from accounting in here. I'll tell him to authorize the travel expenses. I also want to make sure he keeps quiet about this."

"Absolutely," Fenella said. "The last thing we want is for word of this situation to get out to any of our clients. Publicity like this is precisely what they pay us to avoid."

Five minutes later, Al Drummer walked into the office. If Venetia reminded him of his grandmother, Ian thought, Drummer put him in mind of the stern, fire-and-brimstone preacher whose sermons Granny had forced him to endure every Sunday—the one who had shocked the congregation when he was arrested while trolling for prostitutes one weekend in Florida.

Ian gave him the outline of the situation.

Drummer's eyes blazed with what could only be described as righteous wrath.

"I told you that Leon Grady could not be entrusted with a corporate credit card," Drummer said.

Chapter Eleven

She awoke feeling a little groggy but not nearly as wrung out as she usually did after one of the bad dreams. For a few seconds, she kept her eyes closed and tried to make sense of the incessant warbling sound that had awakened her.

Something about the bed felt wrong. It finally occurred to her that she was alone in it. It was unsettling to realize how quickly the feel of Ethan's weight beside her had become familiar and comfortable. One night. Probably not a good thing.

She opened her eyes and sat up against the pillows.

Ethan was gone.

A glance at the bedside clock provided one possible explanation for his departure. It was almost ten o'clock. She stared, disbelieving, at the hands of the timepiece. She *never* slept this late.

The irritating warble interrupted her thoughts. She pushed aside the covers, swung her feet over the side of the bed, and reached for the phone.

"Hello?"

"Did he spend the night?" Arcadia asked without preamble.

"Sort of."

"Sort of? Did he or didn't he?"

"He was here."

"I had a feeling that might happen." Arcadia sounded pleased. "Something about the way he was watching you all through dinner last night. Can I assume matters turned appropriately passionate when you got back to your apartment?"

"He said it was the aftereffects of the adrenaline jag we had both been on all afternoon and evening."

"Adrenaline jag." Arcadia sounded thoughtful. "I suppose that's as good an excuse as any for hot, steamy sex with a virtual stranger."

"That's certainly what I'm telling myself this morning." She got to her feet and reached for her robe. "Heaven knows, I need some kind of rationalization for what happened. I can't believe I did it, Arcadia. I haven't even been interested in a man since—" She broke off. "You know."

"I know."

"And then, last night it was as if the floodgates had been opened. It was a completely surreal experience, if you want to know the truth."

Arcadia chuckled. "It probably just felt a little weird because you've been celibate for so long. Don't worry about it. You had a right to a night of wild abandon. Is he still there?"

"No. He's gone. One is tempted to make the usual snide remarks about men who sneak out without saying good-bye but I suppose I've got to allow for mitigating circumstances in this case."

"Circumstances such as the fact that it's ten o'clock on a weekday morning and he does have a business to operate?"

"Yeah. And so do I. I just remembered that I've got an appointment with a client at eleven, and I've got to arrange for repairs at the Taylor residence. I don't even want to think about what they'll say when they find out what happened to that gorgeous Spanish chest."

"Relax. It will give them a good story to tell at their next cocktail party."

"I certainly hope they take that attitude."

Clutching the phone, she slid her feet into a pair of slippers and padded down the hall toward the kitchen. "I can't believe I slept in like this. And so solidly. I never even heard him leave."

"He probably didn't want to wake you."

"More likely he didn't want to have to make any of the customary polite promises about calling me." She picked up the teakettle and turned on the faucet. "Based on what he told me of his track record, I'm afraid Ethan Truax has a problem with the commitment thing."

"What track record?"

"He admitted that he's been married and divorced three times."

"You're right, it doesn't sound like he goes in for permanency. But, then, you're not exactly looking for a long-term committed relationship, yourself, at the moment, are you?"

It was a depressing observation but entirely valid. A committed relationship implied truth, trust, and a degree of intimacy that she dared not risk.

"Point taken." She plugged in the kettle and opened the ceramic jar that contained her favorite tea. "Still, three marriages and three divorces are a little scary."

"Not even close," Arcadia said quietly. "You and I both know some real scary types. Ethan Truax is not in that category."

"I won't argue with you."

"Not to change the subject, but have you seen the paper this morning?" Arcadia asked.

Zoe started to say no. Then she noticed the morning edition of the *Whispering Springs Herald* lying on the kitchen table. Ethan must have found it at her door and brought it inside before he left. She wondered if she should be touched by the thoughtful gesture. Maybe he had merely brought it in for his own convenience to read before he left for work. That was the problem with a guy who was commitment-phobic. You did not know what kind of spin to put on his actions.

"It's here," she said into the phone. "But I haven't read it."

"You might want to take a look at the story below the fold of the second section."

"Uh-oh. Should I get a bad feeling about this?"

"Depends."

Zoe took a step closer to the high table and saw that the paper had been left folded open to the second section. It was impossible to miss the headline.

DESERT VIEW MAN CONFESSES
TO MURDER OF WIFE

A jolt of unease went through her.

"How bad is it?" she asked. "That nice Detective Ramirez who took our statements yesterday promised that he would do his best to keep me out of it."

"You're out of it, all right. Neither you nor Enhanced Interiors is mentioned by name. The story doesn't name the Taylors, either. It just refers to shots fired at a private residence."

"That's a relief. What about Ethan? This was his first case here in Whispering Springs. Did he get any credit for being the hero of the hour?"

"That's the amusing part," Arcadia stated. "Read the last couple of paragraphs."

Zoe looked closer and saw that Ethan had marked them for her with a heavily inked arrow.

. . . A police spokesperson acknowledged that the murder might never have come to light had it not been for the actions of the private investigator who tracked Mason to the residence yesterday. "His inquiries into the disappearance of Jennifer Mason broke the case," the spokesperson said.

A representative of Radnor Security Systems, a local firm that handles security for Desert View as well as several large businesses in the area, was contacted for comment. He referred all questions to the CEO of the firm, Nelson Radnor, who, in turn declined, citing a long-standing policy of client confidentiality.

"Radnor." Zoe snatched up the paper. "The stupid reporter got the wrong agency."

"He probably just went on the assumption that the investigator was a Radnor employee because everyone knows that company is the big banana in security around here."

"Reporters aren't supposed to go on assumptions." Fuming, she slapped the paper against the edge of the table. “They’re supposed to report facts.”

“Really? Since when? I hadn’t heard that.”

Zoe sighed. “Poor Ethan. He risks his neck, does all the work, and doesn’t get the credit.”

“Look on the bright side. He got you into bed last night. That’s more than any other man has accomplished in a very long time.”

Chapter Twelve

A bell tinkled somewhere in the veils of darkness that hung from the ceiling of Single-Minded Books. Ethan closed the door and waited for his eyes to adjust to the gloom. He had known the proprietor, Singleton Cobb, for only three weeks. He had not yet figured out if Cobb was passionately devoted to the cause of saving a couple of bucks on his electricity bill or if he thought the dingy decor added atmosphere. This was an antiquarian bookstore, after all.

The place was so crammed that he could hardly move. If Zoe ever saw the interior, she'd probably advise Singleton to get rid of all the bookcases. They no doubt messed up the energy flow.

The collection was impressive, especially given the relatively small size of the shop. Out-of-print and rare volumes of all shapes and descriptions filled row after row of shelves that extended from floor to ceiling. The pleasant, slightly musty smell of old books and aged leather permeated the space.

There was a shifting of the shadows at the back of the shop. Singleton materialized, silhouetted against the blue-green glow cast by his computer screen.

If you saw him on the street and did not know what he did for a living, Ethan thought, you would never guess that the guy was an antiquarian book dealer. On the surface, there was nothing of the academic or the scholar about him.

Singleton was built like a rock. Not just any rock, a large chunk of granite. He was the size of a small mountain. He appeared to be in his fifties. Like stone that has been exposed to the elements for a few eons, he had weathered some but he sure as hell had not softened.

His skull was completely shaved. It gleamed, as if it had been oiled. The tendrils of elaborate tattoos peeked out from beneath the rolled-up sleeves of a faded denim shirt. He had the face of a really bad-news pro wrestler.

Singleton peered at him through the lenses of a pair of round, gold-rimmed spectacles. "Got my message, I see."

"It was waiting for me when I arrived at the office this morning."

Singleton snorted. "Heard you come in half an hour ago. Running a little late today, aren't you?"

"Didn't know you were paying such close attention to my schedule."

"Hard to avoid it, seeing as how we're the only two tenants in the building at the moment and your office is right overhead. I hear everyone who goes up or down those stairs."

"I was a little busy yesterday. Out late with a client last night."

Singleton leaned his elbows on the counter and looked interested. "About you being busy yesterday."

"Yeah?"

"I read about Mason and the blood-stained bed and the shootout in the papers. Pretty exciting stuff. By any chance was that you ducking bullets?"

"How did you guess?"

"Not a lot to do around here," Singleton said. "So I sit around and speculate. I remembered your little lady client going up and down the stairs and the paper mentioned an unnamed woman at the scene.

Also, I recall you going out early yesterday morning and not coming back all day. And then you've got the fact that Radnor is more into corporate security and such. Can't see any of his people turning up a blood-stained bed. I sort of put two and two together."

"You should have been a detective."

"Don't think so. Guy could get himself killed with the kind of detecting work you did yesterday."

"It was the client's fault." Ethan crossed to the glass counter. "Personally, I prefer to avoid that kind of exercise whenever possible."

"Blame it on the client, huh?"

"Sure."

Singleton looked knowing. "So you were out late explaining your point of view on the subject of reckless endangerment to your client?"

"Something along those lines." Ethan shrugged. "The good news is that my client's name didn't appear in print. She'll be happy about that."

"I don't blame her. Probably not good for her business to have it going around that she was involved in a situation that got her client's newly decorated house shot up."

"Probably not."

"On the other hand, it would have been a nice bit of advertising for your business if your name had made it into the article."

"Win some, lose some." Ethan braced both hands on the wooden edge of the counter. "Where's my journal?"

"Got it right here." Singleton turned partway around and plucked a large envelope off the desk behind him. He handed the package to Ethan. "Located it through an online dealer I know who specializes in private journals and diaries of the twentieth century. I paid extra and had it shipped overnight."

"I'm impressed." Ethan opened the envelope and removed the slender, leather-bound volume. "I did a search online myself before I came to you. Found some leads to the newspaper coverage of the murder but no trace of the journal."

"The Internet has done a lot for the antiquarian trade," Singleton said. "But like any other business, you've still got to have connections to find the good stuff."

Ethan examined the book. The leather was cracked but the pages were in excellent condition. He examined the first words in the journal. They had been written down in a strong, flowing script.

The Journal of Abner Bennett Foote

Anticipation whispered through him. He turned to an entry at random and read the first few lines.

> ". . . Nightwinds is finished at last. My beloved Camelia now has a setting that befits her extraordinary beauty . . ."

Ethan closed the journal. "I'm in luck. Foote's handwriting is clear and legible."

Singleton's brow wrinkled. "Mind if I ask why you wanted his journal? Is it because you're living in that old house he built?"

"Indirectly." Ethan slipped the book into the envelope. "It's the death of Camelia Foote that really interests me."

"Why's that?"

"I research old murder cases." Ethan pulled his wallet out of his pocket. "It's a hobby."

"Huh. Didn't know she was murdered. The story is that she got real drunk at a big party out at Nightwinds years ago and died in a fall in the canyon."

"That was the official verdict. But the old newspaper accounts imply that there were plenty of rumors of murder at the time. A lot of people, including the local chief of police, apparently suspected that her husband killed her in a jealous rage."

"Unusual hobby," Singleton said. "But when you get right down to it, I guess it's not that much different from playing chess online."

"You do that?" Ethan handed over his credit card.

"Among other things." Singleton swiped the credit card through a machine. "Once upon a time, I used to work for a think tank. Specialized in cryptography. I'm out of the business now, but the chess games are a way of keeping my hand in, so to speak."

"Cryptography? As in computer security and encryption?"

"Yeah."

"You must be good."

"Used to be. I pretty much burned out."

"But you can still find your way around on the Net?"

"Sure."

Ethan took the credit slip and signed it. He picked up the book and paused.

"You ever do any freelance consulting?" he asked.

"Not for a long time. What did you have in mind?"

"I sometimes need the kind of deep background information that it takes a real expert to pull off the Net. I can get the standard info from the usual sources, but I'm not what you'd call a computer whiz. There are times when I need someone who can dig deeper and faster. I can't afford the guy I used to use in L.A. You interested?"

Singleton pondered that. "You can't afford the other guy? That doesn't sound so good."

"Truax Investigations is a small business. Still in the start-up phase. You know how it is."

"Hell, why not?" Singleton grinned. "Might make for a break now and again. The book trade is interesting and I've got my chess games, but I don't mind telling you that it gets a little dull around here from time to time. My social life has been sort of nonexistent since my wife left."

"I know the feeling. Why'd she split?"

"She said I did not show a sufficient interest in upward mobility. Something to do with my refusing to join the Desert View golf club, I think."

Ethan nodded. "My third wife said something along those lines, too."

"Yeah? What did the other two say?"

"First one said she'd married me by mistake. The second one said I was not good at communicating. I think maybe she was trying to be polite."

"What'd she really mean?"

"That I was boring."

The phone rang just before noon. Zoe grabbed it.

"Enhanced Interiors."

"I see you finally made it into work," Ethan said.

The tiny knot of tension, which had settled in the pit of her stomach and which she had been determined to ignore, eased.

"You should have awakened me before you left," she said crisply.

"Figured you needed your sleep. The nightmare you had seemed to take a lot out of you."

"Mmm."

"How do you feel?" he asked.

"Fine, thanks." Time to change the topic. "By the way, I saw the newspaper. Nelson Radnor is a sneaky bastard, isn't he? Imagine him letting that reporter think his company was involved in solving the murder of Jennifer Mason. Talk about nerve."

"I'd rather talk about your bill."

She glared at the photo of Nightwinds on the wall. "You're supposed to be a little more diplomatic and suave when you bring up the subject of money. You sound a trifle mercenary."

"Only a trifle? I'll have to work on that. Look, you operate a small business. You know how important it is to keep up with accounts receivable. You want to come to my office this afternoon after you close for the day? We can go over the details together."

Be still my beating heart. "Why don't you just put the bill in the mail?"

"It's sort of complicated, what with our little agreement to take it out in trade." Ethan paused a beat. "You do remember that part, don't you?"

"I remember."

"Good. I've been thinking it over and I've decided which room I want you to redecorate."

"How big is it?" she asked cautiously.

"Big enough. It's my bedroom. I'll take you out there so you can have a look at it."

His bedroom. Oh, gee.

"I don't know if I've got time this evening," she said uneasily.

"Afterward I'm going to take my nephews and their mother for pizza. You're welcome to come along."

So very casual, she thought. Just a throwaway invitation. But it left her temporarily speechless. Going out for pizza with the family. It sounded so *normal,* the sort of thing that real people, living real lives did.

"I'd like that," she finally said. "I'd like that very much."

At five o'clock that afternoon, she sat in the jaws of Ethan's outsized client chair, the copy of her bill from Truax Investigations on her lap, and fumed.

"Five hundred dollars in miscellaneous expenses?" She raised the neatly itemized bill and waved it in the air. "That's ridiculous."

Ethan lounged back in his chair, elbows resting on the arms, fingers together. His feet, shod in running shoes, were stacked on the corner of his desk. He made a what-can-you-do sound with his tongue.

"Cost of bribes, like everything else, has gone up," he said.

"You should have cleared the amounts with me before you handed five hundred dollars over to that guard and the man at the storage facility."

"Wasn't time to call you. In both instances, I had to make executive decisions on the spot."

"Executive decisions, my big toe. I'll bet you would have been a lot more economical about it if it was your own money you were throwing around."

He tapped his fingertips together and looked authoritative. "The information and access I obtained with the bribes were vital to the successful closure of the case."

"Something tells me you could have obtained that information for a lot less money." She spotted another item on the bill and was immediately consumed with fresh outrage. "What's this about travel expenses? You told me you would cover your own travel expenses."

"Only within the local area. I had to drive outside the city limits of Whispering Springs to investigate the storage locker facility."

"Meals?" She stabbed a finger at another item on the bill. "You're billing me for the sandwich and coffee you had while you were out of town?"

"A man's got to keep his strength up."

Before she could move on to the next ridiculous charge, she heard the sound of footsteps pounding up the stairs. The voices of two young males echoed in the outer office.

"Uncle Ethan, is she still here? You didn't take her to your house yet, did you?"

"Mom made us stop at the stupid mall. That's why we're late."

The door of Ethan's office slammed open. Two boys garbed in jeans, tee shirts, and running shoes charged into the room. Zoe recognized them as the youngsters she had nearly collided with on the stairs on the occasion of her first visit to Truax Investigations.

They halted and stared at her with ill-concealed fascination.

"Oh, wow," the older one said. "She's still here."

Ethan surveyed the two invaders. "Allow me to introduce my nephews. Jeff and Theo, meet Ms. Luce."

"Hi," Theo said.

"Hello, Ms. Luce," Jeff said.

"Nice to meet you," Zoe said politely. She wondered what she had done to warrant so much interest on the part of two small boys.

Jeff turned to Ethan. "Can we go to your place now?"

"Yep." Ethan glanced at his watch. "Where's your mom?"

"I'm right here," said a warm voice from the doorway.

Zoe turned her head and saw an attractive woman with short, curly, light brown hair. She was dressed in a pale yellow blouse and chocolate brown trousers.

"I'm Bonnie Truax." Bonnie smiled. "The mother of these two ghouls. You must be Zoe."

"Yes." *I'm going to like her,* Zoe thought. "How do you do?"

She was about to ask Bonnie why she

had referred to her sons as ghouls, but before she could frame the question, Ethan got to his feet.

"Come on, folks, let's get going," he said. "We'll run over to my place, show Zoe the room she's going to redecorate, and then we'll do the pizza thing."

"Can I ride with you, Uncle Ethan?" Jeff asked.

"Me, too," Theo said. "I want to be sure to see what happens when Ms. Luce checks out the inside of your house."

Ethan looked at Zoe and Bonnie. "Why don't we all go in my car and from there to pizza?"

"Cool." Jeff dashed through the door.

"See you downstairs." Theo raced after his brother.

"Wait for us in the hall," Bonnie called after them.

"Okay," Jeff yelled back over his shoulder.

Both boys pelted down the stairs and disappeared.

Zoe looked at Ethan. "Is there something I need to know about your house?"

"Needs some work." Ethan stood aside to allow Zoe and Bonnie to go through the door.

"Work is right." Bonnie made a face. "Didn't Ethan tell you? He bought Nightwinds, that pink blob just outside of town."

Zoe stopped at the top of the stairs, startled. "That big Spanish Colonial out on the cliffs? Good grief, it's huge. And it was built back in the late 1940s wasn't it? I'm sure it's got a lot of atmosphere, but I'll bet it is one heck of a money pit."

"Got a deal on it from my uncle," Ethan said.

"Victor knew he'd never be able to sell it to anyone else," Bonnie said. "So he practically gave it to Ethan."

"What can I say?" Ethan shrugged. "Uncle Vic saw me coming."

Zoe started down the stairs, following Bonnie.

"Be careful of really good deals when it comes to very old houses," Zoe said. "The upkeep is usually enormous. But I must admit I'll be interested to view the inside. Why are Jeff and Theo so eager to see my reaction to the place?"

Bonnie glanced back over her shoulder. "Ethan more or less promised them that you would collapse and start twitching at the sight of the interior of Nightwinds."

Zoe shot Ethan a disgusted glare. "Thanks a lot."

"He implied that your delicate designer sensibilities would not be able to withstand the shock," Bonnie added.

"Really?" Zoe smiled coolly at Ethan. "Obviously you know nothing about the fortitude required of a successful interior designer."

"I didn't a few days ago when I first made that prediction," Ethan agreed. "But I've got to admit that yesterday was a real eye-opener for me." He lowered his voice and leaned in close, speaking directly into Zoe's ear. "Learned some interesting things last night, too. Do all you decorator types go in for matching underwear?"

It wasn't his words that made her blush, she thought. It was the low, sexy, cheerfully wicked tone. Mercifully, Bonnie, who had reached the bottom of the stairs and stepped outside, had not overheard.

There was no sign of Jeff and Theo at the foot of the staircase.

"I told them to wait in the lobby." Bonnie came back into the hall, looking worried.

Her sudden anxiety was a bit over the top under the circumstances, Zoe thought. The boys could not have gone far and, while Cobalt Street was a little on the shabby side, it was not dangerous.

"Take it easy, Bonnie," Ethan said quietly. "Jeff and Theo are fine. I have a hunch they're in the bookshop."

Zoe heard the calm, steadying note in his voice. He was accustomed to reassuring her, she thought.

At that moment Jeff's voice drifted out of a partially opened door. *"Who wants to buy old books like this?"*

There was a dark rumble by way of a response.

"Do you have any games on this computer?" Theo asked.

The bear in the bookshop rumbled again.

Bonnie relaxed visibly. "Sounds like they've found someone else to pester." She went toward the door. "I'd better rescue the poor man."

"Got a hunch Singleton can take care of himself," Ethan said.

But Bonnie had already vanished through the opening.

Zoe followed and reached the door just in

time to hear Jeff make introductions in an excited voice.

"Mom, this is Singleton Cobb. He owns all these old books."

"He said Uncle Ethan bought one," Theo offered. "And he's got some neat games on his computer."

Zoe peered through the gloom. Her first thought was that Singleton Cobb looked like an aging biker. But there was a quiet good humor in his eyes that did not fit that image.

"I'm Bonnie Truax and these two belong to me. I'm sorry for the intrusion," Bonnie apologized.

"Not a problem," Singleton said. "Always glad to have a little foot traffic through the place." He looked at Zoe. "You're the client, aren't you? The one whose name didn't get into the papers."

"This is Zoe Luce," Ethan said. "Zoe, Singleton Cobb."

Singleton grinned. "You're the client."

"I'm the client, all right." Zoe made a face. "And I've got the bill for services rendered by Truax Investigations to prove it. Do you have any idea how much it costs to bribe people these days?"

"Clients." Ethan shook his head. "They always complain when it comes time to settle the account." He signaled to Jeff and Theo. "Let's go, boys. We've got things to do, and I'm getting hungry."

"We gotta leave now," Jeff said to Singleton. "But we can come back some other time."

"Sounds good to me," Singleton said easily.

"Would you show me some of your computer games next time?" Theo asked. "I could bring you some of Mom's cookies."

Singleton glanced at Bonnie. "It's a deal."

Outside on the street, they all piled into Ethan's SUV. There was still enough late afternoon light left for Zoe to see that Bonnie's cheeks were slightly flushed.

Jeff and Theo chattered about their new acquaintance and speculated on whether or not he owned a motorcycle. Bonnie was quiet for a long time.

"An interesting man," she said eventually. "Not quite what you'd expect."

Chapter Thirteen

Nightwinds stood silhouetted in all its flamboyant pink glory against a scorching sunset. Ethan had a few second thoughts as he halted the SUV in the drive. Maybe this wasn't going to prove to be one of his more brilliant schemes, after all.

The original concept had been simple and straightforward. Encouraging Zoe to pay her bill by redecorating a room in his house had struck him as a particularly crafty maneuver that would allow him to continue some kind of relationship. But what if she concluded that he had incredibly bad taste?

"Let us go inside first," Jeff said with an improbably innocent air. "We can turn on the lights for you."

"Yeah," Theo said. "We know where the light switches are."

"Go for it." Ethan tossed the keys to Theo.

Zoe watched the boys race forward to open the grand door.

"I'm being set up, aren't I?" she said.

"They're going to be awfully disappointed if you don't fall down and twitch," Bonnie said.

"I suppose I could twitch a little bit," Zoe said.

Jeff and Theo got the front door open. Both boys disappeared into the foyer. Lights came on inside.

Ethan watched Zoe approach the threshold. It seemed to him that she hesitated for a split second as though bracing herself. Maybe she had decided to put on an act for Jeff and Theo. Or maybe he was imagining things.

Then he remembered how she had paused briefly before walking into his office the first time. Maybe it was just the way she was about entering a room. Probably a decorator thing.

She disappeared into the glowing pink interior.

He walked into the hall behind her and saw her turn in a slow circle, surveying every ornate, gilded, *pink* detail.

"This is amazing." She sounded awed.

Bonnie laughed. "Pretty incredible, isn't it?"

"Incredible is right." Zoe moved slowly

toward the living room. "I can just imagine an elegant late-1940s party here. All those fabulous clothes and the old cars parked in the drive. What a scene it must have been."

Jeff watched her closely. "Are you going to collapse, Ms. Luce?"

"I don't think so," Zoe said apologetically.

Theo looked disappointed. "You're sure?"

"Pretty sure," she said.

Ethan chuckled. "So much for this evening's entertainment."

"Maybe she'll start to twitch when she sees some of the other rooms," Theo said, still hopeful.

Bonnie looked at Zoe. "Ignore them."

"Come on into the living room," Jeff said eagerly. "There's a picture of Mrs. Foote over the fireplace."

Obediently they trooped into the living room. Bonnie fell into step beside Zoe.

"The story is that the tycoon who built this place, Abner Bennett Foote, was absolutely devoted to Camelia. She was about thirty-five years younger than he was. He showered her with jewelry and furs. After her death he never remarried."

They all came to a halt in front of the portrait. Zoe studied the glamorous woman in the beaded, pink satin evening gown for a long time.

"She was very beautiful," she finally said.

"Yes, she was," Bonnie agreed.

Personally, Ethan thought Camelia looked like trouble. He had a hunch she was the kind of woman who had used her beauty to manipulate others, especially men. But what did he know? A guy who had been married and divorced as often as he had was probably not a good judge.

"Of course," Zoe said, "it doesn't hurt that she's literally dripping in diamonds."

"True," Bonnie agreed. "Good jewelry always adds a certain something."

"Who cares about her jewels," Theo said. "Let's go see the movie theater."

"Yeah, that's the best place in the whole house," Jeff said. "It's got a big-screen TV and a popcorn machine."

The boys dashed off down an arcaded hall. Zoe and Bonnie dutifully followed. Ethan hung back, trying to gauge Zoe's reaction.

So far, so good, he thought. At least she did not seem disdainful. If anything, she looked intrigued. Perhaps she viewed his new home as a decorating challenge.

When they reached the theater, Jeff and Theo tugged on the heavy, curving brass handles of the twin doors.

Zoe examined the elaborate entrance with its orchid-pink panels and gilt trim. "Breathtaking. I don't even want to think about what it would cost to reproduce that workmanship today."

"I told Ethan he couldn't possibly afford to restore this place," Bonnie said. "Just keeping it from further deterioration will be difficult enough."

"Look, there's a curtain to keep out the light if the door is opened while the movie is playing." Jeff hurried into the theater. "And it connects to this curtain over here. If you go through that opening, you're inside the little snack bar."

"Foote probably had it installed to serve the guests drinks and hors d'oeuvres while they watched the film," Ethan explained. He halted beside Zoe, who had made no move to enter the interior of the theater. "There's a carved pink marble counter. The bartender could come and go through his section of the curtain without letting any light into the seating area."

"I see," Zoe said. "Fascinating."

Her enthusiasm had definitely dimmed, Ethan noticed. Her smile was polite but no longer warm. There was a marked tension in her shoulders. She was no longer having fun.

Jeff held aside one of the velvet curtains to reveal the rows of gilded seats.

"There's another curtain over the old movie screen," he explained to Zoe. "Uncle Victor put the big TV in front of it, see?"

"Yes, I see it." She looked into the theater, but she did not enter it. "Pretty cool."

" 'Specially when we make popcorn," Theo told her.

"I'm impressed," Zoe said.

Ethan checked his watch. "Let's go take a look at the bedroom you're going to redo for me, Zoe."

Jeff barreled back out of the theater. "This way, Ms. Luce."

Zoe turned away from the theater doorway with what looked suspiciously like relief.

Not exactly twitching, Ethan concluded, *but almost.*

At the door of his pink-and-gilt bedroom, Zoe halted a second time. But then she walked casually into the space and surveyed it with unmistakable amusement the huge gilded-swan bed, the lush rose-pink walls, and the orchid-print carpeting.

When she turned, Ethan was relieved to see the genuine laughter in her eyes.

"Oh, my," she chuckled. "It takes a very secure man to sleep in a room like this."

Ethan lounged in the doorway. "It's got the best view of the canyon."

"Between you and me, Zoe, I think it looks like the boudoir of a very high-priced courtesan," Bonnie remarked.

"What's a courtesan, Mom?" Jeff asked.

"Time for pizza," Ethan announced.

Could have been worse, Zoe thought. She had been dreading the bedroom, but it was the theater that had taken her by surprise. Fortunately, whatever had happened in that space had occurred a long time ago. The violence and passion locked into the walls was subdued and muted now. She could have handled it if necessary, but she was glad that it was not the room Ethan wanted her to redesign.

The dinner of pizza and salad was no doubt a routine outing for Jeff, Theo, Ethan, and Bonnie, but it had been a special treat for her. She had actually felt normal for a time, as if she was living a real life again.

When the meal was finished, they all walked outside into the balmy night. Fountain Square was festively lit. People strolled among the colorful fountains, coming and going from the other restaurants.

Jeff and Theo wanted to check out a video arcade. Ethan good-naturedly agreed.

Bonnie and Zoe sat on a bench and watched the three males weave a path among the splashing fountains.

Jeff and Theo bounced around Ethan, circling and darting here and there but always returning to his side. They reminded Zoe of a couple of small, eager wolf pups hanging out with the indulgent leader of the pack.

"This may not be any of my business," Bonnie said after a while, "but I have to tell you that I'm delighted that Ethan asked you to join us tonight."

"Are you kidding? I can't remember when I've had such a good time," Zoe said with absolute honesty. "This evening was a real break for me."

Bonnie laughed. "I'll take that with a grain of salt. I can't imagine that eating pizza in a noisy restaurant with a couple of chatty little boys qualifies as a good time for anyone with any serious alternatives."

"Jeff and Theo are terrific."

"Thanks. Sorry about the accident with the pizza sauce. Are you sure you won't let me pay the dry cleaning bill?"

"Don't be ridiculous. That pizza was delicious. Well worth the cost of sending the skirt to the dry cleaners."

Zoe watched the two boys drag Ethan into the video arcade. A wistful feeling slipped through her. In her other life she had known what it was to be part of a family, at least until her freshman year in college when she had lost her parents in a car crash.

After the tragedy, the knowledge that she was utterly alone in the world had been devastating. She had fought the twin demons of depression and anxiety and sought refuge in her studies.

She had emerged from college with a master's degree in fine arts and something else, a kind of sixth sense that she would just as soon have done without.

She had always known that she frequently felt strong emotions in certain houses and rooms. But for the most part, the sensations were very weak and not particularly disturbing. She had accepted them as normal, and perhaps at a low level they were. After all, a lot of people talked about experiencing a sense of déjà vu or some other unsettling feeling when they first entered a certain house or room.

But during those lonely years in college when she had gone inside herself for long periods of time, her reactions to various interiors grew noticeably more acute. Her single trip to Europe, a gift to herself to celebrate her first full year of gainful employment at a museum, had turned into a nightmare. After touring three ancient castles with blood-drenched histories in two days, she had felt so grim and chilled that she thought she had come down with an exotic disease. The following morning she had booked a flight home, borrowing heavily on her credit card to pay the full fare in coach.

She had finally been forced to conclude that, whatever it was she experienced when she walked into a room where violence or some other dark, intense emotion had soaked into the walls, the sensation could no longer be classified as normal.

By the time she met Preston, she had become very adept at concealing her special sense. She had also taught herself a few simple precautions. She always paused before entering a room to make certain she would not be overwhelmed with unwelcome sensations. And, until she met Arcadia, she never, ever told anyone the full truth about her sensitivity, not even Preston.

Preston Cleland had been a kind, caring man who would have tried hard to understand and accept her for what she was: a freak. But his nature had been gentle and scholarly, and she had known, deep down, that it would not have been right to burden him with the knowledge that he had married a woman who sensed things in the walls. She realized that while he would have continued to love her with all his heart, he never would have been able to look at her in the same way again. She had not been able to deal with the thought of seeing pity and concern and anxiety in his eyes.

Preston had had enough problems dealing with his ruthless cousin and the other members of his greedy, avaricious family.

"You know," Bonnie said, lowering her voice to a confidential tone, "this is the first time Ethan has invited a woman out for an evening with the boys and me since his last wife left him."

"Mmm." Zoe kept her response as non-committal as humanly possible.

Bonnie frowned. "Ethan did tell you that he was divorced, didn't he?"

Zoe cleared her throat. "I believe he mentioned that he'd been married and divorced several times."

"Several is a gross overstatement."

"I think he specified that there had been three marriages and three divorces," Zoe said carefully.

"*Three* doesn't qualify as several."

Zoe nodded politely and said nothing.

Bonnie threw up her hands. "Okay, okay, I know what you're thinking. In your shoes, I would come to the same conclusion. On the surface of it, three trips to the altar and the divorce courts does seem to indicate a certain inability to commit. But Ethan is different."

"Bonnie, it's all right. Please don't feel you have to defend him. Ethan and I don't have what you'd call a serious relationship. We hardly know each other. I'm just another client."

"Whatever else you are," Bonnie said, "you are not just another client. If you were, he would not have invited you to have pizza with us tonight. Ethan is very big on keeping his professional life separate from his private life."

"I see." Zoe couldn't think of anything else to say.

"The thing is, Ethan has simply been very unlucky in love." Bonnie held up three fingers. "He married Stacy when he was twenty-two. She was only nineteen. They were both too young. Stacy was coming out of a very chaotic, very dysfunctional home life. She was searching for something solid, and Ethan fell into the trap of playing the knight in shining armor."

"What happened?"

"After about a year, Stacy announced that she was leaving Ethan to follow a, uh, religious vocation."

"Good grief, she became a nun?"

"Not exactly," Bonnie said dryly. "She joined a small, very strict, very fringe religious group."

"A cult."

Bonnie nodded. "I'm afraid so. They got a divorce and got on with their lives. Then, just after Ethan opened his own security agency, he met Devon. It was another serious mistake."

"Why?"

"Devon fell for Ethan because she had a thing for men who have macho jobs. When she found out that most of his work was done behind a desk, on the phone, or with a computer, she left him to marry a professional race car driver."

"Bonnie, I really don't—"

"Kelly, wife number three, came along after he had established his business and was making a lot of money. They did fine as long as he was financially successful. But she couldn't handle the bankruptcy."

"I didn't know about the bankruptcy," Zoe said.

"It was the direct result of a high-profile murder investigation." Bonnie clasped her hands together in her lap and kept her attention on the waters of a nearby fountain. "Certain powerful people in L.A. did not like what happened when he identified the killer and exposed the financial maneuvers that had led to the murder. When it was all over, they made certain that Ethan paid a price for making them take some heavy losses."

"Who got killed?"

"My husband, Drew," Bonnie whispered.

It clicked. Zoe went still. "His brother?"

Bonnie nodded. "Yes."

"So, that's why the children's father isn't here. I wondered. Oh, Bonnie, I am so very sorry."

"Drew was murdered three years ago come November. It took Ethan months to find the killer and the man who had hired him. Just before the trial started, the contract killer, who was out on bail, was shot dead by person or persons unknown."

"The logical assumption being that his employer decided to get rid of him so that he could not testify?"

"Yes. But there was no proof. The trial went on for weeks but in the end Simon Wendover, the man responsible for Drew's death, walked out of the courtroom a free man. The only consolation was that his illegal business activities had been so thoroughly exposed by the media that a large portion of his financial empire fell apart."

Zoe tightened her hands around the edge of the bench on either side of her knees.

"Sometimes a financial blow is the only justice you can get."

"Yes. It's not enough."

"No," Zoe agreed softly. "Not nearly enough."

"In any event, the wealthy men who suffered some of the collateral damage due to the destruction of Wendover's empire felt that Ethan should be taught a lesson. Together they had the power to force Truax Security into bankruptcy. It took a little over a year to destroy everything Ethan had built in ten years. He went down with his ship."

"I can see him doing that."

"In the end, between the loss of his business and the divorce settlement, he was left with almost nothing. He was able to get consulting work with some of his old rivals for a while and a couple made offers. But Ethan is the kind of man who likes to be his own boss."

"That doesn't surprise me."

"We talked it over and decided to make the move to Whispering Springs. We both agreed that it would be good to raise the boys outside of L.A."

Zoe glanced at her. "And where Jeff and Theo go, Ethan goes?"

"Ethan has taken Drew's place in their lives," Bonnie said quietly. "I shall be forever grateful to him. Someday Jeff and Theo will be equally grateful. At the moment, however, they just take him for granted. And I think that's for the best. His presence gives them a great sense of security and stability. He also provides some emotional balance. I still get anxious too easily and I'm inclined to be overprotective. Left to my own devices, I'm sure I would have turned them into little neurotics by now."

"I don't blame you for the overprotective instincts. If I were in your shoes, I'd be the same way."

"What I'm trying to tell you about Ethan is that he is fully capable of making a commitment," Bonnie said. "In fact, I don't think he knows any other way to be. His problem is that no woman has ever really made a commitment to him."

"Mmm." Zoe doubted that was the full story. Three divorces took a little more explaining. But it was not her place to argue the point. What did she know? She had only met Ethan a few days ago. But she had to admit that Bonnie's determined loyalty to him was touching.

"It was knowing that we could all lean on Ethan that helped us get through the worst of the nightmare," Bonnie concluded.

"I'm glad he was there for you," Zoe said. "But what about Wendover? It is so unjust, so *wrong* that the bastard who murdered your husband is walking around free."

Bonnie looked at her with clear, calm eyes. "But Wendover is not walking around free. I forgot to tell you the rest of it. Simon Wendover drowned a few weeks after the trial ended. He fell from his yacht, which was anchored off Catalina. He was alone at the time. Apparently he had been drinking heavily."

A chill of understanding flashed through Zoe. She studied Ethan, who was walking back toward them with his nephews in tow. She had only known him a few days, she thought, but she knew enough about him to realize that if he had set out to find his brother's killer, he would not have let anything, including the vagaries of a less-than-perfect judicial system, stand in his way.

Whatever had happened to Simon Wendover that night on his yacht had probably not been an accident.

She envied Bonnie and Ethan and the

boys, she thought. At least there had been some justice for them. She had not been so fortunate. Preston's murder had gone unavenged. She had plans to balance the scales somewhat, but even if they worked, the result would only be a weak, pale whisper of vengeance.

She wrapped her arms around herself. "I'm glad Wendover drowned," she said fiercely.

"Nobody wept any tears for him, that's for certain."

"What a dreadful time you must have had."

"It was awful." Bonnie rose to her feet. "But looking back, I think the psychic was the worst part."

An unpleasant sense of impending disaster gripped Zoe. She got carefully to her feet. *I don't want to hear this,* she thought. But she had no option. "What psychic?"

"It was my own fault." Bonnie shook her head ruefully. "I should have known better. You see, for a long time after Drew disappeared, I refused to believe that he was dead."

"I understand."

"A so-called psychic got in touch with me

and said she could help me find him. She fed me a lot of nonsense about being able to see him in a small room somewhere, bound hand and foot. She told me she thought he was alive and being held captive. And I was so desperate that I willingly bought into her scam. It cost me a great deal of money, and in the end the false hope only made it harder to deal with the truth."

Ethan, Jeff, and Theo were almost upon them.

"I don't blame you," Zoe said. "I would have wanted to cling to hope, too."

"If you ask me," Bonnie said wryly, "the most remarkable aspect of the whole thing wasn't that Wendover got a dose of really bad karma. It was that the psychic survived Ethan's wrath."

"Oh."

"Ethan detests people who prey on others. After that incident, he absolutely despises people who claim to be psychics. As far as he's concerned, they are all frauds and charlatans. I swear, when he found out how that woman had strung me along, I thought he would strangle her."

Half an hour later Zoe said good night to everyone from the doorway of her apartment.

She looked at Jeff and Theo. "Thanks for a great evening, guys."

"You can come with us again sometime, if you want," Jeff said magnanimously.

"Thank you," Zoe said. "That would be nice. Next time I promise to have some ice cream on hand."

The discovery that she did not keep a supply of ice cream in the small freezer compartment of her refrigerator had produced baffled astonishment. Jeff and Theo had taken the bad news manfully, but she made a mental note not to be caught off guard next time. She was surprised to realize just how much she hoped that there would be a next time.

"I like chocolate chip," Theo said helpfully.

"I'll keep that in mind," she promised.

"I enjoyed talking to you." Bonnie gave her a warm smile.

The temptation to tell Bonnie how much they had in common because of the manner in which they had lost their husbands had been almost overwhelming. But sharing confidences was as risky in this new life as intimate romantic entanglements.

"It was a wonderful evening," Zoe said.

"We really will have to do this again." Bonnie turned to Jeff and Theo and made shooing motions with her hands. "Come on, you two, let Uncle Ethan say good night to Zoe in peace."

Jeff and Theo reluctantly left the doorway and went down the hall. Bonnie followed in their wake.

Theo's voice drifted back along the corridor.

"Is Uncle Ethan gonna kiss Zoe?" he asked.

"That's none of your business," Bonnie told him. "Move, gentlemen."

Ethan waited until the little group had started down the stairs. Then he smiled slowly.

"Yeah," he said, "Uncle Ethan is gonna kiss Zoe."

He put his hands on her shoulders and drew her deliberately toward him. Zoe felt a little fizzy sensation in the pit of her stomach.

Don't get addicted to this, she warned

herself. *It'll never work. Not for long, at any rate.*

But intense curiosity swamped the warning. All day long she had wondered exactly how much of last night's heat had been generated by the aftermath of the adrenaline rush they had both experienced.

He covered her mouth with his own, and she got her answer in no uncertain terms. If it was adrenaline that had sparked last night's passion, the same drug was flowing just as strongly through her veins tonight. How long did it take for that stuff to wear off, anyway?

He sensed her response and deliberately deepened the kiss. His hands moved along her shoulders and then she felt his fingers on the nape of her neck. His thumbs braced her chin, holding her lips right where he wanted them. She was pressed so tightly against him that she could feel the contours of his aroused body.

"Uncle Ethan?" Jeff's voice echoed up the stairs. "Aren't you coming?"

"Hush," Bonnie said. "Let's wait for him outside in the garden."

Ethan slowly raised his head. "I think I just heard my wake-up call. I'd better get moving. Gonna be a little hard to get to sleep tonight, though."

He did the smoldering-eye thing every bit as well as he did the narrow-eyed thing, she thought. She had to swallow a couple of times to find her voice.

"Good night." Reluctant to let him go, she fiddled with the collar of his shirt, pretending to smooth it. "Thanks again for inviting me to join you."

"Any time."

She made herself let go of his shirt. He stepped back into the hall and stood waiting.

Very slowly she closed the door and methodically set all three locks. When she finally fastened the chain, she heard him walk away toward the stairs.

Turning, she slumped back against the door, drew a couple of slow, deep breaths and tried to catalog her reactions objectively. She was definitely feeling a little lightheaded. Giddy, almost. There was a pleasant tingling in certain regions of her anatomy. The fizzy sensation was still strong.

She had to fight the urge to unlock the door, dash out into the hallway, and drag

Ethan back into her apartment. The only thing that stopped her from doing just that was the fact that Bonnie and his nephews were waiting for him.

All in all, it was pretty exciting.

Just like real life.

Chapter Fourteen

"I like her very much." Bonnie spoke quietly, not wanting Jeff and Theo, seated in the backseat discussing Singleton Cobb and his computer, to overhear. "She's different from your usual type."

"You think?" Ethan did not take his attention off the road. "I haven't had a date in so long, I can't remember what my usual type is."

"Don't get me started. If you want to compare dry spells, I'll beat you hands down."

Ethan gave her a quick, searching glance. He did not comment, but the dashboard light revealed the slight curve of his mouth. She knew why her crack about a long dry spell had startled him. It had surprised her, too. She had chided him often enough for not doing more to jump-start his social life, but this was the first time since losing Drew that she had even mentioned her own lack of same.

All of her attention during the past few

years had been focused on maintaining a safe, secure world for Jeff and Theo. The possibility of meeting someone and perhaps even dating again had been the last thing on her mind. She wondered what had put the thought into her head today. Maybe it was seeing Ethan and Zoe together. You could feel the crackle of energy in the air when those two were in close proximity.

"When I said that Zoe was different," she continued deliberately, "I meant that she was not like any of your exes."

"So what? All of my exes were different from each other."

"No, they weren't. Not really. You do tend toward a certain type of woman."

"And that type would be?"

"All three of your ex-wives were pretty and smart and nice enough in their own ways, but they all had two things in common. The first is that they were attracted to you because you look like a pretty cool guy at first glance. Exciting. Mysterious. Maybe even dangerous."

"But underneath I'm boring, right? You don't have to spell it out. Devon did a pretty good job of making that clear."

"No, underneath you are definitely not

boring." She paused. "But you are complicated."

"Complicated." He tasted that word. "That doesn't sound much better than boring."

"Complicated is hard work for a woman. The other thing your exes had in common was that none of them wanted to spend much time dealing with your complexities. They wanted *you* to spend all your time catering to *their* complexities. And let's face it, they were all very high maintenance."

"Huh."

"You are also very controlled. Maybe even a little obsessive about some things. Those factors make you good at your job, but they are not easy to handle in a relationship."

"Obsessive?"

"Forget obsessive," Bonnie said quickly. "That was a poor choice of words. Determined is what I meant. Focused. You keep going until you get your answers. Once you've made a decision, you don't allow anything to deflect you. Look at what the investigation into Drew's murder cost you. Your company and your marriage."

"It was worth it."

She looked at him. "You're always willing to pay the price, aren't you?"

He shrugged. "No such thing as a free lunch in this world."

"That attitude makes you a terrific investigator. But it also makes you a little scary."

"Complicated, obsessive, and now scary. Great. My prospects for renewing my social life are not looking up here."

"What I'm trying to tell you is that those traits have a certain appeal, but they aren't easy for a woman to handle in a serious, long-term committed relationship."

"You think maybe I'm doomed to a lifetime of serial monogamy?"

"What I think," she said very deliberately, "is that you need someone who can deal with the part of you that makes you who you are."

He was silent for a time.

"You think Zoe could handle that part?" he asked after a while.

"I don't know," she said, coming down hard on the side of honesty. "But I'll tell you one thing, I think she's every bit as complicated as you are."

Zoe sat on the edge of the bed, tucked the phone between her shoulder and ear and reached down to tug off her shoes. "The long and the short of it is that because of what happened after his brother's murder, Ethan despises psychics."

"You're not a psychic," Arcadia said. "You're just exquisitely sensitive to the ambience of some interior spaces."

"Let's face it, by any definition, I'm a little weird."

"You don't plan to tell him about your weirdness, though, do you? There's no point. He wouldn't believe you, anyway."

"I know." Zoe flopped back across the duvet and looked up at the ceiling. "He would think I was crazy. Or a fraud. Or both."

"Yes."

"The story Bonnie told me tonight was chilling. The guy who paid to have her husband murdered actually walked free from the courtroom. That's exactly what would have happened even if I had been able to get anyone to believe me about—"

"Don't say it."

"Sorry."

In Arcadia's opinion, events from their

other lives should not be mentioned in any way, shape or form, especially not on the phone. But Zoe found it hard not to talk about them sometimes. Probably because so much remained unresolved, she thought. *No closure,* as her so-called therapist at Xanadu, Dr. McAlistair, would say. And Arcadia was the only one she knew with whom she could safely discuss the past.

"At least in the case of Ethan's brother, there seems to have been some justice of the bad luck variety," Arcadia said.

"Bad luck, my sweet patootie. If Wendover died because he got drunk and fell off his yacht, I'll eat a saguaro."

Arcadia gave one of her throaty chuckles. "So, are you going to see Ethan again?"

Zoe thought about the heat in Ethan's good-night kiss. "I got that impression, yes."

"Good. You need to get out more."

"Getting out is one thing. Playing with fire is something else."

"Just keep it light and have some fun. You deserve some R & R, Zoe. You've had a rough two years."

Zoe levered herself up on her elbows. "Right. Light and fun."

Arcadia made it sound so simple. The truth was, she thought, from where she sat, there was nothing simple about Ethan Truax.

She got to her feet beside the bed and grasped the top of the duvet. “Well, I’d better get some sleep. I’ve got an early morning appointment to look at plumbing fixtures.”

“Sounds exciting.”

“Oh, yeah.”

She tossed the duvet to the foot of the bed.

And froze when she saw the letter-sized sheet of business stationery lying just below the bottom edge of the pillows.

“Oh, my God.”

“Zoe?” Arcadia’s voice sharpened instantly. “Are you okay? What’s wrong?”

Zoe stared at the sheet of stationery, unable to speak. She recognized the logo imprinted discreetly at the top of the paper. It was a small, stylized, black-and-white drawing of an austere brick mansion crouched on the edge of a dark lake.

Beneath the image the name of the establishment was written in elegant type,

CANDLE LAKE MANOR. There was no address or phone number.

Individual letters had been snipped from a newspaper and glued to the page to spell out a message.

> Wish you were here.

Below that line were more words.

> The opportunity to stay out of Room 232 can be yours for a price. You will receive instructions in the near future.

"Zoe?" Arcadia's voice was laced with tension. "Talk to me. Is something wrong?"

"Yes," Zoe said.

Chapter Fifteen

Ethan wrapped both hands around the curved, bronze handles and opened the gilded double doors. He stepped into the postage-stamp-sized lobby and pulled aside the velvet curtains.

For a time, he stood looking into the inky darkness of the unlit theater.

Zoe had not simply paused here on the threshold; she had made an excuse not to enter what had to be one of the more interesting rooms in the house.

He found the bank of switches and snapped a couple upward. The bronze and etched glass fixtures glowed to life. They cast a low, glamorous light that lit the aisle between the two rows of seats.

He studied the gilded, dark pink velvet chairs and wondered what it was about the theater that had caused Zoe to shiver.

Because he was very sure that was what he had seen pass through her when she had looked into this room. A shiver.

After a while, he turned off the lights and

went back along the hall to his study. Abner Bennett Foote's journal was where he had left it on the desk.

He sat down and opened it to the entry he had been reading earlier and picked up where he had left off.

> . . . My beautiful Camelia has invited several of her acquaintances to join us here for a long weekend. The ladies will be beautiful and the gentlemen will no doubt tell excellent stories. There will be a good deal of champagne and gin and everyone will be drunk by midnight. My darling is so young and naïve that she does not see how shallow they all are.
>
> I am not looking forward to the affair but I can hardly object. Camelia's friends are very important to her. When I persuaded my Flower to marry me she made it clear that she would agree only if I would allow her to entertain as often and as lavishly as she wished. This long weekend will no doubt cost me a good deal of money but if it makes my Flower happy, that is all that matters.
>
> There is one bright spot on the horizon

this weekend. I reviewed the guest list this morning and Hill is not on it . . .

"It's a blackmail note," Arcadia said.

"Yes." Zoe wrapped her hands around the mug of hot tea that sat on the table in front of her. But it was no use. Nothing could warm her. She could not seem to stop shaking. These chills were as bad as those she got after she'd had one of her little episodes. "Believe it or not, I did manage to figure that much out."

Conversation and soft jazz swirled around them, masking their tense discussion. The Last Exit was a café that morphed into a nightclub after nine o'clock in the evenings. Zoe and Arcadia occupied a small booth tucked into the shadows at the back. They had a good view of the stage, but neither of them paid any attention to the musicians.

"So much for that special firewall that was supposed to keep me invisible," Zoe commented. "I'd like to get my hands on that broker who sold it to me."

"The Merchant has a sterling business reputation," Arcadia said. "I can't believe he double-crossed you."

Another chill shot through Zoe. She clenched the mug more tightly. "You do realize that if he sold me out, he may have done the same to you?"

"I don't think he sold either of us out. He's been in business for a long time, and there's never been any hint that he might be unreliable."

"Well, *someone* found out where I am, and we have to consider the possibility that whoever it is knows where you are, too."

"Believe me," Arcadia said, "that thought has been on my mind for the past half hour."

Zoe tried to sort through the few facts they had. "If you don't think the Merchant double-crossed us, how do you explain that blackmail note?"

"I don't know what went wrong, but I can think of at least one possibility."

"What?"

Arcadia drew her fingertip around the rim of her tiny espresso cup. "The Merchant operates online. His security is good, but no computer security system is perfect. Maybe he got hacked. Whoever got into his files may have been looking for you in particular or maybe the hacker just grabbed a bunch of names at random and got out."

"I suppose either of those reasons would explain why I got a note and you didn't." Zoe propped her elbows on the table. "Which means that the blackmailer may be the hacker."

"Not necessarily. It's possible the hacker is just another online business person who sold your file to someone who knew enough about you to make use of the information."

Zoe rubbed her temples. "It could be anyone."

"No, not *anyone,*" Arcadia said slowly. "I think we can exclude your in-laws. They have no interest in blackmailing you. If they knew where you were, they would be moving heaven and earth to put you back in Xanadu."

"True." Zoe forced herself to think. "And the same goes for Dr. Harper. If he had discovered my whereabouts, he would have sent his minions to pick me up."

"As quietly as possible," Arcadia agreed. "The last thing he'd want is for Forrest Cleland to discover that you've been running around loose for the past few months."

"Okay, so the blackmailer is probably not Harper or any of my dear relatives."

"No, but whoever sent that note obviously knows a lot about your history with Xanadu."

"The reference to Room 232."

"Yes."

"You're right." Zoe tried to blot out the scenes from her recurring nightmare and stay focused on the logic. "The room number is a very specific detail. Only someone directly connected to Xanadu would know it."

"I think that's a fairly safe assumption."

"One of the orderlies? Ron or Ernie?"

"Maybe," Arcadia said slowly. "Although I would have bet that neither of them is bright enough or sufficiently well connected to have the resources it would take to find you."

"Good point. They're both sociopaths but they are definitely not the sharpest knives in the drawer."

"Doubt if they could afford to buy that kind of information, even if someone offered it for sale to them. Whoever supplied your file to the blackmailer probably charged big bucks for it."

Zoe ran through a few more possibilities. "What about Fenella Leeds?"

"Harper's administrative assistant?" Arcadia gave that some consideration and nodded. "Maybe. Leeds is about as cold as they come and she's smart. I'm sure she knows everything Harper knows. She was sleeping with him for a while, until she got bored and found another victim, remember?"

"Only too well. All right, we'll put her on the list. And don't forget the security chief, Leon Grady."

"I don't know," Arcadia said. "He's not overly smart and besides, I always had the impression that he was Harper's creature. He makes a nice living doing what he's told there at the Manor. Remember the Porsche? And that flashy ring?"

"Maybe he got tired of covering up for his boss," Zoe suggested.

"Maybe."

"We can't overlook Dr. McAlistair, either. Harper was content to lock me away and keep me doped up, but McAlistair was always scheduling therapy sessions. She kept pushing me to tell her exactly what I experienced when I walked into certain rooms. Always trying to conduct one of her little surprise tests."

"She did seem to be particularly interested in your case," Arcadia allowed.

"She had to know about Harper's side business."

"I agree, but, like Harper, I would think her main goal would be to get you back into Xanadu, not to blackmail you."

"You're right." Zoe dropped her head in her hands. "This is hopeless. We'll never be able to identify the blackmailer this way. The most we can do is speculate."

"I think," Arcadia said, "that what we need here is some professional expertise."

Zoe raised her head swiftly, stunned. "Go to the cops? You know that's not possible. The minute they discover that I'm an escapee from a loony bin, they'll fall all over themselves to ship me back there."

"I wasn't talking about going to the police," Arcadia said.

Understanding struck.

Zoe sat back very slowly against the cushions of the booth. "No."

"Got a better idea?"

"No," she said again. "But this is definitely not a good idea either."

"Why not? This is the kind of thing he's

trained to do. He guarantees confidentiality to his clients, and I think you can trust him."

Zoe felt ill. "I don't want him to know about . . . about Xanadu and me and the damned walls."

"You don't have to tell him all the details. He doesn't need to know about your issues with certain rooms."

"But he'll have to be told about Xanadu."

"Yes. I don't see any way around that. You've only got two options as far as I can tell. You either go home, pack, and make a run for it, or you call Ethan Truax."

"When you put it like that . . ."

Chapter Sixteen

Friday . . .

He is here. Hill had the gall to come even though his name was not on the guest list. I confronted Camelia and demanded that she tell him he must leave. But she became very angry and refused to send him away. She says that would be ungracious and that there is plenty of room for one more.

Midnight . . .

I saw them together this evening when the cocktails were served before dinner. I knew from the way he was looking at her that he intended to try to seduce her. Shortly after ten o'clock, they went out into the gardens together. I watched them from my study window. The bastard took my Camelia into his arms and kissed her. She made no effort to resist.

I know now that they must have plotted all along to be together this weekend.

I have been a fool . . .

The phone buzzed, jarring Ethan out of the journal entry. He glanced at his watch and was surprised to see that it was nearly midnight. He had intended to be in bed by now.

He reached for the phone, aware of a small tightening in his gut. There were very few people who might call him at this hour. Bonnie was at the top of the list.

"Truax," he said.

"Ethan? It's me, Zoe."

A whisper of pleasure replaced the unease. He leaned back in his chair. "What's up? Can't sleep?"

"I need to hire you again."

He walked into the Last Exit twenty minutes later and stood in the shadows near the entrance until he spotted Zoe and Arcadia in a remote booth. He watched them for a while. Every few seconds Zoe turned her head, glancing anxiously toward the door, but he could tell that she was unable to see him.

He started toward the booth, deliberately weaving his way through the maze of tables in a convoluted path that kept him out of what little light there was. Neither Zoe nor

Arcadia noticed him until he was almost upon them.

Zoe started visibly when she realized he was looming over the table. Relief came and went in her face. It was replaced by wariness.

"Ethan." She spoke very softly. He got the feeling she was exerting immense control. "I didn't see you."

Arcadia frowned slightly but gave no other indication of surprise. He wondered what it would take to rattle her. A lot, he thought.

"Thanks for coming," Zoe said in the same tone of voice she might have used to express her appreciation for his having turned up at a funeral.

"Not like I had anything better to do."

She flushed.

He sat down next to her, purposefully crowding her a little to see what she would do. She responded by edging back into the corner of the booth. Putting some distance between them. Not a good sign.

"You made excellent time," Arcadia said.

"I like to encourage repeat business, but I've got to admit I wasn't expecting to get rehired quite so fast." He looked at Zoe.

"What's going on? Got another suspicious client?"

"No," Zoe said. "This is a personal problem."

He angled himself loosely in the booth and rested one arm on the back of the bench. "Tell me about it."

She tightened the fingers of one hand into a fist on her lap. "I'm being blackmailed."

Well, shit. He'd better start thinking like a professional here.

"Give it to me from the beginning," he said.

She glanced at Arcadia, as if looking for support. She got a small nod from her companion.

"Two years ago my husband was murdered. Shot dead on the back porch of our vacation cabin."

"I'm listening."

"Preston drove up to the cabin a day before our anniversary. Alone. He didn't tell me. He wanted to prepare a surprise."

"What kind of surprise?"

"Flowers." Zoe smiled wistfully. "Lots and lots of flowers. Dahlias, orchids, huge chrysanthemums. He filled the cabin with them. They were everywhere. The kitchen, the bathroom, the living room. My husband taught art history at a small college in Northern California. At heart he was a true romantic."

"Right. A romantic."

It would never in a million years occur to him to fill a mountain cabin with flowers as a surprise for a woman, Ethan thought. Maybe that was one of his problems.

"There was also a gift for me." Zoe flexed the fingers of her hand and then knotted them back into a tense little fist. "A camera."

Something in her face triggered a hunch. "You found him, didn't you?"

She swallowed. "I was away at a three-day conference in San Francisco, but we had arranged to rendezvous at the cabin. I tried to call him that night but there was no answer. I was a little worried but I told myself that there was a perfectly good explanation for why he wasn't answering his phone. Still, the next morning I left the conference early and drove to the cabin."

"Go on," Ethan said when she came to a sudden halt.

She took a deep breath, steadying herself. "When I opened the door I realized at once that something terrible had happened."

"What did you see?"

"Shattered vases and broken flowers everywhere. The camera had been crushed beneath someone's foot. To me it looked like there had been a fierce struggle. But the police pointed out that Preston had been shot on the back porch. He had apparently gone out to get some firewood. There was no indication that he had even seen his assailant, let alone tried to fight back."

"How did the cops explain things?"

"There had been a prowler in the area hitting empty cabins," Zoe said. "They think he shot Preston from ambush and then went into the cabin to steal whatever he could."

"What did they say about the broken vases and the camera?"

"They concluded that they had been smashed by the killer in a fit of rage and frustration when he failed to find anything significant in the way of cash or valuables."

"What about your husband's wallet?"

She hesitated. "They found it nearby. It was empty. The assumption was that the prowler had discarded it after he took the cards and cash."

"The empty wallet does sort of support the cops' theory," he said gently.

"I realize that," she shot back with sudden heat. "But I refuse to believe that Preston was murdered by a passing prowler."

"What do you think happened?"

"I'm convinced that my husband was killed by his cousin, Forrest Cleland."

"Motive?" Ethan asked.

"Control of a closely held company, Cleland Cage, Inc. It was founded by Preston's grandfather and his great-uncle. Preston himself was not active in management. His passion was teaching. But he held a controlling block of shares, and he took his responsibilities to the firm and the Cleland family seriously."

"What about Forrest?"

"Forrest Cleland is the current CEO. He and Preston did not get along well. Shortly before the murder, Preston and Forrest were engaged in a fight over a major acquisition that Forrest wanted the board to approve. Preston was convinced that Forrest was putting the future of the company at risk. He intended to use his controlling interest to halt the project. Forrest was enraged."

Definitely time to think professionally.

Ethan took the notepad and pen out of the pocket of his shirt. He put them on the table.

"You think Forrest Cleland murdered your husband because Preston was standing in his way with those shares, is that it?"

"Yes," Zoe said evenly. "Yes, that is exactly what I believe. Forrest's plan would have worked perfectly except for one thing. Shortly before he died, Preston made some significant changes in his estate plan. He left me his entire block of shares."

Ethan tapped the edge of the notebook against the table. "You control that block now?"

"Not exactly," she said. "It's a long story. But here is how it works. I think Preston had begun to suspect that Forrest might be dangerous. He left his shares to me in a trust with a proviso that if I died, regardless of the circumstances of my death, the shares would go into another trust to be administered by a bank."

"Who benefits from that trust?" Ethan asked.

"Any and all members of the Cleland family who happen to be under the age of ten at the time of my demise." She looked coldly amused. "The Clelands are a fairly large clan. There are a number of kids under the age of ten at the moment. Fifteen or twenty at least. Neither they nor their parents can access the trust until the offspring reach the age of thirty."

Ethan took a minute to filter that through a fine sieve. Then he nodded, impressed. "It's not that hard to break a will but it's damn near impossible to tear apart a well-constructed trust."

"Yes. Preston knew what he was doing. He was trying to protect me."

"Let me get this straight. The bottom line here is that if something happens to you, Forrest can't get his hands on the shares and neither can anyone else in the family. Very clever."

Arcadia stirred slightly in the corner of the booth. "Not quite clever enough, as it turns out."

Ethan glanced at her and then turned back to Zoe.

"You want to spell that out for me?" he said.

"There was one loophole in Preston's estate plan," Zoe said softly. "It's true that if I die, the shares slip out of Forrest's control.

But the lawyers convinced my husband to set up a mechanism to handle routine business affairs in the event of a temporary emergency."

"Such as?"

She moved a hand slightly. "Say I was incapacitated for a time by a serious accident or surgery. It is conceivable that a situation might arise that would leave me temporarily unable to manage my personal affairs. If that happened, Preston did not want my shares going into the irrevocable trust designed for the children because I'd never be able to get them back."

"As fate would have it," Arcadia said dryly, "a temporary emergency occurred about six months after Preston Cleland was murdered."

Ethan was tempted to follow that tangent, but experience kept him focused. "How does this short-term emergency mechanism work?"

"In the event I am incapacitated for any length of time," Zoe said, "a revocable trust kicks in allowing my shares to be voted by the Cleland board of directors. The revocable trust remains in effect until I revoke it in writing. As things stand now, Forrest controls the board and therefore, the votes."

"Because you are incapacitated?"

"So they tell me."

"You look okay to me. How, exactly, are you incapacitated?"

She looked at him with fathomless eyes. "They say I'm crazy."

There was a beat of silence. The jazz swirled heavily in the darkness.

"You want to run that by me again?" Ethan said softly.

Zoe clenched and unclenched the hand resting in her lap. "My husband's dear cousin managed to get me committed."

"Committed." He repeated the word very precisely and very evenly.

"Yes."

"I'll admit I'm not up on the laws concerning this kind of thing," he said carefully, "but I was under the impression that it was pretty tricky to get someone committed against her will these days."

Zoe's jaw tightened. He could see that she had clenched her teeth. Probably wondering if he was buying any of this. It was a legitimate concern. He was wondering the same thing.

"Forrest had some help with the paperwork and the legalities," she said.

"From?"

"Dr. Ian Harper, the director of a private psychiatric hospital in California called Candle Lake Manor. I have no idea how much Forrest paid him to keep me doped up, locked up, and incapacitated. But I'm sure it was a substantial sum."

Okay, he'd had a feeling this was going to get weird, he reminded himself.

"I can't help but notice that you are not in this Candle Lake Manor hospital at the moment," he said. "You are sitting in a jazz club in Whispering Springs instead."

"Under another name," Zoe said. She fixed him with a determined expression that did not quite hide a hint of desperation. "You are looking at a genuine escapee from an old-fashioned lunatic asylum."

"That's funny, you don't look crazy."

She flattened one hand on the table. "Let me explain how it happened."

"An explanation would be nice."

"The day I found Preston's body at the cabin, I was a basket case. I knew he had been murdered, and I told the cops that I suspected Forrest. They thought I was hysterical. And I can't argue that point."

"Lot of people would get hysterical in that situation," Ethan said.

"True. But I was also sure that I was right. I gave the authorities my statement and then I went home, expecting the wheels of justice to grind. Unfortunately there was no evidence linking Forrest to the crime. No one was arrested. The cabin prowler was eventually picked up, but he refused to confess to murder. After three months I realized that Preston's killer would go unpunished."

"What did you do?"

"I didn't know what to do. I started to wonder if maybe I was wrong and the cops were right, after all. Meanwhile, I was struggling with grief and all of the emotional trauma involved. Then there was the business side of things to worry about. What with one thing and another, it was another three months before I felt I could think clearly again."

"What was your next step?"

"I went back to the cabin," she said.

"To pack up your husband's things?"

"Yes." Her gaze slid away. She looked at the musicians. "To pack up his things. It was the first time I had been there since the day I found him. I sat on the sofa for a long time, remembering how the vases had been shattered and the flowers strewn around the room. And I thought about the broken camera. The more I thought about it, the more I was sure that the pattern of destruction just did not feel like the work of a frustrated murderer who couldn't find enough cash on his victim."

"What do you think that kind of destruction would have looked like?" he asked. He realized that he was genuinely curious about her reasoning.

"I don't know." She shook her head. "It just seemed to me that an angry killer who was furious because he hadn't found enough money would have been more likely to break windows or tear up the furniture."

She was choosing her words very carefully now. Not lying exactly but not telling him the full truth, either. He'd been here before. Clients did this a lot.

He looked down at his notes.

"This is like the thing with the fancy sheets at Davis Mason's house, isn't it?" he asked. "Something doesn't quite fit so you leap to a conclusion that supports your theory."

"I guess you could say that." She looked at him with fierce eyes. "But I do believe that Preston knew his killer. I think he opened the door to him. There must have been a fight. Maybe they argued and came to blows. That would explain all the smashed vases and the camera getting crushed underfoot. I suspect that after the fight, Forrest left and came back later to shoot Preston from ambush."

He contemplated that for a while. It was possible. He had learned long ago that when it came to murder, almost anything was possible.

"I take it you confronted Forrest with your accusations after that last visit to the cabin?" he asked.

"Yes. But I'm afraid that I didn't handle it very adroitly. I made . . . scenes. A number of them. The two most memorable ones occurred when I went to Forrest's home and shouted my accusations at him in front of his wife. The second big one took place when I stormed into a meeting of the Cleland board."

"You accused Forrest of murder in front of his board of directors?"

She sighed. "As I said, I did not handle things in what you'd call a diplomatic fashion."

"No, I can see that. What happened?"

"I don't know what I hoped to accomplish. Maybe I thought I'd get some support from a few of the board members. Instead everyone just looked at me like I'd gone . . ."

"Crazy."

"In a word, yes." She shrugged. "There were a few more incidents in a similar vein. The police were not interested. Forrest convinced everyone that he had an iron-clad alibi for the day of Preston's murder. Everyone else in the Cleland family was content with the cops' theory that the prowler had been the killer. They wanted me to sit down and shut up. I had never been a popular addition to the clan."

"Why not?"

"No money. No background. No social connections."

"Presumably you got increasingly frustrated," he said.

"Oh, yes. Yes, I got very frustrated. So I

got louder. A few weeks later Forrest called in Dr. Harper. I don't know how he found out about him and his hospital. But he told Harper that I had become irrational and was making wild threats. He said that he did not want to turn me over to the cops because, after all, I was *family.* Harper promised him that he would take very good care of me. And he did."

"What did Harper do?"

"He declared me to be a threat to myself and others." Zoe's mouth twisted. "And then he proceeded to medicate me."

"He used drugs on you?"

"Oh, yes, he used drugs."

She closed her eyes. *Fighting back tears or memories or both?* he wondered.

When her lashes lifted, he could see the cold anger that blazed within her. But her voice was unnaturally steady. "The first time I was literally overpowered by orderlies who held me down while I was given a shot of something very strong. I woke up in a little white room in Xanadu."

"Xanadu?"

Zoe exchanged a glance with Arcadia. "Our nickname for the Manor."

Ethan raised his brows at Arcadia. "You were a patient there, too?"

"For a while." Arcadia did not elaborate.

"Another escapee?"

"Mmm."

"Living under a fake ID?"

Arcadia said nothing.

Zoe cleared her throat. "For the record, my ID is not exactly fake. More like concealed."

"You want to explain that?" he said politely.

It was Arcadia who responded.

"I have a connection," she said quietly. "Before I went to Candle Lake Manor, I made some arrangements. Someone I trusted and who is now dead gave me an introduction to an online identity broker called the Merchant. He's very secretive. You have to have a special code just to contact him and he only accepts certain clients. If you make his A-list, however, he offers a variety of services. He'll sell you a complete new life if you want to go that route. But Zoe only needed to stay hidden for a while."

"In fact," Zoe put in, "I have to keep my old identity in order to be certain that I retain control of the Cleland shares. I'm not sure what would happen, legally speaking, to my status as owner of the shares if I assume a whole new ID."

"Zoe Luce is your real name?" Ethan asked.

"Sort of. Zoe is actually my middle name. Luce was my last name before I was married. There's no law that says you can't go back to using it."

"Names don't matter a whole heck of a lot when you're tracing someone," Ethan said. "There are hundreds, even thousands of people with the same first and last names. Numbers are the only things that count. I'm assuming that you're not using your old credit cards or bank accounts. But what did you do about your social security and driver's license numbers?"

"The Merchant offered to provide what he called a spiderweb veil online," she said. "I don't understand all the technical details, but what it means is that he arranged for any inquiries concerning my basic ID numbers to be routed through him. He promised that he would make certain that anyone who searched for me would get the appropriate answers."

"Legitimate inquiries from government or

law enforcement agencies get the truth, I take it."

"Yes, but there haven't been any from those sources." She moved one hand in a crisp arc. "I certainly never gave the government or the law any reason to do a background check on me. As for other online searchers, the Merchant claimed that he would muddy the waters. It seemed to work. Shortly after we escaped, he notified us that an investigator hired by someone at Candle Lake Manor had attempted to find Arcadia and me. He assured us that he had planted a phony story from a Mexican newspaper to the effect that we had evidently died in a hotel fire."

"The Merchant hasn't notified us of any more inquiries," Arcadia concluded. "But someone has obviously found Zoe."

So much for moving to a smaller town where the cases would be simpler and he could have a normal social life, Ethan thought. Business was getting complicated fast here in Whispering Springs, and he was sleeping with a woman who had escaped from a mental hospital.

"I spent six months in Candle Lake Manor," Zoe said. "For all intents and purposes, I might as well have been in prison." She smiled humorlessly. "Except, of course, that I got therapy."

"How did you get out?" Ethan asked.

Zoe put a fingertip in the center of the cocktail napkin and used a second finger to spin the small paper square. She appeared to be giving the question extremely close consideration.

"It's another long story," she said. She stopped spinning the napkin. "Do you really want to hear it right now?"

"It can wait," he said. But not for long, he thought. "All right, let's get to the part that involves me."

"The blackmail threat," Zoe said.

"I assume that whoever has located you is threatening to tell someone else."

"That's the implication." She reached into her large black tote and withdrew a sheet of business stationery. Without a word she handed it to him. "I found this in my bed tonight."

"He got inside your apartment?" He tried to keep the question businesslike, not wanting to alarm her.

"Yes. He knows exactly where I live, and he knew how to get past all my locks."

That was not good news, Ethan thought.

He studied the little etching of the mansion on the lake. "Candle Lake Manor. That's all. No address or phone number."

"Of course not." Arcadia picked up her espresso cup and sipped languidly. "Dr. Harper relies on referrals. He does not believe in advertising. Discretion and privacy are the twin pillars of his business."

"Candle Lake Manor is the kind of place where you can stick your crazy uncle and rest assured that your friends down at the yacht club will never find out you've got some embarrassing genes in the family," Zoe said.

"It is a very, very private institution," Arcadia added.

"A tranquil setting designed to soothe and reassure," Zoe murmured. "A positive environment in which sensitive individuals who cannot cope with the rigors of normal daily life may flourish and thrive in a serene, orderly setting."

"You're quoting, I assume?" Ethan did not look up from the blackmail note.

"I overheard Dr. Harper showing new clients around a couple of times," Zoe said.

Ethan held up the blackmail note. “Mind if I keep this?”

To his surprise, Zoe hesitated. “I don’t know. That’s the only piece of evidence I’ve got.”

It annoyed him that she did not fully trust him with the note. Then it occurred to him that a woman who was accustomed to having her sanity questioned had a right to be cautious about anything that verified her story.

“I understand this is your evidence,” he said patiently. “That’s why I need it.”

She bit her lip, exchanged a glance with Arcadia, and then nodded. “Okay.”

He folded the sheet of stationery and tucked it into the pocket of his shirt. “It looks like you’ll be hearing from whoever left this fairly soon. Any idea who might have found you and how?”

Zoe and Arcadia did some more nonverbal communication. Then Zoe put her hand back into her tote and drew out another sheet of paper.

“We think it almost has to be someone from Candle Lake Manor,” she said. “We made a list.”

“That’s a start.”

"Something else you should know," she said carefully. "I only need to stay hidden for six more weeks."

"What happens in six weeks?"

"I take my revenge for my husband's murder." Her eyes were fierce. "It isn't nearly enough, but it is something."

He chilled. "What are you going to do?"

"Destroy the only thing in this world that Forrest Cleland really cares about. Cleland Cage, Inc."

Chapter Seventeen

Ethan walked through the door of the bookshop shortly after eight the next morning. Singleton loomed in the gloom.

"You're here bright and early," Singleton said.

"Got a new case and I need some consulting work."

"Business is picking up, huh?"

"A repeat customer."

"That would be the interior decorator?" Singleton leaned on his counter. "She got another suspicious client? You know, I see a pattern developing here. Play your cards right and this could turn out to be a full-time gig for Truax Investigations."

"She's being blackmailed."

Singleton sat down on a stool. "Not good."

"No." Ethan put the extortion note on the glass top of the counter. "I'm trying to get whatever I can on this private psychiatric hospital. The director's name is Dr. Ian Harper. I did some preliminary searching online last night and this morning, and I came up with zip. I don't have time to go at it again. Can you do some fishing for me?"

"Sure." Singleton leaned over to study the note. "Not real original. Clipped the letters out of a newspaper."

"The bastard left it in Zoe's bed."

One of Singleton's brows rose. "Which means he's right here in town. Or, at least he was last night."

"It also means he knows his way around locks," Ethan said. "Zoe's got some good ones on her front door."

Singleton looked up. "Could have bribed the manager."

Ethan shook his head. "Zoe told me that she had them changed quietly after she moved in. She did not give the manager the key."

"Okay, so you're looking for someone who can pick a lock and who is probably staying in the vicinity."

"Best guess is that he is associated with this Candle Lake Manor place. Zoe gave me a list of names of some of the people who work there. I'm going to start calling their offices this morning, see if any of them are out of town on business. If he was here in Whispering Springs late last night, there's no way he could be back in his office in Candle Lake yet. I checked the flight schedules."

"Got it. If anyone isn't where he or she is supposed to be, you can start looking for him or her here in Whispering Springs."

"That's the plan."

Singleton got up from the stool. "I'll see what I can find out about this Candle Lake Manor. A private psychiatric hospital, you said? Mind if I ask what Zoe's connection is to it?"

"My client prefers to keep that information confidential."

"Got it." Singleton nodded. "She was a patient there. Don't worry, as your part-time consultant, I consider myself bound by the client confidentiality policies of Truax Investigations, whatever they are."

"Figured you'd see things that way."

"Just out of curiosity, did Zoe get discharged from this Candle Lake Manor because she got better?"

"No, she busted out."

"An escapee from the funny farm. Gotta hand it to you, Truax, when it comes to clients and girlfriends, you sure can pick 'em."

"When you're starting up a new business and a new social life, you can't be real choosy. Oh, yeah, there's another thing." He took out his notepad. "Zoe bought some identity camouflage from an online ID broker who calls himself the Merchant. The guy is supposed to have great security. But someone got the information about Zoe. I'd like to know exactly how that was accomplished."

Singleton was clearly intrigued. "No such thing as perfect security online. You know how to contact this guy?"

"Arcadia gave me a special code." Ethan removed his notebook from his pocket, flipped it open, and read the information to Singleton.

"I'll see what I can do." Singleton studied the code. "Should be interesting."

Ethan went out into the hall and took the stairs two at a time. He let himself into his office, sat down at the desk, and got a notepad out of the drawer.

He picked up the phone and went to work.

". . . I've been referred to Dr. Harper . . ."

"Dr. Harper is with a client at the moment

and his appointment calendar is full this afternoon. May I ask who referred you?"

"This is a very private matter. I'll call back some other time."

Ethan hung up and tried again.

". . . This is Bob at the garage. Is Ron there? I need to talk to him about his lube job."

"Ron's not scheduled to work today. Did he give you this number? He's not supposed to take calls at work . . ."

". . . I need to talk to Ernie about his last rent check. It bounced sky high . . ."

"Ernie has the day off. He can't take private calls on this phone, anyhow. You'll have to get him at home . . ."

He got lucky on the fourth call.

Ethan walked into her office shortly after nine, took one of the client chairs, extended his legs, leaned back, and laced his fingers behind his head. Making himself at home, she thought grimly. Well, she had known from the start that he would probably be irritating at times.

"What can you tell me about Leon Grady?" he said.

A cold wave washed through her. "So he's the one?"

"Could be. The orderlies you mentioned, Ron and Ernie, are not scheduled to work today so they weren't around. I suppose they are possibilities, but Grady is the one who interests me the most. He's definitely not in his office at Candle Lake this morning and the official word is that he is out of town on business."

"He's head of security at Candle Lake."

"You gave me that much last night. Explains how he might have had the resources to locate you and why he might know something about locks. Can you describe him?"

"Short. Heavyset. Thinning hair. Not a spiffy dresser." She broke off, summoning up every detail she could recall. "I'd say he's in his late fifties. He reports directly to Dr. Harper. He probably took a lot of heat from Harper when they discovered that Arcadia and I were gone."

"Is Grady good with a computer? Savvy enough to track you down online?"

She wrinkled her nose. "From what I saw of him, I wouldn't have thought that he was particularly clever at anything, but he might know his way around a computer. I just don't know."

"You mentioned his clothes. How does he dress?"

"Whenever I saw him in the halls at Candle Lake during the week, he was usually wearing a bad suit. But once or twice he came in on a weekend because of an emergency. I seem to remember cheap polo shirts and polyester pants on those occasions. And he had a very gaudy diamond ring. Arcadia is pretty sure the stone is not real."

"Car?"

"A red Porsche. It's his pride and joy. I used to see it in the parking lot, and I overheard some of the orderlies talking about it."

Ethan thought about that and then let it go. "Probably isn't driving it. Too eye-catching. Glasses? Scars? Quirks?"

"Sunglasses. I think they go with the Porsche. I don't remember any scars."

"Right." Ethan unlaced his fingers and got to his feet. "I'm off. If you think of anything else, call me."

"Wait." She leaped out of her chair. "Where are you going?"

"To find out if Leon Grady is in Whispering Springs."

"How do you plan to do that?"

"The traditional way. I'm going to look for him."

He was already at the door, turning the knob. She sensed the controlled energy running through him. On the hunt, she thought. Doing what came naturally.

"Ethan?"

He stopped in the doorway and looked back at her. "Yeah?"

"Be careful."

He looked surprised. Then he smiled slightly.

"Always," he said.

Before she could respond he was gone.

He went back to his office, opened the phone book, and started punching numbers. There were a lot of resorts, hotels, and motels in Whispering Springs and the surrounding area. This was Arizona, after all, a golfer's and sunseeker's paradise. But he cut the list down considerably when he excluded the high-end establishments. He had a feeling that Grady was the kind of guy who would feel more comfortable in inconspicuous surroundings. Blackmail, by its very nature, demanded a low profile.

He thought it was also safe to assume that Grady would not have set up shop too far from his target. He would want to keep tabs on Zoe.

It was amazing how free with information people were when you asked the right questions.

". . . I'm trying to find my uncle. He's got Alzheimer's and he's wandered off again. Big flashy ring. Thinning hair. You'd never know he was ill. Keeps changing his name because he can't remember his own. We're really worried about him . . ."

At eleven-thirty that morning, he drove into the graveled parking lot of the Sunrise Suites motel. Half a dozen cars were parked in the lot. A fast-food chain restaurant occupied the property on the left. There was an old, boarded-up house on the right and, beyond it, a row of dilapidated warehouses that appeared to have been abandoned a long time ago.

Ethan sat behind the wheel for a few minutes, studying the two-story motel. In most of the windows the drapes were open or only partially closed. But one window was completely veiled with dingy curtains that sagged from the rod.

He climbed out of the SUV, collected his tool kit, and went up the outside steps at the far end of the building. He walked along the second-floor balcony, stopped in front of the door that went with the closed drapes, and knocked.

There was a short pause.

"Who's there?"

A man's voice. So far, so good.

"Sorry to bother you, sir," Ethan said, making it sound like he wasn't sorry, just bored. "My company got a call from the manager. There's a leak in the room below. I took a look down there and I'm pretty sure the water's coming from this room. I need to check your shower."

"Come back later."

"Sorry, sir, this is sort of an emergency. The manager is freaking out about the damage downstairs. I gotta get this leak stopped."

"Hell with it. Okay, okay, give me a minute."

A short time later the door opened. A heavyset man with thinning hair peered out through the crack. He was wearing a faded tan polo shirt and polyester slacks. There was a really big, really fake-looking diamond ring on one finger. He surveyed Ethan's gray work shirt and tool kit. Apparently satisfied, he stepped back.

"Make it fast, will you? I'm in the middle of some business here."

Ethan caught the scent of antacid tablets on his breath. He walked into the room and closed the door.

"This won't take long, Grady," he said.

"It better not, I'm trying to work—" Grady broke off abruptly. His mouth opened, closed, and opened again. "What the hell? How do you know my name? Who are you?"

"I represent the lady you're trying to blackmail. She hired me to find you and make sure that you cease and desist." Ethan paused a beat. "That means stop, by the way."

"That's impossible."

"Well, no, it's not. I mean, look at the progress I've made, already. I've located you. That was the hard part. Making sure you stop the extortion will be a piece of cake."

"You're crazy."

"Seems to be a lot of that going around lately."

"Listen to me, you stupid SOB—"

"The name's Truax."

"I don't give a shit what your name is. But here's some free advice. If you're working for the Cleland woman, you're in trouble. She escaped from a psychiatric hospital."

"Yeah, yeah, I know. And you were the guy in charge of keeping her locked up."

"Know *why* she was locked up?"

"I heard about the scam Harper is running," Ethan said. "How, for a price, he arranges to take care of unwanted relatives. A good example of niche marketing."

"Scam? Is that what she told you?" Grady grimaced, his disdain obvious. "And you bought her story. Shit. She's either paying you a lot of money or else she's sleeping with you. Which is it?"

"That's not your problem."

"Let me tell you why her relatives wanted her stashed away out of sight and out of mind," Grady said. "She hears *voices,* man." He aimed a forefinger at his ear and turned it in a circular motion. "In the *walls.*"

"Thought you were in charge of security

back at Candle Lake. Didn't know you were working the shrink side of the business, too. You're a real versatile guy, Grady."

"I'm not one of the quacks, but I made a copy of the Cleland woman's file before I left. I've had a lot of time on my hands since I hit this burg, so I read her records. She wound up in Candle Lake because she accused a big-time CEO of a major company of murdering her husband. Said something about hearing the screams in the room where it happened."

Ethan grinned. "Hey, you really believe those records Harper makes up for his clients?"

"I do in this case," Grady said, talking fast now. "The shrink who was treating her at Candle Lake, Dr. McAlistair, confirmed the delusion in some early notes. In fact, McAlistair took a personal interest in the case. Called it an extremely rare example of auditory hallucination."

"Wow."

"Listen up, pal, Cleland isn't just crazy—she's dangerous. When she and another patient escaped from Candle Lake, they damn near killed two orderlies."

"Let me guess, you didn't report the incident to the cops, did you?"

Grady scowled. "Harper wouldn't hear of it. He's real big on keeping a low profile. His clients don't want any publicity."

"What about the orderlies? Didn't they have some interest in calling in the cops?"

"Nah. Harper made it worth their while to keep quiet. But I'm giving you the facts. The lady's a certified nutcase, my friend. If I were you, I'd cut my losses."

"Strangely enough, I was just about to give you the same advice," Ethan said quietly. "Cut your losses and do it fast because if you don't disappear I'm going to the cops."

"Bullshit." Grady was triumphant. "You can't prove a goddamned thing. What's more, the Cleland woman won't let you call in the police. She knows that once they find out she's a recent resident of a psych ward they'll contact her family and her doctors. She'll be back in Candle Lake before she knows what hit her. Trust me, she doesn't stand a chance. Harper knows how to manage that kind of situation. Man, he's a pro."

Ethan shook his head. "She won't be going back under any circumstances. I've got a plan to take out some insurance for her."

For the first time Grady appeared wary. "How the hell are you gonna keep 'em from hauling her off to the Manor when the good doctors and her dear family all want her put back in a padded room?"

Ethan told him exactly how he intended to keep Zoe out of Candle Lake Manor.

The guy was downright scary. Truax's scheme was breathtaking and damned brilliant. *If he could pull it off.*

But after seeing the stone-cold assurance in his eyes, Leon was pretty sure the son of a bitch would manage it.

Leon stood alone in the middle of the motel room and tried to think his way out of the box in which he found himself. You had to hand it to Truax. He'd come up with a hell of an angle. The Cleland woman might be desperate enough and crazy enough to go along with it. Probably wouldn't even see the trap Truax had set for her.

He knew a slicker operator when he met one, Leon thought. Glumly he dug the large bottle out of his pocket, pried off the lid, and poured a fistful of antacid tablets into his palm. When this was over, he'd better see a doctor about his stomach problems. They were getting worse.

He stuffed a fistful of tablets into his mouth and chewed grimly. It was time to change course. Once Truax made his move, everything would start to come apart. Leon wanted to be in the wind before that happened.

He started to pace the threadbare carpet. He needed to come up with plan B and he had to do it fast. He possessed valuable information. If he could not use it to blackmail the Cleland woman, he ought to be able to find another buyer.

There was at least one other person he could think of who might be persuaded to pay big bucks to find out where the crazy lady was hiding. He hesitated to make that call, though. It was one thing to deal with an escaped patient on the run, but the idea of negotiating with the other potential client worried him.

He stopped pacing and looked at the large envelope that sat on top of the small table. It contained the contents of the Cleland woman's file. He had copied every scrap of paper in the original before leaving Candle Lake Manor. The phone number he needed was there.

He walked across the room, scooped up the envelope, and emptied the contents onto the table.

He picked up the sheet of paper that contained the name and address he wanted, studied it for a while, and then opened the file and reread Harper's original intake notes.

> . . . Subject is obsessed with the delusion that her husband was murdered by Forrest Cleland. She suffers from severe auditory hallucinations, claiming to sense so-called "screams" in the walls of the cabin where the body was found.
>
> Subject made serious verbal threats to Forrest Cleland and has vowed to destroy both him and the firm of Cleland Cage, Inc. Subject is clearly a danger to others and, in her obsessed, hallucinatory state, very probably to herself, as well . . .

Leon put down the notes and popped a few more tablets. The reason he was reluctant to make the pitch to his one other potential target was simple. He knew enough about Ian Harper's business style to suspect that there was a good chance the patient had told the truth. It was very possible that the Cleland woman was right about her husband having been murdered by the CEO of Cleland Cage.

Leon would have preferred not to do business with a guy who was capable of putting a bullet in the brain of someone who got in his way. But he no longer had any choice. Truax had seen to that.

Time was not the only thing that was running out fast, Leon thought. His supply of cash was dangerously low. He'd cleaned out his bank account before he left, but that had only netted him a few hundred bucks.

He had lived on the corporate credit card and his own personal plastic until he'd arrived in Whispering Springs. After that he'd used his hard-earned cash to pay for the crappy motel room and the fast food that was killing his stomach. No telling when Harper might get suspicious and take a notion to trace him via the credit card records. A motel charge popping up from Whispering Springs, Arizona, would be the same as sending Harper a telegram informing him that he was not in L.A. looking for the Cleland woman.

He could try pawning the ring, but he knew enough about pawn shops to realize that he wouldn't get anywhere near its real value.

It had all looked so easy back at the start. He would get in and get out with the payoff from the Cleland woman before anyone back at Candle Lake knew what had happened. He had pictured himself living on a beach in Florida or some island in the Caribbean before Harper even realized he'd been hosed.

But Truax had just screwed things up royally.

The story of his life, Leon thought. There was always someone around who couldn't wait to screw him.

If he was to salvage anything out of this, he had to take some risks. He'd have to put the squeeze on Forrest Cleland before the guy discovered that Truax was about to outmaneuver him.

The burning sensation in his chest was worse than it had ever been. The pills weren't doing a damn bit of good. He reached for the bottle of liquid antacid that sat on the dresser, opened it, tilted it, and drank deeply.

When the fire in his chest eased a little, he pondered his priorities. One thing was crystal clear. He could not hang around this fleabag motel now that Truax had made him.

He needed some more cash to blow town, and he needed it fast. Luckily he had planned for this contingency.

Chapter Eighteen

"What is it? What's happened?" Kimberley Cleland asked.

She sat tensely on the sofa and watched Forrest put down the phone. Something was very wrong. She could see that in his face. He rarely displayed strong emotion of any kind, but whoever he had just finished talking to had managed to anger him. She could tell because he looked even more cold and controlled than usual and that was saying something.

Forrest was fifty-one and very much in his prime. He had the kind of good bones that would draw the eyes of men and women alike until his dying day. At six-foot-four, he possessed a physical presence that did great things for hand-tailored suits. Together with his natural charisma and authority, that presence also helped him keep his board of directors and the members of a constantly feuding, bickering family in line. Most of the time.

She was his second wife. Three years ago

when she had married him, she had made the mistake of thinking that his seemingly bottomless well of cold control was a reflection of his strength. Somewhere along the line she had discovered the enormity of her mistake. Forrest was not strong. He was cold-blooded.

She had been wrong about him. He did not really love her. He had married her because she came from the right social world and because she had the right social connections and because she was attractive and because she was eighteen years younger than he was.

When she hit forty, he would probably trade her in on a newer model. Maybe she wouldn't even last that long. Lately she'd sensed that he was getting restless. She wouldn't be surprised if he was having an affair. He'd had one with her before he'd divorced his first wife.

"That was a man claiming to know the present whereabouts of Sara Cleland," Forrest said evenly.

She stared at him, jolted out of her thoughts. "What on earth?"

"He offered to sell me the information for a considerable sum."

"I don't understand. Sara's at Candle Lake Manor."

"According to the man on the phone, she hasn't been there for the past year."

"But that doesn't make any sense. We've been paying the bills. She has to be at Candle Lake."

"There's one way to find out if she's there or not." Forrest reached into the slim briefcase at his feet and retrieved a small handheld computer. He punched a button and studied the screen for a few seconds. Then he reached for the phone again.

He spoke briefly to whoever answered at Candle Lake.

"I don't care if she's in a therapy session," he snapped. "Get her on the phone."

There was another tense silence.

"Let me speak to Harper," Forrest said in his executive office voice. "Now."

Kimberley got up with a jerky movement and went to the liquor cabinet. She poured herself a shot from the first bottle that came to hand without even looking at the label and listened to the rest of the one-sided conversation in growing panic.

"Don't give me that bullshit about her fragile mental condition," Forrest said softly.

"You've lost her, haven't you? How long has she been gone?"

Kimberley took a long swallow and stared unseeingly at the sweeping view of San Francisco Bay. What she really needed was one of the little pink pills she kept in her medicine cabinet, but she did not dare take them in front of Forrest. He would see it as a sign of weakness even though he was the reason she had been forced to ask her doctor for the prescription.

Forrest hung up and looked at her across the width of the room his first wife had decorated.

"She's gone," Forrest said flatly. "Harper admitted as much. His story is that she managed to slip away a few days ago and that she has been located. He claims that he sent some people to pick her up and that there's nothing to worry about."

"Then it will be okay. Everything will be fine once they have her back at Candle Lake."

"I'm not so sure of that." Forrest got to his feet. "I'll give Harper twenty-four hours. If he doesn't have Sara back by tomorrow, I'll take matters into my own hands."

"You're going to deal with that person

who just called? The one who offered to sell you the information about Sara?"

"If necessary. One way or another, Sara has to be found and returned to Candle Lake as soon as possible. I can't risk having her show up at the annual board meeting."

Kimberley noticed that her hand was shaking. She lowered her half-finished drink with great caution and set the glass down on top of the lacquered cabinet. "Do you really think she'd have the nerve to turn up at the meeting?"

"She's crazy, remember? She thinks I murdered Preston. Her goal is to destroy me and the company. Yes, I think she'll show up unless we get her back into Candle Lake." Forrest picked up the briefcase and started toward the door. "I'll be in my study."

Kimberley watched him walk away from her. It reminded her of the way her father had always walked away when she needed him, the way everyone walked away from her. She tried another swallow of whiskey. The expensive liquor tasted like acid.

Chapter Nineteen

"You told Leon Grady you were going to do *what*?"

Zoe was so stunned that she could barely get the words out of her mouth. It was as if her tongue had just short-circuited. Her brain, too. She stared blankly at Ethan, who sprawled in her client chair, glancing occasionally at his watch. He was making no secret of his impatience to leave. A busy man who had things to do and people to see.

"You heard me," he said. "I told Grady that we're going to get married."

She pulled herself together with a tremendous effort. *"Why?"*

"I thought it was obvious."

"No," Zoe said through her teeth. "It is not obvious. Try explaining it to me in short, single-syllable words."

"Don't worry, most of the words I know are short and single syllable. Okay, here's my thinking on this. You told me that the shares you inherited from Preston are now in a trust that you can revoke at will."

"Yes."

"Your goal is to materialize unannounced at the annual board meeting, paperwork revoking the trust in your hand, and proceed to vote your shares in such a manner as to force the hostile merger of Cleland Cage, right?"

"Yes."

"But if you get picked up by the jolly munchkins from Candle Lake before the annual meeting, your big plans go down the toilet."

"I hired you to keep that from happening, remember?"

"I'm doing my best, ma'am. But in my professional opinion, marriage would buy you a hell of a lot of insurance. It would, in fact, render the entire concept of returning you there null and void."

The logic finally started to sink into her bemused brain. "Because as my husband, you would be able to vote my shares," she said slowly. "You could vote them according to my wishes and achieve the same results."

"True, but practically speaking, it's a whole lot simpler than that. As your husband, I become your new next of kin. I could override any medical decision that Forrest Cleland or anyone else might try to make for you, including commitment to a psychiatric hospital."

"Of course," she whispered. "I never thought of that. Even if they managed to haul me back, you could spring me."

"Right. But I don't think it will come to that. I'm betting that once the word gets out that you're married, everyone involved in this thing will give up on their plans to keep you locked up and slink away into the night."

"You're serious, aren't you?" she said finally.

"When I'm working, I'm always serious. The quickest, cleanest way to do this is to catch a flight to Vegas late this afternoon." He shot another glance at his watch. "We'll get married there tonight and return to Whispering Springs tomorrow."

"You'd really do this for me? Marry me just to keep me safe for the next six weeks?"

"You got a better idea?"

"Well, no, but this seems a little extreme."

"Hey, it's no big deal. Trust me, I've been married lots of times."

No big deal.

"I suppose you do qualify as an expert in the field," she said neutrally.

"Right. I'm an expert. After the annual board meeting, we'll get a quickie divorce and life will go back to normal."

She cleared her throat. "You make it sound so easy."

"It is easy."

She rubbed her temples. "I'm touched, really I am, but I can't allow you to do this."

"Why not?"

She frowned. "Because it's too dangerous, of course."

"I'd like to say that danger is my middle name, but it's not. Relax, this'll work. You'll see."

She shook her head. "I can't let you do it. In essence you'd be putting yourself into the same situation that Preston was in. Don't you see? Forrest killed Preston. Who's to say he wouldn't try to murder you, too, if he thought that you were standing in his way?"

His mouth curved. "You really mean that, don't you? You're worried about me."

"As the saying goes, you don't have a

dog in this fight, Ethan. I don't want the responsibility of putting you in mortal danger."

"You hired me to take care of a blackmail problem," he said gently. "Let me do my job."

"I won't let you take the risk."

"As your husband, I won't be at risk in the same way that Preston was."

"What do you mean?"

"One dead husband who was apparently the victim of an armed burglar can be explained," he said. "A second dead husband at this point would arouse suspicion and invite a lot of questions. Trust me, that is the last thing Forrest will want if he is trying to fend off a takeover. He needs the full support of his board and all of the major shareholders he can get on his side."

He had a point, but she was reluctant to admit it.

"The most likely scenario is that Forrest will try to buy me off when he finds out I'm married to you," Ethan said.

"Hmm."

"It's the only approach that would make sense."

"And if he does try to buy you off?" she asked. "What will you tell him?"

Ethan got up, walked to the desk, and flattened his hands on the surface. He leaned in close. "I will tell him to go screw himself."

"Ethan—"

"Come on, let's get moving. It's going on one o'clock. I'll drop you off at your apartment. You can pack a bag while I take care of some loose ends at the office. I'll pick you up at three-thirty and we'll head for the airport. There are dozens of flights all day long to Vegas, and they take only about an hour. The time change is in our favor."

"What loose ends?" she demanded, struggling to hold on to at least one rational thread.

He shrugged. "There are a few things I want to do before we leave town."

She hauled her ultramarine blue tote out from under the desk and got slowly to her feet. "Such as?"

"I'm going to line up someone to keep an eye on Arcadia while we're out of town."

A new rush of anxiety stopped her in her tracks. "Do you think she's in danger?"

"Probably not. Leon Grady never mentioned her." Ethan was at the door, holding it open. "And I'm inclined to agree with her that the hacker who sold your file to Grady would have offered to sell hers as well if he had it. But I'd rather be safe than sorry."

"I understand your concern, but I think you'd better check with Arcadia before you hire a bodyguard for her."

"Arcadia strikes me as a smart lady. I don't think she'll go stubborn on me."

"Unlike me, you mean?"

"You are a smart lady, too," he said a little too smoothly.

"But stubborn?"

"Very." He looked at her. "You going to walk out of here on your own two feet or do you want to be carried out?"

She raised her chin, clutched her tote very tightly, and marched toward the door with as much dignity as she could summon. "There is one very important little fact that you seem to be forgetting more and more often lately."

"What's that?"

"I'm the client." She poked a finger at his chest as she went past. "You work for me, Truax. That means I give the orders."

"Oh, yeah." He closed and locked her door. "I knew that."

"Getting married again, huh?" Singleton leaned on his counter and regarded Ethan with a meditative expression. "If you'd given me a little notice, I could have organized a bachelor party."

"I appreciate the thought," Ethan said. "Tell you what, you can buy me a beer when I get back from Vegas."

"Sure. Look, I can follow your reasoning here, but I gotta tell you that marrying the client is a little over the top, even for an ace private detective like you."

"That's what Zoe said."

"She's not keen on this plan?"

"I had my hands full talking her into it. She was afraid that she would be putting me in danger."

"And you told her that danger was your middle name, right?"

"How'd you guess?"

"I saw the movie."

"It's a cool line and I've waited all of my professional life to use it, but unfortunately, she was not in a mood to buy it. I had to fall back on reason and logic."

"Don't you just hate when that happens?"

"Yeah. I pointed out that the probability that Forrest Cleland would take the risk of murdering two of her husbands was real low."

Singleton took off his glasses and started to polish them with a cloth. "You think it's all that low?"

"Sure." Ethan lounged against the counter. "But enough about me. Let's talk about you. What have you got for me?"

Singleton replaced his glasses. "Not much, I'm afraid. As far as I can tell Candle Lake Manor is a legitimate private hospital that is wholly owned and operated by Dr. Ian Harper."

"How'd he get enough money to buy his own hospital?"

"He did it the old-fashioned way. He married it."

"Wife?"

"Elizabeth Pangbourne Harper was a spinster most of her life. She inherited a fortune and used it for good works. She was fifty-four when she married Harper. He was forty-two. That was eleven years ago. She died three years later. Heart attack."

"Convenient. Harper got her fortune?"

"Not all of it. A good chunk went to various charities." Singleton consulted some notes. "But he got some of it, and he also got Candle Lake Manor. By catering to a wealthy clientele who will pay dearly for privacy and by steering clear of insurance and government funding, he has evidently found a way to make the place quite profitable."

"A real entrepreneur. Staff?"

"About what you'd expect. Orderlies, aides, housekeepers, kitchen crew, and some security personnel. Turnover seems to be high."

"What about the medical side?"

"As far as I can tell, there's only one full-fledged psychiatrist on the payroll, Dr. Venetia McAlistair. She oversees a small number of so-called therapists. Most of them don't have much in the way of degrees or experience. High turnover in that group, too." Singleton looked up from his notes. "Given the piss-poor patient to medical staff ratio, I've got a hunch that Candle Lake Manor relies heavily on pharmaceuticals to treat the patients."

Ethan nodded. "Drugs are cheaper than doctors, and Harper seems to be a guy who keeps an eye on the bottom line. Anything else?"

"That's about it except for the fact that, as

far as I can tell, none of the patient history or billing records are online."

"You'd expect that from a place that sells the promise of privacy and a very low profile. What about Cleland Cage? Anything new there?"

"Just what you already know. Third-generation commercial real estate development and investment company. Because it is a closely held corporation, there's not much news in the financial press. But there have been rumors that the company has had some serious financial problems lately because of some outstanding debt accrued after it acquired a smaller outfit a couple years ago. Forrest Cleland has been struggling to fight off a hostile takeover from another large development operation for the past year. Big decisions are expected at the annual board meeting next month."

"What about the Merchant?"

"A very secretive type, our Merchant. I used the code that Arcadia provided, though, and I dropped a name. He responded."

"Yeah? What name did you drop?"

Singleton shrugged. "I mentioned the think tank I worked for a while back. He recognized it and was suitably impressed. Reacted like he considered me a sort of peer or colleague. At any rate, he refused to believe that he had been hacked. Takes a lot of pride in his security. But he assures me that he's looking into the matter and that he'll get back to me."

"All right." Ethan pushed himself away from the counter and went toward the door. "If you get more, you know where to reach me."

"Sure. Congratulations on your forthcoming marriage, by the way. You know what they say."

Ethan paused in the doorway and looked back over his shoulder. "No, what do they say?"

"Fourth time's a charm."

"That's good to hear."

He went out into the hall and climbed the steps to the upper floor. He let himself into his office, sat down behind his desk, and reached for the old-fashioned file in which he kept important phone numbers. He flipped through the cards until he found the one he wanted.

Harry Stagg answered on the first ring. "Stagg Consulting."

"I need a baby-sitter for a woman in Whispering Springs and I need him ASAP. Like tonight. You available?"

There was a short pause. "If I say yes, it makes it sound like I'm not doing much business."

"You want the job or not?"

"I'll take it," Stagg said. "Business is a little slow."

"How soon can you be here?"

"Let's see, the flight from San Diego to Phoenix takes about an hour in the air but there's the time change. If I leave now I should be in Whispering Springs by six or six-thirty. That work for you?"

"It works." He gave Arcadia's name and address to Stagg. "I'll talk to her. She'll be expecting you. I'm leaving town with my client as soon as I can get away. We'll be back in Whispering Springs sometime tomorrow."

"Where are you going?"

"Las Vegas."

"I take it this isn't a gambling junket?"

"I'm getting married."

"Yeah? How many times does this make? Three? Four?"

"Four."

"Well, you know what they say," Stagg said. "Fourth time's a charm."

"I've heard that."

He filled Stagg in on Leon Grady and the situation.

"Grady will probably be gone by the time you get here. It doesn't look like he knows about Arcadia Ames, but I don't want to take any chances."

"Got it."

Bonnie walked into the office just as Ethan hung up the phone.

"What's going on?" she asked.

"Congratulate me," Ethan said. "I'm getting married."

"Married?"

"You know what they say, fourth time's a charm."

"A bodyguard?" Arcadia contemplated Ethan. "For how long?"

"A couple of days," Ethan said. "Just until we can be sure that you're not on Grady's blackmail list."

"If he was aware of me, he would have made his move by now."

"It will make Zoe feel more comfortable if

she knows that you're in safe hands while we're out of town."

He was right, she thought. Zoe would worry.

"Okay," she said. "But only until you two return."

"I appreciate the cooperation. His name is Harry Stagg. He'll show up around six or six-thirty if all goes well."

She smiled slightly. "Is he just a big hunk of muscle or is there some brain?"

"There's some brain." He looked into the nearest display case and saw several pieces of unusual looking jewelry. "Got any rings?"

"Yes." She tipped her head to one side. "Don't tell me that you want to buy one for Zoe?"

"When you get married there's supposed to be a ring."

She studied him for a long moment.

"You ought to know," she said softly.

Chapter Twenty

They flew into Las Vegas that evening. At eleven o'clock they were standing in front of the altar of an all-night wedding chapel.

The ceremony was everything one could hope for in a Las Vegas wedding, Zoe decided. The chapel, a glittering little palace decorated with a lot of crystals and candles, was tucked away on a side street just off the Strip. It featured a blue carpet, a white gazebo, and several large vases overflowing with artificial blue flowers.

The minister bore a striking resemblance to Elvis in one of his heavy phases. His assistant, who doubled as bridal attendant, witness, and secretary, was a retired showgirl. The woman cried when the vows were spoken. The tears looked genuine. Zoe was not sure that was a good sign.

The most disconcerting moment occurred when Ethan, at the appropriate moment, produced a gold ring cut with an unusual design.

The best part was that she got to sign her

full name on all the legal paperwork, Sara Zoe Luce Cleland. No more hiding in the shadows.

Fifteen minutes later, Ethan guided her outside into the neon-lit night. They slipped into the endless stream of people moving from one magnificent casino resort to another.

Zoe clutched the little bouquet of real flowers that the assistant had pressed into her hand just before the ceremony. The circlet of gold glinted on her finger.

"You thought of everything," she said, trying to sound blasé. "How did you come up with a ring on such short notice?"

"It's not from any of my previous marriages if that's what's bothering you." There was an edge to his voice.

She felt herself turn red and was grateful for the shadows of night and neon. "I was just curious, that's all."

"I picked it up at Gallery Euphoria before we left. Arcadia knew your ring size."

"Oh." She spread the fingers of her left hand and studied the gold band. "It's quite beautiful. Must have been expensive."

"Arcadia gave me a deal."

"I'm sure she'll let you return it for a full refund," Zoe assured him.

"It's not going on your bill as a miscellaneous expense, so stop worrying about the cost."

She realized that she had insulted him.

"It's just that I'm already so deeply in debt to her," Zoe said, trying to explain. "After we got out of Xanadu I could not access any of my own cash or credit cards. We had to use the money that she had stashed away in an offshore account. I'm making regular monthly payments to her, but the truth is I won't be able to repay her for the costs of using the Merchant's services and my business start-up expenses until I cash out of Cleland Cage. That probably won't happen until a few months after the merger takes place."

Ethan looked intrigued. "Arcadia is into things like offshore accounts?"

"In her other life she used to be a very successful financial trader. She invested for clients and for herself. She knows an incredible amount about really arcane business stuff. She's the one who helped me figure out that Cleland Cage was vulnerable and that a takeover was in progress. She mapped out the strategy for me."

"Huh. Never would have guessed."

Zoe looked at the ring sparkling in the light of a neon-lit doorway. "It was a nice touch," she said, still searching for the right note.

"You don't have to wear it if it makes you feel uncomfortable."

"It's okay."

"Not like the ring makes the marriage any more legal."

"I know." She tightened her grip on the flowers. "I said it's okay. I'd appreciate it if you would not snap at me right now. I'm a little tense."

"Was I snapping at you?"

"Yes."

"Sorry."

"I think we're both tense."

"You certainly seem to be a little high-strung this evening," Ethan allowed.

She resented that. "I'm entitled. It's not like I get married every day."

"Well, maybe *you* don't get married every day," Ethan said gravely. "Some of us, on the other hand, have had considerable experience in that regard and I can assure you that—"

"Oh, shut up. I am not in the mood to joke about your previous experience, so don't start."

"Fine. Not like it's my favorite topic, anyway."

A cloud of guilt settled on her. He had probably been trying to lighten the mood with a little self-deprecating humor, and she had overreacted.

A long stretch limousine cruised past on her left and turned into the spectacularly illuminated entrance of one of the mega resort casinos. A woman dressed in a glittering sequined gown got out. She was followed by a man in black-and-white formal attire.

On the right, people dressed in jeans and tee shirts drifted past on a long, moving walkway that bore an unsettling resemblance to a lolling tongue. They disappeared into the mouth of a giant casino.

Up ahead she could see the brilliant gold and silver sign advertising the hotel where Ethan had made reservations for the night. They had dropped off their luggage earlier when they had checked in, but there had been no time to go to the room before Ethan had hustled her off to take care of the few formalities required to get married in Nevada. She did not know if he had booked two rooms or one and for some bizarre reason, she had found a lot of excuses not to inquire into the matter.

"I'm sorry," she said quietly. "I shouldn't have said that. Especially not after all you've done. I really don't know how to thank you."

"Forget it."

She examined her rapidly wilting flowers and the ring on her finger. "That's a little hard to do under the circumstances."

She expected him to make an acid comment, but he said nothing.

They passed the entrance to a high-end shopping mall built into a hotel. Another doorway invited them to view a world-class exhibition of old masters. Zoe knew that if she and Ethan allowed themselves to be lured into either the mall or the art gallery, they would eventually be fed straight into the resort's casino. That was how Las Vegas survived. The bellies of the great, glittering beasts were the gaming floors, and the creatures required around-the-clock feeding.

"Ethan?"

"Yeah?"

"Do you mind if I ask you a personal question?"

"It's a little late to be asking personal questions," he said very seriously. "You ought to ask those before you marry the guy."

She smiled. "I'll remember that."

"What's the question?"

"How did you get into the private investigation business?"

He said nothing for a few seconds. She thought that he might not answer her at all.

"I was the family screwup," he said eventually. "Took after my Uncle Vic. Dropped out of college. Joined the army. When I got out, I went to work for a large security firm in L.A. for a couple of years and then I went out on my own."

"Bonnie told me about what happened to your brother."

"Figured she said something that night we had pizza."

Zoe looked at the crowds up ahead on

the sidewalk. "I know how it feels to lose someone like that."

"I realize that."

"I understand what it does to your insides to want justice so badly you can't sleep and to have people tell you that you should just keep quiet and let the authorities handle it. I understand how it feels to wake up in the middle of the night knowing that the system isn't going to work for you."

He reached out and took her ring hand, lacing his fingers through hers.

"I know," he said.

"That's why you're going through all this for me, isn't it?" She clutched the flowers. "Because you've been in my position. You know how the obsession for revenge eats at you. How it can make you a little crazy."

"Yeah." He tightened his fingers around hers. "What was he like?"

"Preston?" She summoned up some of the old memories. "He was warm and loving. Caring. Kind. A truly decent man. Pretty much the exact opposite of his relatives. He was the outsider in his family. They're all business people. Preston loved his art history."

"And you loved him." It was a statement, not a question.

"Yes, I loved him. By the time I met Preston, I had been alone in the world for a long time. In his own way, because he was so different from the others in his family, Preston was also very much alone. I think that was the reason we were drawn together." She swallowed. "We promised each other that we would take care of each other."

"And then he got killed."

"Yes. I didn't do a very good job of taking care of him. The only thing I can do now is try to avenge him. While he was alive, Preston cared about the future of Cleland Cage, but as far as I'm concerned, it was Forrest and the company that are responsible for his death."

Ethan kept his grip on her hand. "Drew was four years younger than me. He was everything I was supposed to be. He finished college. He was successful in business and he served on the board of a charitable foundation. He didn't screw up three marriages. He found a woman who loved him. He started a family. He was a fine father and a pillar of the community."

A chill of understanding went through her. "You were his older brother?"

"You know what that means?"

She exhaled slowly. "It probably means that somewhere deep inside, you felt that you were supposed to take care of him."

"Yes. But I didn't do my job. He got killed."

The words echoed all the way through her.

"Do you think," she said very carefully, "that the reason you were obsessed with getting justice and the reason I want revenge so badly is because we both feel that we failed in our responsibilities?"

"Got a hunch that's part of it. What do you think?"

"I think you're right. But it doesn't change anything, does it?"

He squeezed her hand. "No, it doesn't change a damn thing."

Maybe nothing had changed when it came to her need to avenge Preston, she thought, but something was certainly different about her relationship with Ethan. She wondered if he felt the link between them or if it was a product of her imagination.

They walked past a shallow man-made

lake that fronted another giant hotel complex. Small boats, their bows adorned with colored lights, floated across the surface of the water. The little vessels, together with their cargoes of laughing passengers vanished under a bridge into yet another casino.

"You know what?" Ethan abruptly changed direction, dragging her with him. "You were right. It's been a long day and we're both stressed out. What we need is some distraction. Come on."

Surprised, she clung to her drooping bouquet and hurried to keep up with him. "Where are we going?"

"I'm feeling lucky."

"Join the crowd. Las Vegas is designed to make you feel lucky."

"I'm serious."

He whisked her through the nearest casino entrance, plunging them both into a world of flashing lights, tinkling slots, and a sea of card tables. The sounds of laughter, conversation, and lounge music filled the air.

Ethan dragged her to a blackjack table.

"I don't know how to play," she said quickly. "At least not in a real casino."

"Then stand right there and think positive thoughts."

He took a seat. Zoe wrapped both hands around her bouquet and tried to think positive thoughts.

Ethan played with no outward show of emotion, but when he got to his feet fifteen minutes later, he seemed satisfied. He tipped the dealer and pocketed his winnings.

"Good news," he said. "I won't be billing you for the cost of the hotel room. I just won enough to cover it."

Room. Singular.

"It's all right," she said hastily. "I really don't mind. I understand that out-of-town expenses aren't included in your basic fee."

"Think of it as a wedding present." He handed her some quarters. "Here. Try your luck."

"I never win when I play slots."

"Give it a shot."

"Oh, all right." She snatched a few of the coins out of his hand, dumped them into the nearest machine, and pulled the handle.

Quarters tinkled pleasantly in the tray.

"Hey, Ethan, look."

More coins cascaded into the bottom of the slot.

"Oh, my gosh," Zoe whispered.

Ethan lounged against the nearest one-armed bandit and grinned. "Guess this is your lucky night, too."

The quarters continued to rain down into the tray.

"Here, hold my flowers." She tossed the bouquet at him, opened her tote and went to work scooping up her loot.

Ethan waited until she was finished before he took her arm. "Let's get a drink to celebrate."

He led her into the nearest lounge. They sat down in a booth. Ethan put the bouquet on the table.

A waitress dressed in a tiny gold costume appeared.

"Champagne," Ethan said.

The waitress glanced knowingly at the flowers. "Is this a celebration?"

Ethan put an arm around Zoe in an unmistakably possessive move.

"Just got married," he said.

"Yeah, that happens a lot around here." She gave both Ethan and Zoe a genuinely warm smile. "Most of the time I figure it'll last about a week. But you two look good together. Congratulations."

The champagne took some of the edge off the tension, but it did nothing to allay the unsettling mix of excitement and apprehension that Zoe was experiencing. By the time they arrived at the door of the hotel room, the fluttery feeling in her stomach was almost unbearable.

Calm down. It's not like this is a real wedding night. I'm just sort of having an affair with him. Actually, until now, it's been more of a one-night stand.

But that freshly minted wedding license in Ethan's pocket and the ring on her finger made it all seem surreal. What did you call it when you slept with the man who had just married you?

She was concentrating so hard on the question that when Ethan opened the door she walked into the room without her usual pause on the threshold.

The heavy wave of raw lust hit her so hard that she dropped her flowers and nearly fell to her knees.

"What the hell?" Ethan flipped on the light

switch. He caught her arm and steadied her. "Are you okay?" Concern edged his voice.

"Yes."

That was an outright lie. She was not okay. The suffocating essence of recent sex suffused the atmosphere. It was not the kind of earthy, natural emotional energy that sometimes clung to a bedroom for a while. This room reeked of sick and twisted cravings. She breathed shallowly and looked around with a sense of desperation.

On the surface, everything was pristine. The beige-colored carpet had been properly vacuumed. The massive, round bed with its gold-and-black-striped spread and matching, king-sized pillow shams appeared clean and fresh. The bathroom door stood ajar, affording a view of acres of white tile.

But the taint of unwholesome sex clung to the furnishings like a terrible stench.

There was no way she could spend the night in this room. She needed an excuse to ask Ethan to call the front desk and request a move, and she needed it fast.

The answer came when she looked up and saw the large mirror installed in the ceiling over the bed.

"I can't handle that," she said.

Ethan followed her gaze. He saw the mirror and smiled slowly. "Maybe I shouldn't have asked the front desk clerk for the address of the nearest wedding chapel. Got a feeling he tried to do us a favor by upgrading us to a honeymoon suite."

"Would you mind very much if we downgraded ourselves? That mirror is a little over the top for me."

"See, that's the thing about you interior decorators. Picky, picky, picky."

But he was already reaching for the phone.

His request was granted immediately. They collected their bags and went downstairs to get new keys.

"Will you need help with the luggage?" the clerk asked.

"No, thanks," Ethan said. "We can manage on our own."

They made their way back through the casino to the elevator lobby in silence.

Five minutes later they opened the door of another room on the eleventh floor. This time Zoe remembered to halt on the threshold. Nothing intense hit her, just the usual assortment of minor sensations that she could easily tune out.

Ethan watched her walk into the room. "This one okay?"

"Yes, thank you." She was embarrassed but enormously relieved. "Sorry about the fuss."

Ethan hauled her suitcase and his own small flight bag into the room and dropped them on the floor. "I admit that the mirror over the bed was a little on the tacky side."

"Yes, it was." She went into the bathroom, found a glass, and stuck her bouquet into it. "I regret to say that there are a few people in my profession who don't know when to stop when it comes to mirrors."

Ethan came to stand in the bathroom doorway and watched her run water into the glass. "I don't think those flowers will make it through the night."

"Probably not."

But she could not bring herself to dump them into the trash.

"Zoe?"

"Look, there are two sinks," she said brightly. "Which one do you want?"

He walked to where she stood and gently cradled her face in his hands.

"It's okay," he said. "I got one room because I was going on the assumption that we needed only one bed. But if that assumption was wrong, all you have to do is tell me. I can afford two rooms tonight."

A deep warmth flowed through her. She spread her fingers across the front of his shirt, savoring the hard strength in him. The hunger in his eyes was unmistakable, but it was under full control. If she asked him to get another room or to sleep on the floor he would do it.

"Your assumption was not wrong," she said.

He drew his knuckles lightly along her cheek. "You don't know how happy I am to hear that."

He deserved some kind of rational explanation, she thought. She was behaving like a nervous bride on a wedding night.

"I know I'm acting weird," she said.

"The stress."

"That's part of it, but it's more than that. This whole situation just feels so strange. I mean, we've only had one night together and I was just starting to adjust to the idea that we might be sleeping together and wondering how things would go between us and now we're married but it's not a real marriage. I don't know. I can't seem to grasp the concept."

"Listen to the advice of an expert." He kissed her ear. "Forget the license and the ring. Concentrate on the sleeping together part."

Before she could respond, he was kissing her, a heavy, intoxicating kiss—a magic spell of a kiss that set everything inside her gloriously free.

Concentrate on the sleeping together part.

"Ethan." She gripped his shoulders and kissed him back, abandoning herself to the moment with a kind of desperate, feverish need that was entirely new to her.

"That's it," he said against her throat. His voice was thicker and heavier, rich and dense and imbued with dark promises. "You're getting the hang of it."

She leaned into him, absorbing his heat into all the cold places inside her, trying to let him share some of her own warmth.

He scooped her up, carried her out of the bathroom, and stood her on her feet beside the bed. Reaching down, he grabbed a fistful of bedspread, blankets, and sheets and tossed them all out of the way with a single, sweeping motion.

She stumbled out of her shoes, holding on to Ethan to keep her balance. He got out of his own shoes somehow, and then they were falling together, down, down, down.

The next thing she knew she was on her back and Ethan was on top of her, levering himself up on one elbow so that he could strip away her blouse and bra.

She slid her hand downward, got a grip on the zipper of his trousers and lowered it.

When she found him with her fingers, she discovered that he was fully aroused. She cupped him gently.

"Oh, yeah." In the shadows, his smile was both very dangerous and very sexy. "You have definitely got a good grasp of the concept now."

A long time later she opened her eyes. The first thing she noticed was the moonlight dancing on her wedding ring. The pale gleam was as delicate and ephemeral as hope and possibilities for the future.

Ethan stirred against her and gathered her close. "What are you thinking?"

"I'm thinking that I won't go back to using my other name," she whispered. "I'm going to stick with Zoe." A new name and, just maybe, a new future.

"Zoe Truax." He leaned over her and kissed her deeply. "Yeah. I like the sound of that. It suits you."

Chapter Twenty-one

"So," Harry Stagg said. "Come here often?"

Arcadia contemplated the thin man with the deep, world-weary eyes who sat across from her in the small booth. She had never had a bodyguard before and therefore had not been altogether sure what to do with one.

She had agreed to put up with him only because it had been clear that Zoe had had enough to worry about as it was. Flying off to Vegas for a marriage of convenience to Ethan Truax had caused her a great deal of anxiety. Fretting over her friend's safety while she was out of town would only make matters worse.

When Harry Stagg showed up in Gallery Euphoria at six-fifteen, Arcadia had suggested that they have dinner out and spend the evening at the Last Exit. The plan had been to buy as much time as possible before taking him home to her silver-and-white apartment. Unlike Zoe, she had a spare bedroom, but it was hard to picture any man, let alone this one, inhabiting it.

"I like jazz." Arcadia ran her fingertip around the rim of her martini glass. "More than that, I need it. It puts me in another place for a while."

Harry took a swallow of the fizzy water that he had ordered. "Know what you mean."

The trio on stage shifted into a Thelonious Monk tune, "Brilliant Corners." It was a notoriously difficult piece, but Arcadia had heard the group do it before. They could handle it. The piano was leading, the bass and drums moving smoothly into its slipstream.

Harry Stagg blinked a little in muted surprise when the astonishingly clean, compelling music started to flow through the intimate room. Very slowly he lowered his glass. His face was rapt with concentration.

Arcadia gave herself up to the otherworldly sounds, and time shifted into another dimension.

When it was over, neither she nor Harry moved for a while. Then her companion turned slowly back to her.

"Haven't heard anything that good since

the last time I was in New Orleans," Harry said. There was reverent awe in his harsh voice.

"Took me by surprise the first time, too." She smiled slightly. "In response to your question, yes, I do come here often."

"I can see why."

She removed the little stick from her martini glass and put the olive between her lips. No sense wasting the moment, she thought. This was a golden opportunity to do some digging.

"Have you known Ethan Truax long?" she asked.

"We met a few years ago," Harry answered.

"In a professional context?"

Harry appeared to ponder that for a moment. Then he nodded. "You could say that. I worked for some people who wanted me to scare him off a case."

"I assume that plan did not go well?"

"No. Once Truax locks onto a target, he doesn't unlock. And on that occasion, he was investigating the murder of his brother. I'd have had to kill him to stop him."

"Zoe told me about what happened to his brother. I gather that, although the man responsible walked free, he later met with an unfortunate accident."

"Accidents happen," Harry said.

"You told me that you would have had to kill Ethan to stop him. I can't help but notice that you didn't go that far. Does that mean that you draw the line at shooting people?"

"Let's just say I don't do it for money," he said.

"Ah. A small, but profound, distinction."

"As it happened, I did not have to explain that distinction to my employers. They were reluctant to resolve the problem in that way because they were bright enough to figure out that it would come back to haunt them."

"Were they right?"

"Probably. Getting rid of Truax would have made life very difficult for them. You see, Truax had already made a lot of waves by that point. He had a stack of evidence regarding money laundering a mile high. Some of it contained links to my employers. He also had tapes of me coming to see him in his office. After I left, he made sure that a memo connecting me to my employers and them to various shady financial matters went into a safe-deposit box together with the tapes."

"In other words, if he had turned up dead, there would have been more questions than your employers would have wanted to answer."

"Yeah."

"I still don't understand how you and Truax came to be, shall we say, business associates," she persisted gently.

"I did not like the way in which my employers dealt with the Truax problem. When it was all over, I quit. Went into business for myself."

"As a bodyguard for hire?"

"I prefer to think of myself as a consultant." Harry leaned back in the booth and regarded her with his bottomless eyes. "I've answered your questions. Feel like answering some of mine?"

"Depends." She took a sip of her martini. "What do you want to know?"

"I didn't have time to get the whole story from Truax, but I got the impression that you were in that Candle Lake Manor place together with his client?"

"Yes."

He squinted a little, deeply curious. "How'd you end up there? Are you really crazy?"

She smiled. "You could say that. I had myself committed under a false name."

"Huh. Well, you must have had your reasons."

"My husband tried to murder me shortly before he disappeared with most of the assets in my portfolio. I had learned too much about his connections to some illegal activities. I was a loose end."

"Looks like he missed."

"Yes. He missed. But I was afraid that he would try again. So, I faked my own death, got a new identity, established a trust, and used it to have myself committed to Candle Lake Manor. After I escaped I used another new identity."

"Sounds complicated."

"It was."

"Why go through all that?"

"My husband is a very, very clever and extremely dangerous man. Too clever, perhaps, to buy my convenient death. I thought that if he was still trying to find me, a private psychiatric hospital would be the last place that he would look. The plan was to stay at the Manor for a few months and then disappear a second time. Figured two changes of identity would make it harder for him to track me."

"What went wrong?"

"Nothing at first. Candle Lake turned out to be pretty much what I had expected, a nice, remote place where rich folks stashed their embarrassing relatives. It wasn't hard to pretend to be clinically depressed and uncommunicative. They weren't into serious talk therapy there. Just meds. I flushed those down the toilet. Then I met Zoe."

"You two became buddies?"

"Yes. Unfortunately for Zoe, the chief shrink, Dr. McAlistair, took a personal interest in her. Wanted to study her. The result was that she was more closely watched than the rest of us. She had more trouble avoiding the meds than I did."

"But you two found a way out," Harry said.

"Yes."

"What's next?"

"I'm starting over," she replied.

Harry thought about that. "Me, too, I guess. But, then, Truax seems to have that effect on people."

"What do you mean?"

"I dunno. It's hard to explain. Just that if you get into his orbit, things change."

Luminous music flowed into the silence that followed his comment. When the piece was over, Harry looked at her with a long, considering expression.

"Must have been rough there at Candle Lake," he said.

"Zoe had to endure it much longer than I did. We escaped a couple of months after I arrived. She was there, on her own, for four months before that."

"Jesus. Six months."

"Yes."

"Must have left its mark."

"It did," she admitted. "On both of us. We've each dealt with it in our own ways."

"How's that?"

"Zoe signed up for self-defense lessons."

"What did you do?"

"Bought a gun."

Harry nodded. "Works for me."

Chapter Twenty-two

Shortly after midnight, Leon stood on the closed lid of the toilet in the cramped motel bathroom. Through the small window he had a clear view of the group gathering in the alley behind the old warehouses. The drug dealing seemed to be a nightly ritual. It didn't look like a tough crowd. For the most part, the buyers appeared to be teenagers who drifted over from the fast-food restaurant. They bought booze and pills from a couple of older guys who usually showed up around one in the morning.

Tonight Leon planned to arrive before the regular salesmen.

He stepped down heavily and hurried out into the main room. Earlier this afternoon, he had selected several bottles from his emergency stash of stolen Candle Lake meds. His job as security chief at the hospital had given him a good working knowledge of the street value of the pharmaceuticals.

He picked up the sack containing his

wares, a small flashlight, and his key. He paused to hang the tattered privacy sign on the doorknob outside his room and then he made his way down the steps and around to the rear of the building.

There was enough light from the motel parking lot to enable him to find the rutted, unpaved road that ran behind the abandoned house and the warehouses. The glow from a nearly full moon helped. He wanted to avoid using the flashlight if at all possible.

The half dozen or so little dears hanging out around the last decayed loading dock did not notice him until he was almost upon them. The first one who spotted him jumped half a foot.

"Shit, it's a cop."

"We're not doin' anything," another one said, voice rising in that annoying whine that was unique to the teenager of the species.

"Yeah, we gotta *right* to be here if we want."

Kids, Leon thought. *They might be flunking history, English, and math, but they always seemed to know their rights.*

"Relax, I'm not a cop," Leon said. "I've got some candy. Anyone interested?"

Ten minutes later and seven hundred fifty dollars richer, Leon started back toward the distant lights of the motel. *Seven hundred and fifty bucks.* Where the hell did kids these days get so much discretionary income? He'd sure never had that kind of cash when he was a teenager.

He had been planning to leave in the morning because he'd paid cash through tonight and he wanted to get his money's worth. But he was wide awake and in no mood to sleep. Might as well hit the road now. The seven-fifty would see him clear of Whispering Springs, and he had a feeling it would be good to be gone before Truax came back to check up on him.

Everything had gone sour. Again.

That bastard, Cleland, had not been *available* when he had called him a second time to negotiate for the woman's address. When Leon hung up the phone, he had faced the fact that the deal wasn't going to work. The only other angle, as far as he could see, was to try blackmailing Ian Harper. Harper was the one person left who had something to lose and who might be willing to pay for silence.

He would call his ex-boss from somewhere on the road and hope he'd get lucky. At least Harper was a businessman.

If only his original plan to blackmail the Cleland woman had worked the way it was supposed to. Shit. It was like he lived under some dark star or something.

Out of the corner of his eye, he caught the movement in the shadows that clung to the boarded-up house. One of the kids, he thought. Swell. He had some more candy. Maybe he could clear a neat thousand tonight.

He stopped and started to turn.

"Hey, kid. I got what you want right here."

Too late he realized that the figure on the sagging front porch was not a young druggie.

The first bullet took him square in the chest and knocked him down. His first thought was that he could no longer feel the fire of his heartburn. Instead, everything inside him had gone cold.

He was vaguely aware of one of his customers back at the warehouse shouting a warning to his pals.

"Oh, shit, that was a gun. Come on, we gotta get out of here."

He had come so close to the big score,

he thought. But he was screwed again. Story of his life.

He was already losing consciousness when the killer walked closer and put a second bullet into his brain.

Chapter Twenty-three

Zoe put on the white terry cloth robe monogrammed with the name of the hotel and sat in the chair near the window. She picked up the phone and dialed the first number.

"Who is this?" Ian Harper's voice was thick with sleep and irritation.

She could hear the television low in the background. Harper had evidently fallen asleep watching an old movie. A horror film, probably, one with a plot involving a mad scientist working in a lab.

"Hello, Dr. Harper," Zoe said. Just talking to him long distance on the telephone made her skin crawl. "I used to be Sara Cleland, but you can call me Zoe Truax now. You probably remember me as the patient in Room 232. The one Forrest Cleland paid you so well to keep locked up. I wanted to be the first to give you the happy news."

"Sara?" He was fully alert now. "What's this all about? Where are you?"

"I just got married. Say hello to my new husband."

Ethan was sitting on the edge of the bed, watching her. He was naked except for a pair of white briefs. She shoved the phone into his hand. He touched her fingers lightly as he took the instrument from her. She realized she was trembling. Rage and old fears, she thought. She had to get control of both.

"This is Truax," Ethan said into the phone. His voice was colder than the outer rings of hell. "Zoe and I just got married, and we've got a license to prove it. I'm now her next of kin. This call is a formality. I want to be sure you understand that if you try to snatch her I will come after her—and you—and rip apart your business operation there at Candle Lake Manor."

He ended the call and handed the phone back to Zoe.

She took a deep breath and dialed Forrest Cleland's unlisted home number.

Kimberley answered on the fourth ring. She sounded groggy and disoriented.

"Hello?"

"Kimberley, this is Sara."

"Sara?"

"Zoe, now. Zoe Truax."

"I don't understand. Where are you?

What's going on?" There was a slight pause. "Are you all right?"

"I'm doing great, Kimberley. Thanks for asking. I just got married, as a matter of fact. Naturally I wanted to give Forrest the wonderful news right away. Is he there?"

"You're married? But that's impossible. You're . . . you're not well, Sara."

"Call me Zoe. And get Forrest on the phone, please."

There was a brief pause. Zoe heard Kimberley's muffled voice in the background. Then Forrest came on the line.

"Sara? Is that you?"

"I'm no longer Sara Cleland," Zoe said. "Zoe Truax is my name, Forrest. I wanted to let you know that I will be attending the annual meeting and that I will be accompanied by my husband. If anything happens to me before the big day, you'll be delighted to hear that Ethan will be happy to vote my shares."

"What the hell is going on here? Where are you?"

"In a hotel. This is my wedding night."

"Listen to me," Forrest said in his most authoritative tones, "I need to talk to you."

"We can talk at the board meeting. Right now I'd like you to meet my husband."

Ethan took the phone from her a second time.

"This is Truax," he said. "I just spoke with Ian Harper at Candle Lake Manor and gave him the same message. It's real simple. Touch a hair on my wife's head, and I will take you apart."

He ended the call and put the phone down on the bedside table.

"That's that," he said. "Your insurance policy is now in effect."

She sat in her chair and looked at him. "I can't believe you did this for me."

He gave her his slow, sexy smile. "You will when you get the bill."

Chapter Twenty-four

She awoke to sunlight and the glint of gold on her finger. She could feel the heavy weight of Ethan's arm draped snugly around her waist. Mercifully, she had not dreamed last night. She wondered if that was a good omen.

She looked out through the window at the Las Vegas dawn and thought about another daybreak she had witnessed a year earlier. The memories of the escape from Candle Lake Manor rose to the surface.

"Shit," Ernie muttered. "What the hell's the matter with her? She was supposed to get an extra dose tonight."

"Maybe she didn't get enough of it." Ron's voice was low but there was no mistaking the sick lust that reverberated in it. "Don't worry, the restraints will hold her. I brought a needle full of the stuff with me, just in case."

There was another thud followed by a muffled groan. A fist rapped twice, quick, frantic little taps against her door, but she recognized the signal.

She sat straight up in bed, her heart pounding, a cold sweat chilling her skin.

"Use the damned needle," Ernie growled outside in the corridor. "She's too strong."

"It's no fun when they're too doped up to know what's happening. Come on, we can handle her."

She climbed out of bed and grabbed the light cotton robe with the words CANDLE LAKE MANOR stitched on the left breast pocket. Every patient got an identical robe and pair of slippers. There was no belt on the robe and no laces in the footwear.

She went to the door and pressed her ear to the panel. The orderlies had managed to drag their victim to the end of the hallway.

She waited until she was sure they had turned the corner before she went back to the bed and removed the stolen key card from the tiny slit in the bottom of the mattress.

She had obtained the card after weeks of careful observation and plotting. As she had explained to her friend, the plan hinged on the fact that the new orderly who worked the weekend nightshift on this ward had developed a drug habit that he fed by stealing patient meds. The stuff he didn't want to risk taking himself, he presumably sold on the street.

She had done such a good job of looking sedated whenever he showed up with her midnight pills that the orderly had been encouraged to steal some of the new pills that Dr. McAlistair had prescribed. The drugs were intended to induce a cheerful, trusting, euphoric state that McAlistair had hoped would overcome her patient's stubborn refusal to discuss screaming walls and crying rooms.

She had faked swallowing the first few doses and had been only too happy to watch through her lashes when the orderly began to pocket the pills.

She had bided her time. Finally, after five weekends of successful theft, the orderly had grown careless. One Saturday night, after helping himself to the contents of the little paper cup on her tray, he had hurried out of the room in response to a ringing call button and had forgotten to lock her door.

She had given him forty minutes and then she had crept out of the room and made her way down the hall. She had found the orderly smiling blissfully in front of a small television set inside the glass-walled nursing station.

She had pulled the fire alarm just outside the restroom. The orderly, enveloped in a drug-induced haze, had responded to the clanging bells like a confused bull confronted with a striped cape. In the ensuing chaos, it had been no trick at all to grab the spare master key kept in a desk drawer.

The next day she had told her new friend about the acquisition of the key, and they had begun to make detailed plans.

They had decided to make the break on a Sunday night because the weekend orderlies were inevitably more lax than the regular weekday staff.

But this was Thursday night. Ron and Ernie were on duty together. And they had her new friend, the woman with the silvery blue eyes.

She knew where they would take her: the examination room with the medical table fitted with metal stirrups, the room with the screaming walls.

So much for their plan to leave Sunday night, she thought. It would have to be tonight.

She took one last look around the space that had been her prison cell for the past few months. There was nothing worth taking. The personal effects and identification that had been with her when she had been brought to the Manor were locked up in a small room on the first floor.

She used the stolen card key to open her door very carefully. She stood listening for a few seconds. Silence echoed. The hall was empty.

She stepped out into the corridor. The lights were turned down at night but not off. She made her way quickly toward the corner, turned, and went down another intersecting hallway.

At the next junction, she paused again to listen. This section of the hospital did not house any patients, just offices and examination rooms that were supposed to be empty at night.

Muffled noises came from the screaming room. Ron and Ernie were already inside with her friend.

For an instant the fear was so thick that she thought she might succumb to nausea.

Then she moved, hitting the bank of switches at the end of the hall with both hands. The passage went dark but light still glowed beneath the door of the screaming room.

She hurried forward, moving carefully so as to make no sound. The slippers helped. When she reached the fire extinguisher locker, she opened it and grasped the canister in both hands.

She went to the door of the screaming room and banged the extinguisher against it.

"What the hell?" Ernie sounded alarmed.

"Must be one of the loonies," Ron said. "I'll take care of it."

The door of the screaming room opened. Ron took one step out into the hall.

It was at that moment that it occurred to her that her long run of abysmally lousy luck might have finally changed course.

Ron looked first to the left, not the right. He did not see her standing there with the heavy canister raised on high.

"Shit," Ron muttered. "Some crazy turned off the damned lights."

Ron was much taller than she was. She had to swing the extinguisher at an awkward angle, not straight down as she would have much preferred to do. Nevertheless, the heavy canister struck the back of Ron's skull with a satisfying thunk.

He dropped to the floor without a sound.

"What's going on?"

Ernie appeared in the doorway, mouth agape. "What the fuck?"

She pulled the trigger on the fire extinguisher, releasing a gusher of white foam. The stuff caught Ernie full in the face.

He yelped and staggered backward, clawing at his eyes. The fact that he had already unfastened his pants in preparation for rape created a real problem for him.

His feet got tangled in his sagging trousers, and he went down hard. He opened his mouth to yell, and she filled it with foam. Choking, Ernie struggled to breathe.

Sensations stormed through her when she moved into the examination room. She struggled to ignore the psychic noise and raised the canister a second time, preparing to bring it down on Ernie's head.

Her friend was struggling frantically with the restraints. She had managed to rip off her gag. "Help me."

She rushed to the table and unbuckled the leather ties that bound her feet into the stirrups.

Ernie reached out, trying to grab a chair. She turned back, hoisting the extinguisher.

"Wait."

Her friend grabbed a syringe off the desk and plunged the needle into Ernie's arm. The orderly moaned, gasped, and sagged.

"I gave him the full dose. He won't wake up for a while. Let's get out of here."

They took the time to drag Ron back

into the screaming room and locate his car keys. Then they closed and locked the door. They fled to the first floor using the key card to access the emergency stairwells.

The lockers containing the patients' personal effects were located in Leon Grady's office. The magic card key did not work on that lock but it opened the door labeled HOUSEKEEPING AND JANITORIAL SERVICES across the hall. The key to Grady's office was hanging on a hook in the janitorial supply cabinet.

Once inside Security, they found the lockers. The little padlocks that secured them were so flimsy they could have been broken with one of the tools in the janitorial closet, but in the end there was no need to go to the trouble. The keys to the lockers were in one of Grady's desk drawers.

The locker with her name on it opened easily enough. Inside was the handbag she had been carrying the night she had been brought into Candle Lake Manor. To her enormous relief, her wallet, containing her driver's license and some other miscellaneous pieces of identification were still inside. The cash and credit cards had been removed. Those, she knew, had been turned over to Forrest the day she had been admitted. It was standard procedure. But occasionally there was need for a patient's ID, so such documents were retained.

"The credit cards wouldn't do you any good, anyway," her friend reminded her. "You couldn't use them. Too easy to trace."

Outside in the chill of a moonless night, they had climbed into Ron's car. They had driven it to a small house on the outskirts of a tiny mountain town.

"Who owns this place?" she asked her friend.

"I do. Under another name. By the way, from now on you can call me Arcadia."

"Nice name."

"Thanks. I found it in a name-the-baby book."

Arcadia pried up a loose board on the porch and removed a key. She used it to open the door of the house.

Inside the postage-stamp-sized living room, she removed a wall panel to reveal a safe. After working the combination, she took out a packet of documents.

"What's that?"

"A new ID," Arcadia said.

"I'm impressed. You had this all planned before you were sent to Xanadu, didn't you?"

"Yes."

"But, why?"

"It's a long story." Arcadia started toward the front door. "I'll tell it to you after we change cars."

"You've got another car hidden somewhere?"

"In the garage."

The following morning, Arcadia had accessed an offshore account.

"We need a little time to set up a new background for you," she said. "What do you say we take a little vacation?"

"I've heard that travel is broadening . . ."

Ethan raised himself up off the pillows and bent his head to kiss her bare shoulder. "You okay?"

"Yes." She turned onto her back and looked up at him.

Her husband.

He smiled. She felt the tingle all the way to her toes. His face was shadowed with his morning beard, and his hair was rumpled. He was just as compelling in the light of day as he was at midnight. And he was all hers. For a while.

"What were you thinking about?" he asked.

"The escape from Xanadu."

"Tell me about it," he said.

He already knew most of it. He had a right to the rest.

She told him the whole story.

His eyes went cold. "Did those two orderlies ever drag you into that examination room?"

"No. I think they decided that I was too unpredictable in my craziness. They never knew how I would react to the meds."

His smile was coldly approving. "You fostered that impression of unpredictability, I take it?"

"Oh, sure, every chance I got." She stroked her fingers through his hair. "I got rather good at playing the madwoman of Room 232. The orderlies avoided me."

He brushed his mouth across her lips. "I

am very happy to hear that. Otherwise, I would have had to add two more items to my to-do list."

She shivered at the expression that came and went in his eyes.

"I can't take all of the credit for scaring off Ron and Ernie," she said. "They also knew that Dr. McAlistair was particularly interested in my case. They couldn't be sure what I might tell her in a therapy session or what she would choose to believe. She could have easily gotten them both fired."

"McAlistair. That name rings a bell."

"She was the doctor who supervised my so-called treatment plan."

"Right." He looked thoughtful. "According to Singleton, McAlistair is the only real doctor at Candle Lake. She must have her hands full. Why did she take a special interest in you?"

"Officially, I landed in Xanadu because Forrest told everyone that I heard voices in the walls at the cabin telling me that he was the person who had murdered Preston."

"Any of that true?" Ethan asked neutrally.

"Of course not. I don't hear voices." *Just feelings and emotions.* But he wouldn't like that explanation any better, she figured. "I think Dr. McAlistair wanted to believe that I could somehow walk into a room and sense things, though."

"Why?"

"One day during a session, I noticed some paperwork on her desk. It was from the police chief of a small town not far from Candle Lake. The letter thanked her for her consulting services on a recent murder case and said that a check was enclosed."

"What kind of consulting did she do for them?"

"McAlistair saw me looking at the letter and told me that she occasionally did psychological profiles for small police departments."

"Well, hell. She figured that if you really did hear voices in the walls, you might be useful to her, is that it?"

"I think she understood that I didn't hear voices," Zoe said, choosing her words carefully. "But she has a professional interest in the biological basis of human intuition. She's even written some papers on the subject. I think she wondered very seriously if perhaps I might have some sort of extremely sensitive intuition that might be useful at crime scenes. It was nonsense, naturally, but she's really into that kind of thing."

"You think she figured maybe she could use you as an assistant?"

"Either that, or she was simply curious in the academic sense. All I know for sure is that she was constantly testing me. She was always asking me to write down my impressions of a room. She used to experiment with some of my meds, trying to see if certain drugs could boost my sensitivity."

"Sounds like she should have been a patient at the Manor, not the doctor in charge."

"I pretended to swallow the pills." *Most of the time.*

But there had been those two occasions when the meds had been ground up and slipped into her food. Old panic sleeted through her veins. She remembered how she had come to her senses both times in a screaming room with McAlistair standing nearby, urging her to report what she felt.

She pushed the memories aside and saw that Ethan was watching her with a disturbingly intent expression.

"What's the matter?" she asked, trying to lighten the atmosphere. "Worried that you might actually be married to a crazy woman?"

"No," he said. "But it does occur to me that Ian Harper and Forrest Cleland might not be the only ones who had a good reason to keep you locked up at Candle Lake Manor."

A chill ran down her spine. "You may be right. But it doesn't matter now."

"No." He lowered his mouth to hers. "It doesn't matter now."

Chapter Twenty-five

They arrived back in Whispering Springs shortly after three that afternoon. Ethan drove straight to the motel where Leon Grady had rented a room. The phone call he had made as soon as the plane touched down had set off alarm bells. According to Stagg, all was well on this end, but Grady was still registered under a phony name at the Sunrise Suites.

That didn't make sense. He knew Grady's kind. The blackmailer should have cut his losses and been long gone by now.

Zoe sat tensely in the seat beside him. "I can't believe he had the gall to stick around after you told him that there was no way I would pay blackmail. Do you think he came up with another plan? Something to do with Arcadia?"

"He hasn't made any move to contact her according to Stagg, so I think we can assume he isn't aware that she's here in Whispering Springs." Ethan pulled into the motel parking lot.

"Maybe he decided to wait and see if we actually went through with the marriage."

"I didn't think I'd left him in any doubt." He switched off the engine. "But if that's the case, our shiny new license should convince him."

Zoe unclasped her seatbelt. "You know something? I'm glad he stuck around. I'm looking forward to confronting that slimy little worm face-to-face. I've got a few things I want to say to him."

"Might be better if you let me handle this—"

But it was too late. She was already out of the car.

Resigned, he climbed out from behind the wheel and caught up with her just as she started up the steps to the upper level. They reached the landing and walked toward 210. The drapes in 208 fluttered a little. Ethan heard the muffled chatter of a television commercial inside the room.

Zoe glanced back over her shoulder. "Room 210, you said?"

"Yeah." He saw the privacy sign dangling from the doorknob. "Looks like he isn't in the mood to receive visitors."

"Tough." She came to a halt and rapped sharply on the door.

Her enthusiasm for taking on Grady would have been amusing if it weren't for the fact that this whole scene felt very wrong.

There was no response to Zoe's knock. Ethan watched the closed drapes. They did not shift.

"He's probably over at the restaurant, feeding his face," Zoe said.

A bored-looking maid rumbled toward them with her cart.

"Excuse me," Zoe said. "Have you cleaned this room yet?"

"Nope, he hasn't taken the sign down," the woman grumbled. "Far as I'm concerned, I don't care if he never opens that door. Been here almost a week and he ain't tipped yet, even though he paid the manager cash in advance. Doesn't look like the type who'll leave so much as a buck when he checks out."

"We'd like to take a quick look inside that room," Ethan said.

"Can't let you do that," the woman said. "Room's rented and the privacy sign's out. Can't go in as long as the sign's out, y'know. Only the manager can open it when they put that sign on the doorknob."

Ethan reached for his wallet and pulled out a few bills. He folded them in half. "We're a little concerned about our friend. We just want to make sure he didn't collapse or something."

The woman eyed the bills. "I dunno. Not supposed to go in when the sign's up."

Zoe deftly removed the privacy sign and held it behind her back. "There's no sign now."

The maid examined the doorknob. "Damn, you're right."

Ethan shoved the money into her hand. She pocketed the cash with a swift, efficient movement and hefted her key ring.

"Just a quick look," she said.

"Of course," Zoe agreed.

The maid knocked once and then opened the door and peered into the room.

"Housekeeping," she called loudly.

Her wariness gave Ethan the impression that she'd had a few bad experiences opening doors in the course of her career in the lodging business.

For his part, he relaxed a little when he caught a whiff of the air inside the room.

There was a stale, musty odor tinged with the underlying scent of the strong cleaning agent the maid used in the bathroom, but that was all. He realized he had been braced for something worse. He'd had some unpleasant experiences opening doors in his career, too.

The maid stepped back and did a quick survey of the balcony, looking left and right. Satisfied that she was not being observed by the manager, she made a shooing motion.

"Hurry up, take your look. Be quick about it."

Ethan was already inside the room, slipping on a pair of thin plastic gloves. Behind him, Zoe hesitated briefly and then followed.

"Don't touch anything," he said over his shoulder.

She glanced at his gloved hands and raised her brows. "I won't."

Not much had changed since the last time he'd been here, he thought. He rifled rapidly through the contents of Grady's brown duffel bag and found only dirty shirts and socks. The closet was empty. A couple of plastic containers bearing the logo of the fast-food restaurant next door were the only items in the trash.

"My file," Zoe said, sounding outraged.

He looked at her. She stood near the table, examining some papers she had taken out of a manila folder. He could tell that she was furious.

"Thought I told you not to touch anything," he reprimanded.

She ignored him. "That bastard must have copied it before he left the Manor."

"Put it in your purse and don't touch anything else." He went down on one knee to check under the bed. A herd of dust bunnies peeked back at him.

The maid glanced through the doorway. "You gotta leave now," she hissed. "You said you just wanted to make sure your friend wasn't hurt."

"We're on our way." He did a quick survey of the grimy bathroom. Grady's kit bag contained nothing more interesting than a razor, a small can of shaving cream, a comb, and some aged condoms.

He turned away from the bath and followed Zoe out of the room. The maid closed the door very quickly, grabbed the handle of her cart and trundled off without a word of farewell.

Ethan and Zoe went the opposite way, back toward the rear stairs.

Zoe watched him strip the gloves off his hands. "Where did you get those?"

"There was a time when a well-dressed gentleman would not have even considered going out into public without a pair of gloves."

"You're just a throwback to an earlier, more genteel era, is that it?"

"Someone has to try to uphold standards."

"A noble endeavor." She looked at the restaurant. Her mouth tightened. "I'll bet he's over there."

"Maybe." Ethan looked at Grady's car, still parked below the balcony. "Can't see him walking very far. He didn't strike me as the type who worried about getting enough exercise."

The curtain in the window of 208 fluttered when they went past. Ethan caught a glimpse of a face behind the glass.

"Hang on." He stopped and knocked.

The door opened immediately. A cloud of cigarette smoke gushed from the room. A short, bald little man wearing a stained tee shirt and a pair of red-and-white spotted boxer shorts looked out. The front of the shorts gaped wide.

The man had a cigarette in one hand. It was obvious that he had not bothered to shave for the past couple of days.

"You're looking for the guy in 210, aren't you?" he asked cheerfully. "Heard you talk your way past the maid. Pretty slick."

"Have you seen him?" Ethan asked. He was conscious of Zoe looking away from the open front of the boxers.

"How much did you give the maid?" the little man demanded.

Ethan reached for his wallet again and pulled out more cash. He put the money into the outstretched palm. "About half this much."

"Yeah?" The little man stuck the cigarette into the side of his mouth and counted the money. He seemed satisfied. "He went out last night around midnight. Never came back."

"Out?" Zoe frowned. "In a car?"

"Nope. No car. Just went downstairs and went around behind the building. Never came back."

"You're sure it was the man in 210?" Ethan asked.

"Hell, yes, I'm sure. Only the two of us on this floor most of the past week. I rent by the month and I keep an eye on things. Can't be too careful."

The little man took a step back and closed the door abruptly.

Ethan and Zoe went down the rear stairs.

"Gee, you sure get to meet a lot of interesting people in your business, don't you?" Zoe said.

"You didn't think the boxers were a fashion statement?"

"I will never be able to look at a pair of boxer shorts the same way again."

At the bottom of the steps, Ethan turned and went toward the rear of the motel.

Zoe hurried after him. "Where are you going?"

"According to the local block watch captain up there in 208, Grady walked off behind the motel around midnight and never returned. Thought it might be interesting to see if there's any indication that he met someone back here."

She studied the rutted road that ran behind the motel. "You could meet someone secretly behind that boarded-up house or at those old warehouses."

"Let's see if we can find anything."

They walked toward the abandoned house. Ethan took a closer look at it. The windows were covered with sheets of plywood, but the door was partially open. It sagged on rusty hinges.

Should have been closed, he thought. Maybe kids used it as a club house.

He left the road and walked toward the front porch. Zoe followed, wrinkling her nose.

"What on earth is that odor?" she asked.

Ethan was already at the porch, looking at the body that lay just around the corner.

"That odor is the smell of things getting a lot more complicated," Ethan said. "We can stop looking for Leon Grady. Someone else found him first."

Chapter Twenty-six

Early that evening they sat together in Ethan's office.

"I don't get it," Harry Stagg said. "You told the cops the guy had tried to blackmail Zoe, and they still went with the idea that he got shot because he was poaching on another dealer's turf?"

"That's their working theory at the moment," Ethan said.

Zoe exchanged glances with Arcadia, who was sitting in one of the extra chairs Ethan had dragged into his office from the outer room. Arcadia looked as cool as ever, but there was something different about her today. Zoe couldn't put her finger on it, but she knew it had to do with the thin man with the ancient eyes who sat beside her.

They had gathered in Ethan's office following the long session with the police. Ethan had offered coffee. It was good coffee, Zoe thought, but she might have made a serious mistake in drinking some. Her level of tension was already several notches into the red zone.

"I think that, for a while there, Detective Ramirez was looking at me with some serious interest," she said. "He certainly wasn't quite as friendly as he was the last time. But as soon as Ethan informed him that we had a perfect alibi, he came up with his dope dealer scenario. Apparently those old warehouses have recently become a hangout for some of the local kids who experiment."

"Getting married at the time of the murder is one of the better cover stories I've heard in a while," Harry said. "You got witnesses and everything."

"And the staff at the hotel will probably remember us well," Ethan said. "We asked for a room change."

Arcadia glanced at Zoe with a questioning expression.

"The first room had a round bed with a mirror in the ceiling," Zoe said.

Arcadia nodded. "Of course you had to ask for a change."

"Why's that?" Harry asked. "A mirror in the ceiling sounds real nice. You don't see that kind of thing a lot. Leastwise not in the type of places where I usually stay."

"For a very good reason," Zoe said. "It's tacky. Also, in an earthquake zone, it constitutes a serious hazard."

"Las Vegas is in an earthquake zone?" Harry asked with great interest. "Never heard that."

Ethan propped his feet on the corner of his desk. "I didn't have a problem with the decor, myself, but Zoe didn't care for it so we got moved. Bottom line is that our alibi is really rock solid. Which leaves the cops with the dope dealer scenario."

"Is it plausible?" Arcadia asked.

"To be fair, it does make some sense," Ethan allowed. "The cops rounded up a couple of the kids who have a rep for being into the local drug scene, and they admitted that a guy matching Grady's description had approached them around midnight and offered to sell them some of what he said were real prescription drugs."

"They turned him down, naturally," Zoe said dryly.

Harry snorted. "Of course. Just said no, huh?"

Ethan shrugged. "Sure. But under a little questioning, they admitted that they heard sounds that might have been gunshots right after the stranger left them. Said shots came from the vicinity of the old house. They didn't report the gunfire because they weren't sure that's what it was."

"Also, the police found several bottles of various kinds of psychoactive meds in a sack that was found next to Grady's body and more bottles in the trunk of his car," Zoe concluded. "I'll bet he stole them from Candle Lake."

"There was a lot of that kind of theft there," Arcadia said thoughtfully. "So the drug dealer theory is at least somewhat viable."

Ethan looked at Harry. "Not to be indelicate, but just out of curiosity, how good is your story?"

It took Zoe a second or two to absorb the implications of that question. When they hit her, she choked on a swallow of coffee.

"Ethan," she sputtered. "You're not suggesting that Harry . . . that he . . ."

"Just asking," Ethan assured her.

"Don't worry." Arcadia reached over and slapped her lightly on the back. "Our alibi is every bit as solid as yours. The kids heard shots around midnight? Harry and I went to the Last Exit last night. We didn't leave until two, and we've got the bar tab to prove it."

"Oh," Zoe said. "Oh, good."

"The jazz was very fine," Harry added.

"Did the police want to know why you were being blackmailed?" Arcadia asked Zoe.

"Sure," Zoe said. "And we gave them a streamlined version of the truth. I told them that I had spent some time in a private hospital where Grady had worked and that I was anxious not to have that very personal medical information made public to potential clients. The detective was very understanding. We did not mention you, of course."

Ethan examined the tips of his shoes. "There was no reason not to give the cops some of the facts about Zoe. Hell, the more people that know she's married, the better. There was also no reason to drag your name into this mess, Arcadia. But I think it might be a good idea for you and Harry to leave town for a few days."

Arcadia frowned. "Why?"

"As far as we know, Leon Grady was not aware of your new identity. With luck that means that no one else knows you're here in Whispering Springs, either. But at this point we can't be certain of that conclusion."

"He's right," Harry said to Arcadia. "It makes sense to get out of town for a while, at least until Truax figures out what's going on here. He needs to find out for sure who killed Grady."

Arcadia raised her brows. "Is that what you're going to do, Truax? Investigate Grady's murder?"

"Yeah," Ethan said. "I think so. I want to be certain that the cops are right about him getting whacked by a dealer."

"But who else would have a motive?" Arcadia asked.

"Hell, the guy was a blackmailer," Harry pointed out. "Blackmailers always have lots of enemies."

"What about Zoe?" Arcadia asked Ethan. "Will she be safe?"

"My cover is already blown, as they say," Zoe pointed out. "But it doesn't matter anymore. Now that I'm a respectably married woman, hauling me off to Xanadu wouldn't do anyone any good."

"Don't worry," Ethan said. "Zoe will be

staying with me out at Nightwinds at night until this is finished."

Zoe lowered her mug. "I will?"

"Yes," Ethan said deliberately. "You will. I'll take you to work and stay with you as much as possible. I can do some of my research from your office. When I can't be there, I'll make sure you have company. I don't want you to be alone until I've tied up some of the loose ends."

"But according to your theory, I should be okay now that we're married."

"Something is screwy with this situation and I'm not going to take chances," Ethan said.

Zoe opened her mouth to protest.

"Good," Arcadia said before Zoe could manage a single word. "I like that approach."

"I'm glad somebody does," Ethan said. "These are just extra precautions. I do think Zoe is reasonably safe now, but I'd rather she didn't go running around on her own until I get some answers."

"But I've got a couple of appointments with clients at their residences," Zoe said quickly.

"Can you ask them to meet you in your office?"

"Well, maybe."

"Try. If that's impossible, let me know your schedule. I'll escort you to and from the appointments."

She made a face. "I'm not sure this is necessary."

"Trust me, it's necessary, if only for my peace of mind." Ethan turned back to Arcadia. "But it would simplify things if you and Harry disappeared for a while."

"I suppose my assistant could handle the gallery," Arcadia said reluctantly. "Where do you think we should go?"

"Already got a destination in mind." Harry pushed himself out of the chair. "How does New Orleans sound?"

Arcadia looked at him for a long moment. "It sounds . . . interesting."

"Guess we'd better pack," Harry said.

Arcadia rose and walked out of the office with him.

Zoe listened to the sound of their footsteps disappearing down the stairs. She looked at Ethan.

"What is going on with those two?" she asked.

"Don't ask me. The relationship between a bodyguard and his client is confidential."

"Is that a rule from your private detective manual?"

"How'd you guess?"

At nine-thirty that night, he stood in the doorway of his study and watched Zoe examine the titles of some of the books on the shelves.

"Journals, diaries, and records of old murder cases." She pulled a plastic envelope off a shelf, opened it, and removed a slender pamphlet. *"A True Account of the Murder of Harriet Plummer Including a Narrative of the Trial of her Killer, John Strand."* She looked up. "The date is 1870."

"Harriet was a San Francisco prostitute who was killed by one of her clients. Notice the elegant bed in the illustration? Complete with rumpled quilt and lots of fancy pillows? That was the artist's not-so-subtle way of stressing the lady's profession and the sexual undercurrents."

"People bought these pamphlets?"

"Accounts of murders and the trials that followed were very popular throughout the eighteenth and nineteenth centuries. The more lurid, the better, as far as the public was concerned."

"The ones involving sex sold best?"

"Sure." He folded his arms and leaned against the door frame. "Some things never change."

She put the pamphlet back into the plastic container and replaced it on the shelf. "Did they hang John Strand?"

"Yes. Which was, according to my research, a serious miscarriage of justice."

"You don't think he was guilty?"

"Strand was a violent man, prone to fits of rage. He was probably guilty of someone's death, but not Harriet's."

"Who killed her?"

"I think the most likely suspect was a man named George Edward Kingston. He was one of Harriet's regulars, a wealthy, self-made man who planned to marry into a socially prominent family."

"Why do you think he murdered her?"

"She became inconvenient, as they say. I got hold of some letters that Harriet wrote to a friend. She was pregnant and she was sure Kingston was the father. She was furious with him because he was going to end their affair. She threatened to expose the relationship."

"So he killed her."

"I think so, yes. Kingston was worried that his wealthy fiancée might drop him if she and her family learned that he had had a long-standing connection with a known prostitute. There's no way to be absolutely certain at this late date." He paused, searching for the words to explain the silent click of certainty and the rush of satisfaction he felt when he saw the pattern and discovered the answers. "But it feels right."

She watched him closely. "It *feels* right?"

"Kingston as the killer ties up all the loose ends, at least as far as I'm concerned." He came away from the door frame and walked to the desk. "But it doesn't matter anymore. Everyone involved has been dead and gone for a long time."

"Do you do this a lot?"

He lounged against the desk. "Investigate old murders? Yeah. Something to do in the evenings besides watch TV."

"Talk about cold cases." She surveyed the contents of the room. "All of these books and journals and pamphlets and newspapers, they're part of your research library?"

"Yes."

"Why do you do it?"

"Probably because I'm good at it." He paused. "And there's no harm done if I'm wrong."

"Because there's no one left to care about getting the answers?"

"Right. Just an academic exercise." He angled his chin toward the computer. "I'm not the only one who does this. There are others. We write up our investigation reports and post them for people to read and examine."

"Who looks up the results online?"

"We attract a lot of genealogists and people who are interested in their family histories. The site also pulls in a fair number of historians and academics who study the psychological and social issues involved in murder."

"And probably a few weirdos, too."

"Sure. The world is full of weirdos."

She glanced over her shoulder, down the hall toward the theater, and then she looked at him. "I assume you're investigating the death of Camelia Foote?"

"Be hard to ignore it, given that I'm living here at Nightwinds."

"The official story is that she fell to her death in the canyon, right?"

He nodded. "There were rumors at the time that her husband might have pushed her, but nothing was ever proven and the authorities did not go out of their way to pursue the investigation."

"Do you think she was the victim of domestic violence?"

"It's very possible." He picked up the Foote journal. "This is her husband's journal. According to what I've read, he feared that she was having an affair with a man named Jeremy Hill. He was outraged because she invited Hill to a large weekend house party here at Nightwinds. The place was filled with guests. Camelia died sometime during the first night. Her body was found in the morning."

"Who found it?"

He was impressed. "Good question."

"I've heard that the police always take a close look at whoever discovers the body. I know they certainly asked me a lot of questions that day when I found Preston."

"It's very often the killer who reports the

murder. And it could well be that is what happened here." He opened the journal to one of the last entries. "Foote found Camelia that morning. Here's what he wrote a few weeks later.

> ". . . I still cannot believe that she is lost to me, all of her beauty, charm and spirit extinguished forever. I walk through the house and see her lovely, laughing ghost everywhere I turn, mocking me . . ."

"Sounds like an inconsolable husband," Zoe said softly.

"I think he was distraught, all right." He closed the journal. "But the part about the lovely, laughing ghost mocking him is interesting."

"Do you think Foote was suffering pangs of guilt and that he believed Camelia was haunting him?"

"Maybe. I haven't finished the journal yet."

"You've got some doubts?"

"A few, yes." He put the journal down on the desk and scooped up the notebook in which he had written his observations concerning the Foote case. "There is some confusion with the time line. Camelia was very visible off and on throughout the evening until sometime around midnight. No one recalls seeing her after that. But earlier Camelia and Hill had disappeared together for a while. Foote notes in his journal that he saw them returning to the house. He was sure they had made love."

"Did Foote confront them?"

"According to his journal, he was so depressed by the knowledge that he could not compete with Hill for his wife's affections that he went to his bedroom and finished off a bottle of scotch. He remembers nothing more until he awoke the next morning, went for a walk to clear his head and found Camelia's body."

"His claim that he had passed out in a drunken stupor and slept until the next day does sound like a convenient excuse."

"Could be. Or it could be the truth. None of the servants saw him after he went into his bedroom. No one recalls seeing Camelia after midnight."

"If Foote didn't come out of his bedroom until the following morning, that leaves you with all the house guests as suspects."

"I don't think so," he said, "I think it leaves

Jeremy Hill as a definite possibility. The problem is that although Camelia vanished from the party, Hill was seen by many people throughout the course of the evening until the household finally went to bed around three. But he must have gone out a second time because one of the servants saw him return to the house through the gardens shortly before dawn. Hill was alone. Said he'd gone for a walk."

"The lover. Why would he murder her?"

"Because he wanted her very much," he said quietly. "And she refused to leave her rich husband for him. But like I said, there's a problem with the time line. The only two people who are missing from the party at the same time are Camelia and Abner Foote."

"That settles it. I'm betting it was the husband. Such a common pattern." She studied him. "How will you ever get at the truth?"

"Jeremy Hill married a couple of years after Camelia died. Evidently he drank heavily. His wife divorced him and later remarried. Hill fell ill and died a short time after the divorce leaving no offspring. I'm trying to find some of his ex-wife's descendents to see if there are any letters or journals that might shed some light on her first marriage. I'm also trying to find some letters written by people who were guests here that night."

"Good heavens, you could spend months or years tracking down the facts."

"There's no hurry," he said.

"But it's worth it, isn't it?"

He shrugged. "Like I said, it's something to do in the evenings."

"No." She looked at him with deep, knowing eyes. "It's a lot more than that. It's a calling." She walked to where he stood and touched his jaw with her fingertips. "When you do get the answers, you create a little justice. You balance some invisible scales somewhere. Even if no one knows or cares, you've done a good thing, Ethan."

She understood, he thought. His hobby intrigued some people and repelled others. A few took an academic interest in it. But until now he had never met anyone who understood deep down why he investigated the coldest of cold cases.

She raised her mouth and kissed him. He put his arms around her.

He heard the click and felt the rush.

Chapter Twenty-seven

The screams in the walls pierced the drug-induced fog in which she had been drifting all morning. She stopped abruptly, digging in her heels. Frantically she tried to get her bearings.

There was an open door in front of her. Dr. McAlistair had a hand on her shoulder, urging her to enter the room. To her right, a burly-looking man in a uniform watched her with a grim expression. She had a vague recollection of someone having addressed him as sheriff.

"No, please," she whispered. "I don't want to go in there."

"It's all right," Dr. McAlistair said. "You're not alone. I'm here with you."

"No." She tried to escape the hand on her shoulder. Dr. McAlistair tightened her grip.

"You only have to enter the room for a couple of minutes," Venetia McAlistair said coaxingly. "Just step inside and look around. Tell me what you sense."

"No."

The man in the uniform scowled. "I don't know about this, Doc. She seems real upset. You sure you need her input?"

"I'm extremely interested in her reactions to the crime scene."

"She looks like she's gonna be sick. I don't need her messing up the evidence."

"She'll be all right. The drugs I gave her should keep her reasonably calm."

"She doesn't look calm to me," the sheriff said.

Damn right, I'm not calm. She opened her mouth and shrieked.

"Stop it," Dr. McAlistair shook her. "Stop it. You're losing control."

Whatever. Anything to keep from having to enter that room.

She screamed louder.

"Get her out of here," the sheriff snapped. "I haven't got time for this."

Dr. McAlistair reluctantly guided her back toward the car.

She continued to scream. It seemed to be having the desired effect. McAlistair was taking her away from the house with the shrieking walls and that was all that mattered.

"Stop it," McAlistair said, furious now. "Stop it immediately, do you understand?"

"Zoe, stop it. Wake up. You're dreaming."

She came awake in the middle of a muffled sob, opened her eyes, and saw Ethan leaning over her. Perspiration was growing cold on her body. She could feel her heart racing. It took her a few frantic seconds to remember where she was. Then she saw the silhouette of a giant swan wing.

Oh, damn. Another nightmare. At this rate, he was going to conclude that she really was a basket case.

She sat up, clutching the sheet. "Sorry. I told you this might be a problem. If I'm going to stay here with you, I'd better sleep in one of the other bedrooms."

"I don't want you sleeping in another room." He levered himself up against the pillows, reached out, and pulled her into his arms. "I want you in my bed. What was the dream?"

"Just another bad one from the days when I was locked up. Trust me, you don't want to hear the details."

"Yes, I do. Tell me about it."

Maybe it was because it was the middle of the night and he had not turned on the lights. Maybe it was because he had made slow, passionate love to her before they fell asleep. Maybe it was because he had told her about his hobby and she had looked into some deep places inside him that she sensed he did not reveal very often.

Maybe she just needed to talk to someone about the dream.

"I told you there was a doctor who took a special interest in my case."

"McAlistair. The one who did some consulting work for some of the small-town cops in the area and tried to find out if you could do the woo-woo thing at crime scenes."

She winced. "You've got a good memory."

"This McAlistair was in your dream?"

"Yes. The dream was about an incident that happened while I was at Xanadu. McAlistair was consulting on a murder case. She managed to sneak some meds into my food that morning and then she drove me out to the house where the crime had been committed. Tried to make me go into the room where two people had been murdered. I balked."

"Understandable."

"She tried to force me to go inside. Told me I had to learn to control my anxiety."

"As if not wanting to enter a room where people had been murdered was just some kind of normal phobia. Something to get past."

"Yes. Anyhow, the sheriff was afraid that I might throw up all over his crime scene. When I started screaming, he ordered Dr. McAlistair to take me away. I could tell that she was very frustrated and angry but she drove me back to the Manor."

"The sheriff ever find the killer?"

In spite of the fact that her pulse was still trotting along at a brisk clip and her breathing had not yet returned to normal, she smiled. She should have expected that question, she thought. Ethan liked answers. More than that, he *needed* them.

"I saw a newspaper in the hospital library a few days later," she said. "There was a picture of the house and a headline about an ex-husband having been picked up on suspicion of murder."

"Did Dr. McAlistair ever try to pull that kind of stunt again?"

"One other time. With the same results. I started screaming and I kept on screaming until the cops ordered her to take me away. After that, I think she realized I wasn't going to respond to that sort of therapy."

"It wasn't therapy. She was trying to use you."

"Uh-huh."

He settled himself more comfortably against the pillows. "I don't like McAlistair, but I can't see that she has a motive for killing Grady."

She sighed. "You've got a one-track mind, you know that? What does my dream about McAlistair have to do with finding Grady's killer?"

"Nothing probably. I'm just trying to make connections. My gut tells me that Grady's murder relates to your situation." He slid one hand down her arm to her hip. "Think you can get back to sleep or shall we go for warm milk?"

She kissed his bare chest. "I've got a better idea."

"Yeah?"

She kissed him again, closer to his firm,

flat belly, and moved her hand down the front of his body. He was hard and heavy.

"Yeah," she said.

He shoved his fingers through her hair.

"Definitely a very good idea," he said. "Best I can remember in a long time."

She took him into her mouth.

"*Excellent* idea."

His hands clenched fiercely in her hair.

She felt him go hard and tight.

And then he was hauling her up alongside him, rolling her onto her back. When he entered her, she was ready for him. She wrapped herself around him and hung on for dear life.

Chapter Twenty-eight

At eleven o'clock the following morning, Zoe put down the pencil she was using to make a sketch of a living room layout for a client and looked at Bonnie.

"You must be getting pretty bored," she said.

Bonnie closed the romance novel that she had been reading and smiled. "Don't worry, I'm not bored. Actually, it's rather pleasant to spend some time with another adult female. I haven't had a chance to meet too many people yet here in Whispering Springs."

"It's always hard moving into a new community."

"I'm getting involved with some activities at my sons' school and that helps. But what I'd really like to do is find an interesting part-time job. Financially, we're okay, thanks to my husband's insurance policy. But I need to get out of the house more."

"Trust me, I understand. Got any ideas?"

"Before I married, I worked as a librarian,"

Bonnie said. "I've been out of the field for a while, but I'm going to submit an application to the Whispering Springs Public Library and also to the local community college library."

"Sounds like a plan," Zoe said.

"How did you get into the interior design business? Were you a designer before Forrest Cleland shipped you off to Candle Lake Manor?"

"No, I got a degree in fine arts. I was working in a small art museum when I met Preston. He had a special interest in a particular painter we both admired and asked some questions. The next thing I knew—" She stopped.

"You were in love and making plans for a wedding," Bonnie concluded.

"Yes."

"That's how it was for Drew and me, too." Bonnie sighed wistfully. "The first year after he was gone was hell. But in the past few months, I've noticed that I'm starting to think of my marriage as an event that happened a long time ago."

"Another lifetime."

"Yes. It would have been so difficult without Ethan. Especially for the boys."

Zoe fiddled with her pencil.

Bonnie watched her doodle for a moment.

"You're wondering why Ethan and I never moved beyond our current relationship, aren't you?" she asked.

Zoe cleared her throat. "You do seem very close, and his affection for Jeff and Theo is obvious."

"Ethan and I will always be good friends, but that is all we will be."

"You sound very sure of that."

"Some things you know from the start. I think of him almost as the big brother I never had. It works both ways. Ethan views me as a sort of sister, not a potential wife." Bonnie glanced at the photos of Nightwinds. "Did you take those?"

"Yes. I was out walking with my camera that day."

"Great shots. The house looks like it exists in a parallel universe. Very otherworldly. Do you do portraits?"

"Not professionally. Photography is just a hobby."

"Much more than that, at least judging by those pictures of Nightwinds. Rather like Ethan's interest in solving old murders."

"He told me about that last night."

"Is that right?" Bonnie studied her intently. "Did it strike you as a little weird?"

"No. It struck me as very Ethan-like."

"Ethan-like." Bonnie chuckled. "Yes. That is exactly what it is."

"Ethan needs to pursue answers and balance the scales the way other men need to drive fast cars or search for gold. It's part of who and what he is."

"That's almost exactly what Drew used to say about him." Bonnie leaned forward in her chair and folded her arms on her knees. "None of Ethan's previous wives understood that about him."

Zoe wrinkled her nose. "I'd rather not discuss Ethan's previous wives, if you don't mind. It brings to mind the fact that, because of me, he will soon have a fourth ex."

"Not necessarily."

Zoe blinked. "I beg your pardon?"

"Ethan has done a lot of things for his clients in the past, but he's never married any of them."

Zoe waved that aside. "Probably because he never saw the necessity to go that far. My case is somewhat unusual."

"Ethan has had some very unusual cases.

Something else you should know about him. He doesn't sleep with his clients, either."

Zoe was starting to feel cornered. "Yes, well, I wouldn't read too much into the fact that he and I are involved in a relationship. It was just one of those things, you know?"

Bonnie said nothing.

Zoe felt a tingle of inexplicable panic.

"Well." She put down her pencil and got to her feet "I don't know about you, but I could use some coffee. There's a little place around the corner. Why don't we take a short walk?"

"Good idea."

Singleton Cobb showed up at two.

Zoe was interested to see that Bonnie suddenly seemed a bit more animated, almost as if there was some extra energy running through her. For his part, Singleton had a hard time looking away from her. He seemed oddly flustered.

He turned to Zoe. "Looks like I'm your company until closing time. I'll drive you to Nightwinds after work."

"Okay," Zoe said, trying to appear

pleased. This business of having a constant escort was going to get old fast. She wondered how Arcadia was making out with Harry Stagg. Maybe the phrase *making out* was not the best way of putting it.

Singleton cleared his throat. "Ethan invited me to join the rest of you for dinner. Heard tell we're ordering in pizza and salads."

"The basic food groups," Bonnie assured him. She collected her shoulder bag and found her car keys. "I'd better be on my way or I'll be late to pick up Jeff and Theo. See you all later at Nightwinds."

At five o'clock Zoe locked the door of her office and dropped the heavy doorknob key chain into her tote.

"I need to stop by my apartment and pick up some things," she told Singleton.

"No problem."

They walked together to the small lot where Singleton's large SUV was parked. He opened the passenger door for her with a touching gallantry and then he climbed in behind the wheel and fired up the big engine.

"This business of having a constant companion is probably starting to wear thin," he said, reversing out of the parking slot.

"How did you guess?"

"I know how I'd feel if I were in your shoes." He gave her a reassuring smile. "Don't worry. I don't think this situation will go on for long. Ethan will get it sorted out."

"Probably."

"You and Truax going to give your marriage a chance?"

Great. He'd brought up the very last subject she wanted to discuss today.

"This isn't what you'd call a marriage," she said crisply.

"Yeah? What would you call it?"

"Ethan's notion of an expedient solution to a pressing problem."

"Truax says you've got a license and had a ceremony and everything."

"That doesn't make it real."

"Can't argue that," Singleton said. "Makes it legal, though."

"Makes this whole situation very strange, is what it makes it, if you ask me. And getting stranger by the hour."

"I talked to Bonnie while you and Truax were in Vegas. We both think the two of you sort of fit together somehow. Why not let things go on as they are for a while after this is all over? What have you got to lose?"

She was getting that panicky feeling again. Time to change the subject.

"Turn left here," she said firmly. "You can park in front of that green wrought-iron gate."

"Sure."

Singleton did as instructed. She opened the door and jumped down from the high passenger seat before he could get around the front of the vehicle. She walked quickly to the green gate and reached into her tote for the key chain.

Singleton eyed the brass doorknob. "Heck of a key chain ornament. Isn't it a little heavy to haul around in a purse?"

"I'm used to it."

She opened the gate, led the way through the small garden, and unlocked the lobby door.

"You can wait here," she said. "I'll be down in a few minutes."

"Take your time."

She hurried up the stairs to the upper floor, trying to remember all of the items she wanted to transport to Nightwinds. When she reached the top, she turned and went down the hall. She stopped in front of her door and inserted the key into the lock.

The door of the trash disposal room opened behind her. Startled, she turned to greet whichever neighbor had just finished getting rid of his garbage.

But the man who rushed out of the small room crossed the narrow hall in a single stride and grabbed her before she realized he was not a neighbor.

Ron.

"Gotcha, bitch."

He wrapped one arm around her throat, cutting off her air and slapped a palm over her mouth. Her shout to alert Singleton died in her throat.

Another man emerged from the doorway of the vacant apartment on the left.

Where Ron went, Ernie was sure to follow.

"Get her inside," Ernie muttered. "Hurry."

"Take it easy." Ron dragged her across the threshold of her apartment. "None of the neighbors are here."

She struggled, trying to grasp the edge of the door frame. Darkness hovered at the edge of her vision.

"There's someone downstairs in the lobby."

"Got the needle?" Ron demanded.

"Yeah, sure. Just get her inside where we can do this in private."

She became conscious of the weight of the brass doorknob dangling from the key chain clutched in her fist. It centered her as nothing else could have done. She carried this sucker around for a reason, she reminded herself. Her brain cleared a little and some of her training in self-defense kicked in at last. She could almost hear her instructor, *about time you started thinking.*

She swung her arm up and back as far as she was able, aiming the doorknob at the side of Ron's head, praying she would not strike her own skull instead.

She was not sure of her target but she did connect with some portion of Ron's anatomy.

"Shit." He jerked back reflexively, briefly loosening his lock on her throat. "She's got something in her hand."

"Singleton."

Ron tightened his arm around her throat again, hurting her.

She swung a second time, a wide sweeping arc that would have caught Ernie in the chest if he hadn't hurriedly stepped back.

"Just wait, bitch," Ron hissed in her ear. "Just wait until we put you in those stirrups back at the Manor."

"You got her?" Ernie asked nervously.

"I got her. Stick her. Hurry up, damn it, someone's coming."

Ernie closed in, syringe in hand.

She swung the doorknob again, wildly, trying to hit his arm and managed to knock the syringe out of his hand.

The front door of her apartment slammed open. Singleton burst into the room, roaring.

"Let her go."

He grabbed Ernie, hauled him around, and slammed a fist into his face. Ernie hit the wall.

"Get outta here," Ron shouted furiously at Singleton. "She's crazy. We're taking her back to the hospital. We're medics."

"Yeah, she's dangerous, man." Ernie scrambled to his feet, clutching his jaw. "We gotta take her in."

"Bullshit," Singleton said. He rounded on Ron.

"We're medical professionals," Ron snarled.

Zoe swung the doorknob up and back a second time, striking solid flesh again. Ron's ribs, maybe.

"You crazy bitch."

He let her go so suddenly that she had no chance to catch her balance. She tumbled to her knees.

"Let's get outta here," Ron shouted to Ernie.

Ernie did not respond. He was already barreling toward the door. Singleton seized him just as he started through the opening and hurled him back into the room. He slammed into Ron. The two hulks went down like bowling pins.

"Come on." Singleton grabbed Zoe's hand and hauled her to her feet.

Together they ran out into the hall. When they were clear, Singleton stopped, whirled around, and yanked the door shut. He held it closed with a two-handed grip on the knob.

"Call 911," he bellowed. "Then call Truax."

She dug her phone out of the fallen tote and started punching in numbers.

They ate cold pizza and salads on the patio beside the pool. Jeff and Theo had finished their dinner while Ethan shepherded Zoe and Singleton through the police questioning process. When they got back to Nightwinds, the boys had disappeared into the theater to watch television on the big screen.

Ethan was not in a good mood.

"By the time we heard the sirens, the two had managed to lower themselves from my bedroom window," Zoe told Bonnie. "But Singleton and I saw them get into a car. We got a description and a license plate."

"The police arrived just as Ron and Ernie went tearing off down the street." Singleton helped himself to another slice of pizza. "They caught them within two blocks."

"They called Ian Harper from jail." Zoe fortified herself with a swallow of red wine, got up, and started to prowl the patio in front of the pool. "Tried to get him to tell the authorities that they were *trained medical personnel,* if you can believe it. They wanted him to explain to the cops that he had sent them to pick me up."

"Harper denied everything, of course."

Singleton munched pizza. "He called the cops immediately and made it clear that Ron and Ernie were no longer employed by Candle Lake Manor."

"Is that right?" Bonnie glanced at Zoe and then turned to Ethan. "He claimed he'd fired them?"

"According to Ian Harper," Ethan said slowly, "the orderlies were acting on their own."

"But why would they come all this way to get Zoe if someone wasn't paying them?" Bonnie said.

"Good question," Ethan said. "The official explanation from Harper is that the two held a personal grudge against Zoe because of something that happened when she and another unnamed patient escaped. Harper said they wanted revenge."

"Yeah?" Singleton looked interested. "What exactly did happen when you two busted out of the Manor?"

Zoe stopped and gazed down into the pool. "I bashed Ron in the head with a fire extinguisher. Arcadia used a needle full of heavy-duty sedative on Ernie."

"Cool," Singleton remarked.

Bonnie smiled. "Yes. Cool."

"No charges were filed and the incident was never reported because Harper didn't want his clients finding out that Arcadia and I were no longer in residence there."

"Got it," Singleton said.

"But now you're going to press a few charges, right?" Bonnie asked.

"Oh, yeah." She took another swallow of wine. "Assault and breaking and entering, for starters."

Singleton looked at Ethan. "Do you think Ron and Ernie were acting on their own?"

"Not initially," Ethan said. "I'm pretty sure that Harper did send them after Zoe when he found out where she was. He probably also tried to call them off after she informed him that she was married and no longer a good candidate for Candle Lake. But by then it was too late."

"Because by that time Ron and Ernie were in Whispering Springs and lusting for revenge?" Singleton asked.

"I'd rather you didn't use the term *lusting,*" Zoe said with feeling.

"Sorry." Singleton gave her an apologetic glance. "But it does explain why they threatened you in such, shall we say, *personal* terms."

"Mmm." She stopped briefly and frowned at Ethan. "Do you think they might have killed Leon Grady?"

Ethan rested his elbows on the arms of the pink padded lounge chair, stretched out his legs, and pondered the question.

"It's possible," he said. "The cops traced their movements. They arrived in Whispering Springs the same day Grady died. But they don't seem to know anything about his presence here in town. They got a motel room and staked out Zoe's apartment, waiting for her to show up. Evidently that's the only address they had. After waiting for her all afternoon, they took a break that night and went to a bar. The next day, they went back to Zoe's apartment and broke in to the empty place next to hers. Also, there's no strong motive."

"Unless Harper instructed them to get rid of Grady because he was causing problems," Singleton said.

Ethan shook his head. "Like I said, they were in a bar, drinking, that night. Got a hunch their alibis will hold up. Their only goal seems to have been to grab Zoe."

Zoe shuddered. "Bastards. I wonder if they'll actually do any time."

"I think so," Ethan said softly. "Maybe a

lot of it. Detective Ramirez told me that they both have prior convictions for assault and Ron was arrested on a rape charge a few years ago."

"Just the sort of fine, upstanding employees you'd expect Harper to hire," Zoe said through her teeth.

Bonnie winced. "I can't even begin to imagine what it must have been like for you and Arcadia there."

"They're out of the Manor now," Ethan said evenly. "And they aren't going back."

Bonnie nodded. "Understood."

They finished the rest of the pizza in silence. The soft chirps and calls of the night rose from the canyon; somewhere in the distance a coyote howled. Above, the stars were brilliant in a way that Ethan had discovered was only possible in a desert sky.

After a while Bonnie checked her watch. "Well, it's getting late. I'd better get the boys home and into bed."

She got up and started toward the French doors.

"Time I was on my way, too." Singleton hauled himself up out of a pink lounger. "Enjoyed the pizza, Truax." He cast a quick, veiled look at Bonnie, who was inside the living room now. "And the company."

"Any time."

Ethan and Zoe followed Singleton through the house into the entry hall. Zoe hung back, waiting for Bonnie and the two boys.

Ethan and Singleton went outside onto the front patio and stood looking at the parked cars in the drive.

"I owe you," Ethan said.

"No, you don't." Singleton shoved his big hands into his pockets. "You hired me to baby-sit. I was just doin' my job. Hell, didn't even do it very well, when you get right down to it. I should have gone upstairs with Zoe when she went to pick up her things."

"You got there in time. That's all that matters in the end."

"Maybe." Singleton chuckled. "Gotta tell you, though, she was doing a damn fine job of handling both of them with that big ole doorknob she carries."

"There were two of them and one of her. Those aren't good odds. Thanks, Singleton."

"Sure."

The door opened behind them. Theo and

Jeff shuffled outside with obvious reluctance, followed by Bonnie.

"Do we have to go home already?" Theo whined.

"Yes, you do," Bonnie said.

Jeff looked at Singleton. "Mom says you saved Zoe from some bad guys today."

"Zoe helped save herself," Singleton told him.

"Mom says you're a hero," Theo announced.

Singleton blinked behind the lenses of his glasses and turned red. "Nah."

"Yes," Bonnie said. "You are a hero."

"She's right," Ethan said.

Zoe appeared in the opening. "He sure is."

"Cool," Theo said.

"Will you show me how you saved Zoe?" Jeff asked excitedly.

"I've gotta go home," Singleton answered, edging backward toward his vehicle. "Now. 'Night, everyone."

He swung around, hurried to the SUV, got behind the wheel, and revved the engine.

"I think we embarrassed him," Bonnie said.

Chapter Twenty-nine

You could tell a lot about a person from the sound of his or her footsteps. Ethan listened to the steady, determined tread on the stairs. Too heavy for a woman. A man in good physical condition. Used to getting what he wanted. Accustomed to being in charge.

He heard the outer door open and close. The door of the inner office was ajar about a third of the way, as usual. He watched the mirror, studying the reflection of the tall, well-dressed man in the other room. Expensive suit. Expensive haircut. Expensive shoes. Early fifties. Polished. No obvious indication of a weapon.

This was the reason he had placed the desk in this corner and why the mirror was positioned opposite near the window. Okay, so maybe the energy flow was lousy from a feng shui point of view but the arrangement had one humongous business advantage, he reflected. From this angle he could see visitors and clients before they saw him.

"Is anyone around?" the man in the other room demanded in a loud, irritated voice.

"In here," Evan said.

The door opened wider. The man looked around the edge. "Are you Truax?"

"Yes." Ethan sat forward and folded his hands on the desk. "Forrest Cleland, right?"

"How did you—? Forget it."

Forrest walked into the office as if it belonged to him and took the chair that Zoe disliked so intensely. On Forrest it looked more or less the right size.

"Did Ian Harper give you my address?" Ethan asked casually.

"He provided me with the information that you probably lived here in Whispering Springs because that seemed to be where Sara was living, yes. I got your address out of the phone book."

"Getting my money's worth out of that ad lately," Ethan remarked.

"We need to talk," Forrest declared.

"Is this the part where you try to buy me off?"

Forrest was silent for a few seconds. Studying his adversary. Ethan got the impression that he might be adjusting his previous opinion just a shade.

"I think we can come to terms," Forrest said. "My objectives are simple. I want Sara sent back to Candle Lake Manor where she belongs. I also want to be certain that her block of shares are voted in the best interests of Cleland Cage."

"Her name is Zoe," Ethan said. "Zoe Truax."

"She can call herself whatever she damn well pleases. But in case you haven't figured it out yet, Truax, she is not well."

"She looks healthy to me."

"She hears voices in the walls," Forrest said grimly. "She claims those voices told her that I murdered my cousin, Preston."

"Did you?"

"No, I did not."

"Just asking. Someone sure did."

"If you did any research at all before you got involved in this situation, you'd know that the authorities concluded that Preston was shot by an intruder who was after cash and valuables."

"A burglar who then dumped flowers all over the place and deliberately smashed an expensive camera rather than try to fence it?"

Forrest went still. "She told you about the smashed camera and the flowers?"

"Yeah."

Forrest got slowly to his feet and went to stand at the window, looking down into the street.

"Did she also tell you that she was the one who found Preston's body?" he asked.

"Yes."

Forrest glanced at him over his shoulder. "You're a private detective, Truax. You must realize that there is another possible explanation for my cousin's murder. One that accounts for the apparent rage that was exhibited at the scene—the smashed camera and the crushed flowers."

"Are you trying to hint that Zoe might be the murderer?"

"The police considered the possibility and rejected it and that's fine by me. But the truth is her alibi for the day Preston was killed is shaky."

"How's that?"

"She was supposedly attending a three-day conference put on by a private art foundation in San Francisco. It was a big event. It would have been very possible for her to slip away unnoticed."

"Got a handy motive?"

Forrest turned back to the view from the window. He clasped his hands behind his back. "The oldest one of all. Jealousy."

"Was Preston having an affair?"

Forrest hesitated. "Maybe."

"This is getting a little vague, Cleland."

"I don't know the answer for certain. But the possibility exists."

"Got any proof?"

"No," Forrest said quietly. He turned around again. "And I'd just as soon not find out."

"Because it might raise doubts about Zoe?"

"I'd rather not discover that my cousin was shot dead by his wife in a fit of jealous rage."

"You don't want her to go to prison, is that it? You'd rather have her locked up in Candle Lake Manor."

"It's the best place for her," Forrest said quietly. "Dr. Harper will cooperate."

"I'm sure you make it worth his while to be cooperative."

"I would prefer that she be in a hospital where she can be properly treated rather than in prison, yes."

"So much easier to control her shares if she's in Candle Lake than it would be if she went to prison, isn't it? Prisoners have more rights than folks who have been involuntarily committed to a psychiatric hospital."

"Let's get to the bottom line." Forrest came back to stand in front of the desk. "I know why you married Sara."

"Zoe."

"Zoe. You married her because she's the key to a great deal of money." Forrest gave the office a laconic survey. "Probably a hell of lot more money than you've ever seen in one place at one time."

"You don't think we're talking true love here?"

Forrest's mouth curled humorlessly. "No, Truax, I don't think so. I did some checking on you before I came here. Seems this is your fourth marriage. A year ago you lost your business. By the time you paid off the creditors and your third ex-wife, you were flat broke. You're barely keeping your head above water financially. I think the day you met Zoe, or whatever you call her, you saw a way to recover in a hurry and you jumped at it."

"Going to make me an offer?"

"Yes."

"Thought so." It was always gratifying to have it figured right, Ethan thought.

"If you're smart, you'll take it," Forrest said. "I admit you would get more if the merger goes through, but I'm going to fight it every inch of the way. If I do manage to hold Cleland Cage together, you'll be looking at two to five years downstream before you can cash out. And you've got the added complication of having to stay married to a crazy woman for that whole time."

"I get the picture."

"Take my offer now and all you have to do is help me put Zoe back where she belongs. Then you file for divorce. I give you your money, and you're free."

Zoe lowered her camera and stared at Ethan, appalled.

"He offered you *how* much money?" she whispered.

"You heard me."

They were standing near the top of the trail that wound down into the shallow canyon below Nightwinds. The sun was low in the sky. The onset of twilight was streaking the desert with mauve and purple shadows.

Ethan had picked her up at her office a few minutes ago, telling her he needed to talk to her, but he had said little until they had come here.

She had known that, whatever he intended to tell her, it would not be good news. Maybe that was why she had taken out her camera and started snapping off shots of cactus. It had given her something to do with her hands while she waited for him to start talking.

"Yes," she said. "I heard you." She swallowed. "That's a lot of cash."

"Nah, it's a so-so amount, not a lot."

She looked at him. He was in some remote, centered place deep inside himself, she thought. It was probably the same place he went when he was seeking patterns and searching for answers.

"It is a lot," she said dryly, "given your present financial situation."

"Okay, relatively speaking, it's a lot."

There was a slight breeze blowing across the canyon, ruffling her blouse. Absently she raised a hand to hold her hair out of her eyes. "Cleland Cage is the most important thing in the world to him."

"I could see that."

"You did say he would probably try to buy you off."

"Cleland didn't just make me an offer. He said a couple of other things, too."

She watched him, worried by the too-even tone of his voice. "What things?"

"He implied that there was a possibility that Preston was involved in an affair at the time of his death."

For an instant, she was so shocked she could not speak.

"No," she said.

"I tried to pin him down, but he refused to get specific."

"Of course, he refused. That's because there was nothing to be specific about. Preston was *not* having an affair."

"You're sure of that?"

Her stomach clenched. "Absolutely positive. Preston would never have cheated on me."

"What if he did?" Ethan asked, quiet and relentless now.

It dawned on her that he was interrogating her. This was probably the way he dealt with suspects and anyone else when he wanted answers. She did not like being the target.

"I don't understand," she said stiffly. "Where are you trying to go with this?"

"Forrest implied that Preston's involvement with another woman might constitute a motive for murder."

Her insides turned to ice water. "He told you that I shot Preston, didn't he?"

"He didn't come right out and say it. Just sort of let the possibility hang in midair."

She swung around, anger evaporating the chill that had seized her. "But that's not what happened. I didn't kill Preston. I couldn't have shot him."

"Even if you'd discovered that he'd been sleeping with another woman?"

"Even if I found out he'd cheated on me." She felt steadier now that she was on sure and certain ground. "You have to understand that Preston was a gentle man. What we had together, our love, was a very gentle thing."

"Gentle."

She struggled to find the words to explain. "Even if one of us had found out that the other had cheated, the response would have been sadness and disappointment. Maybe grief. But not rage and certainly not violence."

"What would you have done?"

"You're not going to let this go, are you?"

"I can't," he said. "I have to find out where it leads."

She searched his implacable face. "Yes, I can see that. Okay, hypothetically speaking, if I had discovered that Preston had been unfaithful, I would have cried for a while and then I would have set him free. You can't force love. You know that."

"Sure. After four marriages, I know that."

She felt herself turn red. She wondered if he thought she'd deliberately thrown his extensive experience of marriage in his face. That was not what she had intended. It was his own fault if he took it personally, she thought. After all, he was the one who had pushed her into this corner.

"How about marriage counseling?" he asked.

"Counseling?" Startled out of her reverie, she frowned. "What do you mean?"

"Would you have suggested counseling if you had found out that Preston was having an affair?" he asked patiently.

"Oh, no, I don't think so."

"Why not?"

She suppressed the urge to tell him what he could do with his questions and struggled to dredge up more answers.

"I read somewhere that every marriage is based on certain unwritten ground rules," she said carefully. "Those rules are private, usually unspoken, and understood only by the people involved. For some, an affair would be hurtful but not a complete deal-breaker, if you see what I mean."

"Because faithfulness was not one of the bedrock rules of that marriage?"

"Yes. Maybe there are other factors that are more crucial in that particular relationship. Emotional dependency or financial security or social status or a strong religious belief. A person might have a great fear of failure or a dread of being alone. Any number of solid, reasonable things might be more fundamentally important in that marriage than faithfulness."

"But for you, faithfulness would be one of the unbreakable ground rules, is that it?"

"Yes," she said quietly. "For me, trust has to be at the heart of a relationship. Without that, none of the rest of it matters." She paused. "Do you understand?"

"Yes."

The quiet conviction in the single word reassured her as nothing else could have done in that moment. She gave him a tremulous smile.

"Because trust is one of your nonnegotiable rules in a relationship, too, isn't it?" she said.

"Figure you gotta be able to count on something or what the hell's the point of getting married?"

"Yes. Well, the point here is that I did trust Preston. I can't believe that he was cheating on me. But if he had been involved with someone else, I would not have killed him. I would have filed for divorce."

"Understood," he said.

"What's this all about?" she asked. "Did you really think that I might have been the killer?"

"No."

For some reason, that simple answer incensed her. "Then why the third degree?"

"It occurred to me that if Preston was seeing someone else and tried to break it off, that other person might have had a motive to kill him."

She contemplated that for a moment.

"You're thinking about a romantic triangle like the one you're constructing for the murder of Camelia Foote, aren't you?" she said. "I can see the logic, but that doesn't work in this case. Preston was not sleeping with another woman. Trust me. I would have known."

"Okay. Sorry about the inquisition. But I had to be sure."

She looked at him standing there, silhouetted against a dying sun, booted feet braced slightly apart. He reminded her of an oncoming train. You might be able to kill a man like this if you tried really hard and if you were fast enough and lucky enough, she thought, but that was the only way you could stop him.

"I know," she said softly.

She raised her camera and took the picture. Going for the little glimpse of his soul that she saw in that moment.

The photo would give her something of him to keep when this was all over.

....

Preston was a gentle man . . . our love was a very gentle thing . . .

Ethan was wide awake, looking up at the shadows of the ceiling and he knew that he was not going to go back to sleep. He was familiar with this brand of insomnia. It was job-related. It happened a lot when he was closing in on answers.

He had a choice. He could either lie here and brood or he could get up and go into another room and brood.

Beside him, Zoe slept peacefully. He did not sense any of the restlessness that he had come to expect whenever she was having one of her bad nights.

He eased himself away from the warmth of her body, pushed aside the covers, and rose from the winged bed. He found his trousers in the darkness, pulled them on, and padded barefoot out into the dark hall.

There was enough moonlight coming through the windows to illuminate his path. He made his way into the kitchen and turned on a light.

Inside the refrigerator, he found a plastic bowl full of leftover cheese ravioli. Zoe had cooked dinner this evening. She had doused the ravioli in very expensive olive oil and freshly grated Parmesan. He peeled off the lid and helped himself to a sample bite.

As he had suspected, it was just as good cold as it had been hot. Was he a trained detective or what?

He dumped a little habanero-laced hot sauce on the pile of ravioli, located a fork, and carried his treasure to the kitchen table. One of the pads of paper he kept handy in every room of the house was on the windowsill together with a pen.

He sat down, ate some of the ravioli, and opened the notepad.

But the first word he wrote was not what he had planned to jot down.

Gentle.

Well, shit. This was not going to be a very productive night if he didn't get past the gentle thing.

He crossed it out very deliberately and tried again.

People with reasons to kill Leon Grady and Preston Cleland.

"What are you doing?" Zoe said from the doorway.

He put down the pen and looked at her. She was swathed in a white robe and a pair of slippers. Her hair was mussed from the pillows and their earlier bout of passion. His wife.

He was startled by the heated rush of hunger and need that shot through him.

"Are you okay?" Zoe came toward him, concern darkening her mysterious eyes.

"Couldn't sleep. Thought I'd do some work." He indicated the plastic bowl. "Want some cold ravioli?"

"Sure."

She changed direction, opened a drawer, found a fork, and sat down across from him. Leaning across the table, she speared two ravioli and simultaneously craned her head to read his notes.

"What did you cross out?" She sat back and popped the ravioli between her lips. "A bad conclusion?"

"Yeah." He watched her eat for a moment, thinking that this would be a good time to keep his mouth shut. But for some reason, he could not seem to manage that simple feat tonight.

"I'm not like Preston, am I?"

She blinked, stopped chewing, and swallowed hurriedly. Then she cleared her throat.

"No," she said. "No, you are very different."

"You don't see me as a very *gentle* man, do you?"

She hesitated. "Gentle is not the first word that comes to mind, no."

"And our relationship," he said, unable to turn aside now, even though he sensed that disaster was bearing down on him. "You probably would not describe it as a very gentle thing."

"Uh, no. Probably not." She reached across the table to fork up more ravioli. "Mind if I ask what this is all about? Why the focus on our relationship here? It's not like we're really married."

"Yeah, we are really married." He realized his jaw had gone rigid. Always a bad sign.

She flushed. "You know what I mean. Our marriage is just a device. Part of your strategy for dealing with my case."

"And the fact that we're sleeping together? How do you account for that?"

Her cheeks turned a deeper shade of pink, but her gaze did not waver. "We're sleeping together because we're attracted to each other. Not because we've got a piece of paper that says we're married."

"Does that sound a little complicated to you? It sure as hell does to me."

"We seem to be coping."

"Cleland assumes I married you because you hold the key to that block of shares."

"Forrest judges everyone by his own standards and motivations," she said. "He wouldn't understand a man like you in a million years."

"You think you understand me?"

"Not completely. Parts of you are pretty deep and you don't go out of your way to reveal them. But I know you well enough to be sure that you didn't marry me for those shares."

"What makes you so damn certain of that?" he asked.

She paused with the fork full of ravioli halfway to her mouth. "If I say intuition, you'll do that thing with your eyes."

"What thing?"

"You can make them appear amused and scornful and sort of steely all at the same time. Something to do with the way you narrow them, I think. You do a squint that would have looked good on Wyatt Earp."

"A squint, huh? Maybe I should make an appointment to have my eyes checked."

She smiled. "It's not just intuition that makes me sure you didn't marry me in a sneaky maneuver to get hold of those shares. I've got some rock-solid evidence that says I can trust you."

"Like what?"

"I've seen the way you approach your work. I know you crave answers more than you'll ever crave money. Something in you needs to do your bit to keep the karmic scales balanced. I also know that when you sign on for a job, you'll do whatever it takes to see it through. That's who you are."

"You make me sound like some kind of machine."

She put down the fork and folded her arms on the table. "Are you always like this in the middle of a case?"

"Yeah."

She raised her brows.

"Well, maybe not," he said. "This case is different."

"How so?"

"You're different."

"From your usual client?"

"No." He picked up his fork and ate another mouthful of ravioli. "From all the other women I married."

"Oh. Well, now that you've brought up the subject, curiosity compels me to ask, in what way am I different?"

"You're just different, that's all."

"Okay, let's try this from another direction. How do you feel about me?"

"I'm not sure," he said. Might as well be savagely honest. Not like there was anything to lose. "But whatever the hell it is, it isn't exactly soft and gentle."

"I see." Her mouth curved in a slow, inviting grin. "Is that a problem for you?"

"Not if it isn't a problem for you."

She got up, rounded the table, and sank lightly down onto his lap. She put her arms around his neck.

"Trust me," she said into his ear. "It's not a problem."

Chapter Thirty

Radnor Security Systems sprawled across the second floor of a large building located in an office park on the north side of town. The interior resembled an upscale brokerage or insurance firm. The furnishings were sleek. The art on the walls was what Ethan privately termed Southwestern generic—lots of stylized images of red rock canyons, desert vistas, old adobe buildings, and sunsets, all done in shades of turquoise, red, and purple.

He was mildly impressed by the air of important hustle and bustle. Shiny new computers sat on every desk. The employees who came and went from the glass-walled cubicles on one side of the room looked serious and professional.

The receptionist was polished and polite. He sat behind an acre of curved and gleaming wood, lord of a complicated-looking phone system and a really spiffy computer. The little plaque on the desk identified him as Jason.

"May I help you?" Jason asked.

"I'm here to see Nelson Radnor," Ethan said.

"Do you have an appointment?"

"No."

Jason looked regretful in a polished and polite sort of way. "I'm sorry, Mr. Radnor is in a meeting. May I suggest that you make an appointment?"

Ethan propped himself on the corner of Jason's glowing desk and folded his arms. "Tell him Truax is here."

Jason was clearly troubled by this request, but after the briefest of hesitations, he reached for the phone. "Truax, did you say, sir?"

"He knows me."

"Just a minute."

Jason punched in a number and spoke softly into the phone. When he replaced it, he was smiling again. Relieved. He got to his feet.

"This way, please. Would you care for coffee or bottled water?"

"Neither, thanks."

He followed Jason to an office at the far end of the long row of glass-walled cubicles. Nelson's office did not have any glass.

Jason knocked once, opened the door, and ushered Ethan inside.

"Mr. Truax, sir."

"Come in, Truax. Have a seat." Nelson was in his shirtsleeves. He waved a hand toward a padded leather chair. "I wasn't expecting a visit from the competition today. What's going on? Decide to take me up on my offer of some subcontract work?"

"Not yet."

Ethan sat down and did a quick survey of the office. The desk was a hefty, burnished piece of sculpture composed of steel and glass. Nelson's chair was an executive model with a high back covered in black leather. The action was smooth. There was no squeak when he moved in it.

The carpet was dark gray, and the framed southwestern scenes that hung on the walls were suitably masculine. A handsome wooden coatrack stood in the corner. An expensively tailored cream-colored jacket draped elegantly from one of the hooks.

There was no pink anywhere.

The place had an uncomfortably familiar feel, Ethan noticed. It looked a lot like his old office in L.A. He wondered if Radnor had gotten screwed by the same interior decorator.

"What can I do for you?" Nelson asked congenially.

"You can tell me who hired you to find Leon Grady," Ethan said.

"Who the hell is Leon Grady?"

He had to hand it to Radnor, Ethan thought. The guy did not so much as flinch. Then again, maybe the ignorance was straight-up honesty. Radnor Security Systems probably did so much business that the boss didn't bother to pay attention to the small skip trace and missing persons work. It was a good bet he left those sorts of routine jobs to his underlings.

"Leon Grady was staying at the Sunrise Suites motel," Ethan said, making the effort to be patient on the off chance that Radnor actually didn't know what the hell he was talking about. "He turned up dead a few days ago. The cops think it was a small-time drug deal gone bad."

"Yeah, I think I did read something in the papers about a low-end dealer getting shot. But I didn't pay much attention. Radnor doesn't handle security for any of the companies in that part of town." Nelson cocked a polite brow. "One of your jobs?"

"Grady was linked to one of my ongoing investigations."

Okay, so he only had one ongoing investigation at the moment and the prospects of recouping his expenses, let alone getting paid for his time, looked a little dim. *So sue me.* There was no need to spell out the sorry details for the competition. In business you had to present a strong, competent, successful image. The environment had changed over the eons, but the rules of life in the jungle hadn't altered appreciably. Showing signs of weakness was a good way to get eaten.

"I don't get it." Nelson did concerned puzzlement very well. "What makes you think Radnor Security Systems is involved in this?"

"Call it a hunch. The cops are happy with the drug deal scenario but I've got some problems with it. I think it's possible that someone from out of town killed him, and that means the shooter had to find him first. Grady paid his motel bill in cash, presumably because he was trying to hide. I know that no one called me up and asked me to trace him so that leaves you."

"It does?"

"Radnor has the biggest ad in the phone book, so I figure someone calling from out of town would feel more comfortable going with you. I want to know the name of your client."

"I see." Nelson cranked back in his squeakless chair and looked sincerely regretful. "I assure you, I have no personal knowledge of the situation."

"I believe you. We both know that something this small would have been handled by one of your lower level people. A clerk, maybe. We're talking basic trace work here. Nothing complicated."

"I personally review every case that goes through this office at least once a week. I haven't noticed the name Leon Grady."

"Grady got murdered this week, not last. Maybe his file hasn't come up for weekly review."

"Even if we did trace him for a client, you know I can't discuss it with you, let alone give you the name of the person who hired us."

"I know all about your keen regard for

client confidentiality," Ethan said. "You made a big deal of it to that reporter from the *Herald* when you took credit for the Mason case."

"You know reporters. They never get the facts straight. You can't blame me for a journalistic misunderstanding."

"Wouldn't think of it. But I figure you owe me. Did someone from this firm track down Leon Grady?"

"I really can't discuss this, Truax. You know that as well as I do. There's a question of ethics involved."

"Let me put it this way," Ethan said. "If you don't show me the file on Grady, I will be forced to call the president of the Desert View Homeowners' Association and inform him that the association might want to review its contract with Radnor Security Systems."

Nelson sat forward abruptly, no longer projecting polite regret. "What the hell is that supposed to mean?"

"Just that I've got a hunch that the homeowners' association might be interested in knowing that some of the Radnor guards don't take the firm's rules about client confidentiality to heart. Some of them will, in fact, spill their guts about the personal lives of any of the folks living in Desert View for a beer and a couple hundred bucks."

"Are you saying one of my guys took a bribe?"

"How do you think I cracked the Mason case so fast?"

"Shit. You can't prove a damn thing."

"I don't have to prove anything. Like I said, all I have to do is plant a few doubts in the mind of the president of the homeowners' association. Panic will no doubt ensue. Nothing rich folks hate more than knowing someone will sell the details of their private affairs for a lousy two hundred in cash."

Nelson glowered for a full minute. Then he leaned forward and hit the intercom.

"Jason, bring me the case files for the past week. Yeah, I know this isn't the usual day. Get 'em."

Nelson released the intercom button and went back to scowling at Ethan.

"You play hardball, don't you?" he said.

Ethan shrugged.

The door opened. Jason appeared with a stack of printouts. He put them down on Nelson's desk.

"Will there be anything else, sir?" Jason asked.

"No, that'll be all." Nelson reached for the first printout.

Jason glanced thoughtfully at Ethan. There was curiosity and a new level of respect in his eyes. A few seconds later, the door closed softly behind him.

Silence punctuated by the occasional rustle of paper settled on the plush office. Several minutes passed.

"Son of a bitch," Nelson muttered.

He sat back and regarded Ethan with an expression that was not all that different from Jason's. Curiosity and the beginnings of something that might have been grudging respect.

"You guessed right." Nelson shoved the printout across the desk toward Ethan. "We did do a quick trace on a guy named Leon Grady. Client called in from out of town. Paid with a credit card."

Ethan picked up the printout and read the name of the client. "Dr. Ian Harper."

"It was a legitimate case. Harper said that he was Grady's employer and that Grady had disappeared with company funds."

"Yeah?" Ethan read quickly through the file.

"Hey, it says right there that my man verified that Harper was, indeed, Grady's employer."

"Uh-huh."

"Happens all the time, you know that. Embezzlement cases are almost as common as insurance fraud jobs."

Ethan did not look up from the file. He badly wanted to make some notes, but he had a hunch Radnor would come unglued if he starting writing things down on paper.

"Most employers don't gun down the embezzlers once they find them," he said absently. "They just try to recover some of the money. Does it worry you that you might have fingered Grady for the killer?"

"Damn it, don't give me any crap about having set the guy up. Radnor maintains the highest professional standards. All the rules were followed on that case. You can see that for yourself. Hell, you don't know that Harper killed Grady. You just told me yourself, the cops think it was a drug deal."

"You're right." Ethan finished reading and dropped the file on the desk. "I don't know anything for sure. Yet. See you around, Radnor. Consider us square for that little journalistic misunderstanding on the Mason case."

He opened the door.

"Truax."

Ethan paused.

"If you ever decide you want to work for a real agency," Nelson said wearily. "Let me know. I could use someone like you."

Ethan gave the office one last survey, taking in all the familiar, expensive details. "Thanks, but the decor doesn't work for me."

Fifteen minutes later, he walked into Single-Minded and stopped short at the sight of Zoe perched on a stool, heels hooked on the bottom rung. Her head was gracefully bent over an old, leather-bound book in her lap. Light gleamed on her sleekly knotted hair. She wore a purple tee shirt with a scooped neck and sleeves that went as far as her elbows. The myriad knife pleats of a teal green skirt draped elegantly around her ankles.

A hungry, possessive tide rose through

him, tightening his stomach and heating his blood.

This was his wife. At least for a while. And he wanted her.

She looked up at that instant and smiled. "Ethan," she said. "I was starting to wonder what had happened to you. Did your hunch pay off? Did someone hire Radnor to find Grady?"

"About time you got back." Singleton emerged from the gloom at the rear of the shop. "Any luck?"

The small spell that had bound him shattered. He pulled his thoughts back from images of damp, tangled sheets.

"It's a good news, bad news kind of thing," he warned.

"What's the good news?" Zoe asked.

Optimists, he thought. You gotta love 'em.

"I got the name of the person who hired Radnor to trace Leon Grady here in Whispering Springs. It was, wait for it, Dr. Ian Harper."

"*Harper.* Well, isn't that interesting."

"Harper doesn't seem to have made any effort to conceal his identity or his goal," Ethan continued. "Even used his Candle

Lake Manor corporate credit card to pay for the search. Claimed Grady had embezzled funds."

Singleton nodded. "Sounds like a reasonable story."

"It all fits," Zoe said, her expression fierce with satisfaction. "Maybe Grady threatened to blackmail Harper or maybe Harper realized that Grady had become a threat and a liability. Either way, Harper decided to get rid of Grady."

Singleton lounged against his counter. "He must have tracked Grady as far as Whispering Springs and then used Radnor to find out where he was staying here in town. Then he flew in and whacked him."

"Yeah, it's nice and neat, all right," Ethan said. "There's just one small problem."

"What?" Zoe demanded.

"Ian Harper has a real good alibi for the night of the murder, remember?"

She started to argue, and then he saw comprehension strike.

"Oh, damn." She sank back down onto the stool. "You're right."

Singleton frowned. "What's his alibi?"

"Zoe and me," Ethan said.

"We called him from Las Vegas sometime

after midnight on the night Grady was shot," Zoe explained. "I talked to him myself."

"Could have been faking it from his cell phone," Singleton offered.

Ethan shook his head. "Didn't call that number. You gave me both, remember? We dialed up his landline."

"Call forwarding?" Singleton offered.

"I don't think so," Zoe said. "Harper was groggy, like he'd dozed off watching late-night television. An old movie. I could hear it in the background."

"The phone records can be traced," Singleton reminded her, "but it does sound like he was probably back in Candle Lake."

She pinned Ethan with a steely look. "Okay, sleuth, where are you going with this?"

"Funny you should ask that. I do, indeed, have somewhere to go if I don't clear my first big case here in Whispering Springs. Radnor offered me a job."

She made a face. "Get real. You'd hate working for Radnor Security Systems."

He thought about the polished offices and the equally polished staff of Radnor Security Systems. It was a scene straight out of his former life. Zoe was right. He had no desire to return to it.

"Good point," he said. "Guess I'd better get busy and find out who murdered Leon Grady."

"What's the next step?" Singleton asked.

"As it happens, I'm sort of out of brilliant ideas so I'm going to do what a trained, experienced professional detective always does when he runs out of sharp moves."

Zoe looked interested. "That would be?"

"Stir the pot and see what bubbles to the surface."

"What do I get to do?" she asked.

"Nothing. You sit tight right here in Whispering Springs and you do absolutely nothing at all."

She sighed. "You're going to Candle Lake Manor, aren't you?"

"Yeah. Figure it's time to take the offense. Not like I've got a whole lot of choice."

"I'll come with you."

"No."

She slipped off the stool and stood. "You'll need me. I know that place. You don't."

It was true and it would be useful to have

her with him, but he also knew what it would cost her to confront her nightmares.

"No," he said again. "I'll handle it."

She walked to where he stood and touched his jaw lightly. "I understand why you think you have to refuse my help, and I appreciate it more than you will ever know. But I have to do this."

"Damn it, Zoe—"

She went up on tiptoe and brushed her lips across his.

"I'll go pack," she said.

Chapter Thirty-one

She was going back to Xanadu.

The growing tension that was twisting her insides and making her feel twitchy and anxious was normal and entirely expected, Zoe thought. She had known from the outset that it would be like this. She could handle it. She had to handle it.

She gazed steadily through the windshield as the narrow lane that led to Candle Lake Manor unwound in front of the rental car. The scene should have been picture-postcard pretty. The tall trees that arched so gracefully above the drive should have looked like something out of an impressionist landscape. Instead, they seemed to loom ominously, cutting off the light and the safety of the outside world.

Through the trunks of the trees, she caught glimpses of the dark lake. She thought of all the times she had gotten out of bed late at night and stood at her barred window looking out at the cold waters. Some nights she wondered if some evil being lurked beneath the surface casting spells over the Manor. There were times when no other explanation seemed to make sense of her miserable situation. On other nights she had imagined what it would be like to swim out into the middle of Candle Lake and let herself sink down into its depths. The ultimate escape.

The important thing to remember today was that she was not going back alone, she thought. Ethan was with her. There was nothing to fear except fear, itself, blah, blah, blah.

Yeah, sure.

She had been trying to hold back the old memories ever since she had made up her mind to do this. But now she could no longer dam the flood. The images from her nightmares slammed through her.

. . . The small room that had been both her prison and her refuge at night . . . Dr. McAlistair's hushed, shadowy office . . . The chandelier-hung dining room filled with unnaturally subdued patients all eating bland, tasteless food . . . The medical examination room where the hulks had taken their victims on the bad nights . . .

"You okay?" Ethan asked roughly.

She jerked at the sound of his voice and immediately tried to conceal her start by reaching for her tote. She had brought the chartreuse one today. The fierce, edgy color gave her courage.

"Yes, I'm fine." She opened the big bag and rummaged around for a tissue. Her fingers brushed against the heavy brass doorknob key chain. The feel of it calmed her a little. She started to breathe the way her instructor had taught her. *Finding the power source, centering herself.*

This time things would be different, she assured herself. She was no longer helpless. She was not alone.

"You sure you want to do this?" Ethan asked without taking his eyes off the curving drive. "I can take you back to the inn. You can stay there while I talk to Harper."

"No. I'm going with you."

Ethan said nothing, but he took one hand off the wheel and reached across the small space that separated them. He covered her fingers with his own and squeezed once, gently.

Some of the acid-strong tension eating away at her insides was diluted. She did a little more power breathing.

Ethan drove around one last curve, and the Manor came into view.

The three-story brick mansion squatted like a giant toad at the edge of the lake. Prison bars that masqueraded as a handsome, wrought-iron garden fence enclosed the grounds. The scene was just as she remembered it in her dreams.

But there was something different about it.

She gave a soft, muffled cry of surprise.

"What?" Ethan asked.

"It looks smaller than I remembered," she whispered.

Ethan smiled for the first time since they had left Whispering Springs that morning. It was not much of a smile, just a faint curve at the corner of his mouth, but it was real.

"I think that's a good sign," he said.

He was right, she thought. *Maybe this wasn't going to be so terrible, after all.*

A guard dressed in the familiar dove gray uniform of Candle Lake Manor security came out of the tiny guardhouse at the gate. He gave Zoe a cursory glance, not recognizing her.

"I'm Dr. Truax and this is my assistant."

Ethan flashed a business card. "We're here to see Dr. Harper. He's expecting us."

"Yes, sir. You can park in the visitors' section on the right."

The guard went back into the guardhouse and pressed a button. The heavy iron gates swung slowly open.

Zoe was impressed. "That went easily, just as you predicted."

"This place is designed to keep people from leaving, not to stop them from entering."

Ethan parked in one of the half dozen slots allocated to visitors and turned off the engine. He looked at Zoe.

"Ready?" he asked.

"Yes." She unlatched her seatbelt with sudden resolve and opened the door. "Let's do it."

Ethan climbed out from behind the wheel and dropped the keys into his pocket.

She stole another quick look at him as they walked together toward the entrance. This morning when he had dressed for the confrontation with Harper, he had shown her a whole new side of himself, the side that had once run a large, successful business. It was something of a revelation.

Today he looked sleek and intimidating in an elegantly tailored steel gray jacket and trousers. The charcoal gray shirt and silver-and-black silk tie added a not-so-subtle punch of quiet authority. Not that Ethan required any additional sartorial touches to give him that air, she mused. It came naturally to him, even when he was dressed in jeans. But today he looked like a man who could move comfortably in the corridors of power.

No wonder the guard at the gate hadn't questioned the phony business card.

They went up the stone steps and through the thick glass doors. Once inside the formal lobby, some of her fragile assurance slipped. She felt her heart rate kick back up into high gear.

The male receptionist greeted them politely. Zoe remembered him from the old days, but he looked at her with no sign of recognition. Probably because she was not wearing one of the shapeless hospital gowns, she figured. It only went to show how much clothes mattered.

Ethan did his trick with the business card, but the receptionist was not as easy a mark as the guard at the front gate.

"I'll let Dr. Harper know you're here, sir." The receptionist reached for the phone.

"That's all right," Ethan said. "We know the way."

"To the left," Zoe said.

She did not pause, but moved immediately down the hall in the direction of the executive offices, taking charge now that they were on her old turf, just as she and Ethan had planned. Out of nowhere, a rush of adrenaline hit her, filling her with energy and self-confidence. She could do this.

"Lead on," Ethan urged. He fell into step beside her.

"Just a minute, Dr. Truax, please." The receptionist scrambled to his feet, alarmed. "You'll need an escort."

But Zoe and Ethan were already turning the corner.

"Slick," Zoe commented.

"Yeah, the fake doctor thing always works well in situations like this. Makes 'em hesitate a couple of minutes before they summon the goon squad."

"And a couple of minutes is all you need."

"Usually." He looked around. "You know, on the surface, this place looks pretty classy."

"Appearances are deceiving. The first floor is all for show. The patient rooms are on the second and third floors. In fairness, I think Candle Lake Manor may at one time have been a respectable institution."

"But that would have been years ago, before Harper took over."

"Yes." She came to a halt in front of the paneled door of the executive suite and took another deep breath. "This is it."

"Gotta keep moving fast here." Ethan opened the door and ushered her inside. "The receptionist will be frantically trying to get through to Harper to tell him we're on the way."

"Right." She walked ahead of him into the paneled confines of the outer office.

Fenella Leeds, seated at her desk, was talking into the phone. There was disapproval and alarm gathering on her too-perfect face.

". . . Dr. Harper does not have any appointments scheduled for today." Fenella broke off at the sight of Zoe and Ethan bearing down on her. Her gaze brushed briefly across Zoe without much interest and came to rest on Ethan. "Call Richards in Security. Tell him—"

"Forget it," Ethan said. He was already pushing open the door of the inner office. "Harper won't want to be interrupted."

"You can't go in there." Fenella was on her feet now. Apparently realizing she could not physically stop Ethan, she turned back to Zoe who was right behind him. Belated recognition widened her eyes. *"You."*

"Hi, Fenella. It's been a while. Still screwing the guy in accounting?"

Fury blazed in Fenella's eyes. "How dare you?"

"It was no secret," Zoe assured her. "When I was here, all the patients knew how the two of you used to get it on down at the boathouse."

"You stupid little bitch," Fenella breathed. "You don't know what you're getting into."

"I'll take my chances."

She might have hung around to continue the exchange, but Ethan's hand closed over her arm. He hauled her through the doorway.

"Try to stay focused, honey," he said into her ear.

He closed the door firmly behind them and took a split second to lock it before he turned to face Ian Harper.

Harper was on his feet, scowling furiously at Ethan. "I don't know who you are, but I warn you that Security will be here at any moment."

"And when they arrive, you will tell them to go away," Ethan said easily. He steered Zoe into one of the two chairs and took the other one himself. "Two words, Harper. Leon Grady."

"Who the hell are you?" But Harper was staring at Zoe now visibly shaken. "You're Sara Cleland."

"Zoe Truax now." She crossed her legs and smiled at him. "Try to remember that."

"I don't know what this is all about, but I can assure you that you need help," Harper said to her.

"I'll pass."

"Let's get back to Grady," Ethan said.

Harper's jaw jerked once. "What does Grady have to do with this? The police told me that he was murdered by a drug dealer in a town in Arizona a few days ago."

"We know," Ethan said. "We found the body."

Harper was clearly taken aback by that information. "I see."

"The cops think it was a drug deal gone

bad, but Zoe and I are pretty sure we can prove otherwise."

That got Harper's full attention. "What are you talking about? I assure you—"

A loud pounding on the door interrupted him. He opened his mouth to shout something to the people on the other side.

Ethan held up one hand. "We have information that will give the cops reason to think that you're a viable suspect in Grady's murder."

The pounding continued.

"Dr. Harper, are you okay in there?"

"Get on the intercom and tell the pretty lady out front that you don't need security assistance," Ethan said in a level voice that brooked no resistance. "Do it now, or we'll take our evidence to the police."

Harper sat down hard and hit the intercom.

"Tell Security I don't need their assistance," he repeated. "At least not right away. Tell them to stand by in the hall."

"Are you sure, Dr. Harper?" Fenella asked, sounding like she thought he was an idiot.

"Yes." Harper released the intercom switch.

"Good move," Ethan said.

"What is this about me being a suspect in Grady's death?" Harper said hoarsely. "That's not possible."

"Your name and a Candle Lake Manor credit card were used to hire an investigation agency in Whispering Springs to locate Leon Grady. Shortly after the agency notified their client of Grady's whereabouts, he wound up dead. I've got a hunch we are not dealing with a coincidence here. What do you think, Dr. Harper?"

"I didn't kill Grady."

"Was he blackmailing you?" Ethan asked. "Threatening to expose your somewhat unorthodox business and medical practices here at Candle Lake?"

"No."

"Did you hire Radnor Security Systems to find him?"

"No, damn it I didn't hire anyone to find him. Grady went out of town on a business trip. I thought he was on his way to L.A. He was supposed to report back to me when he found—" Harper stopped in mid-sentence. He stared at Zoe.

"He went looking for me, didn't he?" she asked. "Somehow he managed to locate me. But I wasn't in L.A. He lied to you, didn't he? Because he had plans of his own for me. He tried to blackmail me. Wanted me to pay him a whole bunch of money to keep my secret."

"I did not know that," Harper snapped. "All I can tell you is that my administrative assistant became suspicious of Grady's behavior. She got the idea to check his charge card expenses and managed to track him to Whispering Springs. Then she went through his personal email correspondence with a hacker named GopherBoy. Grady had deleted it, but he was not what anyone would call computer literate."

"But Fenella Leeds is," Zoe said. "She found my name and address in Grady's computer files, right?"

"Yes," Harper said wearily. "GopherBoy supplied the information to Grady."

"And you sent the hulks to pick me up," Zoe accused.

"Hulks?" Harper scowled. "What are you talking about?"

"Ron and Ernie. You sent them after me, didn't you?"

Harper looked like he was about to deny that, but then he drew himself up. "We sent two of our trained medical personnel to Whispering Springs, yes. But then you called me, telling me that you were married. I called the motel where Ron and Ernie were staying and left word that they were to forget about you and return here immediately. I am not responsible for any actions they may have take after that point."

"Ron and Ernie tried to kidnap me," Zoe said fiercely.

"That is not my problem," Harper shot back. "I tried to recall them." He turned quickly to Ethan. "Maybe they killed Grady."

"Don't think so," Ethan said.

"Got a good alibi for the night of Grady's death?" Zoe asked.

Harper was clearly panic-stricken. Then his gaze went to his calendar. He appeared to have trouble putting it all together, but eventually he sucked in air and turned an unattractive shade of red.

"Grady was killed the same night that you called me from Las Vegas to tell me that you were marrying Truax."

"Did I call you?" She asked innocently. "I don't remember."

Harper turned purple. "*Yes.* You were gloating."

"Was I?" She made a *tsk tsk* sound. "You know, what with all the meds you fed me during my stay here at the Manor, my short-term memory just isn't what it used to be."

"I was home in bed, here in town that night," Harper said loudly. "You know it as well as I do."

"Are you sure?"

"I don't know what kind of game you're playing here," Harper snarled, "but if you've given the police any reason at all to think that I was involved in Grady's death, you have to tell them the truth. You have to inform them that you talked to me that night and that I was here, not in Whispering Springs."

"Why do I have to tell them the truth?" Zoe asked softly. "After all the lies you told people about me, what possible motive would I have for telling anyone the truth on your behalf?"

"This is your warped vision of revenge, isn't it?" Harper rasped. "I tried to help you and this is how you repay me. You really are a very sick woman."

"So I've been told."

Harper turned back to Ethan, desperate now. "I talked to you, too, that night."

"Did you?" Ethan shifted slightly in his chair. "My memory's a little vague on that point, too."

"You can't do this to me. I'm an innocent man."

"Well," Ethan said, "we would like to find the real killer, naturally. But if that proves impossible, we may settle for giving your name to the cops. They can take it from there."

"I did not murder Grady. I'll be able to prove that I was here that night."

"Sure," Ethan said, "you'll probably be able to clear yourself eventually, but not before there's a lot of really unpleasant publicity. It'll be the kind of PR that will make your clients very nervous. They pay dearly for privacy, don't they?"

"Oh, yes," Zoe chimed in. "Privacy is everything to your clients, isn't it, Dr. Harper? The last thing any of them want is publicity and there's nothing like a juicy, high-profile murder case to draw that, is there? Just think what will happen if you're questioned about your link to the murder of one of your employees."

Harper made an obvious effort to regain his composure. He gave Ethan a flat stare.

"Let's cut to the chase. What's in this for you?"

Ethan tapped his fingertips twice. "I like answers."

"Bullshit. You're in this for the money. That's why you married Sara. It's the only thing that makes any sense in this mess."

"The name is Zoe," Zoe said softly. "Zoe Truax."

Harper ignored her. He kept his attention fixed on Ethan. Zoe could see that he was mentally putting the facts together to his own satisfaction.

"You plan to use her to get your hands on a chunk of Cleland Cage, don't you?" he said to Ethan. "Fine. I wish you luck. But why come to me? I'm out of it."

"No, Harper, you are not out of it." Ethan uncoiled to his feet and reached down to take Zoe by the arm. "When I pick up the phone and call the Whispering Springs cops, you will become a person of interest in the murder of Leon Grady."

"I didn't kill him, and you know it."

Ethan shrugged. "So, you hired someone else to do it to ensure that Grady didn't expose your business dealings. Ron or Ernie maybe."

"No."

"Either way, I'm sure the cops will be curious." They were at the door now. Ethan paused before opening it. "We're staying at the Candle Lake Inn. Give us a call if you come up with any ideas regarding who might have wanted you to take the fall for Grady's murder."

He opened the door. Zoe walked out of the room ahead of him. She had faced down Harper, threatened him in her own small way, with a taste of what he had done to her—and she was feeling quite accomplished.

A small crowd had gathered in the outer office. Fenella Leeds, two orderlies, and two men in dove gray hovered uncertainly. They watched Ethan and Zoe emerge from Harper's lair.

"False alarm, people," Ethan said cheerfully. "Dr. Harper got a little confused. Probably missed his morning meds. But we straightened things out. You can all go back to work."

He kept one hand wrapped around Zoe's arm, moving steadily and swiftly toward the other door. They went past the little gathering. No one made any attempt to stop them.

And then they were out in the hall, heading toward the lobby. Not much farther now, Zoe thought. In another few minutes they would be driving away from Xanadu.

They turned the corner and nearly collided with Venetia McAlistair.

"Sara." Venetia halted, staring in astonishment. "You've come back."

"In your dreams," Zoe retorted. "And the name is Zoe now. Zoe Truax. Ethan, meet Dr. Venetia McAlistair, otherwise known as the Wicked Witch of Candle Lake Manor."

"I don't understand." Venetia looked at Ethan. "Who are you?"

"Ethan Truax." Ethan gave it a beat. "Zoe's husband."

Venetia shook her head. "What is this all about, Sara? If you haven't come back to Candle Lake for more treatment, what are you doing here?"

"Investigating the murder of Leon Grady," Zoe told her. "Know anything about it?"

"Of course not. Why are you concerned with Grady's death? Dr. Harper said that he was killed by some petty drug dealer in Arizona. I can't say I'm stunned with surprise. I always suspected that he supplemented his income by stealing some of the patients' medications and selling them on the street. I told Harper of my suspicions several months ago, but he refused to take action."

"Yeah, well somebody took some serious action against Grady." Ethan studied Venetia with veiled curiosity. "If you've got any ideas on the subject, we'd be happy to listen to them."

"I just told you that I know nothing about the circumstances of Grady's death." Venetia turned away from him, not bothering to conceal her lack of interest in the subject of Leon Grady. She focused earnestly on Zoe. "I've been extremely worried about you, Sara."

"Zoe."

"Zoe," Venetia repeated patiently. "After all the stress you've been through lately, it's safe to say that you are in an extremely fragile state at the moment."

"Good news, I'm getting tougher by the day," Zoe assured her. "If you'll excuse us, we're on our way—" She stopped abruptly, aware that Ethan was gently squeezing her arm. She recognized the signal. He did not want her to blow off Venetia McAlistair. "We're on our way back to the Candle Lake Inn. As Ethan said, if you think of anything that might be useful, you can contact us there."

"I just told you that I can't help you with the Grady business." Venetia glanced at the hallway behind Zoe and lowered her voice. "But it is extremely important that we talk."

The last thing she wanted to do was find herself alone in a room with Venetia McAlistair again, Zoe thought. But Ethan was still squeezing.

"I'll be at the Inn," she said stiffly.

"May I stop by this evening?" Venetia asked eagerly. "I really must speak with you."

"Why don't you come by after dinner?" Ethan suggested coolly. "Say around nine o'clock?"

Zoe was surprised by the odd hour but she said nothing.

"That's a little late," Venetia said hesitantly.

"It will give us a chance to enjoy dinner in peace," Ethan said. "Zoe's had a long day. She needs some time to relax."

"Oh, yes, of course." Venetia nodded approvingly. "Yes, I understand. I'll come by around nine. We'll have a nice, cozy chat."

"Oh, boy," Zoe muttered. "Can't wait."

Still grasping her arm, Ethan whisked her around Venetia, down the hall, into the lobby, and out of the Manor.

"What was that all about?" she asked a few minutes later when Ethan was piloting them back down the tree-lined lane. "Why do you want Venetia to come to the inn this evening?"

"So you can keep her occupied while I see what I can find at her place."

She straightened abruptly in the seat. "You're going to search her house? What on earth do you expect to find?"

"Haven't got a clue. It's like I told you before we came here, in the detective business, when you run out of ideas, you start stirring things up."

"The detective business seems to have a few things in common with my business."

"Yeah? How's that?"

"One of the little tricks I've discovered as an interior designer is that when I can't figure out what's wrong with the energy flow in a room, I start shifting the furniture around until things start to feel right."

"Shifting the furniture around." He thought about that. "Yeah, that's exactly what I'm doing." He gave her a quick, searching glance. "Are you going to be okay alone with McAlistair this evening?"

"I can handle her."

He nodded, satisfied. "Figured you could."

Chapter Thirty-two

Zoe watched Venetia McAlistair bustle toward her across the cozy inn lobby and tried to suppress a chill of unease. For the first time that evening, she conceded to herself that she might have been somewhat hasty earlier when she had assured Ethan that she could handle this meeting.

It was one thing to face down an old adversary with Ethan by her side. It was going to be another thing altogether to do it on her own with this long-standing enemy.

After giving the subject a great deal of thought, Zoe had decided to meet her here in the lobby. The fire on the massive stone hearth gave off a reassuring warmth. In addition, there was a scattering of other people around. While none would be within immediate earshot, she would have the comfort of knowing that she was not completely isolated.

Just the sight of Venetia's grandmotherly features and rumpled-looking suit was enough to tighten her breathing tonight. The story of Hansel and Gretel flashed across her mind. On second thought, perhaps it would have been wiser to sit a little farther away from the cheerfully blazing hearth.

Stop it, she scolded herself silently. *You've got a job to do here.* She was pretty sure Ethan could handle a simple search of Venetia's house without getting into trouble, especially since she would be keeping her busy while he worked. But she was feeling a lot of unease this evening and not all of it had to do with the forthcoming conversation. If Ethan was right, there was a killer running around loose.

"Sara." Venetia came to a halt in front of her. "Thank heavens. I was afraid you might change your mind about talking to me."

"I will if you don't start calling me Zoe."

"Yes, of course, dear. Zoe." Venetia sat down in a large, padded chair and looked around. "Where is Mr. Truax?"

"My husband is upstairs in our room," she said smoothly. "He felt we should talk in private."

"I see. I'm so glad he appreciates that a conversation between a patient and her therapist should be confidential."

"Let's get one thing straight here, Venetia,

I'm not your patient. As far as I'm concerned, I never was your patient. I was a prisoner at Candle Lake Manor."

"That is a very unrealistic view of the past, my dear."

"Yes, but it's my view. I agreed to see you this evening because you said it was important that we talk. So start talking."

Venetia sighed. "You still appear to have a lot of hostility issues."

"You don't know the half of it."

"That is only to be expected, under the circumstances. I want to assure you that I have only your best interests at heart. I'm here to help you."

Ethan clenched the penlight between his teeth and aimed the narrow beam at the file folders in the drawer. Each was neatly labeled. No surprise there. Having gone through the bedroom and the kitchen of the neat little house, he had already discovered that Dr. Venetia McAlistair was the methodical type.

The files Venetia kept here in her home office were mostly connected to her outside business as an occasional consultant to law enforcement. She presented herself to her clients as an expert in forensic psychology, but he could see from her private notes that Zoe was right. McAlistair flirted a lot with the woo-woo stuff.

Her records of half a dozen murder investigations contained a lot of personal observations and some wild speculation but very little in the way of hard facts. It looked like the good doctor wanted very badly to believe in her own psychic abilities.

> . . . Possible sexual overtones to the sensations experienced at the scene. Victim may have had sexual contact with the killer . . .
>
> . . . Sensed that victim knew the killer. Distinct aura indicating a personal connection . . .

"Bullshit, Dr. McAlistair." He closed the folder and dropped it back into the drawer. "Pure, unadulterated bullshit."

He was about to give up when the beam of light struck the label on the last file. CLELAND.

"I realize this is a very difficult subject for you, Sara, I mean, Zoe. But I feel that until you confront this aspect of your nature, you will be unable to move forward."

Zoe smiled coldly. "I did move forward, Venetia. I moved right out of Candle Lake."

"What I'm trying to explain to you is that I believe you have a certain intuitive ability that enables you to pick up information in some situations that might escape the notice of others."

"Gee. You think?"

"I understand you as no one else can, my dear." Venetia lowered her voice to a confidential tone. "Because I have a similar ability."

"Oh, wow. Maybe you're even crazier than me. What a thought."

"Do you recall the two occasions when I took you to crime scenes?"

"Frequently." Zoe flexed the fingers of her right hand. "In my nightmares."

"If you have nightmares it is because you are attempting to deny the reality of your nature. As long as you refuse to deal with it, you will be conflicted. I know this because I, too, attempted to deny my own talents for a very long time. Why do you think I was drawn to the study of psychology in the first place?"

"So you could torment people like me?"

"Don't be ridiculous." Venetia's brow wrinkled a little. "I went into the field because I felt an overwhelming need to find a logical, scientific explanation for the sensations I occasionally experience in certain places where great violence has been done."

"You really believe you've got some kind of psychic ability, don't you?"

"I don't like to use the term *psychic* because it carries a lot of negative connotations," Venetia said. "I prefer the word *intuition.* And, yes, I do feel that some people have stronger amounts of it than others. You and I are among that small number of powerfully intuitive individuals."

> . . . Although the dose was doubled in an attempt to overcome her phobic-like reaction, the subject refused to enter the room where the crime had taken place. She began screaming and would not stop until she was removed from the scene.
>
> I suspect that the hysteria was, in part, staged by the suspect as a means of ma-

nipulating the situation so that she would not have to enter the room. But even if that is the case, such extreme resistance indicates just how powerful her ability may be. Why else would she have refused to go forward?

Ethan flipped through the remainder of the notes, a storm of dark anger brewing in his gut. From what he could see, it was a near miracle that Zoe had survived her time in the Manor with her sanity intact.

Maybe it hadn't been such a good idea to leave Zoe alone with Venetia McAlistair tonight.

He removed all of the notes from the file and dropped the empty folder back into the drawer. When McAlistair eventually discovered that her records had been stolen, she could use her keen intuition to solve the crime.

He took the penlight out from between his teeth and checked the time. Ten-fifteen. Zoe had been with McAlistair for more than an hour. He had learned nothing useful here. Time to go.

He slipped out of the house the same way he had entered it, through the kitchen door, and went back through a stand of trees to the place where he had left the car.

He got behind the wheel and tossed the notes he had taken from the Cleland folder down onto the passenger seat. He sat for a while, considering possibilities and probabilities. He had counted on finding something related to Leon Grady in Venetia's cottage since she was so strongly linked to this thing, but he'd come up empty.

He thought about the cast of characters he had seen today at Candle Lake Manor. Then he thought about corporate credit cards and people who might have access to them.

He fished the notebook out of his pocket and checked an address. He located it on the map of Candle Lake that he had brought with him. Probably couldn't accomplish anything useful there tonight, he figured. The odds were that the house would be occupied at this hour. But you never knew.

No harm taking a look on the way back to the inn.

"I am offering you more than therapy," Venetia said. "That's important, of course.

You need to learn how to handle your experiences. But there's a financial aspect involved here that you may not have considered."

"Ah. Now we get to the good part." Zoe sat back in her chair, feeling more in control. "How much do you intend to pay me to do your consulting work for you?"

"You will not be doing my consulting work for me." Venetia showed a flash of annoyance for the first time. "You will be *assisting* me. I am willing to negotiate a reasonable fee for your services."

"What do you consider reasonable?"

Venetia cleared her throat. "I will be providing you with counseling services to help you deal with your issues. My fees for those services are similar to what I charge my law enforcement clients. So I think we can arrange a sort of trade here. For every hour of therapy I make available to you, I would expect an hour of your time at a crime scene."

Zoe laughed. "You actually expect me to pay you for the privilege of doing your woo-woo stuff at crime scenes? This is a joke, right?"

Chapter Thirty-three

To his surprise, the two-story Victorian-style house was dark. He could not see a car in the drive, but there was every possibility that it was inside the garage. Might be a dog, too.

Problems, problems.

But as long as he was in the vicinity, it wouldn't hurt to get a little closer.

He left the car in another stand of trees, this one near the edge of the lake, and prowled back toward his objective.

No dog barked when he got close to the house. He stopped to peer into the garage window and saw the dim outline of a vehicle inside.

Damn. The owner was home and no doubt asleep.

He wandered around to the back and saw a screened porch. On the other side of the screen, he could see the kitchen door.

So near and yet so far. He wondered if the occupant was a light sleeper.

No, he was not going to go in, he told

himself. That would be really, really dumb. He would come back tomorrow after the occupant left for work. That was the smart thing to do.

He examined the knob on the screen door. It would be a piece of cake. The rest of the locks were probably just as old and just as simple.

He took the gloves out of his pocket, tugged them on, and fiddled a little with the screen door. Experimenting.

The knob turned easily. Unlatched.

As long as he was this close, he might as well check the lock on the kitchen door. That way he would know what tools to bring tomorrow.

He opened the screen very slowly and crossed the porch. In the shadows, he could see the outline of two aging rattan chairs and a freezer. There was no hum from the freezer. It looked old. A large, half-filled garbage can stood immediately next to the kitchen door.

The kitchen door was unlocked, too. Not only unlocked but slightly ajar.

He eased the kitchen door open. From his vantage point, he could see through another doorway into the darkened living room.

Something was crumpled in a pool of moonlight on the floor in the front room. From where he stood, it looked a lot like a body.

There was always the possibility that the occupant had fallen asleep on the rug in front of the television, but he'd seen scenes like this one before.

He was pretty sure Fenella Leeds was not asleep.

He listened to the silence for a moment and then he entered. Maybe Leeds was not yet dead.

"You may as well know that I'm planning to hand in my resignation soon," Venetia said. "I will be leaving Candle Lake Manor. I intend to pursue my consulting work full-time. If things go as I believe they will, I may be able to use a junior partner."

"Don't look at me," Zoe said. "I've already got a day job, and I like my new life in Whispering Springs. I'm not looking for another career with or without free therapy."

"I'm not asking you to make a decision

right now. But I want you to think about it. Speaking as your therapist, I can tell you that if you don't learn to deal with your special abilities, you will face the possibility of a serious mental breakdown."

Zoe glanced surreptitiously at the antique tall clock in the corner. It was going on eleven. What the devil had happened to Ethan? He should have been back by now. How much longer did he expect her to keep Venetia occupied?

"The closest I ever came to an honest-to-goodness real-life meltdown was during my stay at the Manor," she said. "If I survived that, I can survive anything. Which reminds me. I've got a question for you."

Venetia brightened. "Yes, dear? What is it?"

"I know you must have been aware of Harper's scam, how he arranged to keep certain inmates, people like me, for example, safely doped up and tucked away for a price. But I've wondered all along how actively involved you were in it. Did he split some of the profits with you?"

Venetia blanched. "I have no idea what you're talking about."

"Ah, come on, Doc. It's just us girls talking here. You can tell me. Did you actively assist him? Maybe provide second opinions when they were needed? Or did you just look the other way?"

"Are you suggesting that Dr. Harper deliberately misdiagnosed some of the patients at Candle Lake?"

"Uh-huh."

"That's ridiculous. And, I must tell you, that it is an indication of a serious form of paranoia. You really do need my help."

"Good thing I didn't take you up on your offer of a partnership, isn't it? Just think, you might have found yourself working with a crazy woman."

Fenella Leeds was dead. The rug beneath her was very wet. She had been shot at close range. Recently. The killer had no doubt entered the house the same way he himself had, Ethan thought. Through the kitchen door. He had probably left via the same route.

In the moonlight, he could see some signs of an intensive search. Not a desperate, chaotic toss. The manner in which the shelves had been emptied appeared methodical and orderly. Someone who knew what he was looking for and knew the places in which it was most likely to be found, he decided.

Time to call the cops.

Just as he started toward Fenella's phone, he noticed the three suitcases parked near the front door.

Fenella must have come straight home from work and started packing for a hasty departure from Candle Lake. There was only one good explanation for that move, as far as he could see: The arrival of Zoe and himself on the scene.

It fit with the scenario he had come up with after leaving Venetia McAlistair's house, he decided. As Harper's executive assistant, Fenella had inside knowledge and access to his corporate credit card number. She could have been the one who hired Radnor to track down Grady. But judging by the fact that she was now dead, it was pretty clear that she had not been working alone. And Grady's file indicated that it had been a man who had called the agency to request the trace.

The ceiling squeaked faintly overhead.

The flood of adrenaline in his veins suddenly became a full-blown tsunami.

Someone else was in the house.

He could make the call to the cops just as easily outside in the safety of the trees as he could standing here in the middle of the living room, he reminded himself.

He drifted back toward the kitchen door. The winking red light on the answering machine stopped him.

Had the killer called first to make sure Fenella was home?

He hit star 69.

Somewhere in the deep darkness at the top of the stairs, a phone rang.

That settled it, whoever was up there was probably the killer, and Ethan was pretty sure he knew who it was now.

It stopped ringing.

Ethan ran for the back porch. He pushed open the screen door and let it clatter shut, trying to give the impression of a man rushing away from the house.

But he did not go down the steps. He stayed on the porch, settling into the well of night next to the large garbage can.

An eternity of at least three minutes passed.

The stair treads creaked.

Another pause.

Footsteps inside the kitchen. The door opened cautiously.

After a few seconds, a figure exploded out the door.

Ethan had the garbage can ready, partially tipped on its side, balanced on the bottom rim. He shoved it straight into the fleeing man's path.

The figure shrieked in surprise and rage and then went down hard, tangling with the spilled garbage and the heavy can. A gun thudded heavily on the wooden floor of the porch.

Ethan moved, pinning the killer in a pile of food scraps and empty cartons.

"It's over, Drummer," he said.

Al Drummer started to weep. "I loved her. I did it all for her. But she betrayed me. I had to kill her, don't you see? I had to do it."

Chapter Thirty-four

Zoe saw him the instant he walked into the lobby. She had been watching for him from her post near the fire. He had phoned her twice, once just before he talked to the police and again when he had finished and was in the car driving back to the inn. She had gotten only the barest outlines of the situation from him on both occasions.

She flew across the room toward him, heedless of the crew working the front desk, and threw herself into his arms. He wrapped her close and kissed her hard.

"Are you okay?" she whispered.

"Sure." He tightened his arms around her.

For a moment she clung to him, wanting to stay this close as long as possible. But eventually it dawned on her that they were in a public place. "The lounge is still open. We can talk in there."

"I could use a drink."

They sat at a small table overlooking the black-and-silver surface of the moonlit lake. The lounge was nearly empty. The bartender brought two glasses of brandy. Zoe let Ethan have one sip before she started in with her questions.

"Al Drummer?" she said. "He was the killer?"

"He had a lot at stake," Ethan said slowly. "For the past few years, he had been quietly skimming some of the profits off the top of Harper's business enterprise. Harper wasn't a good enough businessman to detect the embezzlement and of course he never called for an audit because he didn't want anyone finding out about his own scam."

"Drummer had the perfect setup. An embezzlement operation that was not likely to ever be detected by his boss."

"It was damn near perfect until Fenella Leeds came to work for Harper. Evidently she started sleeping with the boss just to get a handle on possible angles. She figured out the game he was playing with certain clients real quick."

"Arcadia and I were pretty sure that she was aware of what was going on."

"She realized the potential for embezzlement, dropped Harper, and seduced Al Drummer."

"Only to find out that Drummer already

had a nice little skim operation up and running." Zoe nodded. "Arcadia and I used to watch the pair of them sneak down to the old boathouse. We always wondered what Fenella saw in Drummer."

"They made a deal. She offered extensive inside knowledge of Harper's activities and pointed out ways of upping the take from the embezzlement. They became business partners. At least, it was all business on Fenella's side. Drummer, however, fell in love."

"But it all started to come apart when Leon Grady located me and decided to start up his own little blackmail business, is that it?"

"Yes. Fenella may not have had a degree in psychology, but she was obviously quite shrewd when it came to judging people. She guessed almost immediately that Grady was up to something when he told Harper that he was going to try to find you in L.A. She knew he was chronically short of cash and that he would probably use the corporate card as much as possible."

"So she went straight to Drummer and told him to keep tabs on Grady?" Zoe asked.

"Yeah. According to Drummer, she was sure that Grady had become a loose cannon and that he threatened the highly profitable operation she and Drummer had going. She decided that he had to be stopped as soon as possible. Drummer tracked him as far as Los Angeles, but lost him there. Then Fenella provided him with Grady's personal credit card information."

"How did she get it? Off Grady's computer?"

"Yes, together with your address."

Zoe shuddered. "So she and Drummer were able to determine that Grady's real destination was Whispering Springs."

"Yes, but Grady was living on cash at that point, which meant that they couldn't use his credit cards to pin down a location in Whispering Springs. So Drummer did the logical thing. He called up the largest security and investigation firm in Whispering Springs and used Harper's name and credit card to hire Radnor to do a quick search."

"And Radnor found him."

"Yes. But Fenella also realized that it was just as important to get you back. She had no way of knowing what you might do and she considered you a potential threat to the embezzlement scam."

"And besides, I was a high-profit patient," Zoe said bitterly.

"Very true. So she went to Harper and told him that she knew where you were. But she did not mention that she had also located Grady. Harper sent Ron and Ernie to pick you up. Fenella and Drummer made their own private plans to take care of Grady."

"Which one of them went to Whispering Springs to kill him?" Zoe asked. "Fenella or Drummer?"

"Drummer," Ethan said. "I get the impression that Fenella was opposed to the notion of taking personal risks, if she could avoid it. Also no one took much notice of Al Drummer. He could call in sick for a day or two and not raise any eyebrows."

"She convinced Drummer to do the dirty work, is that it?"

"There was a certain logic to the decision." Ethan took a swallow of brandy and lowered the glass. "Drummer had been a hunter all of his life. He knew how to handle a gun."

"I see. So Ron, Ernie, and Drummer were

all in Whispering Springs on the same day, but the hulks didn't know about Drummer."

"No. And neither did Harper. Later, with Grady out of the way, Drummer and Fenella hunkered down here, hoping the whole thing would blow over."

Zoe felt a rush of fierce satisfaction. "But things didn't blow over because we got married, Ron and Ernie got arrested, and you insisted upon investigating Grady's death."

"The minute she saw us barge through the door today, Fenella must have known her problems were just beginning. She routinely listened in on the conversations that took place in Harper's office. She heard us tell Harper that we were looking into Grady's murder and that we figured the killer was someone who had access to his credit card information."

"She realized we were going to pull it all apart, didn't she?"

"Probably." Ethan turned his glass between his hands. "She had to know that eventually we would find out that Al Drummer was in Whispering Springs the night of Grady's death. And she heard us tell Harper that we were going to make sure that the scandal got into the media. So, after we left, she went home and started packing."

"And Drummer followed her?"

"Not immediately. He did not know what was going on at that point. According to him, Harper came to see him after we left and demanded to know if someone had used his corporate credit card to hire an investigation firm in Whispering Springs. Drummer got the rest of the story about our visit to the Manor from office gossip. By the time he figured out that there was a huge problem, Fenella had left for the day. He went by her house to see her."

"That would have been, what? Five-thirty or six?"

"Right," Ethan said. "They quarreled. She told him she was ending their relationship. Drummer left. He went home, had a few drinks, and worked himself into a fury. Called her on the phone. She did not pick up. That really maddened him. He got a gun and went back to her house. Confronted her and shot her."

"Why did he hang around? What was he doing upstairs when you arrived?"

"Before he shot her, she taunted him with the fact that she had recorded a couple of their conversations, including one in which he told her that he had killed Grady. She told him that if he gave her any trouble she would turn it over to the cops."

"He was searching for the recording when you arrived?"

"Yeah." Ethan looked out at the black lake. "He had just found it upstairs in a suitcase that Fenella had not finished packing when he realized that I was in the house."

She closed her eyes against the knowledge of how close Ethan had come to getting killed. "My God."

Ethan said nothing. When she opened her eyes, she saw that he was still watching the dark waters of the lake. She could feel him moving deeper into that place inside himself where he could be alone and still.

"Ethan?"

"Mmm?" He took another sip of brandy, but he did not take his attention off the lake.

She reached across the table and put her hand on his arm. "Ethan, listen to me. I know what you're thinking, but you're wrong. You could not have saved Fenella. You are not responsible for her death, do you hear me?"

He did not say anything for a while.

"If I had gone there first, instead of hitting Venetia McAlistair's cottage . . ."

"No." She put both hands on his arm and tightened her fingers to get his attention. "You can't second-guess yourself like this. You were right to check McAlistair's place first. It was the logical thing to do. Yes, Fenella is dead, but don't forget that she conspired in the murder of another person. Grady is dead because of her."

"I know."

She did not like the sound of that. He was agreeing with her, but she could feel him sinking deeper into the dark place.

She rose, went around the table, and hauled on his arm. He did not seem to notice.

"Ethan. Get up." It was like trying to levitate a large chunk of granite.

He frowned. "What?"

"Let's go."

"Where?"

"Upstairs."

He shrugged, finished his brandy, and got to his feet.

She took him by the hand and led him out of the lounge and up the stairs to their room on the second floor. Pausing, she took out her key, opened the door, and drew him into the cozy interior.

She closed the door, turned, and went into his arms.

"Kiss me," she ordered softly.

He did the narrow-eyed thing and finally started to focus on her. She could feel him resurfacing.

She raised her mouth, twined her arms around his neck, and kissed him with everything that was in her.

He came back from wherever he had gone with a sudden rush of heat.

"Zoe."

He tumbled her down onto the bed.

A long time later, he awakened and saw that the pattern of moonlight streaming through the window had shifted. It now slanted across the bed, silhouetting the graceful curve of Zoe's hip as she lay curled on her side.

He felt warm again. That came as a surprise. Earlier he had felt himself sinking into the familiar ice zone. It was a place he had visited off and on over the course of his life, but he had not discovered the true depths of the zone until after Drew's death.

Tonight, when he had sat with Zoe looking out over the lake, thinking of how he should have gone to Fenella Leeds's house first, he had figured he would be in the ice zone for a fairly long period. He had wondered if Zoe would leave while he was there. He wouldn't have blamed her. Others had made it clear that he was not great company when he was off in that other place.

But he hadn't had a chance to go deep tonight. Zoe had dragged him back. He knew himself well enough to know that the bad time had passed. He would be okay until the next trigger incident, whatever that might prove to be.

But meanwhile, he had Zoe.

He put his arm around her waist and pulled her close against him.

He slept.

Chapter Thirty-five

"You know what really frosts me about all this?" Zoe said.

"What?" Ethan used his fork to push some of his scrambled eggs onto a slice of rye toast.

He was certainly eating a hearty breakfast this morning, she thought. She took that as a good sign. Last night she had been worried about him.

They were sitting in the inn dining room. A handful of other tables were also occupied. Through the windows she could see a slice of the lake. The water looked like hammered steel beneath the cloudy sky.

She really hated this place, she thought. She could not wait to leave. But today she and Ethan were scheduled to give statements to the local police. They would probably not escape Candle Lake until tomorrow.

"What bothers me is that Ian Harper is going to walk away from this mess," she said.

Ethan paused in mid-chew and shook his head. "No, he won't. He's going to go down in flames, financially, at least. His scam will be exposed. The publicity surrounding the murder of Fenella Leeds will cause his special clients to run for the hills. Lawyers will swarm and some rough justice will be done."

"You really think so?"

"Trust me."

"I hope you're right."

"Harper will no doubt try to disappear, but I'll keep an eye on him. If he pops up somewhere else, I'll pull the plug on him."

Her mood lightened somewhat. "Promise?"

"Promise. He'll never rest easy again. He'll always be looking over his shoulder."

"Okay," she said, satisfied. If there was one thing she was entirely certain of these days, it was that Ethan kept his promises. She went back to eating her oatmeal.

The Candle Lake chief of police was waiting for them in his office the next morning. He informed them that Ian Harper had vanished. Ethan could see that Zoe was outraged, but he tried to be philosophical. On the plus side, Harper had not gotten away with any of the funds in the Candle Lake Manor accounts. Fenella Leeds had arranged to transfer most of the available Manor assets into her own account shortly before she was murdered. Getting the money back was going to be a legal nightmare.

"It's not our problem," Ethan told her as they drove away from the small municipal building that housed the Candle Lake police department.

"There are a lot of folks who will be staking claims to that cash." Zoe looked a little more cheerful. "By the time the lawyers are finished, I doubt if there will be a dime left."

"Right."

His phone chirped and he answered. "Truax here."

"Everything okay there?" Singleton asked.

"We're still ass-deep in cops and statements. Anything new there?"

"I'm tying up some loose ends, too," Singleton said. "The Merchant made contact again. He says he's satisfied that he has identified the files that were hacked by GopherBoy. Zoe's was among those that got snatched, but Arcadia's is clean and untouched. It was a full-identity package and the Merchant stores them in a different, more securely encrypted database on a different computer. He is anxious to assure all of his clients that he has taken measures to make certain that this sort of incident does not happen again."

"Measures?"

"He says he used a specially designed virus to destroy the hacker's hard drive." Singleton cleared his throat. "I got the impression that the hacker won't come out of this in good shape physically, either. But I didn't want to go there so I didn't ask any more questions. The bottom line is that I think we can be reasonably sure that Arcadia isn't any more at risk than she was before this whole thing started."

"Talked to Stagg?"

"He and Arcadia are on their way back from New Orleans. Got the feeling Harry Stagg wasn't in a rush to return though. I think he may be enjoying his work."

"Into every life, a little sunshine must fall, I guess."

"Don't think Stagg is a sunshine kind of guy. When are you and Zoe coming home?"

Home. It would have sounded very good if not for the fact that when this was over he was going to be faced with the end of another marriage. He had gotten through three previous divorces, he reminded himself. But he had a feeling that this one was going to be harder than the others. He was not looking forward to it.

"It's getting late," he said. "We'll stay here tonight and leave after breakfast tomorrow. We should be back in Whispering Springs around three or four tomorrow afternoon."

"See you when you get here," Singleton said and hung up.

"The hacker didn't get Arcadia's file," he said.

"Thank heavens."

"She and Stagg are on their way back from New Orleans."

She nodded and fell quiet for a moment.

"The meeting of the Cleland board is only a few weeks off," she said eventually.

"Yeah."

"And then we can get our divorce."

"Guess so."

"You'll be free again," she said a little too brightly.

"So will you."

"Probably one of the shortest marriages in history."

"Maybe we'll get into one of the record books," he said.

"I'll be able to pay your full bill in cash in a few months after the merger takes place," Zoe said.

He tightened his hands on the steering wheel. "Our deal was that you would do the design work on Nightwinds."

"Well, yes, but that was back when we weren't sure how this would turn out. I didn't know if I'd have the money to pay you then. But now it looks like I will."

"I'm satisfied with the original bargain."

She flashed him a quick, searching glance. "You still want me to work on Nightwinds? Why? You told me yourself it would be a long time before you could afford a lot of major remodeling."

"I know, but in the meantime, I could at least paint some of the rooms. Maybe pull up some of that orchid carpeting. I've got to do something. I can't go on much longer surrounded with all that pink."

She sat back in the seat. "Okay."

He relaxed his hands a little on the steering wheel. The arrangement was a little weird and there was still the divorce to get through. But at least he would be seeing her on a regular basis for a while.

Something to be said for having your own private interior decorator.

They got back to Whispering Springs at three-thirty the following afternoon. Ethan parked in front of Zoe's apartment building, opened the trunk, and removed her suitcase. Another wave of uncertainty went through her. She had been tense and edgy ever since she had gotten out of bed this morning and things were not improving.

Ethan's mood was just as prickly. They had both been overly polite in an attempt to avoid snapping at each other during the trip home.

Now what? She wondered, twisting her key in the gate lock. She could invite Ethan to join her for dinner this evening, but she was not so sure that was a swell idea. He had other obligations. There were Theo and Jeff and Bonnie to consider. Also, he did have a business to run. He would probably want to check his messages and go through the mail.

He would no doubt appreciate some space, she thought. They had been living very closely together for the past few days. The man did have a private life. In spite of what he kept saying about that damned wedding license, it wasn't as though they were really married. They were involved in an affair that just happened to have a fancy piece of paper attached to it.

Ethan frowned as they went up the stairs. "You feeling okay? You've been acting strange all day."

"I'm fine."

"You don't look so fine."

"I said I'm okay." She stopped in front of her door and rummaged through her tote for the heavy key chain. "I'm just a little tired, that's all."

"You're tense."

"I'm not tense," she said evenly.

"I know tense when I see it. You want to tell me what's going on?"

"I'm not the only one who's on edge here. I feel like I'm walking on eggshells around you."

"I'm doing just fine," he said. "You're the one who won't communicate here."

"Don't worry about me." This was ridiculous. They were on the brink of a full-scale quarrel and there was absolutely no reason for one. "You've probably got things to do."

"Sure." He put the suitcase down with a thud, grasped her arm, and turned her around to face him before she could unlock the door. "Things to do. Like figuring out where the hell this relationship is going."

That was too much. "Why ask me? How should I know where it's going? I've never been in a situation like this."

"Neither have I."

"Look, the last thing I want to do is argue with you. Let's talk about this later when we're both in a better mood."

He braced one hand on the door frame. "You know what? I think I want to argue about this right now."

"Well, I certainly don't."

The door opened without warning. Singleton loomed.

"Better argue about it later," he advised in low tones. "There's a party going on in here."

Zoe was so startled she nearly dropped the heavy key chain on her own foot.

Then she saw the large white banner draped across her tiny living room. CONGRATULATIONS ZOE & ETHAN was spelled out in big red letters accented with a lot of glitter. Arcadia, Harry Stagg, Bonnie, Jeff, and Theo were grouped around the banner. A small pile of packages wrapped in silver-and-white paper were stacked on an end table.

Ethan frowned at the sign. "What the hell?"

"Surprise, Uncle Ethan," Theo called.

"We got a giant cake," Jeff said proudly. "They put your names on it, too."

"And ice cream," Theo said.

Singleton smiled benignly. "It was all Jeff's and Theo's idea."

"It's not my birthday," Zoe said blankly.

"This isn't a birthday party," Arcadia said dryly. "It's a wedding reception."

Chapter Thirty-six

Bonnie sank deeper into the bubbling spa pool and gave Zoe an apologetic look. "Sorry about catching you by surprise yesterday. Jeff and Theo came home from school bubbling over with the party concept. Apparently one of their classmates got to be a ring-bearer in a major production last week, and the kid went on and on about the big reception after the wedding."

"Don't tell me—let me guess," Zoe said. "Jeff and Theo got into the competitive mode, right?"

"Something like that. They concocted the notion of throwing a surprise party for you two. Unfortunately, they talked to Singleton about their scheme before they brought it to me. By that time they had Singleton on their side. I was outnumbered."

"Don't worry about it," Zoe said. At some point she had decided to adopt a mature, philosophical stance toward the whole thing. "They meant well. It was just one of those little awkward social moments that happen in life."

"Speaking personally," Arcadia murmured from the other side of the simmering spa pool, "I had a lovely time. Great cake."

Bonnie chuckled. "Chocolate with Zoe's and Ethan's names spelled out in red frosting. Definitely a culinary statement."

"It was quite dramatic," Zoe said. "Not your usual wedding cake."

Bonnie was amused. "You can say that again."

Zoe leaned back and put her hands out to either side on the underwater bench to brace herself. The roiling waters felt good. She had not realized just how tense she had been during the past forty-eight hours.

Arcadia was the one who had suggested that they all meet at her health club that afternoon. Bonnie had jumped at the invitation and promptly made arrangements to pack her sons off to Nightwinds with Ethan. Zoe had joined the other two women because she needed the company of women for a time. Life with the male of the species had become tricky.

The interior of the elegant spa room was a vast, elaborately tiled and delightfully decadent space. The club was heavily into water features. A variety of small- and medium-sized hot and cold pools were grouped around a larger one. Waterfalls and fountains splashed in the corners. Fluffy white towels were stacked in convenient locations.

Women, some nude, some in swimsuits, lounged in the waters. In the alcoves, others stretched out on padded massage benches, allowing themselves to be pummeled into a blissful state.

"To be perfectly honest," Bonnie admitted, "I didn't try very hard to shut down the party planning."

"It's okay," Zoe tilted her head back. The philosophical thing was working, she thought. "I know you've been taken with the idea of seeing Ethan married again."

"What I'm taken with is the notion of you and Ethan giving this marriage a chance," Bonnie said seriously. "I mean, you're already having an affair and you've got the license. Why not just, you know, let things go along as they are for a while? See what happens?"

"She's got a point," Arcadia said. "Divorce is expensive, even when no one wants to fight over the assets. Neither you nor Ethan need a lot of lawyers' bills right now."

"I'll be able to pay for the costs of the divorce when I cash out my shares in Cleland Cage," Zoe said quietly. "I certainly don't expect Ethan to have to pay to get out of this situation."

"Ethan will insist on covering his half of the costs," Bonnie said. "I can guarantee it. It will be a point of honor for him."

"This isn't a matter of honor. It's business."

Bonnie moved her legs under the surface of the water, scissoring them languidly back and forth. "Maybe Ethan doesn't want to be rescued from the marriage. Have you talked to him about it?"

"Of course he wants out." In spite of the soothing waters, Zoe could feel the place between her shoulders tighten. On top of that, she was getting cross. So much for her newfound philosophical approach to the situation. "Why on earth would he want to be trapped in this marriage?"

"Because it's very convenient for him?" Arcadia raised her platinum brows. "After all, you two are sleeping together, so what's the big deal with staying married until you're both ready to split?"

"Believe me, it's a big deal," Zoe retorted.

"Why?" Arcadia asked.

Zoe drew up her knees under the water and wrapped her arms around them. "It just is, that's all. Marriage is always a big deal."

"I'm not so sure Ethan is looking forward to another divorce," Bonnie said. "When you get right down to it, he's a little old-fashioned about some things."

"Old-fashioned? Ethan?" Zoe asked in amazement. "The man's been married *four times.*"

"Probably just a long run of bad luck," Arcadia said. "Hey, it can happen."

"You're attributing all four marriages to bad luck?" Zoe was starting to feel cornered. "That's a bit of a stretch, don't you think?"

"I've explained the first three marriages to you," Bonnie reminded her. "And you know the circumstances surrounding the fourth. This one is not exactly Ethan's fault."

"What do you mean?" Zoe shot back. "It was his idea."

Bonnie ignored that. "Speaking as his concerned sister-in-law and the one person who knows him better than anyone else in this spa, I don't think it would be good for Ethan to go through the stress of a fourth divorce. Not right now, at any rate."

"Don't worry," Zoe muttered. "Ethan can handle the stress factor."

"I'm not so sure. He's vulnerable."

"Ethan? Vulnerable?" Zoe made a face. "Give me a break."

"This is a rough time for him," Bonnie insisted. "Starting up a new business is always difficult. You know how it is. He's got some serious competition with Radnor to worry about. He has to establish new contacts in the local police department and on the street. And then there's the problem of attracting paying clients."

"Hey, just a minute here, I'm a paying client." Zoe broke off. "At least, I will be very soon."

"Maybe, but in the meantime, you have to admit he hasn't seen any profit on this job. In fact, you've cost him a bundle out of pocket."

"And forcing him to pay his share of the divorce costs will definitely be an added financial burden that he doesn't need right now," Arcadia said.

"Aaargh." Zoe glared at her companions. "I don't believe I'm hearing this. You duped me into coming here today, didn't you? It was a plot. I thought I was going to be able to relax and instead I get ambushed."

"Take it easy," Arcadia said. "All Bonnie and I are saying is don't rush into anything. Where's the harm in letting the situation ride for a while?"

"We're talking about marriage here," Zoe said. "This is serious stuff. Maybe not to someone who has been through it four times, but it certainly is to me."

"Ethan took every single one of his other marriages seriously," Bonnie countered. "In fact, it's my guess that you'll have to make the first move to end this one. I doubt if he will."

Zoe swallowed. "Then I'll do it."

Arcadia extended one foot above the bubbles and examined a platinum toenail. "You want out that badly?"

Zoe hesitated. "I don't want to feel like I'm holding him in a cage."

Bonnie laughed. "If and when Ethan wants out of the cage, you'll know it. Trust me on this."

Zoe gave up. Time to change the subject.

She pinned Arcadia with a look. "Enough about me. Let's talk about you."

"What about me?"

"How was New Orleans?"

Arcadia slowly lowered her foot back into the water. An odd smile curved the corners of her full mouth.

"New Orleans was good," she said.

They sat in the shade of the patio and watched Jeff and Theo bounce a giant, inflated ball around the pool.

Stagg reclined on the lounger. Singleton occupied a webbed chair. Ethan sat on another chair, leaning forward a little, forearms resting on his knees, hands wrapped around a can of soda. He watched the boys splash exuberantly in the water.

Earlier, he had put out a bowl of chips and pretzels and a cooler filled with iced pop. He knew Bonnie would not be thrilled with his choice of after-school snacks, but he consoled himself with the thought that Jeff and Theo were working up a healthy appetite for dinner. He figured he'd done his duty by reminding both boys to put on plenty of sunscreen.

"Don't see why you gotta rush this divorce thing." Harry Stagg leaned back in the pink padded lounger. "Looks to me like the two of you are getting along okay. Besides, divorces cost money. I got one once a long time ago. I still remember writing the check to pay off the lawyer. It was painful."

"The man has a point." Singleton leaned a little way out of his chair and helped himself to a handful of potato chips. "You don't need any extra expenses right now. Got enough as it is. Start-up phase of a new business is always dicey. You need to conserve your cash."

"It's not the money," Ethan said. "It's more complicated."

"You sure?" Harry was clearly skeptical. "Has Zoe told you that she wants a divorce?"

"Not yet," Ethan admitted. "But I'm sure she'll bring it up after the board meeting."

"You looking forward to a fourth divorce?" Singleton asked around a mouthful of chips.

"No," Ethan stated. "Been there and done that three times. No matter what they tell you, it's never simple. It's always messy."

"Right." Singleton downed a mouthful of pop. "So why push for it? Like Stagg said, you and Zoe are okay together right now. When things are no longer okay, you can worry about filing for a divorce."

"I don't think it's going to be that easy," Ethan said.

"Arcadia says Zoe agreed to do up some new interior designs for this house," Harry remarked.

"Yeah." Ethan ate some chips. "Part of our business arrangement. So what?"

"Well, you sure as hell don't want to go through a divorce while she's working on this place," Harry said. "She might get distracted and that could be dangerous."

"Dangerous?" Ethan elevated one brow. "How?"

"Stagg's right," Singleton said, munching. "Wait until Zoe finishes her design work before you start talking about a divorce. People get emotional in the middle of a divorce. They become weird and unpredictable."

Ethan contemplated his previous three divorces. No doubt about it, there had been some weird and unpredictable aspects. And those had been what people liked to call *good* divorces.

"You don't want to jeopardize the remodeling here," Harry said. "I mean, let's face it, you gotta do something about all this pink."

"Right. A man can't live with this much pink," Singleton said. "Not for long, at any rate. It's not healthy."

"You get used to it after a while," Ethan said.

Harry and Singleton swiveled their heads toward each other and exchanged glances through their dark glasses.

"He's getting accustomed to it," Singleton said ominously.

"Oh, man," Harry exhaled heavily. "Not a good sign. Time is running out. His brain is starting to rot."

Singleton turned back to Ethan. "Look, forget the pink problem for now. Maybe you're trying to make this whole situation a lot more complicated than it really is. Let's look at the facts here. Neither you nor Zoe is looking over the garden fence yet, right?"

"I've been too busy since I got to Whispering Springs to look over any fences. Same for Zoe. Neither of us have had a chance to develop anything resembling a normal social life."

Singleton turned a can of pop slowly between his palms and looked wise. "Not sure there is any such thing as a normal social life."

"Huh." Harry was obviously taken with that observation. "You may be right. I sure as hell never had one."

Ethan glanced at him. "What about New Orleans?"

"New Orleans was different." Harry's wraparound sunglasses made it impossible to read his eyes.

"Normal?" Ethan pressed.

"Don't know that you'd call it normal." Harry's mouth twitched a little in what might have been a smile. "But New Orleans was definitely good."

"Tell you what," Singleton said, "let Zoe bring it up first. That way you'll know if she really wants a divorce."

"I'll think about it," Ethan said.

But he was not sure he could take the uncertainty. Marriage was a strange phenomenon in his experience. Sort of like being pregnant. Either you were married or you weren't. He had never been good with anything that required inhabiting a mushy middle ground.

Chapter Thirty-seven

Zoe stood in the center of the sprawling, lush, pink living room, a grid-printed sketchbook in hand, and drew a rough floor plan. It was not easy envisioning the space without the flamboyant furnishings. It was amazing how overpowering the color pink could be in all its variants and mutations.

The bones of the house were good, though, she thought, mentally stripping the interiors of furniture and drapes. The dimensions of the rooms were pleasing and well situated to take advantage of the natural flow of energy.

Maybe she could even do something about clearing out the bad vibes in the theater. One of the things that she had discovered during the past six months was that there really was something to the feng shui and Vastu theories. She could modify the invisible auras of some rooms by changing the design.

She had the house to herself this evening. Ethan was at a school function with Bonnie,

Jeff, and Theo. She could feel the potential in Nightwinds. Maybe it was because it was the first time that she had been alone in the residence, the first time that she had not had to worry about the enormous distraction created by the owner.

It had been a strange feeling letting herself into the big house tonight. In the legal sense, this was her home, too. She was Ethan's wife, for a while, at least.

She finished the sketch of the living room and looked up at the painting hanging on the wall above the mantel. Camelia Foote smiled down, taunting, mocking, and yet somehow tragic. She had married for money and maybe the bargain had seemed like a good one at the time. But it had brought her no happiness.

Zoe turned away from the portrait and walked into the formal dining room. Beyond the yards of rose-colored drapery, she could see the shades of shadows that defined the desert night. The moon was bright, washing the canyon in silver. The lights of other homes glittered in the distance like so many bright, sparkling little gemstones tossed carelessly about.

She stood looking at the scene for a long time.

The doorbell chimed, breaking the trance. She had been so lost in her reverie that she had not heard the car arrive in the drive.

She went quickly toward the door, wondering if the school function had ended early.

But when she peered through the small glass peephole she saw Kimberley Cleland.

Damn. She did not need this. She was tempted not to answer the door, but her car was parked in the drive. Kimberley would know that someone was home.

Reluctantly, Zoe opened the door. "What are you doing here?"

"Sara." Kimberley smiled tremulously. She was dressed in black trousers trimmed with a black silk shirt. Her pale blond hair was pulled into a ponytail. An expensive-looking bag made of soft, pliable black leather was slung over one shoulder. "May I come in? I need to talk to you."

"The name is Zoe and if you've come to offer another bribe to Ethan, you'll have to return some other time. He's not here."

Kimberley shook her head. Her eyes darkened with some strong emotion that might have been pain. "You're the one I want to talk to."

"How did you find me?"

"I went to your apartment first. When you weren't there, I knew you would probably be here."

"Where is Forrest?"

"Home. He doesn't know I'm in Whispering Springs. I left a message telling him that I went to visit my mother for a few days."

"If you've come to plead with me not to vote in favor of the merger, you can save your energy."

"Yes, I've come here to plead with you." Kimberley's voice was cracking at the edges. Tears glistened in her eyes. "I'll get down on my knees, if that's what you want. Please, listen to me, that's all I ask. There is so much at stake."

Kimberley was one of the many family members who had refused to talk to her in the wake of Preston's death, Zoe reflected. She had stood by her husband and the rest of the Clelands while Zoe was committed to Candle Lake Manor. *I owe her nothing. Not one single, damn thing.*

But just as she was about to slam the door in Kimberley's face, Ethan's words came back to her. When in doubt, stir the pot and see what bubbles to the surface.

Kimberley just might be the one person who could break Forrest Cleland's alibi. What did she have to lose by talking to her? Zoe thought. If Kimberley was desperate, it was possible that she might forget herself and say too much if pressed hard enough. Maybe she would drop some small clue that would provide an opening to find proof of Forrest's guilt.

"All right." Zoe stood back. "Come in."

"Thank you." Relieved, Kimberley stepped quickly into the large hall. She stopped and looked around with an air of surprise and gathering distaste. "How . . . unusual."

"The original owner did it for his wife. She liked pink."

"I can see that."

"The living room is this way." Zoe led her into the front room and waved Kimberley toward the sofa. "Have a seat."

She took the chair on the other side of the pink marble coffee table. Damned if she would offer coffee or tea, she decided. Not unless Kimberley really started to get chatty and informative.

Kimberley sat down somewhat gingerly.

She put her black purse on the sofa beside her and examined Zoe with a tiny frown.

"You look . . . very well," she said, breaking the small silence.

"For a crazy woman, do you mean?" Zoe gave her a bright, brittle smile. "Oh, hey, I'm in great shape. Been working out and eating right. But you know what, Kimberley? I barely survived Candle Lake Manor. I blame all of the Clelands for putting me in there, of course, but most of all I blame Forrest."

Kimberley's face was drawn and tight. "I swear, he only did what he thought was best for you. You were so very ill."

"Please do not add insult to injury by lying to me. We both know why I wound up in there. Forrest paid Ian Harper a lot of money to keep me out of the way."

Kimberley laced her fingers very tightly together. "I understand your anger and resentment, but what else could we do? You weren't yourself in the weeks and months following Preston's death. And after you made that last visit to the cabin, you seemed to take a turn for the worse. All those accusations against Forrest. What happened to you that day when you went back there? What was it that put you into such a state?"

"I thought you came here to talk to me about my shares of Cleland Cage."

"I'm sorry." Kimberley twisted her hands. "It's just that I've always wondered why you lost it the way you did after that second visit to that cabin. Claiming to hear voices in the walls. It was frightening, if you must know."

"In point of fact, I never claimed to hear voices in the walls."

"You said something about hearing an argument."

"No, I did not. I said I sensed rage. I didn't have to hear voices in the walls to know that whoever murdered Preston had been crazy with it. It was pretty obvious, Kimberley. The smashed flowers and the broken camera. All of it was evidence of a *really* sick mind."

"The police said that whoever killed Preston was probably furious because there was so little money in his wallet. That would be logical in a terrible kind of way." Kimberley tightened her fingers. "But it wouldn't mean the killer was crazy."

"This one was definitely nuts."

"How can you be sure?"

"Maybe it takes one to know one," Zoe replied.

Kimberley stared at her, shocked. "You admit that you're not well?"

"Let's get back to why you came here to see me tonight. I'm especially interested in the fact that you didn't tell Forrest about this visit."

"He would not have let me come here," Kimberley whispered. "He'll be very angry if he finds out what I've done."

"What, exactly, are you going to do?"

Kimberley got to her feet, hands still clenched. She bowed her head. "I'm here because I can't stand the guilt any longer. Please forgive me, Zoe."

Zoe went very still. Then she rose cautiously from the chair. It was suddenly very hard to breathe.

"What guilt?" she whispered. "What are you talking about?"

"I've tried so hard not to think about this, but I can't pretend any longer." Kimberley raised her head. She looked as if she was drowning in her unshed tears. "You're right. I'm afraid that Forrest may have . . . that he might have shot Preston."

"Dear God."

"But not because of the shares."

"What other reason could there possibly be?"

"I think he may have discovered that I was—" Kimberley paused to wipe her eyes with the back of her hand. "This is so hard."

Zoe went around behind the high, gilded chair and gripped the back very tightly. "What are you trying to say?"

"I'm so desperately sorry, but the truth is that I had an affair with Preston." Kimberley was sobbing full out now. She reached down, opened her bag and took out a handful of tissues to blot her tears. "And I think Forrest got suspicious and that he went to the cabin that day and . . . and shot him."

Ethan's phone rang just as he bent over to examine the robot Jeff was demonstrating.

"It picks up this little stick," Jeff explained proudly. He pushed a button to set the robot in motion. "Watch this."

The robot whirred into jerky action. Ethan watched it clutch the small strip of wood while he fished his phone out of his pocket.

"Excellent," he said to Jeff. "Most excellent."

Jeff beamed.

"Let me get this," Ethan said, indicating the phone. "I'll be right back."

"Okay."

"Truax," he said into the phone, working his way cautiously through the maze of low tables that had been set up in the classroom.

"This is Singleton. I've got—"

The high-pitched voices of some twenty youngsters excitedly explaining their science projects to their parents created a background din that made it impossible to catch what Singleton said.

"Hang on until I get outside," Ethan said.

Bonnie, standing on the other side of the room, talking to Jeff's teacher, saw him and gave him an inquiring look.

He let her see the phone in his palm. She nodded and went back to her conversation.

Ethan went past a demonstration of capillary action, which featured purple-and-orange tinted water and some drooping stalks of celery, and a handmade replica of the solar system.

"Okay," he said, stepping out of the room into the balmy night. "What's up?"

"I don't know if this is important or not,"

Singleton said. "But you told me to let you know if any of the Clelands made any moves. I've been monitoring their online activities to see if anyone bought any tickets."

"Forrest?"

"No. His wife. She got on a flight to Phoenix this afternoon. I didn't pick up the red flag until I checked my computer a few minutes ago."

Ethan went cold. With a slamming jolt of deep certainty, all the pieces of the puzzle came together.

"Well, shit," he said very softly. "I should have seen it coming."

"Mama, Mama, that man said the bad 's' word," a high-pitched voice declared in ringing accents. "I heard him."

Ethan looked down and saw a person of very small stature staring up at him. The short person's mother was frowning.

"You're in trouble," the small person announced.

"You can say that again," Ethan said.

He ran for the parking lot.

Chapter Thirty-eight

An unseen ice storm swirled through the big house. It gave no outward indication of its presence. No papers fluttered in the draft. The drapes did not billow. The chandelier in the hall did not tremble beneath the driving sleet. But Zoe could feel the heavy, chilling sigh as it passed through her, whispering along her bones.

"You're telling me that Forrest killed Preston because of you," Zoe repeated very evenly.

"Yes. This has all been such a nightmare for so long. I can't stand it anymore. I can't sleep. I can't eat. I'm living on pills. I'm terrified of my own husband because of what he did and what he might do. It has to end. Don't you understand?"

"Oh, yes, Kimberley. I understand all of it now."

Kimberley pulled herself together with a visible effort. "The truth has to come out, or I'm afraid that I'll be the one who will end up in Candle Lake Manor."

"I called it Xanadu." Zoe released her death grip on the back of the chair and moved back a step toward the arched opening of the central hall. "It was an unreal place in some ways, you see? A place of sunless seas and caves of ice, just like in the Coleridge poem. There were so many nights when I lay there in bed looking out at the lake thinking that this couldn't be happening to me, that I was living in a nightmare."

"Yes." Kimberley raised her tear-smudged face. "Living in a nightmare. That's what it feels like. I should never have gotten involved with Preston. But he wanted me so much and I was so unhappy with Forrest."

"Really? How strange." Zoe took another pace back. "Say, I've got an idea. Would you like a tour of this house? It has a fascinating history. Maybe even what some people would call a ghost."

"A ghost?" Kimberley was confused now. Anger sparked in her eyes. "Come back here. I don't want a tour of this damned house. I'm trying to explain how it was between Preston and me."

"But I don't care anymore how it was between you and Preston." She was at the arched opening. She turned and walked away down the long, grand hall. "That's one of the things I learned during my stay in the Manor, you know. Not to care. It's better when you don't care. That way there's no pain. No sense of loss."

"Don't walk away from me."

Zoe kept going.

Kimberley followed. Zoe looked back and saw that she had retrieved her black bag.

"You know, Kimberley, if you really are going crazy, you might want to consider checking into Candle Lake yourself. I'm sure for certain types of people, it would be a lovely place for a vacation. You can have all the pills you want."

"I have to tell you about Preston." Kimberley hurried after her, clutching the purse. "I know this comes as a shock to you. But the truth is we had been seeing each other in secret for some time. Preston begged me to leave Forrest. But how could I do that?"

"Really, Kimberley, you're not being at all logical here. Why would it have been so difficult to leave Forrest if you no longer loved him?"

"Oh, please, Sara—"

"Zoe. I really must insist that you call me by my new name. I left the old name behind at the Manor." Zoe laughed, a high, sharp, edgy sound that echoed eerily in the long hall. "Yes, indeed, that place made a new woman of me."

"I couldn't possibly walk away from my life with Forrest just to marry a man who teaches art history, could I?" Kimberley's voice rose. "I had everything I wanted. I couldn't turn my back on it all."

"How sad. Now you'll never know what you missed, will you? You're doomed to live out your perfect life with Forrest." Zoe started to hum.

"Stop it. You're acting crazy."

"Probably because I am crazy. Just ask any of the folks back at the Manor. They'll tell you how crazy I am."

"You have to listen to me."

"One of the great benefits of having been declared insane is that I no longer have to listen to anyone unless I really, really want to listen and I don't think I want to listen to you, Kimberley. Now, then, where was I? Oh, yes, I was giving you a tour of this magnificent residence. A man named Abner Bennett Foote built it for his wife. That's her over the mantel in the living room. Did you happen to notice? She was lovely and, I think, just a little bit crazy, too. She married Foote for his money, you see. Don't you think that's a crazy thing to do?"

"I don't want to hear anything about her. I don't care about a dead woman. I want you to know about Preston. How he cheated on you with me."

"Then again, maybe you don't think it's crazy to marry for money. After all, that's what you did, isn't it?" Zoe stopped in front of the pair of elaborately worked theater doors. She winked at Kimberley. "Wait until you see this room."

She flung open both doors, took a deep breath, braced herself, and stepped into the darkened theater.

The whispers of old pain and rage that still clung to the walls stirred the small hairs on the nape of her neck. She forced herself to take three more steps into the room and flipped one of the light switches at random.

She stepped through the heavy, velvet curtains into the seating section.

Kimberley trailed after her, fumbling her way through the hangings. When she emerged on the other side, her face was a mask of anger.

Somewhere in the distance a phone rang.

"You can't face the fact that Preston loved me, can you?" Kimberley said in a low, fierce tone. "*Me,* not you. He wanted me."

"She died in here, you know." Zoe leaned back against one of the seats in the last row and stretched her arms out to the sides. "This is where he murdered her."

"Murdered who?" Kimberley peered around the shadowy theater. "What are you talking about?"

"Camelia Foote. They all thought she died in a drunken fall in the canyon, but that's not what happened. She died in this very room. I know that because I can sense the killer's rage. It's still locked in the walls." She looked up. "And in the ceiling and floor, too, I suppose. Still so strong, even after all these years."

"You're lying. You can't feel anything. You're making it all up as you go along."

"I wish that was true." Zoe pushed herself away from the row of seats and strolled slowly toward the marble bar in the corner. "But the unfortunate fact is that I really do feel things sometimes. And what I'm picking up in this room is very similar to what I picked up at the cabin after Preston was killed. A sick, uncontrolled rage. I went back the second time a few months later just to make sure."

Kimberley watched her nervously. "You really are crazy, aren't you?"

"Maybe." She grasped the edge of the velvet curtains that hung next to the bar and pulled it aside. "Maybe not. But I'm pretty sure they met here around midnight."

Kimberley scowled, trying to follow the shifting currents of the conversation. "Who met here?"

"Camelia and her lover, Jeremy Hill. They had both been drinking heavily all evening. Flirting madly. Maybe they had made love in the gardens earlier. At any rate, Hill was desperate. Probably begged her to leave her rich husband. But Camelia refused."

"You don't know any of this. You're just telling a story. One that I don't want to hear."

"Are you sure you can't hear it in the walls?" Zoe went behind the high, polished marble bar and folded her elbows on the cold stone. "Listen closely, Kimberley. Maybe if you try real hard, you can feel some of what Camelia felt that night because the two of you had something in common."

"I have nothing in common with that woman. Stop it, right now."

"You both married for money. You both got everything you thought you wanted in life. Wealth. Social connections. A spectacular home."

"I don't want to hear another word about that old murder."

"Both of you told yourselves that you had everything you desired, but that wasn't true. You each tried to have your cake and eat it, too. You wanted love and passion, but you did not want to risk your cozy little financial setups to get them. So you and Camelia went looking for love on the side."

"That's not true."

"Neither of you found the real thing. Oh, sure, Camelia managed to find a man who could give her something that looked like passion, but he became obsessed and in the end he killed her."

"Shut up." Kimberley sounded calmer now. She reached into her purse. But this time she did not take out some tissues. When her hand reappeared there was a small, silvery gun in it. "Just shut up, do you understand?"

Zoe's mouth went dry. She hoped the heavy marble bar was thick enough to stop a bullet because it was all that stood between her and Kimberley.

"What sent you over the edge, Kimberley?" she asked in a conversational tone. "Was it seeing how happy Preston and I were together? You wanted to be happy too, didn't you?"

"I deserve to be happy."

"You've been reading too many self-help books, I'm afraid. But getting back to your little story, I assume that you tried to convince Preston to have an affair with you. Naturally he turned you down. Gently, of course. He was a very gentle man."

"He did not turn me down." Kimberley kept the gun trained very steadily on Zoe. "He loved me. We had an affair."

"No, he did not love you, and you did not have an affair."

"You can't be sure of that."

"I am sure of it. Very sure. Preston would never have betrayed me."

"That's what you want to believe."

"I know it deep inside. I have no doubt,

however, that you threw yourself at him. But when he refused to get involved, you became desperate, didn't you? You followed him to the cabin that day and tried one last time to convince him to have an affair with you. But he turned you down again. And you couldn't stand it."

Something crumpled in Kimberley's face. "He wouldn't listen to me. I tried to tell him how much I loved him, and he wouldn't listen."

"Of course not. Because he loved me. And you couldn't stand that, could you? I was the little nobody from nowhere. No family, no social background. No money. Yet Preston loved me, not you."

"It should have been *me.* All those flowers he bought, they should have been for *me.* He should have picked out a special gift for *me,* not you."

"This is all about you, isn't it?"

"I tried to tell him, but he refused to listen. He actually told me to go away. *Me.* I loved him and he told me to go away."

"And you did go away, didn't you? But you returned later."

"I left the car at the side of the road and walked back through the woods to the cabin and I waited. After a while, Preston came out onto the back porch to get some firewood. I had the gun."

"When he turned to carry the wood into the cabin, you shot him in the back. And then you put another bullet in his head, just to be sure."

"He needed to die."

"Because he had rejected you."

"Yes. *Yes.*"

"After you killed Preston, you went into the cabin and tore it apart. It was your insane rage I felt in those walls, not Forrest's."

"Don't you dare call me insane."

"Camelia's lover went over the edge, too." Zoe touched one of the heavy candlesticks. "Lost it big time. He must have been as obsessed as you were, Kimberley."

"*I was not obsessed.* Only crazy people are obsessed."

"I can't hear you because I'm listening to the silent screams of rage in these walls. Surely you can pick up some of the energy? They say crazy people can do that."

"I don't hear anything. I'm not like you."

"After that last quarrel, I think Jeremy Hill picked up the nearest heavy object." Zoe closed a hand around each candlestick and hefted them experimentally. They were not much heavier than her tote when it was fully loaded.

Kimberley seemed irritated by the candlesticks. “Put those down.”

“Camelia turned to walk away and that’s when he struck her. From behind. The same way you attacked Preston.”

“Preston deserved it, I tell you.”

“Got news for you, Kimberley, only crazy people talk like that.”

Zoe heaved the candlestick she held in her right hand across the top of the bar, putting everything she had into it.

Kimberley shrieked and jerked back reflexively, scrambling to avoid the long metal object hurtling toward her.

The gun roared.

Zoe ducked behind the bar, clutching the second candlestick. The heavy marble shuddered under the impact of the bullets.

Kimberley fired again.

Zoe moved. Keeping her head beneath the level of the top of the stone counter, she ran for the curtains that veiled the bartender’s entrance.

She plunged through the thick hangings

into the tiny lobby and raced out into the hall.

Behind her, she heard Kimberley running toward the entrance.

She whirled and tugged frantically on the heavy, gilded doors. Kimberley burst through the curtain, stark madness in her eyes. The doors swung ponderously closed a split second before she reached them.

Heart pounding, Zoe angled the second long candlestick through both elaborately curved handles, effectively barring Kimberley inside the theater.

Half a second later, the heavy doors trembled. In her fury, Kimberley had thrown herself against them.

Zoe fled down the hall.

She rounded the corner into the living room and collided with Ethan.

"What the hell?" He grabbed her arms. "Are you okay?"

Muffled shots thundered at the other end of the hall.

"Kimberley," Zoe gasped. "I locked her inside the theater. She's got a gun. But I don't think she can get out."

Ethan eased her aside and went to the

arched opening. He looked cautiously around the corner. Another shot boomed.

"Oh, man," Ethan said. "She sounds really pissed."

"Actually, she's really crazy."

Chapter Thirty-nine

They gathered in Ethan's office the following morning. It was a large crowd, including as it did Zoe, Arcadia, Bonnie, Singleton, and Harry Stagg. Ethan went across the street to the small café and bought six cups. What was one more item under miscellaneous expenses?

"I was wrong about Forrest all along," Zoe said soberly.

Ethan frowned. He had been worried about her today. She had come through the dangerous events last night with flying colors, but this morning she was definitely looking depressed. Now he finally understood why.

"Don't blame yourself for picking the wrong bad guy." He sat forward at his desk. "You were right about the fact that Preston was murdered by someone who knew him. The police should have looked deeper than they did."

"For two years I blamed Forrest, though. No wonder he thought I was a real nutcase.

Preston didn't change his will because he thought Forrest was dangerous in the physical sense. He was just afraid that his cousin wouldn't do what was best for the company."

Arcadia, seated on the window ledge, swung one foot in an absent motion. "Ethan is right, you can't blame yourself for thinking that Forrest was the killer. It was a perfectly logical assumption under the circumstances."

"I agree," Bonnie said forcefully. "Logical enough that the cops should have probed the alibis of everyone connected to Preston Cleland much more thoroughly than they did."

"If they had done their job," Singleton said, "they would have turned up the interesting fact that the one person who did not have a good alibi for the day of the murder was Kimberley Cleland."

"No one even considered her, least of all me," Zoe said.

"Because there was no obvious motive," Arcadia pointed out. "After all, you knew that Preston was not involved with anyone else, so why would you even consider the possibility that a woman might have murdered him?"

"When you come right down to it," Stagg said, examining the café logo on his plastic cup as if it contained the key to a great secret, "Forrest has a lot to answer for, even if he didn't pull the trigger."

"Damn right, he does," Ethan said. "If he'd mentioned his theory that Preston was having an affair, the investigation would no doubt have gone in a different direction. One that could have led straight to Kimberley."

Zoe wrapped both hands around her cup and studied the contents. "That brings up another question. If he suspected that his wife was having an affair with his cousin, why did he look the other way? I can't see Forrest putting up with a cheating spouse."

"Maybe he loved her too much to face the truth," Bonnie suggested.

"Forrest Cleland?" Zoe gave a ladylike snort. "Passionately in love with anything except Cleland Cage? Get real."

"You know what?" Ethan said softly, "The question of why he chose to ignore the possibility that Kimberley was having an affair with Preston, or anyone else, is a good one." He looked at Zoe. "What do you say we ask him?"

Forrest met them in the lobby of Las Estrellas resort. He looked weary and grim when he sat down across from them in a quiet section of the spacious room.

"I hope this isn't going to take long," he said, glancing at the face of his titanium watch. "I just got back from a long session with the police and in a few minutes I have to call the lawyer I hired for Kim."

"Gee," Ethan said. "We sure do apologize for wasting your valuable time. After all, it's not like we've got any right to a few answers. Your wife did try to murder mine last night, but what the heck, not like we're talking about anything *serious* here."

"Save the sarcasm, Truax. What do you two want?"

Zoe looked at him. "We want to know why you chose to look the other way if you thought Kim was having an affair."

Forrest clearly looked startled. "But I never thought Kim was having an affair with Preston or anyone else. And, in point of fact, she wasn't."

"No, but she was obsessed with Preston," Ethan said.

"Apparently." Forrest rubbed his temples. "But I was unaware of that. I had my hands full with the negotiations for a new acquisition at the time. I wasn't spending much time at home."

"So how did you arrive at the conclusion that Preston was involved with someone?" Ethan asked.

Forrest paused, evidently searching his memory. Then he shrugged. "Kim mentioned it in passing one day shortly before Preston was—" He stopped and came at it again. "Shortly before she killed him. She just said it very casually. Like it was gossip she had picked up at the country club. I don't know why she would do that if it wasn't true."

"Maybe you weren't paying attention," Ethan suggested softly.

Anger flared in Forrest's face. "What the hell is that supposed to mean?"

Zoe shook her head. "Maybe unconsciously Kim dropped some clues hoping that you would pick them up."

"Why would she want me to think she was involved with Preston?" Forrest demanded. "She must have known that if I believed anything of the kind, I would have filed for divorce on the spot."

"I'm sure she did know that," Zoe said quietly. "Which is very likely why she just hinted carefully around the edges. She was crazy, but she wasn't stupid. A part of her was still sane enough not to want to jeopardize her cushy position as your trophy wife."

"I still don't get it," Forrest said. "Why hint at all?"

"Don't you see?" Zoe asked. "If you believed that Preston was having an affair with someone, *anyone,* it would have made her private little fantasy that much more real to her."

There was a short silence while Forrest absorbed that.

"Hadn't thought of it that way," he said at last. "When she mentioned the possibility that Preston was seeing someone on the side, the only thing that occurred to me was that you—"

"Had a motive for murder," Zoe concluded.

"I'm sorry," Forrest said evenly. "But I could see what the two of you meant to each other. I was afraid that if you had found out that Preston was cheating on you, you might have gone a little crazy."

"But you never mentioned that possibility to the cops," she said.

"No," he said.

"Because you knew that I could still control my shares from prison?"

Forrest flattened his hands on his thighs. "I know you won't believe this, but I honestly thought that you would be better off at the hospital. Harper said he was sure he could help you."

Zoe took some deep breaths. "I will never forgive you for that. Do you have any idea of what it was like there? Harper did not even allow visits from the patients' friends because he said it interfered with the course of therapy. Not that anyone outside the Cleland family even knew where I was, thanks to you. Everyone I ever knew vanished from my life."

His jaw tensed. "Maybe if I had been paying more attention to what was going on at home, I would have realized that Kim was the crazy woman, not you. Perhaps I could have stopped her before she went too far."

Zoe did not know how to respond to that

so she kept silent. Ethan did not move in his chair, but she could feel him analyzing the currents that flowed both above and beneath the surface.

"Things have not been going well between Kim and me for the past few months," Forrest said eventually. "She's been drinking a lot. There was a scene at the club a few weeks ago. She flew into a rage with no warning. I was planning to talk to my lawyer about a divorce, but I had decided to put it off until after the board meeting. I knew it was going to cost me a bundle to get rid of her, and I needed time to work out a strategy. Looks like things will be even messier now."

"Probably," Ethan said without any trace of detectable sympathy.

There was another heavy pause.

After a while, Zoe reached into her crimson tote and pulled out an envelope. She gave it to Forrest.

He accepted it with a frown. "What is this?"

"A proxy made out to you so that you can vote my shares at the annual board meeting. I know you'll do what's best for the company."

His hand clenched around the envelope. "You know I'm going to reject the merger."

"I know."

"That means I won't have the cash to buy you out for another two years, at least. Maybe longer."

"I sort of figured that. Luckily I've got a day job." Zoe got to her feet and hitched her tote over her shoulder. "Shall we go, Ethan?"

"Sure." He rose from the chair and took her arm.

Together they walked out of the lobby and into the warm, bright glare of the desert sun. In the distance, the mountains raked the endless blue sky.

Ethan opened the door of the car for her. "What made you decide to do that?"

"Give him the proxy?" She slipped into the passenger seat. "The Clelands aren't a nice family but they *are* a family. That company belongs to them. More than that, it's what holds them together as a clan. Now that I know that Forrest didn't kill Preston, I don't have any reason to destroy them."

"Even though they treated you like a second-class Cleland?"

For some peculiar reason, she felt lighter

and happier than she had in a long, long time. She smiled up at him, blinking a little against the dazzling light.

"I'm not any kind of Cleland now," she said.

"Damn right," he said. "You're a Truax."

He closed the door.

Chapter Forty

Three days later, on a warm, scented night, they went out onto the pool terrace after dinner and reclined on two of the padded loungers.

Zoe braced herself as she did every time things got quiet between them, wondering if this would be the moment when the subject of the impending divorce came up.

"How did you know that Jeremy Hill killed Camelia Foote in the theater?" Ethan asked.

The question startled her. It wasn't the one she had been expecting.

"I was just guessing," she said carefully. "Making up a story to lure Kimberley into confessing. Did Hill kill Camelia there?"

"I think so. I finished Foote's diary, and I put together some information I found in some letters that were written by people who were guests here that night. I also got lucky and turned up some personal notes written by the chief of police who investigated Camelia's death."

"What did you discover?"

"Jeremy and Camelia were seen going into the theater sometime around midnight by at least two different people. No one remembered seeing Camelia again after that although Hill was very much in evidence. The chief considered all of the guests' statements extremely shaky because everyone was drunk. But he also talked to the members of the household staff. Remember I told you that one of them noticed Hill returning to the house from the direction of the gardens just before dawn?"

"Hill went outside the second time to dispose of the body in the canyon?"

"Probably. I think that after the quarrel in the theater, Hill hid Camelia's body behind the bar and locked the theater using her keys. He went to bed late, along with everyone else. When the household finally seemed quiet, he went back downstairs, unlocked the theater and carried Camelia outside to the canyon. Probably cleaned up whatever blood there was, too. He would have found water and sponges and towels in the bar. Could have packed the soiled stuff in his suitcase."

"It was a risk," Zoe said. "What if he had been seen with the body?"

"He could have wrapped her in his jacket and carried her in his arms as if she had passed out drunk. I doubt that anyone would have looked twice. It was probably common knowledge that they were having an affair."

Zoe thought about it. "It fits."

"I'm satisfied with it."

"Going to publish the case at that web site you told me about?"

"Not as long as I'm living here," he said dryly. "I sure as hell don't want curiosity seekers knocking on my front door asking to see the murder scene."

"I can understand that."

Ethan folded his arms behind his head. "You didn't answer my question. How did you know that Hill killed her in the theater?"

"I told you, it was just a story I was spinning for Kimberley. I wanted to rattle her a bit, make her incriminate herself."

"Try again," Ethan said.

She had known that, sooner or later, this moment would arrive, she thought. But she had hoped it would be later. She looked out into the moonlit night and thought wistfully about what might have been.

"You'll think I really am crazy if I tell you the truth," she said quietly.

"So, it's true? You do sense things in rooms?"

"Sometimes."

"I was afraid of that." But he sounded resigned to the inevitable. Not angry or disbelieving.

She waited for the other shoe to drop.

The silence deepened.

"Intuition," Ethan said.

"I'm weird, Ethan."

"The older I get, the more I realize that everyone is a little weird in some way." He shifted on the lounger. "So, have you got a plan for rescuing me from all this pink?"

She turned her head on the padded lounger and looked at him. But it was impossible to read his expression in the warm darkness.

"I'm working on one," she said cautiously. "Not all pink is bad, you know."

"I have it on good authority that prolonged exposure to it can rot a guy's brain."

"Only if the brain in question is very weak to begin with. Yours is not."

"You're sure about that?"

"Positive."

"Good to know that." Ethan paused. "How long do you think it will take?"

"To draw up all the plans and select all of the furnishings? Months, probably."

"Maybe by then I'll have enough cash to pay for some of the remodeling and some new furniture. If nothing else, I can at least paint the place."

"Bonnie mentioned that you got a new client today," she said.

"Insurance job. They want me to verify some facts concerning a suspicious claim. Strictly routine, but it's the kind of bread and butter business that keeps a small agency going."

"I like the sound of the word *routine*. We've all had enough excitement lately."

"Uh-huh."

Zoe waited, but Ethan did not offer anything more.

"So," she said. And stopped.

"So, what?"

She gathered her nerve. "About our divorce."

"It occurs to me that neither of us can afford one right now."

She held her breath. "Are you suggesting

we stay married until we can afford to get divorced?"

"It isn't just the money," Ethan said. "I gotta tell you I'm not looking forward to becoming a four-time loser. No one looks kindly upon guys who have been married and divorced four times. We appear shallow to the untrained eye."

"And then there's the problem of replacing the bed," she offered.

"Don't remind me. I don't even want to think about having to buy a new bed right now. You know how much they cost?"

"Sure. I'm an interior designer, remember? I can tell you exactly how much a new bed costs. What you're saying is that we should stay married partly because of the financial aspects and partly because you don't want to deal with another failed marriage."

"There's also the fact that we're sleeping together," Ethan said softly. "Looks to me like things are working pretty good in some areas right now. Why fix it if it ain't broke?"

She pondered that. It was, she realized, the first time in a long while that she had dared to think about her own future. Hope and possibilities, tantalizing and bright, glittered at the edge of her vision. If she stretched out her hands, she might be able to touch them.

"Those are all sound, sensible reasons for staying married," she said, trying to keep her voice very even.

"I thought so."

The desert night settled around them like dark silk.

She got up from the lounger, took the small step that separated them, and slowly lowered herself until she was lying on top of him, her legs tangled with his.

He framed her face with his hands. "Ah, Zoe."

"It wouldn't be easy, you know," she said, wanting to get it all out into the open. "We would be wise to take it very slowly. Keep our own homes for a while. Give each other some space. Get to know each other before we try living together."

"Sure." He traced her cheekbones with the edge of his fingers. "Nice and slow."

She felt his body responding to hers, and she caught her breath. "We'll have to make up some of the rules as we go along. You're not the only one who's bringing a lot of heavy baggage to this marriage. I'm a genuine escapee from Xanadu, remember? It's true I was there for all the wrong reasons, but there's no getting around the fact that I've never been what most folks would call normal."

"Neither have I."

"I'm probably going to continue having some of my bad dreams, and I'm not going to stop sensing things in walls."

He touched the edges of her mouth. "I've got a few bad habits of my own. Been known to be moody at times. Bonnie says I'm complicated."

"So am I."

"And you're a decorator."

She smiled ruefully. "We all know your opinion of interior *designers.*"

"I agree it won't be easy and that we'll have to invent some of the rules." He brought her mouth very close to his. "But maybe that's a good thing in our case. What do you say?"

Hope and possibilities glittered.

"I say yes."